The shining splendo  *cover of this book reflects th... le. Look for the Zebra Love... omance. It's a trademark tha... reading entertainment.*

UNTAMED DESIRES

Her hand trembling, Rachael reached out to brush her fingertips across Storm Dancer's cheek. He turned his head slightly so that his lips touched her fingertips. She could feel herself trembling, frightened and yet captivated by his presence.

She knew he was going to kiss her. She knew she should step away from him. Yet as he wrapped his arms around her waist, she felt her hands fall to his bare, bronze shoulders. She sucked in her breath.

His lips touched hers ever so lightly and Rachael melted in his arms. Her entire body was alive with the first sensations of desire. When his kiss deepened, she swayed toward him, molding her body to his. Thoughts of the sins of lust and burning in everlasting hell tumbled in her mind, but she was out of control. All she cared about was this man and his touch. . . .

SAVAGE SURRENDER

COLLEEN FAULKNER

ZEBRA BOOKS
KENSINGTON PUBLISHING CORP.

ZEBRA BOOKS

are published by

Kensington Publishing Corp.
475 Park Avenue South
New York, NY 10016

First printing: March, 1992

Printed in the United States of America

Chapter One

Pennsylvania Colony
May 1761

Lady Rachael Moreover slipped her hands into her velvet-soft kidskin gloves as she glanced out the window. An awkward silence hung in the air casting a pallor over the occupants of the carriage that bumped along the rutted roadway.

"I . . . I don't understand, Rachael," Viscount Gifford Langston finally said, his face notably paler.

"I mean what I say," she repeated firmly. "I shan't marry you." She took a deep breath. She had vowed she would be honest with Gifford, but she didn't want to injure him unnecessarily. This was her fault as much as his. He had led her down the path, but she had followed like a smitten dairy maid. She tucked a lock of rich chestnut hair beneath her silk traveling bonnet. "I can't marry you because it would be wrong."

Gifford glanced from Rachael to his cousin the Reverend James who sat beside him, and then back to

Rachael again. "But the banns have been read, my dearest. The ceremony is but a formality." He slipped across the carriage to the opposite upholstered bench so that he might sit beside her and he took her gloved hand. "It's as if you already *were* my wife."

Rachael pulled her hand from his, suddenly loathing his touch. Slowly she turned from the window until her blue-eyed gaze settled on Gifford's strikingly handsome boyish face. "I am no man's wife," she said with determination, "until I make my vow before God." Her gaze shifted to Gifford's cousin sitting nervously on the opposite bench. "Is that not true, Reverend?"

The dark-haired man cleared his throat, taken off-guard by the sudden turn in conversation which had been entirely pleasant until a moment before. He had never cared for his cousin Gifford and had accepted his offer to ride along to their aunt's only because the woman was so gravely ill. John James should have known he would be caught in something unpleasant like this. Events always seemed to turn unpleasant when they involved Gifford Langston.

The reverend took a moment to consider the young woman across from him. She was a beauty, indeed, with her honeyed complexion, rosy lips, and thick shining glory of dark hair, but it was in her eyes that John saw true beauty . . . a beauty of the heart . . . of the soul. His first impression of Lady Rachael upon meeting her six months ago when she'd arrived from London to marry Gifford was that she was entirely too good for his conniving cousin. Like many other women before her, she had been fooled by Gifford's handsome good looks and his smooth-tongued ways. Fooled, but apparently *not fooled for long,* John thought. He turned his attention back to his cousin. "Yes," he answered evenly, "before the Lord, that is where a man and a wife are joined unto death. Our government in its all-knowing wisdom seems to believe that it is they who should govern such sacraments, but it is not as the Lord instructed us."

Rachael flashed him a grateful smile.

Gifford scowled. Because it was obvious the *good* reverend wasn't going to come to his defense, he took a different tack. "Surely you're not serious, Rachael, love. Twice before you've said you'd changed your mind but both times—"

"I came to my *senses?"* she injected. "It's not going to work this time. I've made my decision."

"Tell me why it is you can't marry me. The house I built for you is nearly complete." When he touched her damask sleeve, she stiffened.

Rachael glanced out the window again, taking in the panorama of the dense forest of the Pennsylvania colony surrounding them. Never, until she'd come to the American colonies, had she seen such stark beauty as this. There was something about the sight of the trees, about the sound of the woodland birds, and the heady smell of the humus that intrigued her. Its magic lured her from her bed at night to sit in the window and listen, imagining what it would be like to wander through the ancient oaks and elms on a starry night.

"I cannot marry you, Gifford, because I don't love you." Rachael clenched her jaw. There. She'd admitted it finally . . . to Gifford, but more importantly to herself.

"Love me! Of course you love me. And I you. I should think I would perish without you at my side."

He clasped his hands to his breast in emphasis.

Rachael rolled her eyes heavenward. To think she had once found his histrionics romantic. Now she simply found them irritating. Unconsciously, she shook her head. How could she have been so easily beguiled by Gifford? Why hadn't she listened to her brother Thomas when he had warned her that the Viscount Langston was not the husband for her? Thomas had tried to warn her of her intended's dishonesty. He had tried to tell her that Gifford was a man who played a part, any part you wanted him to, but only long enough to get what he wanted from you. But Rachael had been fooled by Gifford's lavish attentions. The extravagant gifts, the evenings at the playhouse, the stolen kisses, they had all masked his true self behind a veil of girlish dreams.

"Rachael, please," Gifford insisted under his breath. "Let's talk about this later." He shook his head ever so slightly. "But not in front of my cousin. I'm hurt that you would bring up such a delicate matter in the presence of another."

Rachael pulled an embroidered handkerchief from her sleeve and mopped her perspiration-dotted forehead. She had purposely waited to break the news to Gifford in John's presence, thinking he might soften the blow. Perhaps that had been a mistake. Perhaps even an act of cowardice. She tucked the handkerchief back into her sleeve. "There's nothing to talk about. I made a mistake in thinking I wanted to marry you. I'll not double the error by doing so."

"It's your brother, isn't it?" Gifford ran his index finger along the line of his blond mustache. "He comes into port long enough to fill your pretty little head with these notions and then sails away again. He doesn't like me. Of course he told you not to marry me. I suppose he even had the audacity to call me a fortune hunter."

"He did," she conceded quietly. "But Gifford—" The sound of a man's scream froze her voice in her throat.

"Christ, what was that?" Gifford muttered as the carriage lurched to one side throwing him against Rachael.

A second scream rent the air followed by several thumps that rocked the carriage.

Rachael grasped the seat as the vehicle swayed suddenly out of control. "The coachman!" she cried as she stared out the window in shock as the carriage raced by the crumpled body of the liveried driver. She sat back hard in her seat, squeezing her eyes shut, praying this was all a terrible nightmare, but knowing it wasn't. Arrows . . . Those had been feathered Indian arrows protruding from the coachman's chest.

At the sound of an ear-splitting howl Rachael's eyes snapped open. "Do something!" she shouted. "We're under attack! Indians! The carriage is going to overturn!" She could see the savages now, naked redskinned men running beside the careening vehicle, howling like wild beasts.

"Our Father who art in heaven," the reverend began to murmur as he went down on his knees on the carriage floorboards, "hallowed be Thy name . . ."

"Gifford!" Rachael screamed.

But Gifford was shaking so hard that all he could do was clutch his silver-tipped walking cane, his face terror-stricken.

She pressed her face to the window just in time to see one of the loin-clothed heathens leap into the air. The carriage lurched beneath the added weight of the man and quickly began to slow down.

Indians! Rachael's mind raced. She knew she should pray, humbly preparing herself for the hereafter, but no words came to mind. White-hot anger bubbled inside her. Attacked by Indians so near to Philadelphia! Impossible! Only two days ago Gifford had been telling friends how safe Philadelphia was despite the trouble with the French and the Indians.

"Lead us not into temptation . . ." Reverend James went on.

When the carriage jerked to a halt, Rachael swallowed against her immobilizing fear. She wasn't ready to die. Not yet. There were too many things left to do in life. She wanted to marry. To love. To cradle a child in her arms. She didn't want to die, and certainly not at the hands of brutal savages.

". . . For thine is the kingdom and the power and the glory forever. Amen."

The door slammed open and a hideous face painted in black and white thrust through the doorway. Gifford cringed. Reverend James clasped his hands and bowed his head in prayer. Rachael defiantly lifted her lashes to meet the red devil's gaze. If she was going to die at this redskin's hands she wanted to see his face.

The savage shouted in a gruff voice, his words monosyllables and utterly foreign to Rachael's ears. The redskin grabbed Reverend James by the collar of his coat and hauled him out of the carriage.

"Please! Please!" Gifford cried. "Don't hurt us! We've money. A great deal of money! You can have it! Have it all!" His hands trembled as he jerked a coin purse from his belt and jingled it.

A moment later the redskin reached for Gifford. He tried to retreat, but in the tiny carriage there was no where to go. Gifford tripped on Rachael's skirts and fell, striking his forehead on the window sill. Rachael watched, horror-stricken as the savage dragged the unconscious Gifford from the carriage and threw his motionless body to the ground below.

Rachael knew she was next. Thrusting out her jaw, she rose as the heathen grasped her ankle. "I can walk," she spit.

The redskin barked something as he took her by her forearm twisting it unmercifully. Rachael nearly tripped as she leaped down out of the carriage. "What do you want?" she demanded. "We've done you no harm! You must free us at once! You have no right!"

The painted-faced man slapped her hard across the face and Rachael felt a drop of blood trickle from the corner of her mouth. A sob escaped her lips as she wiped her mouth with the sleeve of her new ivory damask gown, staining it crimson.

"Yo ra se," the painted man said, reaching out to stroke her cheek.

Rachael recoiled. "Don't touch me!" she shouted in his face. "Kill me, but don't touch me, you filthy creature!"

There was a cackle of laughter from two other savages standing nearby, but the painted man made no attempt to touch her again. Rachael's gaze darted from Gifford's crumpled body to the small clearing where the carriage had come to a halt. For God's sake, where was Reverend James?

At the sound of more guttural speech, she turned toward the horses that were being unhitched by a savage wearing a beaten cocked hat. The reverend was on his knees, his hands clasped, tears running down his cheeks as two redskins attempted to rip his clothing from his back.

"Stop that! Stop it at once," she screamed running toward Gifford's cousin.

"Run!" John James shouted. "Run for your life, Lady Rachael."

"No!" she cried, grasping John's quaking shoulders. "We try to run and they'll kill us!" A redskin pulled free his black frock coat as another tugged at his heeled shoes. "They're going to kill us anyway," John moaned.

"No! No! Stop it!" Rachael sobbed. She turned to the nearest redskin and pummeled his bare back with her balled fists.

Reverend James took that moment to leap to his feet and run.

"No, John!" Rachael screamed as she tried to twist from her capture's grasp. "Don't run, John!"

But as the words slipped from her mouth, so did the arrow from the Iroquois bow. The arrow cut through the morning air with a swish striking the Reverend James square in the back.

Rachael screamed as she brought her gloved hands to her face to shield her eyes from the sight, knowing the Reverend John James was dead before his body hit the ground. As she lowered her hands she saw his life's blood flowing onto the soft carpet of green moss. "No! No, you can't do this," she begged. "We've done nothing to you!"

"Nothing?" A strangely accented voice came from behind.

Rachael whirled around, expecting to see a white man, shocked to see a savage uttering the English words. He was an ugly man with a bald head save for a thatch of black hair that sprouted from the center and fell over one ear in a scalplock. He had a scar that ran across his cheek to a terribly disfigured ear. Rachael's lower lip trembled. The savage's onyx eyes were filled with hate . . . hate of her.

"You say you have done nothing," he snarled. "You killed my three sons. You raped and tortured my wife leaving her in pieces so that she could not rise into the heavens. You call that nothing!"

Rachael stumbled backward. "I did nothing! I've never laid eyes on a red man until this moment!"

Broken Horn gestured toward Gifford who still lay unconscious on the ground. "Your men. Your people." He spat on the ground. "Someone must be responsible. Someone must pay."

"Pay? I can pay. I have money." She brushed away a piece of hair that had fallen across her bruised cheek. "Let me go back to Philadelphia and I'll bring you coin."

"Coin?" Broken Horn sneered. "You white men, you think coin can right the wrongs of a hundred years!"

When he swept out his hand to catch her, Rachael darted left, but he snagged the sleeve of her damask gown. A sinister smile crept across Broken Horn's scarred face. "You are pretty, white woman." He nodded. "And brave. I think I should not kill you."

Relief flooded her face. "No. Don't kill me. Let me go." She glanced sideways at the men who were leading away the carriage horses. Someone was inside the carriage ripping up the seat with a knife, in search of valuables no doubt. "Take the horse. My fiancé and I . . . we'll walk back into Philadelphia."

Broken Horn's gaze shifted to Gifford's limp form and then back to Rachael. "Let you go?" He gave a little laugh. "No. You will come with me."

"No!" Rachael cried trying to tear from his grip. "You can't. That's kidnapping!"

"That is life. More than he has," as he indicated the Reverend James, "eh?"

Rachael squeezed her eyes shut for a moment, trying to think. Should she run? They would only shoot her down as they had the reverend. Was it better to die quickly than to wonder when the arrow would come? Her eyes fluttered open. If she ran now, there was no chance of survival, but if she waited . . . perhaps that chance would come.

Broken Horn waved a broad hand signaling his men to hurry. He still held Rachael by the sleeve of her gown.

"Where are you taking me?" she demanded. "If it's ransom you want—"

"Shut up before I shut you up," Broken Horn snapped. "I have had enough of your words. Keep quiet and do as I say and perhaps you will live until we reach the Watashia River."

Rachael opened her mouth to speak again, but the look on the redskin's face warned her to keep silent. A savage approached Gifford and whipped out a jagged-edged knife.

"What is he doing?" she murmured more to herself than her captor. Suddenly realizing that the savage meant to cut Gifford's throat she bolted, tearing from Broken Horn's grasp. "No! Don't touch him! Let him be!" She reached Gifford's body and grabbed the savage's bare forearm. She looked back toward Broken Horn. "Please don't kill him."

"He is your husband?" Broken Horn asked.

She lowered her head. "Husband to be . . . he was, I mean."

Broken Horn contemplated his choices. The girl he could trade for muskets and whiskey. The man . . . ransom perhaps. Then of course a white captive was always a good diversion for the Mohawks. "He cannot walk," Broken Horn scoffed. "We must travel fast."

Rachael fell to her knees, grasping Gifford's face. His forehead was split open where he'd hit the window sill. The blood had congealed but his forehead was already turning purple with bruising. "He can travel. I swear he can! Please don't kill him!" She patted Gifford's pale cheek. "Gifford, Gifford, wake up!" she insisted in a half whisper. "Gifford if you don't wake up, love, they're going to kill you."

He groaned, his eyelids fluttering. "That's right," she urged. "Wake up." She patted his cheek harder.

"Kill him!" Broken Horn barked.

"No!" She turned back to Gifford slapping him hard across the cheek. "Gifford, if you don't wake up, damn you, they're going to kill you!"

The sharp slap in the face made Gifford open his eyes. "Rachael . . ." he mumbled groggily.

"Gifford, get up!" she insisted, rising to her feet, trying to drag him up with her. "They're going to kill you if you don't get up."

"Kill me?" Slowly Gifford's eyes focused. The realization of where he was and what had happened quickly washed over his face. "Rachael!" He wrapped his arms around her, leaning heavily on her shoulders. "John?"

"Dead." She brushed his cheek with her hand. "They're not going to kill us, not yet at least, but you have to walk. Do you understand what I'm saying, Gifford?" She grasped his chin, forcing him to look into her eyes.

Broken Horn shouted another command and the savage standing closest to Rachael gave her a shove forward.

"Gifford, we have to go with them. You have to walk now," she said, forcing him to stumble forward. ". . . Or we'll never live until sunset."

Chapter Two

The sun faded slowly in the western horizon until it was naught but the sweep of an artist's brush. The air chilled and nocturnal animals began to crawl from their resting places in the dense underbrush to hunt, to drink from the slow-running creeks, and to peer at the humans who marched northward.

Heavenly Father! will they never stop, Rachael thought as she forced one foot in front of the other. Her captors were inhuman! No man could walk from sunrise until well beyond sunset at this relentless pace and not tire! No one but these savages . . .

Iroquois was what Gifford said they were. Mohawks of the Iroquois Nation, People of the Flint Country, said Broken Horn, the leader of the red men who had kidnapped them.

Rachael wiped her forehead with the back of her ivory damask sleeve, or what was left of it. In the two weeks that had passed since her capture she had walked twelve to sixteen hours a day. Her leather-heeled slippers were in shreds, her feet blistered. Her face was sunburned despite the bonnet she wore. Her gown, her beautiful damask morning gown, was a tattered, soiled rag.

On the third day of traveling she had insisted Broken Horn loan her his hunting knife so that she might cut the hem to make it easier to walk. He had balked, thinking she meant to kill herself, but Rachael had only laughed as she sawed at the once beautiful fabric, exposing her calves. She hadn't walked those hundred miles through the mosquito-infested forest to kill herself. No. At that instant back at the carriage when she had decided not to run, she had made the choice to live, no matter what it took.

Rachael turned tiredly to glance over her shoulder. Gifford was lagging again. If he didn't pick up the pace, it would surely mean punishment. She swallowed the knot that rose in her throat. All of Gifford's handsome good looks had disappeared in a day. With his hair dirty, his upper lip split in two places, the purple-green shade of bruising across one cheek, and red mosquito welts covering his face, he looked more like some urchin from the back alleys of London than a viscount of a popular family in Philadelphia.

"Gifford!" Rachael whispered, her voice raspy. It had been hours since they'd stopped to drink from a muddy spring. "Gifford," she signaled with her hand behind her back, "Gifford, come on!"

"I can't," he moaned, his head hanging from his shoulders. "I can't walk another mile."

Rachael eyed the savage walking a few feet ahead of her. Painted Face had been assigned to guard her, but he was lost in conversation with the Indian who wore the cocked hat. She slowed her pace, letting Gifford catch up. She dropped a hand on his waist. "It's nearly dark. We'll stop soon for certain. I know it!" She tried to sound cheery.

"And then what?" he asked, his voice on the edge of hysteria. "You should have let them slit my throat and have been done with it."

"Don't say that!" She gave him a squeeze. "You have to hold on, Gifford. We're going to get away from these beasts. Someone will realize we're missing and come searching. My brother! Surely Thomas will come for us!"

Gifford rested his bruised cheek on her shoulder. "I'm so tired, Rachael. It would be so much easier to just lie down." His knees buckled and Rachael grasped him by the waistband of his pants, pulling him up. It was funny how two weeks ago she could never have done anything so intimate. But two weeks ago seemed now like two hundred years.

In the first days of travel she had quickly learned that survival was not for the squeamish. In a day's time she had learned to eat half-raw rabbit with her hands, to relieve herself on the path just as the men did, and to sleep on the ground with nothing but a lump of moss for a pillow.

"You've got to walk!" Rachael insisted angrily as she gave Gifford a shake. "I can't carry you, Gifford! You lie down and they'll kill you."

"No reason to live," he muttered.

"You have to live for me," she said impulsively.

He lifted his head to look at her. "For you? You said you wouldn't marry me. Without you there's no need to go back to Philadelphia. Without you, I'm lost."

Rachael rubbed her forehead with her free hand. If there was one thing she learned in this ordeal, it was that she was certain she didn't want Gifford for a husband. He should have been caring for *her* needs! He should have bene protecting *her* from the savages. Instead, from the very first moments, it had been the other way around.

No. If she and Gifford survived this nightmare, she would not marry him. Coming so close to death had made her realize how important life was. Somewhere in the world there was a man who would love her. When she escaped—and she would escape—she was going to find that man. Given the situation she and Gifford were in, she didn't consider lying too great a sin. If a few lies would keep him alive, they would be worth the penance, wouldn't they?

Rachael stroked Gifford's mosquito-bitten forehead with her soiled fingertips. If it wasn't love she felt for him, at least she had compassion. Gifford was a weak man; she could see that now. He needed her if he was to live. "Oh, Gifford. Don't worry about what I said. What you need to worry about now is keeping yourself alive. You have to drink and eat—"

"I cannot eat raw flesh! Squirrel burned on the outside and bloody on the inside." He tried to spit but his mouth was so dry that he had no saliva.

"You have to eat to keep up your strength. And you have to walk. You have to do what Broken Horn and his men tell us. If we're going to be rescued, we just have to hang on!"

He hung his head again. The sun had set and

darkness had settled on the forest. "It's past dark," he complained. "And still they keep walking."

A barked command startled Rachael. It was Painted Face. *"Kax aa,* no talk!" He brandished the spear he carried, waving her forward.

Rachael released Gifford, giving him a quick hug. Hurrying until she walked just behind Painted Face, she studied the darkening forest. More than a week ago she had given up hope of her and Gifford simply escaping. Broken Horn and his companions had given them no chance, watching their every movement. Besides, where would they run to? The second day of her capture the Indians had skirted a crude log cabin that she assumed was occupied by farmers, but she'd not seen another sign of civilization since. Once Rachael had realized escape wasn't possible, she had concentrated on the thought that someone would come for them. When she and Gifford hadn't arrived at his aunt's surely her brother Thomas had been notified. And once he found the carriage and the reverend's body with the arrows protruding from his chest, he would have surmised that she and Gifford had been captured. Thomas was looking for her now. She just knew it.

Night settled on the forest in an inky blanket of darkness. The moon appeared above the treetops casting a pale light across the craggy faces of the Mohawks. Still they pushed on, a sense of eagerness in their moccasined footsteps. When Rachael asked Painted Face when they would stop for the night, he had only grunted threateningly. She lost all sense of time as she trudged forward, occasionally offering a word of encouragement to Gifford.

Rachael was thankful for the small bit of diversion the darkened forest offered. Rather than being frightened of the eerie sounds, they tapped her attention. She tried to imagine what kind of animal made each sound and what it meant. She was fascinated by the raccoons and opossums that scurried across her path and the deer the travelers scared up out of the brush.

The sound of a turkey gobble suddenly startled Rachael. A turkey? She had heard no turkeys before. Turkeys weren't night creatures. The bird sounded again, and to her surprise one of the Mohawks in the group repeated the sound with remarkable likeness.

Several Indians appeared out of the darkness and the group came to a halt. Broken Horn fell into conversation with the tallest of the greeters. When they turned to look at her she felt her face flush. That evil grin of Broken Horn's make her shiver wondering just how long it would be before she would have to fight for her virtue.

Broken Horn and the other man spoke for another moment or two and then the group moved forward, Broken Horn falling back to walk beside her.

"We enter the village," he told her, his head held high. "My mood is good. Crow's Wing offered me two rifles, English-*manake* whiskey, and a buffalo hide from the great western lands for you."

Rachael could feel her throat constricting. Her heart palpated so rapidly that it pounded in her ears. "You cannot sell me!" she managed. "I am a human being! You cannot sell *people.*"

"You are not *people,"* he said incredulously. *"We* are the people." He glanced at her. They were of the same height so he could look directly into Rachael's eyes with his. "As I told you, Crow's Wing offered me great wealth for you," he shrugged, "but I was thinking you would make a good woman for Broken Horn." He nodded, liking the idea. "I would take you into my longhouse with your skin of white." He caught a lock of her hair and rubbed it between his thick fingers. "You and I we would make sons to fight the English."

She gave a little laugh. "I won't be *your woman!* I belong to no man red or white."

"You refuse Broken Horn, son of the Bear Clan's shaman!" He grasped her arm tightly.

Through the pale light of the moon Rachael could see Broken Horn's scarred face. She had insulted him. Her survival instinct told her to go along with whatever she must to live, but she couldn't give herself to this man. No matter what. "I refuse."

He sneered. "Then you will be sold." With that he stalked off, moving ahead of the others and once again taking the lead.

Gifford fell in beside Rachael. "What was that all about?" he asked.

Rachael exhaled, the feeling of doom heavy on her shoulders. "He offered to take me as *his woman."*

"His woman! But you already belong to me, Rachael, love. You said so yourself."

She turned on him. "Belong? I don't *belong* to anyone!"

Gifford brushed back a string of his dirty hair. "I only meant—"

"Enough." She lifted a hand defensively. "I've had enough today. Please, don't say another word. Not a single, blessed word."

Gifford fell silent and they trudged along side by side. Soon the sound of barking dogs filled the night air. The forest began to clear and after passing single file through a thicket of thorns they entered a village.

Rachael came to a halt, Gifford bumping into her. "We're here," she whispered.

Painted Face pushed them forward roughly. Rachael dragged her feet, suddenly as frightened as she had been the day the carriage was attacked. Several men and bare-breasted women appeared from the long wood huts that were illuminated by small campfires.

They were all talking at once in angry heated tones. Rachael shrank back in fear as the crowd descended on them. Broken Horn was shouting and laughing, obviously proud of his captives. A tall woman with a severe harelip stroked Rachael's hair then gave her a sudden, hard push, nearly knocking her to the ground.

Gifford caught her. "I say! That will be quite enough!"

The harelipped woman brought her face close to Gifford's, babbling in her native tongue. Laughing, laughing at him . . .

Trembling, Rachael covered her ears with her hands. She feared she was going to faint. She was deathly tired and the noise, the confusion, was more than she could stand. Everyone was talking, talking about her and Gifford. They were touching her clothes, her face, her breasts.

"Stop it! Stop it!" she cried. She threw a glance in

Broken Horn's direction. "Make them stop!"

Broken Horn stepped toward her and several Indians made way for him. "You change your mind, white Rach-ael? You wish for my protection?" He caught a lock of her tangled hair and raised it to his lips. "Please this man and I might make you wife." He eyed his first wife, the woman with the harelip. "Please this man much and you might take Pretty Woman's place."

The woman with the harelip shot Rachael a threatening glance.

Rachael looked from Pretty Woman to the sea of dark eyes all staring at her, waiting. She could hear Gifford inhale sharply. To turn Broken Horn down again, here in his own village would mean—She lifted her dark lashes. "I have done nothing to you and yet you took me against my will. You dragged me through the forest for more than two weeks and then—"

Broken Horn slapped her hard across the mouth silencing her. "Enough! Either you accept the generosity of this man of the Bear Clan, or you become one of the others."

Rachael's gaze followed Broken Horn's. She heard Gifford cry out in protest. Two men were dragging him toward the far side of the camp. For the first time she saw by the dim light of the moon and the glowing cookfires that there were people tied to poles in the ground . . . white men and women.

Rachael bit down on her lower lip to stifle a sob of terror. So she and Gifford were not the only captives. . . .

Broken Horn lowered his hideously scarred face within inches of hers. "I say again, do you accept this man's generosity, because if you do not, you will be sold to the French with the others. Sold as the whores that you are!"

Rachael looked at the captives across the camp. The men dragging Gifford had reached the spot and were securing him to a pole. She looked back at Broken Horn. "I do not accept your generosity," she said quietly, the venom plain in her voice.

Broken Horn paused for an instant, almost in disbelief. Then he gave a curt nod and walked away.

Pretty Woman and another immediately descended on Rachael, grabbing her hands and dragging her toward the other captives. Out of the corner of her eyes, Rachael saw a man standing in the shadows of a campfire. His eyes met hers and for a moment she thought she saw a glimmer of compassion in his heathen black eyes. Then suddenly he was gone, just a shadow in her mind making her wonder if she had truly seen the man at all.

Pretty Woman gave a grunt, jerking Rachael. "Come!" she ordered. "Come to see your new home."

The other woman laughed.

They tied Rachael to a pole with another woman, opposite of Gifford's pole. They twisted her hands behind her back, seeming to enjoy her cries of pain. Then they secured her wrists together and left her.

For a moment Rachael sat huddled on the ground in shock. She had never in her life felt so alone, so frightened. She could hear the even breathing of the woman tied behind her. Through the dim light of the moon she could see the outline of Gifford's slumped body.

"Gifford," she whispered.

"Rachael . . . Rachael, love . . ."

"Gifford, what are we going to do?"

"I don't know," he whispered back. Then a pause, then, "Rachael, I'm thirsty."

"I told you, you should have drank back at that last stream."

"Stream!" he laughed, his voice raspy. "That was no more than a slow-running sewer!"

"It was water, Gifford."

He gave a grunt of disdain and then was silent again.

Rachael took a deep breath and lifted her chin to gaze up at the stars. Her grandmother had always told her life was fate. The day you were born, she said, a life was mapped out from birth to death. She said it was in the stars. Rachael wondered as she stared up at the bright pinpricks of light whether or not her death at the age of twenty-two was in the stars.

Storm Dancer ducked into Broken Horn's longhouse and stood in the doorway. Gull, Broken Horn's second wife, was serving him a platter of roasted venison and honey-sweetened corncakes with her one good hand. The other, a knot of useless flesh, rested on her hip. Pretty Woman was busy tucking her husband's children by Gull into their sleeping platforms at the rear of the longhouse. At the sight of Storm Dancer, Gull and Pretty Woman lowered their lashes appropriately, taking care not to make eye contact with their superior.

"Storm Dancer," Broken Horn grunted, cramming

an entire square of corncake into his mouth.

"Brother . . ." It was an accusation.

Broken Horn glanced up irritably. "Sit, sit," he said in English. "My woman will get you food."

Storm Dancer broke the plane between him and his brother with an even stroke of his bronze hand. "No food."

"Then at least do not be impolite," Broken Horn went on in English despite the fact that his brother spoke their native tongue as was appropriate. "Sit while I eat." He turned to his second wife. *"E a yon te ant."*

Gull quickly dropped a wooden trencher of food at her husband's feet and backed her way past Storm Dancer and out of the wigwam, leaving the men to be alone.

Storm Dancer crouched before the small, glowing fire in the center pit. Its burning embers cast a glow of eerie light on the two brothers, the two enemies. "You have brought more captives . . ."

Broken Horn grinned as he reached for another hunk of venison. "Fine white bitch, isn't she? Crow's Wing offered me plenty for her, but I think I might keep her for myself."

"You have four wives, *ak ya tat cke a ha.* You are a greedy man."

Broken Horn gripped his bulging loin cloth with a greasy hand. "My needs are great." He laughed at his own joke as he licked his wet fingers. "You yourself should take a wife, take two, and then you would understand the needs of a true man."

Storm Dancer scowled. "You must let her go."

Broken Horn glanced up curiously. "Her?"

"All of them, of course," he replied without skipping a beat. In the recesses of his mind he wondered why he had said *her* . . . he had meant the woman of course, the brave woman who had stood up to the Mohawks when they might well have cut her down with one sweep of a war club.

"I will not let them go. The French offer guns and whiskey for the women. It is a profitable business."

"And the man? Why did you bring him? The French do not pay for men."

Broken Horn shrugged. "A diversion." He lifted a finger. "And Rouville still pays for yellow-haired scalps with or without balls."

"You sicken me, Brother."

Broken Horn threw down his wooden platter. "And you me! You shame our father with your woman's ways!"

"You're going to kill us all with your troublemaking, your warring." Storm Dancer lifted a finger. "The Mohawks will die; the six nations will fall. I see it in the storm clouds."

His brother spat on the hearth. "You see nothing but what you want to see." He slapped his bare chest. "You forget, I, too, am the son of a shaman, and I see victory, I see the English-*manake* blood run red over this land until they are no more."

Storm Dancer shook his head venomously. "False dreams, false hopes. You listen too much to the Senecas across the river. The French are not with us. We are but instruments in their fight with the English. We can be sacrificed."

Broken Horn slipped his blade from his belt. "Any man who crosses me will die painfully."

Storm Dancer looked away. He knew this was a useless conversation. How many times had he had it in the last year with his brother? And always the same conclusion. Broken Horn hated the English and was not only willing to die, but to sacrifice his entire nation to drive the white men off. Storm Dancer couldn't convince him that it was useless battle. Though he'd been to the cities and seen the expansion, he still believed the Iroquois could beat the English. He didn't realize that sheer numbers made such a feat impossible.

Storm Dancer stood. "I ask you again to release the prisoners. All of them. They are innocents."

"They are white," Broken Horn reached for a flask of whiskey from a basket on the floor and popped the cork, "so they are guilty."

"I will go to the council."

"So go. You know what they will say. They will say Storm Dancer, son of a shaman, is a coward. They will say he is not man enough to do what must be done to defend his people. They will say he is not fit to be a Mohawk with a stomach so weak."

"It is wrong to kidnap, to torture, to kill, to sell human beings."

"They are not human beings," Broken Horn shrugged as he took a deep sip from the bottle and then grinned, "so no wrong has been committed."

"This is not the end of it, Brother. I have sat by long enough and watched you lead our people astray."

Broken Horn gave a wave of his hand. "You call me brother, but you forget, we are only half-brothers.

Your mother, She-Who-Weeps is Lenni Lenape." He chuckled. "So that makes you only half-human, half-brother."

Without another word, Storm Dancer ducked out of the longhouse and into the night air. He stood for a moment in the shadows of the structure, his hands clenched at his sides as he tried to control his anger. What was he going to do? How was he going to convince his people that Broken Horn was wrong? How could he make them see the annihilation of his people he saw in his dreams? How could he make them understand that if they did not cease this warring and try to live beside the white men, that they would all die?

A soft, feminine sigh caught Storm Dancer's attention and he turned toward the place where the captives were kept. He could see the young woman who had just been brought in. She was tied to a pole, slumped over in restless sleep. Her head rolled to and fro as she murmured something.

Storm Dancer knew he should not go to her. He should not look at her or speak to her. She would die or be carried off like the rest and he was powerless to stop it. He himself walked too narrow a line between life and death among the Mohawks to dare try to save even one life.

But something drew him toward her, perhaps the fine line bones of her face or the soft sweep of hair that fell over her shoulders. As he drew closer he could hear her. Water. She was asking for water. It had probably been hours since she last drank and Pretty Woman certainly would not have bothered to give prisoners food or water.

Storm Dancer made a sharp turn and went to his own lodge. A moment later he came out carrying a gourd of cool water. Without bothering to look to see if anyone else watched him, he went to the woman captive and squatted. He touched her cheek gently and then lifted the gourd to her lips.

Rachael's eyes fluttered. Water . . . she was so thirsty. Half asleep, she didn't know where it came from or even if she was dreaming. She didn't care. Perhaps if she dreamed her thirst was quenched, she would sleep better.

Taking several gulps, Rachael breathed deeply. Someone was there. She forced her eyes open and was met by the same compassionate gaze that had followed her across the compound earlier in the evening.

"Thank you," she whispered, offering the barest smile.

"More?" the red man asked in strange, lilting English.

Rachael's smile broadened. Her angel of mercy was a handsome man with high cheekbones and sensuous lips. His skin, it was a most perfect shade of red, like new-turned soil. He smelled of pine and the forest just after dusk. He seemed so gentle.

"No more," she whispered, "but Gifford, please." Her eyelids fell as she struggled to remain conscious.

"Gif-ford?"

She lifted a hand, pointing toward the man she had intended on marrying. "Please, give him the rest."

On impulse, Storm Dancer tenderly brushed her cheek with his fingertips. The thought occurred to him that he could cut this white woman free and carry her off. He could save them from the tragedy that he knew lay ahead for them both. But his duty kept him here. His love for his mother, his responsibility to the children of the village held him back. He knew he had to stay and try to save his people.

Storm Dancer rose and walked toward the other captive with the gourd of water still in his trembling hand.

Chapter Three

Rachael woke slowly to the unfamiliar morning sounds of the Mohawk camp. Voices filled the air as women and children went about their first-light chores. Firepits crackled and men murmured greetings to one another as they gathered outside their lodges to break the fast.

Even before Rachael opened her eyes she could feel the May sun shining down on her. Its bright light invaded her thoughts, casting swirls of patterns inside her eyelids. Already her head ached. Slowly lifting her lashes, Rachael took in the sights that surrounded her.

By the light of day she could see that the Indian camp was large, with perhaps twenty longhouses arranged in three rows. Several small lodges stood at the ends of the rows. There were redskinned Mohawks everywhere. Children ran across the compound carrying bark buckets of water while half-naked women hurried about tending to meals at their individual family fires.

Men with heads shaved save for long scalp locks sat cross-legged, some busying themselves, others idle, while they waited for sweetened mush and the bread Rachael could smell cooking.

Her gaze strayed closer. A few feet away Gifford lay sleeping, his head awkwardly propped against the wooden post he was confined to. She couldn't see the woman tied behind her, but there were several female captives: a blond-haired woman in a yellow shift; a young Indian girl, her naked body barely covered by a dirty pelt; a brunette with a bloodied head, part of her hair and scalp obviously missing. Rachael swallowed against the bile that rose in her throat. The captives looked half dead. She couldn't help wondering how long it would be before she looked like them . . . or worse.

Rachael licked her dry lips, thinking how thirsty she was. An image flashed in her mind. A man, an Indian with haunting obsidian eyes. Had he really come to her last night, or had she imagined it all?

Rachael squeezed her eyes shut. She had dreamed so many strange things last night. She had been a bird soaring in the sky. A thunderstorm had come. She'd flown through the clouds looking down on the Indian village. She saw death everywhere and her heart had ached for her captors. She gave a grunt, opening her eyes again. How she could have felt anything for these people, even in a dream, she didn't know.

"Rachael?"

She immediately glanced across the space between her and Gifford. "Gifford?"

"It's morning? They haven't killed us yet?" he said

in disbelief.

"Not yet," she murmured afraid to speak too loudly for fear she would draw one of her captor's attention.

"Well thank God that heathen brought me water last night or I'd have never lived until morning."

Rachael stared at Gifford. *So she hadn't imagined him. . . .* "Someone brought you water last night?"

"At least one of these beasts had the good sense to realize that I'll be worth naught as ransom if I'm a dead man." He brushed his mouth against the tattered cloth at his shoulder. "You think we dare call to someone for food and water."

Rachael chewed her lower lip thoughtfully as she glanced out at the Indian camp. She wanted to ask Gifford about the man who had brought him the water, but something made her keep silent. "I think we'd best keep quiet, Gifford."

"Like hell! I'm thirsty and I need use of the privy." He looked toward the busy camp. "Excuse me! Say there, could someone come here. We've needs to be taken care of."

A young boy passing with a bucket of water picked up a stick and hurled it at Gifford, striking the post he was tied to just above his head. There was an echo of laughter as Gifford cringed.

"You'd best tell that boy to hush 'is tater-trap else we'll all be in the stew pot . . . ," a voice said softly from behind Rachael.

A moment of silence hung in the air. "What did you say?" Rachael whispered.

"You heard me. I said hush 'im up before they make us all into supper. They do that you know. Eat people."

A shiver of fear crept up Rachael's spine. "My name's Rachael, Rachael Moreover. Who are you?"

"The name's Dory. My mam named me Doreen but I decided it just wasn't a name fittin' for a slattern like myself so it's just Dory."

Two weeks ago Rachael would have been shocked by such talk. But she was so anxious for human contact that she didn't care who Dory was. This woman obviously knew something of these redskins; perhaps she could be of some help. "I'm glad to meet you, Dory. Across the way is . . . is my fiancé, Gifford Langston."

"Langston, eh, well you'd best tell your fancy man that if he doesn't keep quiet them Mohawks'll cut off his possibles and roast 'em on a spit. These is bad ones, this bunch. That Broken Horn bastard, he's got everyone all stirred up. Got the Injuns riled for a hundred miles. See, the way I understand most of the Mohawks goes with the English, but them Senecas across the St. Lawrence River, they's with the Frenchies. Broken Horn's somehow convinced the whole village to go that a way. The fool," Rachael heard her hock and spit on the dusty ground, "thinks he and the Frenchies are gonna wipe out every Englishman in the northern colonies."

"How . . . how long have you been a captive?"

"Of this bunch, or the last?"

"Broken Horn didn't kidnap you?"

"Won me on the dice. It was a gaggle of Senecas that done stole me nigh on a year ago. They weren't bad. Didn't beat on me too hard and they were a hell of a lot kinder than old Jesop I was bonded to."

"You were a bond woman?" Rachael urged with morbid fascination. Dory's will to live was obviously strong and Rachael admired her for it.

"Was sold in London three years ago for stealin' to feed my dyin' babe. Instead of hangin' me or throwin' me into Newgate to rot, I was sold into indenture for seven years. Old Jesop bought me in Connecticut. I hated the winters and his stinkin' fish hands all over me every night, bleedin' or not. Didn't care for his wife much, I suppose . . ." She chuckled. "So when the Senecas stole me, I figured I was movin' up in the world."

"But then these other Indians lost you to Broken Horn?"

"Sad tale, ain't it?"

"So what now? What will Broken Horn do with us?"

"Women he sells to the Frenchies for muskets and sech."

Rachael hesitated for a moment before lowering her voice to be certain Gifford didn't hear her. "And men?"

"Be tortured and killed most likely." Her voice was matter-of-fact.

Rachael leaned back against her post, closing her eyes. Damnation! This was all her fault. She had told Gifford they would be better off to come peacefully with Broken Horn. Now what was she going to do . . . what were they going to do? She couldn't let Gifford die at the hands of the heinous creatures!

When Rachael didn't speak again, Dory twisted her hands until she could touch Rachael's bare arm. "Rachael-honey."

Rachael took a deep breath. This wasn't a time to

feel sorry for herself. If they were going to get out of here alive she had to be able to think with a clear head. She smiled. The woman Dory's touch was comforting.

"That were mean of me to spit it right out. But it's the plain truth. These Mohawks are a foul pod a peas. A week ago I seen 'em kill a man and eat his flesh right off the bone."

"We have to escape then."

"Ain't no escapin', 'cept by dyin'."

"I don't believe that. Not for a minute. My brother, Thomas, he's coming for us. I know he is. I just have to hang on. Thomas will rescue me and Gifford and you too, Dory."

"You're a lady, ain't you? Money? Papa titled?"

"He's an earl of little importance. Why?" she asked, not seeing the point to Dory's questioning.

"You just sound like a person who's always got what she wanted. Believe in fairy tales I'd guess."

"I believe in the Father Almighty and His protection," she said firmly.

"So where was His protection when Broken Horn was thievin' you? Use your head, girl. You got no one to protect you; you got nothin' but your wits."

"God hasn't and will not abandon me—"

"Shht!" Dory interrupted. "Here comes that hare-lipped bitch. She's a mean one. The Mohawks call her Pretty Woman on account she's so ugly. First wife to Broken Horn. He's got four, you know. Don't cross 'er. She'd cut out your tongue soon as look at you."

Rachael's gaze went to Gifford. She shook her head ever so slightly in warning. She knew he intended to confront the Mohawk. She could see the arrogant glimmer in his eyes.

Gifford ignored her warning. "About time someone came," he said haughtily. "My fiancée and I, we need water, food, and time to get up and stretch our legs. We're not beasts to be tied to a tree!"

"Water?" Pretty Woman approached Gifford with a bark bucket hung on one arm and a gourd ladle in her hand. "Here water." She dipped a generous portion and threw it in Gifford's face.

Rachael gasped.

Pretty Woman turned to Rachael. "You water?" she asked, grinning.

Rachael lowered her gaze. "Please," she said, trying to sound meek. She knew when to challenge and when to keep silent. Years in the home of her strong-willed father taught her that much.

Begrudgingly, Pretty Woman dipped another portion of water and raised it to Rachael's lips.

Rachael drank greedily, not knowing when she would drink again. When Pretty Woman pulled away, Rachael wiped her mouth on the tattered sleeve of her gown and stretching her neck she was able to dampen her face with the cool wet cloth. She listened to Dory drinking thirstily. Then Pretty Woman moved on.

"She's in charge of the captives," Dory whispered when the Mohawk woman walked away. "You want anything, it has to come from her."

"There . . ." Rachael chose her words carefully. "There was a man who came last night. Black eyes," she said quietly.

"Black eyes! You're talkin' about every redskin in the colonies, Rachael honey."

"I would know him if I saw him again. He brought me water in the middle of the night. He . . . he was kind to me."

"Must have been dreamin'," Dory scoffed. "Ain't no kindness in this village. White-haters they are. All Indians hate us, I guess, but these people, they got a grudge. Seems there was a raid a few years back when the men were out hunting. Everyone slaughtered. Women and children. Even the dogs and horses."

"No. No, I wasn't dreaming. He came to me. He took water to Gifford too. Gifford said so."

"Strange thing. I been here two maybe three months and no redskinned angel of mercy came my way."

An image of the savage who had brought her the water flashed in the back of Rachael's mind. Then, as if she had conjured him from her own imagination, she spotted him, walking across the compound.

Her breath caught in her throat. It was the color of his skin that fascinated her. And his hair . . . Unlike most of the men who had those inhuman-looking scalp locks, he wore his like a woman in a thick blue-black blanket down his back. He was the most provocatively masculine man she had ever laid eyes on.

As if sensing her attention, the Indian turned. His bare bronze chest was broad and planed with muscles, his arms and shoulders corded with strength. Against all reason, Rachael's gaze strayed to the small loincloth that barely covered his groin. She swallowed hard, both frightened and fascinated at the same time by the man's obvious virility. Slowly she lifted her lashes until their gazes met. For the briefest moment she sensed compassion in his face . . . interest, perhaps even lust.

A warmth in the pit of her stomach began to radiate outward. Her tongue darted out to moisten her lower lip.

The Mohawk frowned and suddenly walked away.

Rachael's face reddened in shame. What was wrong with her! These people had captured her and now held her prisoner! That man was a godforsaken heathen! A savage! How could she allow her thoughts, her body to betray her like this?

Against her will, she glanced back to the place where he had stood only a moment before, wishing he was still there.

"All of this work and no servant, Husband. It is not fair," Pretty Woman complained in her native tongue as she knelt before her husband and began to remove his moccasins. The longhouse was empty save for Pretty Woman and Broken Horn and their baby daughter who lay sleeping on a pile of furs against the back wall. "You have given that second wife Gull with the crippled wing a servant, why not me?"

Broken Horn watched his wife as she tugged off his moccasin and rubbed his foot between her palms. "Gull deserves servants; she takes good care of them. The last two I brought you both died unnaturally. I heard whispers that you drowned the little Shawnee girl, and that it was you, Wife, who fed the white woman the poison berries."

Pretty Woman laughed as she ran her fingernail across the sole of his foot. "They had eyes for you and you them."

Broken Horn's eyes narrowed. "Then you do not deny you had a hand in their deaths?"

"Give me another servant to carry water and chew your hides," she lifted his foot, brushing it against her sagging breast, "and I will have more time to care for my husband as he should be cared for."

He flexed his toes, pinching her brown nipple. "I could give you one of the captives . . ."

She raised his foot and licked his big toe. "Yes."

"The new woman. The Rach-ael."

"No. The fat one." She took his toe in her mouth and sucked it.

Broken Horn lay back on a pile of skins, moaning softly. He thought of Rach-ael and her perfect unmarred ivory skin and wondered what it would be like to lay with her here in the warmth of his longhouse. He glanced up at Pretty Woman through hooded eyes. She was a good wife; she pleased him well sexually, but she was ugly. Of course that was why he'd married her in the first place. He ran a finger over his scarred face to the place where his ear had been sewn back on. He hated physical perfection in a man or a woman and would not stand for it in his own lodges.

The white-*manake* Rach-ael was perfect, as perfect as any woman could be. But of course that could be altered. He smiled. Pretty Woman was now licking the bottom of his foot, tickling him with her pink tongue. He groaned, slipping his hand beneath his loincloth.

No man would be interested in the white Rach-ael if she was no longer pretty, would they? She would then be Broken Horn's, and his alone. . . .

Broken Horn signaled to Pretty Woman and she

lifted her deerskin skirt and climbed astride him. "Yes," he murmured in her ear as he squeezed her breasts with both hands. "Yes, I think you will have that servant." His eyes fluttered as his wife settled on his manhood. "We will welcome the Rach-ael into our home tomorrow."

"Gifford!" Rachael whispered loudly. "Gifford, wake up. I have to talk to you!" She watched the camp for any signs of movement, fearful someone would overhear her. She heard nothing but the crackle of campfires and the low murmur of two night sentries as they conversed in the moonlight. Directly behind Rachael, Dory snored.

All day long Rachael had half sat, half lay in the hot sun watching the Mohawks, trying to figure out how to escape. If she and Gifford didn't get out of here, it would be her fault when they killed him. It was her idea to come along peacefully, so it was her responsibility to get Gifford out of here.

"Gifford!"

"Hmmm?" he asked sleepily.

"Gifford, are you listening to me?"

There was a moment of silence before he answered. "I'm listening, Rachael, love."

"Gifford, we have to escape. We have to get away from these people before it's too late!"

"There's no way to escape," he said tiredly. "We're watched every moment."

She shook her head, unwilling to take no for an answer. She had to get away from here! She had been plagued all day with thoughts of the gentle-eyed Indian. The sight of him across the compound had made her stomach queasy, her head light. With the coming of darkness, she had realized that she was as terrified by him as by the others. Only for different reasons. Broken Horn, Pretty Woman, the other villagers made her fear for her life, but that other savage, he made her fear for her soul.

"No, you're wrong, Gifford. There are horses tied in those trees." She indicated the woods behind them with a toss of her chin. If we could get loose, we could take a horse and ride out of here."

"Ride? You saw the terrain we crossed. The forest is too dense to ride in! We'd not make a mile before those red beasts were on us!"

"I thought of that. But there were game trails. We crossed hundreds of them! They're wide enough for a single horse. We could just take a horse and ride east. Surely we'd hit civilization in a day or two."

"I thought you said we shouldn't try to escape." There was a tone of accusation in his voice. "I thought you said Thomas would find us. I thought you said that damned brother of yours would rescue us!"

"Shhh!" Rachael insisted. "Someone will hear you!" She took a deep breath. "I know what I said, but I . . . I was wrong. We can't wait for Thomas. We have to start out on our own."

"I just don't see how we can do it, Rachael. I'm weary from lack of food and water. I don't know that I can travel."

"Gifford, listen to me. We have to try! It's our only chance . . ."

There was another long silence. Rachael knew he was thinking. Finally his voice came again in the dark. "You say there are horses, but how are we to get to them?"

"I don't know. One of us will have to get loose and then untie the other." She thought of her Indian and wondered if she could somehow convince him to untie Gifford. *Her Indian!* Heavenly Father! What was wrong with her to think like that? She forced herself to concentrate on thoughts of escape. "We just have to make it to the horses, Gifford. It's the only way."

"You two's crazy to be thinkin' that way," Dory whispered.

Rachael wriggled her fingers until she touched Dory. "You, too, Dory. You have to come too!"

"Oh, no. Don't be cuttin' me in on any such deals. Word is, the Frenchies will be comin' through in a few days. I aim to get sold to one of them. Once I get closer to white folk, that's when I'll make my move. 'Course you never know," she chuckled good-naturedly, "might get sold to some handsome young Frenchie I could take a likin' to. Bein' a whore to a Frenchman's a sight better than bein' a whore to a fish man!"

Rachael closed her eyes, resting her head on the pole she was tied to. "I can't leave you here when we go, Dory."

"Go? You ain't goin' far. Listen to Dory and stay put." She lowered her voice. "One livin' is better than two dyin'. 'Sides, it don't sound to me like you got any love for Fancy Breeches over there. He talks to you more like he would a little sister than a lover."

Rachael could feel her cheeks burning. At least that

was one wise decision she'd made. Gifford had said that because the betrothal papers were signed, he could legally bed her. When she'd refused him he'd offered her an emerald necklace as a gift, in exchange for the gift of her virginity. Rachael had toyed with the idea of giving in and bedding him before they were wed. She had to admit she was curious about the *wifely duties* her mother had hinted at and the young women at tea had tittered about, but it just hadn't seemed right, the way Gifford had made the offer. It hadn't *felt* right.

"Don't you understand, Dory? I have to try to escape. It's my fault Gifford is here."

"Goose feathers! I say look out for yourself. You don't see *him* makin' any plans to get *you* out a' here, do you?"

Rachael glanced out at the Indian camp as she rolled onto her hip, trying to find a more comfortable position. Perhaps when Pretty Woman untied her and led her into the woods to relieve herself, she could get free then. If she hit the Mohawk woman over the head with something . . . With an exhausted sigh Rachael lay back against the post. Her wrists were raw from the leather bindings, and her feet were all pins and needles from lack of circulation. She had barely been able to stand this evening when Pretty Woman had untied her and taken her into the forest. How in heaven's name was she going to make an escape when she couldn't even walk!

The melancholy sound of a single bone flute broke the stillness of the night air. Where the flutest stood or who he or she was, Rachael didn't know. It was a magical sound that hung in the silence of the night, seeming to blend with the sway of the trees and the chirp of crickets. The lonely tune drifted through the camp, touching Rachael's heart. A smile crossed her sun-chapped lips. Even in the midst of pain and suffering, there was goodness. God had not abandoned her as Dory suggested. Rachael knew she would somehow survive this ordeal, if by nothing else, than by sheer will.

Chapter Four

"Up! Up, English-*manake,* Rach-ael!" Pretty Woman ordered.

Rachael blinked in confusion. It was barely dawn. The bright pinks of sunrise were just cresting over the treetops. The Mohawk camp was still quiet. Only a few women were up and about, trying to get a head start on their morning chores.

"I say, up!" Pretty Woman repeated as she menacingly slipped a knife from the waistband of her short summer skirt.

Unconsciously, Rachael cringed. But her captor did nothing but slice the bindings that secured Rachael's hands behind her back. "What do you want with me? What are you doing?" Rachael challenged, trying not to sound as fearful as she felt. She rubbed the raw rings the leather had cut into her wrists. Pretty Woman was taking her somewhere. Somewhere the others weren't going.

"What are you doing?" Dory demanded, awakened by the voices. "Where are you taking her, Pretty Woman?"

"Get up," Pretty Woman urged, pressing her moccasined foot into Rachael's thigh, left bare by her tattered damask gown. "Get up, English-*manake* Rach-ael. This woman has need of you."

"Take me," Dory argued as Rachael stumbled to her feet. "Take me, you harelipped bitch."

Rachael turned to get her first glimpse of Dory. The woman was heavyset with a thatch of shorn orange hair and wide-set blue eyes. Her face was pockmarked and haggard, but there was a sparkle in those blue eyes, that same sparkle of life that Rachael had heard in her newfound friend's voice.

"No talk!" Pretty Woman shouted, slapping Dory with the back of her hand. "No talk. You talk, I cut out your tongue and feed it to my dogs!"

"It's all right," Rachael told Dory as she flexed her legs, trying to get some of the feeling back in them. "I'll be all right." She wanted to reach out and wipe away the trickle of blood that ran from the corner of Dory's mouth, but she knew that would only make Pretty Woman angrier.

"I say! What's happening here?" Gifford insisted, awakened by the commotion. "Where are you taking my fiancée? I demand to know what you're doing with Rachael!"

"Hush, Gifford," Rachael snapped under her breath. "Shut up, or you'll have us all killed!" She immediately regretted lashing out at him. He was only trying to protect her, but for heaven's sake, didn't he realize they were at this savage's mercy?

Pretty Woman gave Rachael a shove forward. "Go! You walk my lodge."

Rachael threw a fleeting glance over her shoulder at

Gifford and Dory and hurried ahead of Pretty Woman. The Mohawk directed her to a longhouse on the end of a row. Painted above the door was the picture of a bear, its mouth gaped wide with ferocious teeth.

"In!" Pretty Woman ordered gruffly.

Rachael ducked inside. Built of elm saplings and bark, the house seemed even larger inside than it had from the outside. There were woven baskets and dried herbs hanging from the ceiling. The lodge smelled faintly of pungent herbs and smoke. Neat piles of animal skins and more baskets lined the long walls, as did eight narrow sleeping platforms. Rachael spotted several children still asleep in their beds. Two platforms down, Broken Horn lay snoring.

Rachael wondered where the other three wives were that Dory had told her about, but she assumed they were busy outside with their morning chores.

Pretty Woman slapped a trowel-like wooden tool into Rachael's hand and tapped a bark bucket resting near the cold firepit in the center of the wigwam. "You clean ashes." She pointed in the direction of the door. "Outside. Start fire. Get water." She grasped Rachael's chin with two pinching fingers and brought her face inches from Rachael's. "You work, but no touch man." She indicated Broken Horn who was still sound alseep. "You touch man, my man, I kill you and eat you." Her coal black eyes narrowed dangerously. "You understand this woman's words?"

Rachael paled. Slowly she nodded her head.

Pretty Woman gave a nod in return and then started for the door. Just before she ducked outside, she spun around looking back at Rachael. She seemed to be studying her captive's ragged attire. Finally she said,

"You take off."

Rachael's eyes widened, her hand going protectively to her neckline. True, the remains of her damask gown exposed more than it covered, but at least it offered some protection. She eyed Pretty Woman's pendulous breasts, wondering if the woman meant to make her to go half naked like the other savages in the camp. Rachael didn't know that she could do it . . . not in front of Gifford.

Rachael lifted her dark lashes to meet Pretty Woman's gaze.

"Take off! Take off!" the Mohawk insisted, leaning over to rummage through a pile of animal skins.

Rachael's lower lip trembled. "Take off my clothes . . . here?"

Pretty Woman tossed her a piece of tanned hide.

Instinctively, Rachael caught it. "You want me to wear this?" she asked, setting down the fire trowel so that she could look at the Indian clothing.

Pretty Woman clapped her hands. "Now! Dress! Do work!" She crossed her arms over her chest, waiting.

After only a moment's hesitation, Rachael turned away for privacy's sake. At least Broken Horn still slept. She stood for a moment with the hide dress in her hands. She knew she had no choice but to follow Pretty Woman's instructions. Still, tears of humiliation stung her eyes as she shed the remnants of her dress and underclothing.

Dropping her English clothes to the hard-packed dirt floor, Rachael shook out the piece of hide. It was a sleeveless sheath made of some sort of animal skin that had been scraped clean of any fur. Though it was tattered around the edges, the seams were well sewn, and it would cover her breasts. Rachael slipped the dress over her head, amazed by how soft the leather felt as it fell over her nude body. Self-consciously touching her knees, Rachael turned back toward Pretty Woman. "Don't . . . don't you have anything longer? It doesn't even cover my knees. I'm tall for a woman, too tall."

Pretty Woman snatched up Rachael's clothing.

"Wait, you can't take those. They're mine!" Even as the words slipped from Rachael's mouth, she knew how foolish she sounded. Of course Pretty Woman could take her clothes. She could do anything she wanted. Rachael was her prisoner.

Pretty Woman started for the lodge door again, Rachael's discarded clothing tucked under her arm. "Fire. Water. Hurry fast, English-*manake* Rach-ael."

Rachael couldn't help but heave a small sigh of relief as the Indian woman took her leave. Apparently all Pretty Woman wanted of Rachael for now was for her to be her slave. Rachael could do that. She could work. She could work while she laid plans for her and Gifford's escape!

"Very pretty," came a voice, startling Rachael.

She whipped around to see Broken Horn still stretched out on the sleeping platform, but with his head propped up with his hand. He waggled a finger. "You wish to change your clothing, you may do so in this man's lodge any time." He gave a wave of his hand. "Any time."

Rachael gasped, embarrassed, mortified that this heathen had seen her naked body, but her embarrassment was quickly replaced by anger. "How dare you look at me!"

He sat up. "A beautiful woman unclothes herself in a

man's home and he is not to look?"

"Pretty Woman made me take off my clothes! Your wife made me put this dress on and you know it." She ground her teeth. "I thought you were asleep, but you were just pretending, weren't you?"

He grinned. "Very nice, yes, very nice." He reached out pretending to cup her breasts with his hands.

Rachael squatted by the firepit and with jerky movements began to scoop the ashes into the bucket Pretty Woman had left for her. "I'm warning you," she said in a low voice. "You touch me and I'll tell your wife."

"You are warning me?" He ran his fingers over his scarred face, taking in her ivory-skinned beauty. "If she thinks you and I have rolled on the bedskins, she will kill you." He watched her for a reaction and when there was none, he went on. "She's killed other slaves I've given to her before."

Rachael looked up. "Innocent women you forced yourself upon, no doubt."

He shrugged, getting up to stretch lazily. His skin blanket fell to the floor exposing his nude male body. "A man cannot help it if his needs are great." He gave a slight thrust of his hips.

Rachael was shocked only for a moment by Broken Horn's purposeful exposure of himself, but she didn't look away. That was what he wanted. He wanted to shame her, to humiliate her. "I warn you then," she said, her gaze never breaking from his. "You touch me and I will take that knife you carry and I will kill you, but first,"—it was her turn to point a finger—"I will cut off that which you are obviously so proud of, though for what reason I'm unsure . . ."

The grin fell from Broken Horn's face. "Do not threaten me, English woman!" He reached for a belt and piece of cloth and tied on his loinskin. "You are at my mercy. You live or die by my word!" He struck his chest with his bare fist. "Not even that brother of mine can save you!"

Brother? Rachael held the trowel in midair. *Could he mean the Indian who had brought her the water? The man who long after dark watched her from the shadows of the longhouses? The savage she could not stop thinking of?* She lifted her lashes to meet Broken Horn's devil black gaze. "Your brother?"

"Storm Dancer?" He lifted a bushy eyebrow in recognition. "You know who I speak of?"

She lowered her gaze, turning her attention back to the ashes in the firepit. *Storm Dancer . . . His name was Storm Dancer . . .*

Broken Horn moved toward the doorway. "I do not know what your interest in my brother is, English Rach-ael, but I can tell you he would be of no use to you. Better to cast your eyes in this man's direction. I could make your life easy . . . or very hard."

Rachael swallowed against her fear. He was threatening her. He was trying to scare her into submission, no matter how subtlely.

"Think about my words," Broken Horn said as he moved toward the door. "You please me well and I might even make you my wife."

Rachael lifted her head to retort, but when she did, she saw that he was gone. Enraged, she stabbed her trowel again and again into the soot of the firepit. God help her, but she hated that man. Never before had she wished a man or woman ill, but she hated Broken Horn and his wife Pretty Woman and she wanted them dead. A chill covered her skin in gooseflesh. Would it come to that? Death? If so, would it be hers or theirs? *Theirs* she decided surprised by her own tenacity. Most definitely theirs.

For more than a week Rachael played slave to Pretty Woman and Broken Horn's other wives. She cleaned their firepits, hauled water up from the river, washed their dirty clothing on the rocks, and even skinned and cleaned dead rabbits and squirrels. She served Broken Horn meals and was forced to withstand his lewd comments. He had tried to touch her once, but Pretty Woman had walked into the longhouse. Rachael knew she had seen something, because, though she said nothing, the Mohawk woman had lit into her accusing her of doing some menial task improperly. She had struck Rachael across the arm with a piece of firewood, and Rachael had the bruises to prove it.

Still, the hours of hard, unfamiliar labor had given Rachael time to think. Her relative freedom to move about the camp had given her a chance to keep track of the number of sentries and the pattern of their rounds at night, the best time she thought for her and Gifford to make their escape.

The thought of Gifford made her lift her head and stare out across the camp from where she kneeled cutting up squash for the evening meal. Gifford wasn't doing well. He refused to eat what was offered. He drank only because after dark when Rachael was returned to the place where the captives were tied, she insisted.

Pretty Woman came out of the longhouse with a metal pot and several wooden utensils in a wide woven basket and dropped them in front of Rachael. "Wash."

"I'm cutting the squash you told me—"

"Wash now," the Mohawk insisted.

Slowly Rachael rose. Thank goodness the day was nearly over, because she was ready to drop. "Wash, now," she mumbled. "Yes, I'll wash now."

"You find way?" Pretty Woman asked, her lips pursed in annoyance.

"Yes, yes, I can find my way to the river and back." Rachael tried to sound too tired to care, but inside her heart was pounding. For the first time, Pretty Woman was going to let her out of her sight! This might be a chance to get a better look at how the horses were hobbled.

Pretty Woman caught Rachael's arm and forced her back around. "You no run."

Rachael shook her head. "Run? Run where?"

The woman stared malevolently. "You try to run, I kill."

"I know, I know," Rachael muttered, too tired to care if Pretty Woman slapped her for insolence. "You'll kill me and eat me, that or feed me to the dogs."

Pretty Woman scowled but released her. "Come back fast."

With a nod of understanding, Rachael headed down the neat row of longhouses and toward the river. Passing through the briar wall she had entered through the first night in the village, Rachael followed a narrow path toward the small river which she understood joined farther upstream with the St. Lawrence. She passed one of Broken Horn's lesser wives on the way and obediently lowered her gaze. It had taken her several days to realize that the women of Broken Horn's longhouse were slapping her for making eye contact with them.

Reacing the river, Rachael took her basket of dirty cooking utensils and walked down the slick bank to a favorite rock. There was no one to be seen save for three teenage boys fishing a quarter of a mile down the river. *Good,* she thought. *A little time to myself.* Rachael hadn't realized how much she had once enjoyed her private time until it had been taken away. Now it seemed as if prying eyes were always upon her. People were always watching her, waiting for her to do or say something wrong. Even Gifford.

Squatting on the rock as she had seen the other women do, Rachael pulled out a dirty stirring spoon and began to rinse it. The clear, cool water felt so good on her hands that she wished she could dive right in. She was so hot and sticky that her skin felt grimy. With the few moments of time that Pretty Woman gave her to get ready in the morning, she barely had time to wash her face and run her fingers through her hopelessly gnarled hair before the woman was commanding her to get to work.

As Rachael raised the clean spoon from the water, she splashed herself. The water felt so wonderful against her heat-prickled skin that she cupped a handful and poured it down the front of her dress. With a giggle, she reached for another handful, splashing it on her face, then her arms, then her bare legs. Before Rachael realized what she was doing, she had slipped off the rock and was standing in the waist-deep water, laughing and splashing.

She didn't know what made her look up, but suddenly he was there, standing on the opposite bank, smiling . . . smiling at her. She froze, her blue-eyed gaze meeting his.

Storm Dancer didn't know what had made him follow his brother's white slave down to the river. Storm Dancer was not generally a man of impulses, nor a man to seek out the company of others. He was a loner who enjoyed the solace of his days. He didn't know what he had come looking for either, but his reward had been great. He was amazed by this woman called Rachael, who had splashed in the water with such carefree abandon, for despite the overwhelming odds against her, she had somehow managed to find a bit of light in the darkness of her desperation. Despite the fact that she was a prisoner held in a strange land by strange people, she had found the barest moment in time to pluck a bloom from the thorns of her fate.

By the Gods, but she was beautiful, even with her pale white man's skin. Her face was the most perfect shape, and her hair, all dripping wet was like a dark curtain of satin silk. His gaze met hers and for a moment she held him spellbound. Though he'd seen blue eyes before at the St. Regis Mission where the Jesuit priests had taught him of their language and their God, Storm Dancer still wondered how anyone could see out of sky-eyes. Brown was the proper color for eyes, everyone knew that.

Rachael crossed her hands around her waist as if to protect herself, yet she made no move to back away. There was something about this man that drew her to him, that made her think terrible, lustful thoughts.

Storm Dancer walked slowly down the bank and into the water and still Rachael didn't move. He cupped the water with his hands and splashed it over his broad bronze chest, his muscles rippling with each movement. He watched her watch him. "The mother river is cool today," he said in lilting English.

She tried to ignore the way the water ran in rivulets down one of his sinewy arms. "Yes," she answered, not knowing what else to say.

He took a step forward; she took one back. He offered her his hand. "I would not hurt you."

"Would . . . Would you help me escape?" she dared.

Storm Dancer smiled. Bold she was, and clever. She could look at the enemy, see his weak spot, and strike for it. "Would that I could, but I cannot. You belong to Broken Horn. I cannot interfere. It is the law of the People."

She lowered her head, confused by the tears that suddenly clouded her eyes. "I understand." She tried to hide the hurt in her voice. What had made her think the savage would help her? What had made her for that instant feel as if her life depended on *him,* the enemy?

"You don't," he said softly, losing himself in the depths of her sky-eyes, "but I wish that I could make you understand. I wish that I could take you in my arms and carry you from this place. I wish that I could hold you, love you, make love to you on a bed of moss." Storm Dancer didn't know what had made him say such a foolish thing, but the words were out of his mouth before he could stop them.

Rachael watched a stick float by her, Storm

Dancer's words echoing in her head. *I wish that I could hold you, love you, make love to you on a bed of moss,* he had said. Rachael waited for the feelings of shock, of resentment, of utter disbelief, yet they didn't come. If an Englishman had said such a thing to her she'd have slapped him flat across the face for the insult, yet from this savage, she felt no affront. His words made her flush with . . . with what she didn't know.

Rachael turned and began to walk back up the bank where she climbed up on the rock. He followed.

"I have to go," she said more for her own benefit than his. "Pretty Woman will be angry. I've been here too long." She began to quickly wash the other utensils in the basket, water still streaming from her wet hair.

Storm Dancer came up the bank toward her. He wanted to comfort her, but he didn't know how. He looked away, fighting his anger. He was angry with his brother for doing this to this beautiful woman, but he was even angrier with himself for being unable to help her. If he helped the slave escape, the other captives would be tortured and killed. Storm Dancer would be brought before the council for disobeying the laws of the People. He would be punished, perhaps even cast out, and then how could he be here to help his people?

"Another time, another place . . ."

His voice was a whisper on the wind to her ears. She looked up. "Another time, another place, what?"

"Another time, another place and I—"

The shouts of men and the barking of dogs interrupted him. Suddenly the camp sounded alive with excitement. There was laughter and the sound male voices . . . French voices.

Rachael looked up at Storm Dancer. "The French, they've come to buy us, haven't they?"

Storm Dancer turned away so that the woman would not see his face. *"Kahiila,"* he murmured in his mother's native tongue. "Yes, little one, they have come for you."

Chapter Five

From the shadows of the doorway of Broken Horn's longhouse, Rachael watched the Mohawks. The pounding of the ominous hollow drums were wearing her nerves raw. Though it was long past the time that the village normally retired for the night, the adults had gathered at the community campfire and were caught up in some sort of welcoming celebration that was growing more frenzied by the hour. Intoxicated by French whiskey, the villagers seemed to be losing control by the hour. Men were fighting hand to hand, rolling in the dirt. Shots were fired continually as braves handled French weapons. Only an hour earlier, a brave with patchy skin had been accidently shot in the stomach and now suffered, moaning in a nearby lodge.

The Frenchman, Rouville, who had come into the camp earlier in the evening, seemed to be responsible for the festivities. He was an officer with the French army, but Rachael suspected he had broken off from the legalities of his government. Surely France didn't allow its soldiers to participate in the buying and selling of human beings!

By the time Rachael had finished washing Pretty Woman's cooking utensils and had returned to the longhouse, the Frenchman was deep in conversation with Broken Horn. Rouville was a tall, wiry man with a thinning hairline and a pointed red beard. He wore a uniform, stiffly starched and adorned with metals of valor that glistened in the firelight. He and Broken Horn had passed a bottle of whiskey back and forth as they spoke.

Pretty Woman had ordered Rachael to serve Rouville's men, who waited outside, but Broken Horn had intervened. "No, Wife," he'd said with a wave of his hand. "Leave the English-*equiwa* to serve my guest. You care for the soldiers."

Pretty Woman had lashed out rapidly in Iroquois, but Broken Horn had ignored her, making some comment in French about a woman's anatomy to Rouville, and waved her away. Rachael had then been forced to bring Broken Horn and the Frenchmen plates of rich venison stew and corn bread sweetened with clover honey.

She had served the men quickly and then retreated to the far end of the longhouse. She had no sooner stepped back when Rouville had made an offer to buy her. Rachael's mind had spun in anger as she had listened to the two men argue in French as if they were talking about a horse! She'd also heard them refer to Gifford, then laugh, but she hadn't been able to hear them clearly enough to know what it was they intended to do with him.

With the coming of darkness the drums had begun to

sound. Pretty Woman came into the longhouse and ushered her husband and his guest outside, ordering Rachael to remain and clean up after the meal. The woman had tucked her infant daughter into bed and then gone out to join the other Mohawks who were gathering in front of the community longhouse.

Once the leftover food was stored and the wooden trenchers, utensils, and pots were rinsed, Rachael sat down to wait for Pretty Woman to return for her. But the music had become more erratic, the laughter louder. White soldiers and Mohawk men and women alike became drunker as they passed the whiskey flasks provided by the French around and around.

Rachael hung in the doorway of the longhouse watching the Mohawks dance and sing. It had been at least two hours since Pretty Woman had left her to finish her duties in the longhouse. *She's forgotten me!* Rachael thought. A ripple of excitement coursed through her. *This could be it,* she realized. *This could be our chance to escape!* Her first instinct was to run to where the captives were taken and untie Gifford—and Dory, too, if she was willing to go along. But Rachael knew she needed a definite plan; she also surmised that if her captors were drunk now, they'd be drunker later. She didn't want to take any unnecessary chances. When they escaped, they would have only one chance. If the Mohawks caught them, they would all be tortured and killed.

From the doorway of the longhouse, Rachael watched the savages. No one took any notice of her as she stepped outside into the moonlight. Rouville was seated beside Broken Horn, laughing, as a drunken

Pretty Woman thrust her fleshy, sagging breasts into the Frenchman's face.

Taking care not to draw any attention to herself, Rachael crossed the compound to where Gifford, Dory, and the others were tied. Slowly, she lowered herself to the ground at her pole and tucked her hands behind her back. *Let them think I'm tied up,* she thought as she turned to get a better view of the camp. She had to count on Pretty Woman being too drunk to remember whether or not she'd retied her captive. As for the other Mohawks, they would just assume she'd been tied up for the night.

"Good God, Rachael, what are you doing?" Gifford's voice came through the darkness.

"Shhh," she answered. "Pretend you're asleep."

"Rachael, you're loose. Come untie me! Quickly!"

"Not yet," she whispered as she glanced into the light the huge community fire cast. Men were dancing around and around the flaming tower they'd built, wearing hideous wooden masks painted with leering faces and jester grins. The men sang as they danced intricate patterns into the powdery dirt with their moccasins. The French soldiers and Indian women sat in an outer circle clapping and hollering. Flask after flask of whiskey was still being passed. Several soldiers had cornered women and were fondling them roughly. No one seemed to notice the soldiers' behavior, or at least care.

"Let's wait a little longer," Rachael told Gifford. "If they're drunk now, they'll be drunker in an hour. We'll have a better chance of getting away."

"Rachael! Have you lost your senses? Untie me

this moment!"

Rachael looked up through the darkness at Gifford, hurt by the tone in his voice. She considered untying him, but he wasn't thinking clearly! If she let him go now, he might jeopardize their successful escape.

"Rachael!"

"Just a little longer, Gifford, and then I'll come. I'll untie you and I'll get the horse and we can ride right out from under their noses."

"No . . ." he whispered, then paused. "No . . . I'll get the horse. You'd better sit back down like you're still tied just in case someone comes this way."

"Gifford, I—" Rachael clamped her mouth shut. Someone was coming toward them—a soldier and a brave. The two men were laughing. Rachael closed her eyes, holding her breath as the men passed her and walked out of her line of vision.

Suddenly there was a scream. One of the other women captives. "No! No, let me go!" she cried. "Please leave me alone!"

Rachael's lower lip trembled. A moment later the men passed her again, this time half carrying, half dragging the captive in the yellow dress. Anna, Dory had said her name was. She'd been kidnapped from a farm in the New Jersey Colony.

A sob rose in Rachael's throat as she watched the men drag poor Anna through the camp, the girl screaming and begging.

"Just look away," Dory whispered, her fingers finding Rachael's. "Just look away, Rachael-honey. Ain't nothin' can be done for that girl now."

"The . . . the soldiers, they bought her r . . . right?

They . . . they're just taking her with them, r . . . right, Dory?"

"I'm 'fraid not. Looks to me like she's a samplin'. They like her, they'll be willin' to buy the rest of us. I wouldn't expect that poor child to live through the night."

The men and Anna disappeared into the darkness, her sobs drowned out by the beating of drums and the sound of the Mohawks singing. Too frightened to move, Rachael sat in silence, her head against the post as she ignored Gifford's frantic calls. Then, suddenly she heard the girl one last time. A terrifying shriek pierced the night air. It was a sound of pure terror, a sound of defeat. One scream, and then silence . . .

"All right," Rachael hissed. "All right, Gifford. Let's go."

Dory caught Rachael's fingers in her own steady grip. "Don't be a fool, Rachael-honey. You'll not make it a mile. You want them filthy animals to do to you what they done to poor little Anna?"

"They're going to do it anyway! I can't just sit here and wait for them to come for me—for Gifford. I have to try." She pried her fingers from Dory's grasp. "You come with us."

Dory chuckled. "As wide as my ass is, Rachael-honey, you expect me to get on that Indian pony with you and Fancy Breeches? The nag wouldn't make it from here to Broken Horn's longhouse!"

"You could take your own horse!" Rachael fell onto her hands and knees watching the Mohawks closely. God knew she wanted Dory to go with them, but even without her friend she knew she had to go. She knew she had to try to get away before it was too late.

"Hurry, Rachael!" Gifford urged.

Watching the frenzied Mohawk dancers and keeping her eye out for Pretty Woman, Rachael crawled the distance between her and Gifford and knelt, reaching around him with both hands.

The smell of urine on Gifford was strong. She wrinkled her nose as she fumbled for the leather bindings that held him to the pole.

"Ah, Rachael, love, it's so good to feel you so near again," Gifford crooned, burying his face in her clean hair. "You smell so sweet."

"You smell bad." Rachael knew it wasn't his fault, but she just hadn't been able to hold her tongue.

"Just wait till I've been bathed properly. Just wait until I'm clothed again properly. I'll be as good as new." He brushed his mouth against the peak of her breast.

"Gifford!" The knot came loose in her hands and she jerked back. "There." Self-consciously she brushed her hand over her leather dress. There was a wet spot where Gifford had touched her with his mouth. Her stomach rolled in disgust. "Let's go."

"No. You stay here. I'm in charge now!" He wobbled to his feet. "You go back to Dory and wait until I give you the signal. Once I've freed the horse and mounted, then and only then do you come."

Her eyes met his and for the hundredth time she wondered what she had ever seen in the Viscount Gifford Langston. "All right," she conceded. "But hurry. They might be coming back any moment."

"Yes, yes." He turned to go and then turned back,

grabbing Rachael by the bare arms and pulling her hard against him. Before she could protest, he pressed his lips to hers in a forceful, hurtful kiss.

"Giff—" Rachael struggled against him, disgusted by his fetid smell and wet, cold lips. "Gifford!" she cried out, pushing him away. She wiped her mouth against the back of her hand, staring at him with stormy, accusing eyes. "Go on!" she muttered. "Hurry! We have to get out of here before anyone discovers we're loose!"

"Right." Gifford brushed his fingertips against her chin and then turned and ran toward the place where the Mohawks kept their ponies and horses hobbled.

Her heart pounding, her blood rushing with adrenalin, Rachael ran back to her post and squatted down, tucking her hands behind her back. "You certain you won't go with us, Dory?"

"Think I'll keep my scalp a little longer."

"You understand that I have to go? I have to get Gifford out of here."

"You don't owe him nothin'."

"Not after tonight I won't," she said resolutely. "Never again after tonight."

A full minute ticked by and then another. Rachael shifted her weight from one foot to the other. *For God's sake, where was Gifford?* She stared into the darkness. She could hear the horses naying and moving their hooves on the hard ground, disturbed by something . . . disturbed by Gifford. *But what was taking him so long?*

Rachael glanced uneasily in the direction of the Mohawks. One of the braves glanced toward the trees where the horses were kept. He'd heard something too. Another brave called to him and he laughed and turned away.

Rachael heaved a sigh of relief. "Come on, Gifford, come on," she murmured. "Please hurry!"

"Your last chance to stay, Rachael-honey," Dory said gently.

"Your last chance to get away."

"I'll take my chances with the Frenchies. I 'spect Broken Horn sold us all but Fancy Breeches."

"I want to thank you for all you did for me," Rachael whispered.

"I don't know what you're talkin about."

Rachael came around the pole so that she could see Dory one last time. "Thank you for being my friend." She looked down. "I've never had any real friends before. Not someone who cared about me."

Dory's blue-eyed gaze met Rachael's. "I hope that God of yours protects you."

She lifted up on one knee and touched Dory's pockmarked face with her palm. "He will, Dory. I'm certain of it."

A Mohawk howl jerked Rachael's attention. On her hands and knees, she crawled back to her post. Suddenly there were Mohawks running and screaming. Several had grabbed up spears and were hurrying toward the place where the horses were kept.

Rachael hesitated for only a moment and then took off running. This was it. This was her chance. Either she got away now or she was dead.

"Gifford!" Rachael screamed running toward the horses. "Gifford! They've seen us! Hurry, Gifford! I'm coming! I'm here!"

Rachael came around a tree and spotted Gifford just lifting the reins over a roan mare's head. "Oh, thank God! Gifford," she cried still running toward him. "They're coming! We have to hurry!"

He spun the horse around just as Rachael reached him. She raised her hands up. "Help me get on!"

But instead of reaching out for her, he sunk his heels into the horse's sides and the frightened animal bolted.

"Gifford!" Rachael screamed. "Wait! Wait for me!" She ran blindly through the woods after him, the briars and branches tearing at her hair and clothes.

"The horse can't carry us both, Rachael, love. I'll come back for you," he called over his shoulder. "I swear it!"

"Oh, God! Gifford. Don't leave me! They'll kill me!" She tripped on a root and went halfway down before she righted herself again. "Gifford!" she moaned, flailing her arms. "Don't leave me! I wouldn't leave you!"

"I'll be back," he called as he disappeared into the darkness.

A sob of terror escaped Rachael's throat. The Mohawks were coming. She could hear them. She could hear their dogs baying excitedly at the scent of her. She wanted to fall to the ground in utter defeat. Gifford had left her! The coward had left her behind!

There was nothing left to do now but run. Run!

Rachael dodged a tree and raced down a narrow deer trail she knew led down to the river. One of her slippers flew off her foot but she kept running. Perhaps they would shoot her. That wouldn't be such a bad way to die. It would be fast and relatively painless. Anything was better than being caught and tortured to death.

Down the path to the water, Rachael flew with the Mohawks getting closer by the minute. There was laughter and howling as they gained on her. This was a game to them! An amusement! She had become the night's entertainment.

Reaching the edge of the riverbank, Rachael threw herself in. The cold water revived her. She was terrified, but she still had the will to live. She didn't want to die, not here alone in the woods!

Without looking back she waded toward the far side. She heard a splash and a shout as one brave leaped into the river. She had just reached the bank when he caught her by the hair on her head and swung her around.

"Te a yonts ka hou o twe ah sa," the Mohawk hollered.

Eat. Rachael recognized the word. *Eat . . . he said he was going to eat her liver!*

With a scream of desperation, Rachael twisted in his grasp, ignoring the pain he caused as he pulled viciously at her hair, trying to lift her out of the water.

The Mohawk wore a painted black and white face with a hideous tongue protruding from the mouth.

"Let go! Let go of me before I eat *your* liver!" she screamed, clawing at the bank. Her hand touched the cold hard surface of a rock and she grabbed it as he raised her out of the water. She gripped the rock with both hands and, with a scream, brought it down as hard as she could over his head.

The Mohawk fell back unconscious into the river taking Rachael with him. She went under, but came back up instantly. She spit and sputtered as she grabbed for the bank and began to pull herself up by the roots of grass that stuck out from the muddy slope.

Just as her cheek touched solid ground, she saw Broken Horn. She didn't know how he'd gotten there or how much he'd seen. Slowly she lifted her head to stare into his lifeless black eyes.

"You should not have tried to run," he said haltingly. "I am disappointed. You and I, English-*equiwa,* could have had a good life. We could have had many sons. Now you must die."

"Gifford," she murmured, dropping her head to the ground. Die? She was going to die. The words really didn't sink in. She wondered if Gifford had escaped.

"The coward is gone. But my men, they will find him and then he, too, will join you." Broken Horn reached down for Rachael and she lashed out at him, kicking, biting, and scratching. It took Broken Horn and Two Crows to subdue her.

Finally, when there was no fight left in her, Rachael relaxed. Broken Horn had to pick her up and carry her back to the village thrown over his shoulder.

When they entered the light of the roaring campfire, the Mohawks of the camp were waiting. They shouted at her, throwing sticks and stones. Two men bound her to a pole like a hog tied for slaughter.

Pretty Woman approached her as the men sank the pole into the ground, uprighting Rachael. "I told you no run. I told you no touch my man." A smile crossed her misshapen mouth. "Now you pay price."

With a nod, Pretty Woman stepped back and men began to pile branches around Rachael. Rachael watched for a moment through lowered eyelashes not understanding what they were doing. Her wet hair clung to her face distorting her vision. Her heart pounded so loudly that she could barely hear the Mohawks as they screeched and screamed in excitement.

Then she saw it. A torch.

The Mohawks were beginning to dance again, this time around her as the drums began to pound in an ominously slow, steady beat. Fire. They were going to burn her to death.

Drums rolled as Broken Horn lowered the torch to set the brush on fire. Rouville stumbled forward, barely able to walk for his drunkenness. "I'll still take her," he told Broken Horn, grabbing at his arm. "I'll still take the bitch, but not if she's charred."

Broken Horn slapped Rouville hard, knocking him to his knees. "She disobeyed. The man got away. She dies!"

Black clouds of thick, suffocating smoke rose and curled heavenward. The smell of the burning wood filled Rachael's nostrils. It was all happening so quickly. Her skin grew hot and prickly. She could smell her hair singeing as the flames licked closer. She couldn't breathe. She couldn't think. She coughed, struggling for one final breath of cool night air.

The smoke stung her eyes, but she opened them one last time. She wanted to see the man, the men and women who had done this to her. She forced her eyes open so that she could see them all clapping and laughing as they danced faster and faster around her, taking joy in her pain.

In the midst of the terror, something drew Rachael's attention. A sound . . . a single bone flute. She struggled to see through the haze of smoke and the confusion in her mind. Then she saw him. Her savage. Though he had not been willing to save her from the other Mohawks, he had at least expressed his compassion. Though he had tried hard to make her think he was as they were, she sensed a difference. A bittersweet smile crept across her face. She was losing consciousness now. She could feel herself slipping. Storm Dancer had come to play her way into heaven.

Chapter Six

Storm Dancer pressed his lips against the bone flute, letting his eyes drift shut as the sweet resonant notes filled the night air. Rachael was dying. *Rachael.* That was the first time he'd allowed himself to think of her by name. *Rachael . . . the wife of Jacob.* He remembered the name from his teachings of the Bible back at the mission. His father had insisted that he and Broken Horn go to the Jesuit Mission so that they might learn the language of the English and their ways. Storm Dancer had brought those things back to the village with him, but tucked safely in his heart he had also brought their God.

As Storm Dancer released a soft, haunting note, he suddenly realized that he could not let Rachael die. But if he snatched her from the flames at this moment, how could he protect her tomorrow, the next day? Broken Horn would never allow him to take her from the village to a white settlement. The law of the People would not allow it. The laws were the Mohawks' and Storm Dancer was a Mohawk, bound to those laws till death. *Would it not be better,* he wondered, *to let her soul rise into the heavens so that she might be with her God?*

Storm Dancer glanced over the heads of the frenzied Mohawks. They were dancing and singing, celebrating Rachael's death and their power over her. His Rachael had been so brave. She had not cried out with fear when Broken Horn had lit the flames, nor had she begged to be spared. She was at this moment as fit for death as any warrior. Yet as Storm Dancer studied her ashen face, as he watched her struggle for her last breath, as the smoke suffocated her, he saw a vision. Amidst thick billows of smoke he saw a child. He heard his own laughter mingling with Rachael's.

The power of God had spoken. Storm Dancer and Rachael were bound by destiny. He lowered the flute. The vision faded, the voices diminished until he wondered if he had heard them at all. He stared through the wall of flames that separated him and the white woman. Perhaps today was not the day she was to meet her God.

Storm Dancer tucked his flute into his quilled vest and pushed forward through the circle of dancers. As he stepped through the curtain of flames, he heard shouts of protest. The drums slowed and became erratic. The smoke was so thick that Storm Dancer couldn't see his Rachael. He felt for her with his hands and when his fingertips touched the soft leather of her dress, he grunted with relief.

Pulling the knife from his belt, Storm Dancer slit the leather ties that bound her feet and hands to the pole. Rachael slumped forward into his arms. Storm Dancer couldn't breathe. His eyes burned and his chest burned.

He could feel the heat of hell on his bronze flesh.

Lifting the unconscious Rachael into his arms, he emerged from the wall of flames and came face-to-face with the crowd of angry villagers.

"You have no right to take this slave," Broken Horn shouted coming toward Storm Dancer. "She tried to escape; the man got away. She must be punished." Broken Horn pointed an accusing finger. "Return her to the fire of her death."

Storm Dancer looked down at Rachael. Her face was pallored save for the smudges of black soot across her cheeks. Her wet hair, streaked with ashes, clung to her shoulders in thick lumps. Her wet doeskin dress clung to her breasts, her nipples evident through the well-tanned leather. He raised his head to meet his brother's hostile gaze. "I have the right to take this woman as wife because I no longer have a wife to cook and clean for me, is that not true?" Storm Dancer spoke in softly accented Iroquois, but his voice was razor-edged.

"Not this woman!" Broken Horn bellowed in English. "You may not have this woman! This one must die."

"I have the right," Storm Dancer insisted evenly. He lifted his gaze to meet his fellow villagers'. "Is that not right, my *friends?* To take this woman to replace She-Who-Is-Gone?"

For a moment no one spoke. Storm Dancer wondered if tonight was the night his own people would turn on him. They had threatened to do so before. Would tonight be the night he would have to raise a weapon against his own blood? His beliefs were so different from theirs in so many ways that it sometimes seemed as if he could no longer be a part of the tribe he had been born into, and that thought pained him greatly. Again and again he and his fellow Mohawks had clashed head against head. Again and again he had petitioned the council for one reason or another trying to make his thoughts understood. But his father, Two Fists, the shaman, and the old chief, Meadowlark, had allowed Broken Horn to take too much power. They had allowed his hatred for the white men to become their hatred. It had always been held against Storm Dancer that he was half Delaware on his mother's side. The Mohawks said the Lenni Lenape blood weakened his spine. The Delawares were not fighters; they were reasoners. It was that reasoning, that attempt to end the strife between the red man and the white man with words, that the Mohawks and his half-brother despised in Storm Dancer.

Storm Dancer's gaze went from one villager to the next. Angry black eyes watched him, their hatred evident on their whiskey-flushed cheeks. *Would not one man or woman agree that it was indeed law that he could take a slave as wife?*

"This man speaks the truth," came a voice from the crowd.

Storm Dancer's eyes sparkled though he did not smile . . . His mother . . . She-Who-Weeps, he should have known she would speak up, even if none other would.

"This man speaks the truth of the law," She-Who-Weeps repeated, coming through the crowd. Despite her years, she was still a beauty to behold with her petite frame and thick dark hair peppered with white. "For shame! Your English fire drink makes you forget who you are. We have our laws." she went on in Iroquois. "You cannot change them on whim. You cannot change them because it does not suit you this night. If you do not like this law, you take it to council and you change it, but this man," she raised a hand toward her only son, "has a right to take the slave as wife and even if you vote tomorrow to change the law, you know she will still be his wife."

"She's right," mumbled Two Crows standing next to her.

"She-Who-Weeps tells the truth," Gull admitted begrudgingly. "Storm Dancer has a right to take the slave as wife."

"No!" Broken Horn insisted, turning to the crowd. "The English woman was mine, mine to do with as I wished."

"You did not marry her," Storm Dancer said, "so she is free to marry me."

Broken Horn whipped around to face his brother. "She will not have you!" he scoffed. "She must agree. Is that not the law?" He crossed his arms over his bare chest in triumph. "She hates us. She hates you for your red skin, half-brother, just as she hated me. I offered to marry her but she would not have me, just as she will not have you."

"I will take the white woman," Rouville offered stepping forward. He took a swig from a flask. "I say sell her to me cheap and be done with her. No woman is worth a brother's argument."

Storm Dancer looked at Rouville, his violent distaste for the man obvious. "I would kill her myself before I would give her to you."

"Enough, enough," Meadowlark, the chief, said

from the rear. The villagers stepped back to make room for the old man. The feeble Meadowlark walked slowly under the weight of a buffalo hide cloak decorated with gold coins, his Englishman's cane thumping on the hard ground. "Storm Dancer is right," he said, lifting a wrinkled hand.

"Sir," Broken Horn protested, "the slave was mine. She tried to escape and she allowed another slave to escape. My men, at this moment, search for him. She must be punished."

Meadowlark shook his head. "She-Who-Weeps is right, the law is the law, my son. I cannot change what our great great grandsires wrote."

"You are weak, old man!" Broken Horn spit.

A sudden hush fell over the villagers. They all stared at Broken Horn, their jaws slack.

There was a moment of utter silence and then Meadowlark turned away, ignoring Broken Horn's ghastly comment. Slowly he shuffled away.

At that moment Storm Dancer felt a sorrow in his heart as he had never felt sorrow before. Meadowlark should not have allowed Broken Horn to speak to him in such a manner and live. With that comment, Meadowlark had lost what little power he had over the village. From this night forth until his death he would be naught but a figurehead.

Storm Dancer considered coming to Meadowlark's defense. He considered challenging Broken Horn for the disrespect he had expressed for their chief. But then blood would flow . . . Broken Horn's blood, and Storm Dancer could not bring himself to kill his brother. Not yet.

Raising the still unconscious Rachael closer to his

chest, Storm Dancer broke through the crowd of villagers and strode toward his lodge on the edge of the village. He ducked inside and lowered Rachael gently to a hide mat spread on the packed dirt floor. Tenderly, he lifted her head and placed a soft pillow of goose down beneath it.

From the bucket of clean water by the door he poured a portion into a bowl and retrieved a precious square of linen. Squatting beside Rachael, he bathed her face, washing away the soot, wishing he could wash away the pain so evident on her ashen face.

Marry this Rachael? I have agreed to marry a white woman? his voice echoed in his head. *I cannot marry a white woman. I have no desire to marry anyone ever again!* Yet with those words he had spoken before the village, he knew he had pledged himself. He had said he would marry her to save her life, and now marry her, he would.

Somewhere in the depths of her mind, Rachael could feel herself rising out of a pool of blackness. The burning heat of the flames were gone. Now there was only the coolness that rolled over her face, her arms, even her legs. She no longer heard the crackle and pop of the flames, but rather a soft tenor voice crooning some strange unintelligible song.

Rachael took a deep shuddering breath. Her lungs burned. She coughed, choking on the smoke that still filled her chest.

"Easy," the singing voice murmured. "Easy, my Rachael. He brushed her hair back, caressing her cheek with his cool hand.

She tried to force open her eyelids, but they seemed so heavy. The man's voice was so comforting. It would have been so easy to drift back into the dark unconsciousness that sucked at her. But Rachael struggled. She had to know what was happening.

She willed her eyes open. For some reason she was not surprised to see her Indian leaning over her, bringing a dish of water to her mouth. "Drink," he urged.

Rachael lifted her head to sip the cold water and then lay back again. Her eyes slowly focused. She was in a lodge she had not been in before. It was small and dome-shaped rather than long and narrow like the longhouses.

"Storm Dancer?" It was the first time she had spoken his name aloud though she'd said it a thousand times to herself.

"Yes, *ki-ti-hi?*"

Her gaze searched his black eyes for understanding. "What happened? How did I get here?" She ran a palm over her face. "The fire?"

Storm Dancer sat back on his heels to look at her, this woman who would be his wife. "You are safe now, Rachael." Her sky-eyes were filled with uncertainty.

"You saved me?" She ran a hand through her wet, sooty hair.

He wondered what her hair would feel like on his fingertips when it was freshly washed and dried in the sun. "Today was not a good day to die for a woman warrior."

"I belong to Broken Horn. He must be very angry."

"Very angry," Storm Dancer said in lilting English.

"He let you cut me down and carry me away?"

"It is the law."

Rachael sat up. "What is the law?"

"That if I claim you as wife, you live."

Rachael's eyes widened in sheer shock. "Wife! I'm not your wife!"

"The ceremony will be tomorrow when the great mother sun sets in the western sky."

She gave a little laugh born of hear-hysteria. "I'm not marrying you! I'm not marrying Gifford and I'm certainly not marrying that animal brother of yours!" She stared at Storm Dancer, somehow feeling betrayed by him.

He stood and busied himself in the small lodge putting away the bowl. "I am sorry for you, then," he said matter-of-factly. "Because you will have to be returned to Broken Horn."

Her eyes followed him as he moved about the lodge. Though small, it looked comfortable. A pewter punched lamp hanging from the ceiling cast golden candlelight to see by. Like Broken Horn's longhouse, baskets and dried herbs hung from the ceiling rafters and there was a small firepit in the center of the structure. But Storm Dancer's lodge definitely lacked a woman's touch. Bowls, animal pelts, tools, and hunting weapons lay haphazardly about. He had to step over a broken cooking basket to return a spear to its proper place against the wall.

"You're blackmailing me," she accused. "You can't do that. That makes you no better than Broken Horn!"

He turned to face her, irritated that she should be so ungrateful. "I did what I could to save you."

"And saying you would marry me was the only way?"

He shrugged. "It was the only way." Then he paused,

his dark eyes never straying from hers. "I give you the choice, Rachael. I will not force you. I would never force you."

"Choice!" She shoved the light linen sheet he had draped over her. "You call that a choice! Die or marry a savage?"

Storm Dancer's jaw tensed. "I did not say it was a good choice."

Rachael drew up her legs so that she could hug them with her arms. She rested her forehead on her knees, squeezing her eyes shut. What did she do now? What could she do? Here it was, a way to save herself? She had told Dory that God would protect her, that he would save her from Broken Horn, but never in her wildest imagination did she think that this would be the solution.

She lifted her head. "If I marry you, Broken Horn can't take me back."

"No. As my wife, you have my protection . . . always."

The way he said the word *always* made Rachael shiver. *Always? Just until I escape,* she thought. *Just until Thomas comes for me. After all, how much longer can it be, a week or two at the most? It wouldn't be a real marriage,* she rationalized. *It would just be a way to protect myself until Thomas comes for me, or until I find a chance to get away on my own.*

Rachael watched Storm Dancer ring out the square of cotton she knew he had touched her body with when he had bathed her. "All right," she said quietly. "I'll marry you, but only because I don't want to die."

"There are many different reasons to marry."

"Yes, and what is yours?" she challenged. She was angry that he had forced her into this position. She was angry that she had no better solution.

He turned away so that she could no longer see his strikingly handsome bronze face. "I had a wife, but she is gone."

So the widower wants someone to cook and clean, she thought. *A slave.*

"I would not hurt you. I do not believe in striking women."

"Only forcing them to marry you?" The moment she said it, she regretted her words. She knew she should be thankful. For God's sake, the man had risked his own life to save hers!

When he made no comment, she softened her tone. "Gifford, did they find him . . . the man who was with me."

He shook his head. "No, not yet. Broken Horn sent men looking for him." He brought a bowl of fresh berries and set them down in front of her. "They will kill him when they catch him," he said.

She lowered her chin, reaching for a few berries. "I know."

"He was not your husband?" Storm Dancer had to ask, though it didn't really matter. The white man would never make it out of Iroquois territory with his scalp intact.

She swallowed the berries, but they went down hard. "No. He was meant to be, but . . ." she let her voice trail off, not seeing the point of continuing. If Gifford was not already dead, it would only be a matter of hours. It seemed almost sacrilegious to speak of the trouble between them now. What was the point of saying she hadn't loved him. What was the point of saying that Gifford had never made her blood stir, not like the red-skinned man here in this lodge. Not like Storm Dancer.

Storm Dancer squatted and reached for their berries. His fingertips brushed hers and she pulled back. He wondered if Rachael loved the man, Gifford. "They say he left you behind," he said, aware of the lightning that had arced between them when they had touched.

Tears sprang to Rachael's eyes. "Not . . . not on purpose. Gifford wouldn't do that to me. I wouldn't do that to Gifford."

Storm Dancer chewed thoughtfully. "You are not responsible for another man's cowardice."

She looked up. He was so close. She could hear him breathing; she could smell that odd, provocative woods smell that clung to him. She wondered if she had made a mistake in agreeing to marry this heathen. She wondered if she had lost her soul the moment she had said yes.

"Gifford was not a coward. He was frightened. He got confused."

"They say he said he would come back for you. You know that is not true."

Again, tears stung her eyes. She lowered her head so that he could not see her weakness. "He will come," she whispered.

"I warn you, Rachael. If you become my wife, you will be mine unto eternity." His voice became sharp, almost threatening. "I will not let you go. I will not lose another wife. The choice is yours, my brave warrior."

Rachael knew it was a sin to lie. *It's the only way,* her inner voice screamed. *The only way to survive.* She hung her head asking for God's forgiveness even as she spoke, "I will be your wife," she whispered. "Forever."

He reached out to stroke her cheek. "There will be plenty of time to become familiar with each other. I do not expect you to come to my bedskins our first night as man and wife." His fingertips explored her smooth skin . . . the curve of her trembling lips. "I am a patient man."

She let her eyes drift shut, frightened by the warm sensuous feeling that had started deep in the pit of her stomach but now rose, curling like smoke to warm her limbs. *At least he doesn't expect me to bed him,* she thought. *Not yet, at least,* she reminded herself.

Rachael clasped his hand and lowered it. His fingers found hers, but she did not pull away immediately. "You said we would marry tomorrow?"

He stroked her fingertips with his, surprised by his own obvious desire for this pale-skinned woman. "Yes. Tomorrow *ki-ti-hi.* Tomorrow you will be my wife."

She withdrew her hand and lay back on the bed he had made for her, drawing the sheet protectively over her shoulders. "Tomorrow, then," she said, as if she spoke her own death sentence.

He stood and blew out the candles, leaving the lodge in total darkness. "I will leave you here tonight. It would not be fitting for me to stay with you still a maiden, but I will be just outside the door if you need me. Call and I will come."

Rachael pulled the rough linen closer, closing her eyes. These savages had a strange sense of honor. They could burn a woman to death, they could force her to marry them, but they couldn't sleep in the same lodge with the woman who was about to become their wife. The thought seemed so absurd that she couldn't help but smile in the darkness.

Storm Dancer glanced one last time at Rachael's still form, and then, grabbing his spear, he ducked out into the night air.

Chapter Seven

Rachael heard the Mohawk drums begin to beat steadily, signifying that the marriage ceremony was about to take place. She shivered despite the warmth of Storm Dancer's lodge. No matter how many times she reminded herself that this heathen rite was no true marriage, deep inside she was frightened by the thought of pledging herself to Storm Dancer.

The Mohawks had not caught Gifford, but what if he was killed in the forest before he could make it back to safety? How would anyone know where she was to rescue her? What if Thomas gave up searching for her? If no one came for her, would she be this brooding redman's wife for the rest of her days?

No. If no one comes for me, I'll escape on my own, she told herself. *I'll wait a few days, a week at most, and then I'll set out on my own. I'll play the good wife of the savage, make him trust me, and then I'll slip out of the village and then I'll be free, free from all the men who want to possess me.*

The beat of the drums outside Storm Dancer's lodge

accelerated. Rachael wiped her damp palms on the new doeskin dress she wore . . . a gift from the bridegroom. Like the ragged sheath Pretty Woman had given her, the dress was sleeveless, falling just short of her knees. But this dress had been intricately quilled, as had the new moccasins on her feet. She wiggled her toes looking down at the soft doeskin leather. She had to admit that they were a sight more comfortable than the heeled slippers she walked into the camp wearing.

She-Who-Weeps came through the flap in the lodge. "It be time," she said in her best English.

Rachael smiled at the older woman. She-Who-Weeps was the one Mohawk in the village who had been kind to her. This morning she had brought her a meal and then taken her to the river to bathe. Her mother-in-law-to-be had waded out with Rachael into the cool water and washed Rachael's hair with some thick white pith from a plant stalk. To Rachael's surprise the Indian shampoo smelled wonderful, and left her hair shiny and clean. After washing her hair, She-Who-Weeps had offered Rachael a small cake of soap so that she could wash herself. Rachael had spent nearly an hour in the shallows of the river trying to soak off the weeks of grime.

Finally, when her skin tingled from the scrubbing, Rachael had waded out of the river and allowed She-Who-Weeps to dry her off with a linen towel. Back at Storm Dancer's lodge, the older woman gave her the dress and moccasins explaining that they were a wedding gift from Storm Dancer.

Rachael had spent the remainder of the day resting. She-Who-Weeps remained at her side, at her beck and call. Once, Rachael had asked where Storm Dancer was, because she'd not seen him since the night before. The older woman had laughed, explaining that it was ill-luck for the bridegroom to see his bride before the ceremony, else she might realize how truly ugly he was and refuse to marry him.

Ugly? Storm Dancer was many things, arrogant, frightening, complex in personality, but never ugly. So, Rachael had spent the last few hours contemplating her situation and wondering what would happen after the ceremony. Would Storm Dancer keep his word and not insist on intimacies, or would Rachael be forced to fight for her virtue?

"Rach-ael," She-Who-Weeps said gently. "It is time. Your warrior waits."

Rachael nodded her head, her hair brushed shiny sweeping over her shoulders. She-Who-Weeps had insisted on fixing it this way for Rachael, in the style of a bride, the Delaware woman had said. Fanning out Rachael's hair with a porcupine quill brush, She-Who-Weeps had made small braids that lay on top, with shells and beads woven into them.

Rachael lifted her head to meet She-Who-Weeps' gaze. "I'm ready."

The elder woman took Rachael's cold hand in her own warm one. "My son is good man. Brave. He will give you sons to be proud."

"I'm certain he is a good man, at least for a Mohawk," Rachael answered honestly. "But I'm being forced to marry him to save myself. You cannot expect me to be happy about it."

She-Who-Weeps rubbed Rachael's hand between her wrinkled ones. "I understand your words. This woman was taken from her family when she was no more than fifteen summers. Two Fists took this woman far from her people and made her one of his. This woman found much sadness." She squeezed Rachael's hand. "But so did she find much happiness. She longed for home for many years until the day she knew she was home."

Rachael withdrew her hand. She couldn't tell She-Who-Weeps that she had no intentions of remaining here in the village. She couldn't let anyone know that to her this marriage was a farce. It was a way to survive. "Thank you for your kindness," she said.

She-Who-Weeps nodded. "This woman see much happiness for you, Rach-ael. She only hopes that you know it when you see it."

A shout from outside the lodge made Rachael stiffen her spine. "We'd best go before they drag me out," she murmured.

She-Who-Weeps lifted the skin flap and Rachael stepped out into the fading light of dusk. Most of the village had gathered if not in celebration, then for curiosity's sake. They stood opposite each other in two lines leading to the community firepit which burned brightly. Broken Horn and his four wives were noticeably absent. At the end of the two columns of villagers stood Storm Dancer and two old men, the shaman, Storm Dancer's father and the chief, Rachael assumed from what She-Who-Weeps had explained.

Storm Dancer drew her attention, and mesmerized by his gaze, she began to walk toward him, her moccasined feet finding the step in the drumbeat. Storm Dancer was indeed a sight to behold in his wedding garb. Dressed in a small loin cloth and a quilled vest, he stood with more bronze, muscular flesh bared than hidden. His blue-black hair had been pulled to one side and tied with a ribbon of sinew and dangling feathers and beads. On each bulging bicep he wore an engraved copper band. His face was solemn, his black eyes intent on her.

She took the last steps toward him and stood at his side as directed. The shaman began to chant softly, swinging a smoking pot of pungent ash as the chief spoke with great flourish. Storm Dancer replied once in his native tongue, but no one asked Rachael anything, so she kept silent. She tried to think of other things besides the wedding and the virile heathen who stood beside her, holding her cold, trembling hand in his steady one. She tried to tell herself again and again that this was no true marriage, but deep in her heart, she felt a tie binding her to this stranger as the foreign words of the ceremony were spoken.

When the wedding was over, there was no kiss. Rachael didn't know if that was the way an Indian ceremony was, or if Storm Dancer had simply spared her, knowing her feelings. Either way, she was relieved. The villagers did not gather around for congratulations, but rather scattered, the women heading for their lodges, the men gathering near the firepit and passing around bottles of whiskey. Rachael stood watching the Mohawks for a moment and then turned to look up at Storm Dancer.

"It's done," she murmured, not knowing what to say, but feeling some words were necessary.

"Done," he echoed. "You will be safe now. I, Storm Dancer of the Bear Clan, will protect Rachael, his wife."

She lowered her gaze, unable to stand the scrutiny of

his obsidian eyes. "I didn't thank you for saving me."

He brushed his fingertips against her pale cheek. "I ask for no thanks. I ask only that you accept fate."

She lifted her lashes. "Fate? It's fate that men will control my life forever? First my father, then Gifford, then Broken Horn, now you?"

Several braves glanced their way hearing the tone of her inappropriately raised voice. Storm Dancer took her by the arm and led her toward his lodge. "I will not control you unless you have need of control." He lifted the door flap and gently but firmly pushed her inside.

"Need of control, what does that mean?"

"It means I expect you to behave as a wife of a Mohawk would behave. You do not show disrespect for me or for my family before others. You are to be honorable in all ways and words."

She crossed her arms over her chest. "Honorable. You call the buying and selling of humans honorable?"

"I do not take part in the sale of English-*manake.*"

She laughed humorlessly. "So that makes you innocent? Broken Horn is still kidnapping and selling women! You are allowing it to happen. My friend Dory is tied to a pole out there!"

"I cannot help the others. Only you, Rachael."

Tears stung her eyes and she turned away so that he wouldn't see her weakness. "Why me?" she whispered. "Why then me?"

"I cannot say." Storm Dancer lit the tallow candles in his pewter lamp filling the lodge with soft light. "Fate I would suppose." He paused letting his words sink in. "Now come and eat. My mother has left us a wedding feast."

"I'm not hungry."

He sat cross-legged on a hide mat. "Then sit while I eat."

The tone in Storm Dancer's voice made her obey. She sat across the cold firepit from him, as far away as she could get in the small lodge.

Storm Dancer took a piece of venison covered with mushrooms from a platter and a healthy serving of corn cut from the cob. "I understand that it will take time for you to adjust to our ways. As I told you, I have much patience. But I do not have patience for sullen, pouting children." He lifted an eyebrow. "I have kept my side of the bargain. I took you from the flames and I made you my wife so that your life might be spared. You must now fulfill your part as wife."

She watched him spear a mushroom with a knife and bring it to his lips. "Tell me what you wish me to do and I'll do it."

He scowled. "I think I like better the shrew than the mouse." He plucked the mushroom from the knife with his teeth and chewed. With a nod he indicated a small bundle near the firepit. "For you, a wedding gift."

She touched her bosom. "But you already gave me the dress and moccasins."

"Open it." He sliced the venison and bit into a succulent piece.

Rachael picked up the hide bundle and unrolled it. Inside was a soft tanned belt covered with blue beads, and a woman's knife. She looked up at him.

"Every wife must have a knife. To do her work, to protect herself. You will wear it whenever you are not in sight of me."

She ran her hand over the breathtakingly beautiful beaded belt, trying to hold tightly to the anger she felt for Storm Dancer. But it was so difficult to be angry when he had given her such a beautiful present.

"Thank you," she whispered.

He dipped himself a ladle of water. "Now come, eat, and then we will sleep. Tomorrow She-Who-Weeps will begin to teach you of a woman's ways. She will teach you to be a good wife to Storm Dancer."

Relucantly, Rachael ate. Though she wasn't hungry, she knew she had to eat to keep up her strength. If she was going to escape she had to remain strong of body as well as mind. After the meal, Storm Dancer took up his flute and began to play. Lazy with food and drink, Rachael sat cross-legged, her eyes drifting shut with fatigue. For a long time she sat in the soft candlelight listening to her new husband play his bone flute.

All too soon, he laid it aside and began to prepare for sleep. With her eyes half closed, Rachael watched Storm Dancer shed his quilled vest and moccasins. She watched the way the candle light played against his bronze skin as it rippled with each motion.

Seeming to sense that she watched him, Storm Dancer turned. "Time to sleep, Wife," he said, his voice so low that she felt rather than heard his words. Slowly he offered her his hand.

She felt compelled to take it, though why she didn't know. "Yes, I am tired," she said lamely as his fingers curled around hers and he lifted her to her feet.

He nodded to the pile of soft skins and furs spread on the floor. No doubt that was a bride's bed left by the well-meaning She-Who-Weeps.

Rachael's gaze moved from Storm Dancer to the bed and back to Storm Dancer again. Before she could protest he pressed a finger to her lips.

"I said I am a patient man, and though I desire you Rach-ael, I will not take you against your will. To force a woman is not the way to begin a life together."

She lowered her gaze feeling guilty for the accusations that she had held on the tip of her tongue. "I truly am thankful for what you have done for me," she whispered. She lifted her gaze.

He caught a tiny braid of her hair and twisted it around his finger in a strangely intimate gesture. "Do not be afraid of me, Rach-ael. You are my wife now. I would kill any man who brought harm to you."

As she looked into his dark eyes, she came to the stark realization that he meant what he said. Her mind strayed to thoughts of Gifford and the sight of him riding away to leave her behind. She knew it was foolish to compare a savage to a viscount, but she couldn't help herself. She couldn't help wondering that if placed in the same position, what Storm Dancer would have done. Would he have ridden out of the camp without her? She thought not.

Her hand trembling, Rachael reached out to brush her fingertips across Storm Dancer's cheek. His skin was soft and warm. He turned his head slightly so that his lips touched her fingers.

Fascinated by the feel of his skin, she explored the contour of his lower lip with the pads of her fingertips. She could feel herself trembling, frightened and yet at the same time, captivated by his presence.

He lowered his head. She knew he was going to kiss her. She knew she had to step back. Yet as he wrapped his arms around her waist, she felt her hands fall to his bare bronze shoulders. She sucked in her breath.

His lips touched hers, ever so lightly, as if testing the

waters. Instead of stiffening, Rachael felt herself melting in his arms. She told herself one kiss was a fair price to pay a man who had just saved her life. But the truth was that she wanted the red man to kiss her. She wanted to kiss him.

His tongue touched her lower lip and she parted her lips, her entire body alive with the first sensations of desire. When his kiss deepened, she felt herself sway toward him and mold her body to his. Thoughts of the sins of lust and burning in everlasting hell tumbled in her mind, but she was out of control. All she cared about was this man and his touch.

When he withdrew, she was breathless. She was embarrassed. She was mortified. She had practically thrown herself into this savage's arms!

She took a step back, pulling away as if his warm bronze skin scalded her. "I—" She didn't know what to say. She knew her cheeks were burning bright red.

Storm Dancer laughed, but not unkindly. "Go to bed, my Wife," he murmured, pointing to the pile of furs. "I will not come to you, no matter how much I would like to."

Rachael made a quick retreat to the far side of the lodge, and keeping a careful watch on his movements, she slid into the bed. There was more rich male laughter as he lowered his hand to his loinskin to remove it and she rolled onto her side so as not to catch a glimpse of his naked maleness.

"Good night, wife," Storm Dancer murmured softly as he dropped his loinskin and blew out the candles. "Dream well."

Rachael lay motionless as she listened to him shake

out a hide mat, and lay down to sleep on the far side of the firepit, and it was not until she heard the rhythmic breathing of sleep that she finally relaxed and surrendered to her own exhaustion.

Gifford plodded forward, his stolen horse's reins still tangled in his limp hand. It was near dawn. He had been riding, then walking, for three or four days without stopping for more than an hour's rest. He was too frightened to stop. He knew that if he didn't reach civilization, the savages were going to catch him. They were going to torture him, then kill him, then eat his flesh from his bones. To Gifford, every whistle of the wind sounded like a Mohawk war cry. Every night shadow, every fallen tree in the distance looked like a savage waiting to pounce.

Just a little further, Gifford tried to comfort himself. *Just another step, another mile. There's got to be someone out there who will know how important I am. Someone who is looking for me. Someone who can help me.*

A branch snapped and Gifford came to a sudden halt, peering into the semidarkness of dawn. He was too exhausted to go on, too tired to care if the Indians ate him or not.

Another branch snapped. Gifford could hear faint footsteps now. He knew he should run. He meant to run, but his limbs would no longer obey him. His horse nickered as the reins fell from his hand. "Horse. Horse, don't leave me," Gifford muttered as he went down on his knees. "Horse don't leave me here with the Indians.

Don't let them eat me."

Gifford felt himself fall forward, pushing his face into the soft humus ground of the woods. The smell of rotting leaves and damp wood filled his nostrils. *Get up! Get up!* his mind shouted. But he was beyond trying. He wanted nothing more than the peaceful blackness of sleep. Perhaps death.

"Pa! Pa!" Gifford heard a faint voice call. "Pa! Come look what I found!"

Gifford heard a dog bark as the footsteps drew closer. He knew he should sit up, but he just couldn't manage it. The dog's wet nose pushed at his face.

"Pa, look," the distant voice said. "I found a man!"

"Holy Mother Mary," another voice, deeper this time, more mature, said.

Someone touched Gifford's shoulder. He felt himself being rolled over. He tried to open his eyes.

"Still breathin'," the deeper voice said. "I'll give him some water. You fetch your ma. Now!"

Gifford heard the footsteps crunching in the dead leaves as someone ran away. The dog followed.

Water touched Gifford's lips and he drank in great greedy slurps.

"You all right, sir?"

"Viscount Langston," Gifford managed. "My name is Viscount Gifford Langston. You must . . . must notify my family in Philadelphia of my whereabouts. They will pay you. Pay you well."

"Injuns?" the man asked.

Gifford cracked open one eye to see a bearded man in buckskins. "Yes. Mohawks."

The man in the buckskins gave a low whistle. "The Holy Virgin must of been with you! I ain't never heard of no one getting away from a Mohawk. Not alive." The man paused and then spoke again. "Was . . . was there others? Other captives, I mean?"

Gifford nodded, his eyes slipping closed. "Yes." He took a deep breath. "My wife, Rachael, but . . . ," he shook his head, "but she's dead. The bloody redskins murdered her."

Chapter Eight

Storm Dancer stood at the door of the ceremonial longhouse setting his thoughts in order. Tonight he would once again present to the council his opinion on the war between the French and the English and the village's choice of sides. Somehow he had to make the chief, his father, and the other elders of the council understand the danger of continuing the raids on the English forts that were being encouraged by Rouville and carried out by Broken Horn and his men.

Storm Dancer knew he was fighting an uphill battle, but just the same, it was his duty to his people to try his best. He took a deep, cleansing breath, trying to focus on the discussion to ensue.

This last week he'd had a difficult time concentrating on anything. Since his marriage to the white woman, Rachael, the female had haunted his every waking moment. It was not that she encouraged his attention. In fact, she avoided contact with him whenever possible. Rachael gave the illusion that she was trying to behave in the proper manner of a Mohawk wife, with She-Who-Weeps offering instruction, but Storm Dancer knew she was not a woman to be so easily changed. Rachael was there for him in body, but most definitely not in soul. She responded when spoken to, but made no effort to speak to him on her own.

He knew it was only a matter of time before she tried to escape. He saw it in her sky-eyes. Most captives in her position would have attempted already. But Rachael was patient. She was smart. Storm Dancer, of course, could not allow her to escape; she was his wife now. But just the same, he admired her for her cunning.

He couldn't help wondering if she was repulsed by the thought of being wed to a red man. During his time at the mission, he had learned of prejudice and its evils. But when he thought of that one kiss on their wedding night, he was certain he had not forced her. He was certain she had responded to him as a woman who desired a man would.

Storm Dancer took another deep breath. This was why he had never intended to marry again. Women took up too much time in thought and deed in a man's life. They were often more of a vexation than a benefit. He was convinced that men spent too much time concerning themselves with female matters. Hadn't he spent the last two years thinking of Ta-wa-ne, going over and over in his mind how he could have made her happier? How he could have kept her from—

He refused to think of her now. Tonight's council meeting was too important to lose himself in self-pity or recrimination.

Holding his head high, his tanned body erect, Storm Dancer entered the ceremonial lodge and took his place in the spot designated for a guest. He nodded politely first to the chief and then to his father, the shaman. He pointedly ignored his half-brother who sat between the two elderly men.

A clay pipe of pungent tobacco was being passed around. Storm Dancer did not care to smoke, but he took an obligatory puff before passing it on to the next man. When the pipe had been passed around full circle to each council member and then back to the shaman, the chief cleared his throat and began his customary welcoming speech.

For nearly an hour the council prattled on with village concerns of a domestic nature; a quarrel between One Eye's second wife and Pretty Woman over a pewter pot, the naming of a new man-child, the visitation of the priest from St. Regents Mission the previous month, and other trivial matters. Storm Dancer sat quietly listening as each subject was discussed and solved. Though Meadowlark attempted to run the council meeting, Broken Horn spoke most often. Other council members voiced their opinions, but the old chief and his shaman, each time, came to a decision based on Broken Horn's conception of the matter.

Finally, when Storm Dancer thought that he would go insane from all the useless babble, Meadowlark addressed him.

"So, son of Two Fists, you ask to speak to our council," Meadowlark said in Mohawk. "What is it you wish to discuss?"

Storm Dancer paused for a moment, waiting for all eyes to turn on him before he spoke. "I come to ask that the council reconsider our position with the French, Chief Meadowlark. Rouville is a cheat and a liar. The man is dangerous. We should follow the ways of our fellow Mohawks in other villages and try to make peace with the English-*manake.*"

Broken Horn groaned. "Week after week my brother comes to us with the same words." He addressed the council members. "How long must we endure before he is no longer welcome before this council fire?"

"A man of this village is always welcome before this fire. It is the law," stated Two Fists.

"That is a man who speaks out of pity for his half-son," Broken Horn accused.

Storm Dancer waited for his father's reply, half-hoping his father would take up for him, knowing he would not. Though Storm Dancer knew his father's weakness concerning Broken Horn, Storm Dancer still had the childish need for approval by his father. When the old shaman said nothing, Storm Dancer went on. "I see destruction for our people. I see blood, I hear screams of pain. I taste death on my tongue."

"Why does our father, the shaman, not have these premonitions, half-brother? Tell the council members why not. He is our shaman, not you."

Because he is old. Because he has lost the sight. Because he has been so influenced by his favorite son's hate and greed that he has lost his power, Storm Dancer thought. But out of respect for the father he still loved, he did not reply. Instead he stood and addressed the other council members. "I ask only that you think about what we are doing when we raid English villages and forts. The English are bringing men, women, and children to our land by the great boatful. They are coming whether we like it or not. And if we anger them enough they will come with their great armies of muskets and kill us while our children sleep. We have no choice, honored councilmen, but to learn to live side by side, else there will be no life left within us."

"That is woman talk!" Broken Horn accused, violently swinging his fist. "These are the words of a man who is a coward. With the help of our friend Rouville we can drive the white men from our land. We can soak the soil with their blood!"

"White men? Is Rouville not a white man as well?" Storm Dancer reasoned aloud. "Are not the French as great a threat as the English?" He scanned the circle of council members, excited by the looks on their faces. They were listening to him! He had them thinking!

"You have wasted enough of the council's time with your whining." Broken Horn pulled a silver flask from his beaded belt and popped the cork. "Dismiss him," he suggested to Meadowlark as he took a swig of the French liquor.

Meadowlark looked up at Storm Dancer apologetically. "We have heard your words and will take them into consideration."

Coward! Storm Dancer thought. *You are a coward not to stand up to Broken Horn. Not to at least come to your own conclusion!* But Storm Dancer could not bring himself to dishonor the old man. He had been too good to Storm Dancer as a child. He still deserved respect from his braves.

Storm Dancer nodded. "Think well on my words, brothers of the Iroquois nation. Bring in other brothers so that we might discuss this dire situation. Call a council of all Mohawks. I tell you our lives depend on the decisions we will make in the next few months."

Storm Dancer stood for a moment letting his words reverberate in the ceremonial longhouse and then with a nod of thanks, he made his exit, his head still held high.

Outside the longhouse, the fresh cool air of sunset hit him with a refreshing blast. Tonight would have been a good night to fish, but he just didn't feel up to it. He contemplated going to his mother's longhouse to visit with her, but found himself heading toward his own small lodge. He did not realize he sought out his new wife until he saw her standing in the shadows of dusk staring up at the darkening sky.

She was indeed a beautiful creature, this English woman, Rachael, with her crown of shiny dark hair and round eyes the color of the summer sky. Even her pale skin seemed beautiful to Storm Dancer tonight. It was not red like the mother earth but instead the color of moonlight reflected off the great lakes of his homeland.

Storm Dancer watched her as he approached the lodge. She stood like a warrior, her head held high, her breasts thrust out. She was definitely not the submissive creature Mohawk women were expected to be. He smiled. How many complaints had he heard this week from the other wives about his wife not knowing her position among the women? The entire village was divided into hierarchies, not just among the men, but the women as well. If Rachael was to become a Mohawk, she would have to learn the rules of their way of life, but all in good time, he reasoned.

Rachael refused to obey or even consider obeying anyone but her husband and even then, Storm Dancer made his wants requests rather than demands. It was true that eventually Rachael had to learn her place, but he had no desire to break her spirit in the process. She'd been too brave through her entire ordeal. She deserved a certain amount of respect that, in Storm Dancer's eyes, few woman deserved.

"The stars will be bright tonight," Storm Dancer said to Rachael, watching the way her lips turned in the slightest smile.

"Yes," she murmured. She wrapped her arms around her waist, holding herself tightly as if to protect herself from him.

"A good night to fish."

When she made no response, he gazed up into the heavens with her. After a moment of silence, he touched her arm lightly. "Come." He motioned her into the lodge and quickly began to throw some items into a canvas sailor's bag he had bought from a white trapper several years ago. He dropped precious fish hooks and a line into the bag, an extra skinning knife, a rolled cotton blanket, a waterskin, and several other miscellaneous objects.

Rachael hung in the doorway watching Storm Dancer pack the knapsack. "Where are you going?"

"We." He added a small medicinal pouch to the canvas bag.

She took a step back. "No. I . . . I'll stay here. I'm not afraid." She brushed back a lock of silky hair. She was afraid of staying in the village without Storm Dancer's protection, but she was more afraid of being alone with him. "I'll be fine."

Slinging the knapsack over his shoulder, and retrieving his favorite bow and quill of arrows, he took her gently by the wrist and led her out of the lodge. "No. I have a mind to go fishing this night with my wife. Come."

She dragged her feet trying to twist her arm from his grasp. "Please. I . . . I don't like to fish."

He stopped in midstep, turning his black-eyed gaze on her. "Have you ever gone fishing?"

She looked away. "No," she confessed, "but—"

"Then how can you say you do not like to fish?"

She turned back to the handsome brave who called her wife. The heat of his hand penetrated her thoughts. A part of her wanted to break free and run from this savage, but a part of her wanted to reach out and trace the line of his sharp jaw. She knew it made no sense, but a part of her wanted to taste his lips on hers again. "Where are we going fishing?"

"A special place." He tugged on her wrist and this time she followed. "A special place my father took me and my brother when we were children." He winked at her. "A magical place."

She took a hurried step so that she might walk beside him and he dropped her wrist. She could tell by the stubborn look in his eyes that he would not allow her to stay behind, so she decided to make the best of it. Perhaps she could even do a little exploring. If she was going to be forced to escape on her own, she had to know the area. "I don't believe in magic," she told him.

"Don't believe in magic?" His rich tenor voice was laced with a childlike wonder. "How can you live in a world as beautiful as this and not believe in magic?"

"Magic is for babes. Magic is naught but an illusion."

He laughed. "You are too serious, Rachael. You must learn to accept life's gifts and give thanks for your riches."

"I don't feel very thankful," she told him honestly. It was funny how she could never recall having ever had a conversation like this with Gifford. A conversation friend to friend. "My carriage was attacked. I saw a man die. I was dragged across half a continent by a crazy man. I was nearly burned at the stake and then I was forced out of circumstances to marry a man I did not wish to marry."

Storm Dancer was not offended by her words. In his heart he knew that in time Rachael would learn to accept him as her husband just as She-Who-Weeps had learned to accept Two Fists. "It is true that you have been through great trials, but you are alive, Rachael. You are healthy. You have a chance to make a life for yourself."

They reached the edge of the village and passed through the briar wall into the forest. She was caught between wanting to shout at Storm Dancer and knowing it was best to keep silent. She wanted to tell him she hated him. She wanted to tell him she would not stay. She was not his wife and would not be his wife.

As if reading her mind, Storm Dancer spoke. "He will not come back for you, you know."

Rachael tripped on a hidden root and he put out his arm to prevent her from falling. She pushed his arm away, catching herself. "I don't know what you're talking about."

He smiled in the moonlight. "I am no fool. I see you watching . . . waiting. I am sorry that he left you behind. You think that he will return for you with an army and guns, but he will not. That English-*manake* was a coward. He did not care if you lived or died, 'else he would never have left you." He paused for a moment giving her time to think, then added softly, "You deserve a better man to warm your bedskins, to father your children."

Rachael's cheeks burned at the thought of intimacies with Storm Dancer. He meant to have her. She could hear it in his voice. If Gifford didn't return soon with help. If her brother Thomas didn't find her—" She swallowed hard.

He's right, an inner voice warned. *Storm Dancer is right. Gifford will not come back for you. Gifford lays dead somewhere in the wilderness. Thomas has given up on you. It's been too long. He thinks you're dead.*

A sense of panic surged in her chest constricting her throat and making her feel dizzy. *No one's coming for me. Not ever. If I don't escape on my own, I'll never escape.*

She glanced aside at Storm Dancer. He had been so kind to her that she almost felt guilty. Of course that was absurd. The man was holding her against her will. He'd forced her into marrying him and if she didn't escape he'd force her into his bed.

For a long time Rachael and Storm Dancer walked side by side down a game path that led northwest. Occasionally, Storm Dancer would point out a scurrying nocturnal animal or a curious bush or tree. After a while Rachael began to relax and enjoy the sights and sounds of the dark forest. Feeling she was is no immediate danger of Storm Dancer's ardor, she allowed herself to forget for a few moments that she was the captive and he the captor. For the briefest time, she allowed herself to become one with her surroundings, just as Storm Dancer was one with this world of his.

"I never knew the forest could be such a beautiful place at night," Rachael ventured, ducking a low hanging branch. Though the elm and sycamore trees were closely knitted, a three-quarter moon shone through the treetops, as if God held a lantern to illuminate their way.

Storm Dancer nodded. He could feel Rachael becoming more at ease out here away from the village, which was exactly what he had hoped for. Perhaps alone for a day or two they could begin to get to know one another. Storm Dancer's first marriage had been a dismal failure, so dismal that he had intended to never marry again. But now that he was married he was committed to make it work. If he and Rachael could build a foundation to their relationship, as a man built a foundation for his longhouse, he was certain the marriage could withstand the winds of change and the snowfalls of time.

"What I have told you of magic is here, Rachael," Storm Dancer said. "You have but to look to see the magic others take not the time for." He came to a sudden halt and pressed a finger to his lips, pointing in front of them.

Rachael's eyes widened with pleasure at the sight of a gray fox skittering across the path followed by several half-grown kits.

She smiled, mesmerized by the bushy tails and glimmering eyes. She'd never seen a fox except for the red ones men and women in elaborate riding costumes chased while riding to the hounds outside of London.

When the foxes had disappeared into the undergrowth of the forest, Storm Dancer started forward again. "Come," he said, catching Rachael's hand.

It occurred to Rachael that she should pull her hand from his, but it seemed so natural that she didn't. She told herself that she let him hold her so as not to annoy him, but the truth was that she liked the feel of his touch. It was comforting, but at the same time it sent a thrill of excitement through her. Perhaps it was the thought of the forbidden. Perhaps she was just lonely.

For another hour Rachael and Storm Dancer walked. Then, before long, the woods began to thin. Anxious to see what was ahead, Rachael walked in front of Storm Dancer, climbing over jutting rocks and vaulting over fallen trees as if she'd spent a lifetime in the forest. Pushing through a thicket of hemlocks, Rachael rocked back on her feet in surprise. "Oh," she murmured, "it's beautiful!"

Even in the darkness of midnight, she could make out the outline of the lake's edge. "What's it called?" She walked down to the water's edge so that the water could lap at her moccasined feet as she stared out into the darkness wondering just how far the lake stretched.

"Called? It is called nothing." He put down his knapsack and bow. "It is a funny thing the way whites must name every place." He came to the water's edge and knelt to scoop a handful of water and bring it to his lips.

Rachael squatted beside him. "I guess it is rather silly, isn't it?" She laughed, her voice carrying on the wind.

Storm Dancer scooped two handfuls of water and offered it to Rachael. Her gaze flicked to his, then to the water cupped in his broad palms. She lowered her head and drank, tasting the cool wetness of the water and the saltiness of his hand. It was an innocent enough gesture and yet here in the darkness with this red man it seemed eminently intimate.

When she pulled back, he reached out and touched a drop of water that ran down her chin. She watched as he caught the drop with his fingertip and brought it to his own lips.

Suddenly Rachael was lost in the depths of his heathen black eyes. She could feel his light, fresh breath on her face. She could smell that deeply masculine woodsy scent that clung to him, haunting her every waking moment.

He's going to kiss me again, she thought. Do I allow him? But her mind was already made up, perhaps even before his. He leaned toward her. She met him halfway, their lips brushing like the wings of a night moth.

Rachael had expected, almost craved more. She nearly fell off-balance as Storm Dancer stood, breaking the kiss. "Come to my magical place," he said, offering her his hand.

"You mean this isn't it?" The kiss seemed so natural to her, as if she had been kissing the tall redskinned man her entire life.

"No. I'll be right back and then I will take you there." He left her alone by the side of the lake and disappeared into the forest. Rachael sat down on a jutting rock to wait for him. It was funny that she felt no fear sitting here in the darkness in the middle of the wilderness with nothing to defend herself but the knife she wore around her waist. It would never have occurred to her to go out alone in London or even in Philadelphia after dark without a proper male escort, but from here on this rock, both cities seemed far more dangerous than this peaceful forest.

When Storm Dancer came out of the treeline he was carrying a large object over his head. A boat!

Rachael jumped up. "We're going onto the water?" She'd always loved the water. Even the ocean crossing to get from London to Philadelphia had been enjoyable.

He carried the boat to the lake's edge and lowered it into the water without so much as a splash. "Get the bag," he told her, "and climb in. You must take care, though. Step only on the spine or ridges. The canoe is watertight, but the skin shell is very delicate." He offered her his hand. "Kneel across the ribs and you will not fall through."

Rachael stepped hesitantly into the canoe and it began to rock violently. She gazed anxiously up at him, but he tightened his grip on her hand and nodded. Slowly she lowered herself to the floor of the paper-thin canoe. Once she was seated, Storm Dancer waded out into the water until he was chest-deep and then with a leap, he stepped into the canoe, barely rocking it as he fell onto his knees. Laying down his bow and quiver of arrows, he lifted a two-sided oar from the canoe's hull and began to paddle.

Rachael was hypnotized by the single fluid motion of man, paddle, and water that sent the canoe gliding through the lake with each powerful thrust of Storm Dancer's arms. His bare back rippled with each stroke, his muscles straining against his skin with each motion as the canoe eased soundlessly across the lake.

Moonlight fell in a band from the dark sky across the water illuminating the deep blue-green of the spring-fed lake. It was the most beautiful place, the most beautiful moment in time Rachael had ever experienced.

"This is it," she whispered, afraid her voice would break the serenity. "This is your magical place," she declared after several minutes.

"No." He pointed with one muscular arm. "There is my magical place."

Out of the darkness rose the outline of land. "There we can be alone." he told her. "There we can see what it is to be man and wife."

Chapter Nine

The moment the canoe hit the soft sand of the bank, Rachael jumped out. She was caught between the fear of the ominous words Storm Dancer had spoken and her excitement over the special place he had brought her to. Never in her life had she ever experienced the emotional turmoil this heathen caused in her. Before she'd met him she'd always known exactly what she wanted, how she felt. These days, nothing was clear, nothing made sense.

"Oh, it's beautiful," she sighed, choosing to ignore his last words. She turned in a circle taking in the panorama of the water, the curving beach, and the moonlit sky.

"I told you it was magical." He smiled. He delighted in seeing her happy and carefree, if only for a moment. Turning back to the canoe, he dragged it well onto the shore and retrieved his bow, quiver of arrows, and knapsack. "Come," he told her, slinging the quiver and knapsack over his broad, bare shoulders. "There is a good place to fish around the bend. A deep place cut into the land where the fish like to hide and grow fat and delicious."

Rachael fell into step beside him. Just as Storm Dancer had promised, around the bend in the shoreline, the water cut inward making a small lagoon. The moonlight shone on the private pool, basking it in soft light. The water rippled with fish as they came up to strike at the long-legged insects that skated across the flat surface.

Storm Dancer sat down to retrieve his fishing line from his sack. "You could find wood and we could make a small fire," he suggested.

Anxious to explore the area around the lagoon, Rachael went in search of dry kindling and brown grass. If there was one thing she'd learned in the last week from She-Who-Weeps, it was how to make a good fire. Once she got back to Philadelphia, she'd have a thing or two to teach the sullen maids who usually built the fires in her brother's home, making more smoke than flame.

For half an hour or more Rachael climbed over rocks, made her way through prickly bushes, and walked along the sandy beach gathering small limbs. She was curious about what lay further along the shore, but she didn't stray out of sight of Storm Dancer, for fear she would cause suspicion. By the time she returned to his side, he had two plump trout at his feet and was pulling in another.

"So many fish!" she laughed as she dumped her armful of firewood in the sand and went to retrieve flint and steel from the knapsack.

Storm Dancer dropped the third fish onto the ground and it flopped up and down on the dry land.

"I'm hungry. Aren't you?" He held up a trout by its gills. "Fish is best if it goes from water to fire."

Actually, for the first time in weeks, she was hungry . . . famished. "You didn't bring a pan. How can we eat them?"

He pulled the long, thin knife he carried on his belt and began to scrape the scales off the trout. "I will show you how to clean and cook the fish so that you might do so for me in our lodge."

She looked away, thinking that if Gifford or Thomas didn't come for her soon, she would have to set out on her own. Storm Dancer was making too many plans. He really thought she meant to be his wife. Though she had no intentions of being a savage's spouse, she didn't want to hurt Storm Dancer. In the last week, he'd made more effort to make her comfortable with the idea of marriage than Gifford had in the last eighteen months.

Rachael turned her attention to the fire, building a tent of dry grass. With the flint and steel she lit the kindling and soon had a bright blaze burning.

Storm Dancer nodded his approval as he approached her, the cleaned fish hanging from his finger. He squatted beside her in front of the fire and pointed at the pile of wood she'd gathered. "Give me a strong, green stick."

By the light of the campfire she rifled through the pile and came up with an appropriate piece of wood.

He accepted the stick and pierced the length of the fish with it. Then, taking two forked sticks, he pushed them into the soft, damp bank on each side of the fire and hung the fish between the two by the skewer. Now the fish hung just above the blaze so it would cook but not burn.

Rachael rocked back on her feet and sat down, hugging her knees. "I didn't know you could do that. It looks so easy."

He sat down beside her to wait for the fish to cook. "No task is difficult once taught and learned."

She watched the flames lick at the fish. Already she could smell the heavenly aroma of baked trout. "But there's so much to remember. Before I came here I never lifted a finger for myself. If you'd thrown me out here six months ago I'd have starved to death or been eaten by wolves."

He turned his head so that he could watch the expressions change on her face. "But not now."

She shook her head ever so slightly, afraid to turn and look at him. "Not now," she said softly.

"Tell me about your life," he urged. His voice was as gentle as the summer breeze that blew in off the lake. "Tell me where you lived. Tell me what you did with your life before you came to me, wife of mine."

She shrugged. His endearments made her uncomfortable. They made her want to call him *husband of mine.* "There's little to tell. My father is an earl. We lived in London in a small house."

"You miss your family?"

She stared into the orange flames that were spitting with the fat and juices of the baking fish. "Not really. Only my brother." She looked at Storm Dancer who sat so patiently listening. Gifford had never been one to listen. *Stop doing that,* she told herself. *Stop comparing Storm Dancer to Gifford. You cannot allow yourself to soften to him. You cannot be this savage's wife. The thought is ludicrous!*

She went on with her story. "Thomas and I were

close, even as children. But then he bought into a shipping business with friends and spent most of his time sailing between Philadelphia and London."

She sighed. "I was very lonely when he left. Mama died. Papa started spending most of his time at the gaming tables."

"You crossed the great sea to be with your brother?"

"No." She began to draw patterns in the sand with a twig. "I came to marry Lord Langston—Gifford. We met in London. He was madly in love with me. He wanted to marry me the first night we met at the playhouse."

"He said he wished to wed you, but he did not."

She gave a nervous laugh. Storm Dancer made her think about things she didn't want to think about. He made her feel when she didn't want to feel. "He would have married me, but I said no. I wanted to get to know him a little better." She took a breath. "That's a lie. Actually Thomas wouldn't let us marry right away. We compromised and he brought me to Philadelphia so that Gifford and I could spend time together before we were married. Gifford started building a house. The wedding date was set twice, but I postponed it both times." She could hear a quiver in her voice. "I think he began using some of my dowery for the house. I think that's why he was so anxious to be wed."

Storm Dancer reached out and stilled the hand that was digging into the sand. "You changed your mind about marrying this Giff-ord?"

"Over and over again." Somehow his fingers found hers and they intertwined. "It just didn't *feel* right."

"You did not love the coward."

She lifted her chin defiantly. "He's not a coward. He

wasn't. We just weren't suited to be man and wife."

Storm Dancer lifted her hand to his lips and kissed her knuckles. "It is not your fault, my brave Rachael. It is not your weakness, it is his."

Her gaze locked with his and she was mesmerized. "No, he's not my weakness, but you are," she heard herself say.

Storm Dancer threaded his fingers through her hair, drawing her close. Rachael's eyes drifted shut as their lips touched. She knew this was wrong, and yet she couldn't help herself.

His mouth was warm and tender against hers. Somehow her hand found his bare shoulder and she stroked the hard, muscular flesh that rippled beneath her fingertips.

When Storm Dancer's fingers brushed her breast through the thin leather dress she heard a sigh escape her lips. Never had anything felt so heavenly, so sinfully good.

He teased her lower lip with the tip of his tongue and she moaned. Her tongue touched his in a slow-building dance of sensual awakening.

"Ki-ti-hi," he murmured in her ear, his warm breath sending shivers of gooseflesh down her neck. *"K'da-holel, n'dochqueum."*

She lowered her hand to his, guiding it over her breast as she kissed him. "Gifford never—"

"Shh," he hushed. "Do not speak of the coward." He kissed her chin, the tip of her nose, her forehead.

"But I can't help it." She ran her fingers down his sinewy arm, reveling in the feel of the hard maleness of his biceps. "I compare him to you again and again. You are a savage and yet you are more a man than Gifford

Langston ever was."

He smiled, toying with a lock of her sweet-smelling hair. She rested her head on his shoulder, her hand on his bare chest. "It is good for a wife to appreciate her husband," he whispered. "It is good that we could learn to like each other." He kissed her once more and then reached for the fish. "Come, wife. Let us eat before the fish burns."

Rachael could feel her cheeks growing warm as she awkwardly pulled away and sat down. She didn't know how she could look Storm Dancer in the face after behaving so wantonly. But he went on as if nothing had happened . . . as if it were commonplace for a man and woman to kiss as they had kissed, even to touch as he had touched her and then sit and share a late night meal.

So Rachael sat in the soft, warm sand and ate the delicious trout Storm Dancer had roasted over the fire, pretending that it was perfectly natural to kiss a man and then sit down to supper. She talked with him as if they had known each other for a lifetime. Very quickly it became obvious to her that though their ways were very different, this man was no mindless savage. Storm Dancer was intelligent and witty. Though his thoughts and actions were gentle, he was a fierce man with fierce convictions.

At first they spoke of meaningless things. They laughed and talked of their childhoods. Though Storm Dancer's life was entirely foreign, there was something about the Indian ways that fascinated Rachael, making her almost wish she'd been born a Mohawk. After a while the conversation grew more serious.

"Tell me why your people have become a part of the

fight between England and France," Rachael urged. She had never been interested in politics before, but suddenly this seemed important.

Storm Dancer took his time in answering, as Rachael noticed he often did. "As you know the French and English fight for land . . . land that cannot be owned, not by Frenchmen, not by English-*manake,* not even by Ganiengehka, our Iroquois brothers." He tossed the bones of a fish picked clean into the flames. "Most of the Mohawks have sided with the English. Like it or not you have come to stay. Your people come across the ocean in great canoes and settle to the south and to the east of us. Each season that passes, your foothold in this land becomes stronger." He paused. "I say, my brother Mohawks from other villages say, learn to live beside the English-*manake* or become extinct."

Rachael wiggled her toes in the sand, glad she'd removed her moccasins as Storm Dancer had. "So why does your village deal with Rouville? Why have you become a French ally if the other Mohawks are all English allies?"

Storm Dancer's dark gaze met Rachael's and she was captivated by the fierceness in his voice. "My brother, Broken Horn, has a hate in his heart for the English-*manake.* Three summers ago they came to our village while the men hunted, and they slaughtered our families. Broken Horn lost two wives and three sons that day."

Rachael felt a flutter of pity in her stomach for Broken Horn. "So in his eyes, the English deserve to die. It's revenge."

Storm Dancer reached out to take Rachael's hand in his. Slowly he traced the lines in her palm with his finger. "It is not that simple, you see the English attacked our village in retaliation. Not a week before Broken Horn led a raid on a fort. He burned it to the ground with women, children, and old men still alive inside." Storm Dancer squeezed his eyes shut against his painful memories. "I can still hear their screams."

She stiffened. "You didn't take part in it?" she asked, fearful of what his answer might be.

He shook his head. "No. Broken Horn knew I would have stopped him. I had made a trip to St. Regents Mission to heal a dying priest. Father Drake was good to me when I studied at the mission. I owed him. By the time I reached our village, Broken Horn and the other men had already set out for the fort. By the time I reached the fort it was too late."

Rachael found herself smoothing his broad bronze hand, savoring the warmth of his touch. "It wasn't your fault. You're not responsible for Broken Horn's evils."

"My head tells me this is so, Wife, but my heart,"—he touched his chest—"my heart finds me guilty. I should not have gone to the mission to see Father Drake. I should have been in my village. I knew what my brother was capable of." He glanced up into the starry sky. "I should have been there to stop him."

Not knowing what to say, Rachael remained silent. In the last week Storm Dancer had taught her that sometimes quiet was better than talk.

He gave Rachael's hand a squeeze and then released it. "I feel like swimming," he told her, standing up to stretch his legs. "Let us bathe and then lay down to sleep." His voice had lost that tightness she had heard only moments before. "It will be dawn in a few hours time."

Rachael stood. She had quickly taken to the Indian way of bathing once or even twice a day. She'd even taken some swimming lessons from She-Who-Weeps and done quite well, but she was still uncomfortable with the custom of bathing nude.

"You go." She wrapped her arms around her waist, suddenly feeling chilled. "I'll watch."

Storm Dancer unlaced his vest and dropped it to the ground beside the firepit. His hand fell to the strings of his loincloth and Rachael went to turn away as she always did, but something held her back.

Storm Dancer's gaze locked with hers as his fingers found the leather thongs. Rachael heard the leather ties and loin cloth hit the hard ground. By the light of the moon she could see the smallest hint of a smile on his face.

He was daring her!

She didn't know what made her do it. Perhaps the night air, perhaps the memory of the feel of his hand on her breast. Deliberately, her gaze slipped downward. She studied his broad, bronze chest, corded with muscles which led to his flat waist flaring slightly to his hips. Her stomach knotted. She almost looked away, but she could feel his eyes on her. Color diffused through her cheeks as her attention fell to his sparse sprinkling of dark hair and his semirigid shaft.

Storm Dancer paused for moment, letting her become familiar with the male anatomy and then it was he who turned around and walked away, the well-defined muscles of his buttocks flexing as he strode.

Rachael exhaled. That wasn't as bad as she'd imagined it would be. Though odd, Storm Dancer's male parts were not completely unintriguing, in fact . . .

Rachael groaned aloud at the path her mind was taking. Six weeks with these amoral heathens and she was thinking like them!

She heard a splash and looked up to see Storm Dancer sliding gracefully under the water. He surfaced in a puddle of moonlight and waved. "Come to me, Wife."

She walked to the water's edge and let the water wash over her bare toes. The lake did look inviting.

He waved again. "I give you my word as a warrior that I will not lay a hand on you, Wife. Come in and enjoy the water. It's part of the magic."

A mischievous smile broke across her face. *Who would ever know?* she thought. *Once I'm back in Philadelphia, who would ever know I'd swum naked with my savage?*

No one.

Rachael touched the lacing of the vest she wore. She had only the vest, a short skirt, and the woman's loincloth to remove. Storm Dancer was watching her. Even in the moonlight she could see his black eyes riveted to her. She lowered her gaze to the leather bodice. Her hands trembled as she untied the rawhide lace. She stalled by pulling the lace from each eyelet until finally the vest hung open revealing much of her breasts. Afraid she would lose her nerve, she shrugged it off and dropped it beside Storm Dancer's clothing.

The cool night air hit her breasts, making her nipples pucker. Unable to look at Storm Dancer, she found the tie of her short skirt and in a moment, it too lay on the ground. Her hand went to the loincloth. Two weeks ago she had been almost frightened of this undergarment, but now it was her only protection.

"That is enough," Storm Dancer urged gently, as if knowing the thoughts that flew through her mind. "Join me and we will bathe together."

Though she wanted to run, Rachael took her time in entering the water. She tried to savor each sensation and cast it to memory—the smell of the night air, the touch of the cool breeze, the sight of Storm Dancer waiting in waist-deep water, the feel of his gaze on her naked flesh.

Rachael waded out until the water was thigh-high and then she lowered her body, covering herself with the security of the dark water.

"Brr, it's cold," she said, her own voice sounding odd to her ears. She came within three feet of him and stopped.

Storm Dancer reached beneath the water and brought up a handful of sand and began to scrub himself as was the custom. Rachael did the same. The grainy sand was abrasive to her tender skin, but left her entire body covered with tingling sensations. Storm Dancer leaned back to wash his hair. Rachael did the same, but each time that she went underwater, he appeared a few inches closer.

Then somehow he had her hand. He opened his arms, inviting her into his embrace. Rachael shivered as much from fear as cold. "I—"

"I want only to hold you, Rachael-wife. I told you. I would never force a woman to give of herself what she did not wish to give, and certainly not my wife."

At that moment, Rachael trusted Storm Dancer wholeheartedly. He wrapped her nude body in his arms beneath the water and it seemed the most natural thing to her. His warmth drew her closer until she snuggled against his chest, her cheek resting on his shoulder. She glided her hands over the curves of his muscular forearms feeling wickedly bold. If she was truly his wife, there was no sin in their touching, was there?

But was she his wife? Rachael had told herself time and time again in the last week that she was not. Yet the smallest part of her told her she *was* married to this strikingly handsome red man.

Storm Dancer lifted her off her feet, cradling her with his own body. By the light of the moon she could see him gazing down at her, his dark eyes filled with the fire of his longing.

When he leaned down to kiss her, she turned her face toward him. She threaded her fingers through his wet hair, savoring the taste of him, lips against lips, tongue touching tongue.

This time when his hand made contact with her breast, she allowed herself to enjoy the strange sensations that rippled through her entire body. Floating in his arms, her head in the crook of his arm, she watched his hand as he stroked her.

When Storm Dancer lowered his mouth to her breast, she sucked in her breath, stiffening. He murmured something in Mohawk and she relaxed, not knowing what he said, yet understanding his reassurance. The feel of his wet, hot mouth tugging at her nipple sent tremors of delight through her veins. She wanted him to stop, but she wanted him to go on forever.

"Storm," she murmured.

"Wife," he answered in a teasing voice.

"Storm, you have to stop."

"Why?" He kissed his way up between the valley of her breasts. "Tell me why, sweet wife of mine."

"Because . . . because . . ." Flustered, she gave into the laugher that bubbled up inside her. "Oh, because I don't know why, just because."

One moment he was laughing at her, then suddenly he was lowering her into the water. She could feel his body stiffen as he released her, his muscles bunching as he eased her to her feet in the waist-deep water.

"What is it?" Suddenly she was frightened. He was watching the shore as he waded toward it.

"Stay, Rachael," he ordered briskly.

She covered her bare breasts with her arms. The laughter and excitement of the moment was past and now all she had left was fear and shame. "Storm—"

He brought a finger to his lips. "Shhh. Stay where you are and you will be safe."

She waded toward him, not wanting to stay in the water alone.

The moment his bare feet hit the dry land he was sprinting the few feet to the campfire. By the light of the dying flames she could see him reach for his knife.

Rachael still saw nothing or no one. What was wrong with Storm Dancer? There was no one out there!

"This isn't funny. Wait for me!"

He turned toward her, crooking a finger. "Get on your clothes and wait for me here. Do not forget your knife, Rachael." He turned back toward the darkness of the land that spread from the shoreline.

She had nearly reached the bank when she heard a terrifying war cry. Someone sprang out of the darkness and Storm Dancer whirled around, his knife glinting in the moonlight as he faced his attacker.

Rachael's hands flew to her mouth to keep from crying out as she saw through the shadows of night, the face of Broken Horn.

Chapter Ten

Storm Dancer fell beneath the weight of his brother, but twisted out from under him and bounced up into a crouching position. Broken Horn rolled and flipped into the same stance, imitating Storm Dancer.

Storm Dancer barked something in Mohawk and Broken Horn broke into a grin. He laughed jokingly, but Storm Dancer did not.

Rachael covered herself with her hands as best she could and stalked out of the water. The bloody bastard Broken Horn had been spying on them! He'd watched her and Storm Dancer. She could feel her face growing hot with embarrassment at the thought of what had taken place in the lake . . . what someone had watched them do.

"Damn him," she muttered hurrying for her clothes on the bank, not caring if Broken Horn saw her stark naked. At this point what was there left to see?

Broken Horn tossed his knife to the ground and Storm Dancer followed suit. Without weapons, the two men circled each other like caged beasts. Broken Horn hissed, moving his hands in a circular motion, daring Storm Dancer to make the first move.

Ignoring the men, Rachael yanked on her vest and reached for her leather skirt. She wasn't certain whether Storm Dancer had known Broken Horn followed them or not, but she didn't care. At this moment she hated Storm Dancer as much for luring her into the water and making her want him to touch her like that as she hated Broken Horn for watching them.

As Rachael jerked on her skirt she could hear Storm Dancer speaking in harsh, low tones. He was angry. No, by the sound of his voice he was enraged. Her gentle lover had become the vicious savage that she'd known he was all along. The logical conclusion would be that Storm Dancer was furious with his brother for following him, but Rachael wasn't interested in logic. She strapped her beaded belt and knife sheath around her waist. There was no room in her head for logic when her heart was so overwhelmed by emotion.

She sat down on the ground to pull on her moccasins, not caring that the sand stuck to her wet skin. She wasn't staying here, not with these crazy red men. She wanted to go home to Philadelphia, and if Thomas or Gifford weren't coming for her, she'd find her way home on her own!

Broken Horn straightened, looking past Storm Dancer to where Rachael stood dressing. By the light of the campfire he could make out every feminine curve of her body. "She is a beautiful woman in her pale-skin way, Brother," he said in English so that she might hear. "Responsive to a man's touch, eh?" He laughed. "As brothers share of the hunt, let me share of the feast." His tongue darted out to touch his upper lip. "I have a taste for white honey."

Before Rachael could shout a reply, Storm Dancer swung his fist and connected with his brother's jaw. Broken Horn went reeling backward, taken completely by surprise.

"Do not insult my wife again, Brother," Storm Dancer threatened. "Or I will be forced to kill you and hang your scalp from my lodgepole for all the world to see."

"Kill me!" As he got to his feet, Broken Horn stroked his prized scalp lock mockingly. "You would not kill me and you and I both know it. You are too soft for the Mohawk way of life and everyone knows it. That is why they will not listen to you at council."

"They will not listen to me at council because you have filled their minds with lies and their hearts with hatred."

This time it was Broken Horn who attacked, but Storm Dancer dodged the assault and swung again, slamming Broken Horn in the stomach. With a sharp exhalation of breath, Broken Horn went down on one knee clutching his midsection.

Storm Dancer rested his hands on his bare hips. "Leave now before I am forced to dishonor our father and hurt you!"

"Hurt me?" Broken Horn rose slowly, trying to catch his breath. "You don't have the balls. Now come, Brother, hand over the woman and let a real man give her a ride,"—he thrust out his hips—"a ride she will be long in forgetting."

Storm Dancer dove forward wrapping his arms around Broken Horn's waist and sending them both crashing to the ground.

Rachael went on lacing her moccasins. She didn't care if the two of them killed each other. She wasn't waiting around to see the outcome.

The two brothers rolled over and over in the sand pounding each other with their fists.

Rachael stood up and grabbed the knapsack Storm Dancer had brought with them. Taking the waterskin as well, she started off in the opposite direction of the two fighting men. Perhaps if she was lucky they'd both roll into the lake and drown each other. As she disappeared into the darkness she could hear the muffled thumps of Storm Dancer's fist connecting with Broken Horn's face as he struck him again and again in uncontrolled fury.

"I'm going home," she muttered beneath her breath as she stalked off into the darkness, fighting tears. "I just want to go home."

Storm Dancer hit his brother in the jaw and Broken Horn's body went limp. Breathing heavily, Storm Dancer rose, leaving Broken Horn lying unconscious in the sand.

"Rachael?" Storm Dancer called, wiping away the blood that trickled from the corner of his mouth. *"Maata wischasi, n'dochquem."* When he heard no response, he walked to the campfire. It was beginning to die out.

Rachael's clothes were gone, as were her knife, the waterskin, and his knapsack. Storm Dancer smiled. So his English-equiwa wife had fled finally, had she?

A part of him could not help being hurt by the thought that despite what they had shared here on the shore and in the water, despite the obvious feeling between them, she did not want to stay with him. He thought of Ta-wa-ne and had to fight the bitter anger that rose in his throat threatening to choke his reasoning.

Rachael was not Ta-wa-ne. Rachael was a woman who had been held captive and was forced to marry him to save herself. In her eyes she was still a captive. In truth, she was. Storm Dancer had to keep that fact in mind when judging her actions.

But the fact remained that she *was* his wife and though he had lost one, he would not lose another.

Storm Dancer glanced over his shoulder at Broken Horn. Storm Dancer knew he should feel some sense of remorse for losing his temper as he had. Broken Horn's face was a bloody pulp. Several ribs were probably broken. It was not the Mohawk way for brother to fight against brother in this manner. But Storm Dancer felt no remorse, only an ominous fear that this was not the end of their argument. Since Broken Horn had brought Rachael to the village the chasm between him and Storm Dancer had only widened.

Storm Dancer put on his loincloth and moccasins and then went to Broken Horn. He pushed his brother's shoulder with the toe of his moccasin. *"Ickalli aal!* Away with you brother before I lift your scalp and hang it from my lodgepole."

Broken Horn groaned but made no attempt to rise.

Storm Dancer glanced off in the direction of Rachael's footprints. She would not get far. First he would deal with his brother, then his disobedient wife. He walked down the beach around another bend and there on high ground was Broken Horn's canoe. Had Storm Dancer been less enthralled with his wife and more observant of his surroundings he'd have heard or at least felt Broken Horn approaching by water.

Storm Dancer dragged the canoe down to the water and floated it back around the bend to where his brother lay unconscious. Pulling the canoe far enough up on the bank to keep it from floating away, Storm Dancer went back to Broken Horn.

Standing over him, he stared at his face. Though they had once been friends a long time ago, they were now enemies and that thought saddened Storm Dancer. Broken Horn had dishonored him too many times in word and deed for them to be anything but adversaries. *The wise thing would be for me to kill him now,* he thought. *Before he destroys what chance I have with Rachael . . . before he destroys our entire village.*

But Storm Dancer could not do it. They were still blood brothers, if only half-brothers. No, if he was going to kill Broken Horn it would be in fair battle, warrior against warrior. Storm Dancer leaned over and slung Broken Horn's limp body over his shoulder. His brother was beginning to stir, but was still unconscious.

Storm Dancer dumped Broken Horn unceremoniously into the canoe and gave it a shove into the water. For a moment he held the bow of the boat, staring down at Broken Horn. On impulse, he took his knife from his belt and with one slice of the razor-sharp blade he held Broken Horn's precious scalplock in his hand. He had threatened to hang Broken Horn's scalp from his lodgepole for the insult thrown on his wife. Was this not even better revenge? Now Broken Horn's scalplock would fly from Storm Dancer's lodgepole for all to the village to see and Broken Horn would be forced to hear their laughter.

Storm Dancer tucked the long black scalp lock into his belt and then gave the canoe a shove, setting it adrift. Returning his knife to its sheath he cast a final glance over his shoulder at the canoe and then took off in an easy trot in the direction Rachael had fled.

Rachael sat on a log half buried in the sand staring out at the lake that she now knew surrounded them. Storm Dancer had known she would try to escape! That's why he'd brought her here. She picked up a broken branch that had drifted ashore and hurled it angrily into the water. She was trapped on the island surrounded by water, just as she was trapped in the village surrounded by hundreds of miles of wilderness.

An unfamiliar sound made Rachael leap up off the log. Someone was approaching. Broken Horn? As much as she wanted to get away from Storm Dancer, she prayed it was him and not his brother. Broken Horn was evil and he was dangerous and Rachael had no desire to tangle with him on a deserted island in the middle of the night.

Peering into the darkness, Rachael slipped her knife from its sheath. Her first impulse was to call out into the darkness but she didn't. *Never call attention to yourself,* Storm Dancer had just told her the other day. *See and know the enemy before he sees you.*

So Rachael waited, without moving. Though her heart was pounding in her chest, she breathed easily, listening, watching the beach. The footsteps grew closer and then suddenly stopped. She thought she could see a dark form, but she wasn't certain. She squinted, her knife clutched in her hand, her body tensed.

"Yuh Kehella, kikileuotte," came a voice from the darkness.

Rachael felt herself immediately relax, if only slightly. It was Storm Dancer. She lowered her knife. "You didn't tell me this was an island!" She was shocked by the harshness of her own voice.

"You gave me your word a week ago, Wife, that you would not try to escape." He came toward her. "I am disappointed in you."

She flailed her knife. "Come a step closer and I'll slit your throat."

He laughed. "Brave and fierce as well."

"I'm entirely serious."

He stopped an arm's length from her. She could see him now. He was dressed in his loin cloth and vest, his wet hair clinging to his muscular shoulders. He had several cuts on his face that oozed blood. He was the most frighteningly handsome man she had ever seen in her life.

"You have nothing to fear from me, Rachael. Why do you try to run?"

"He followed us. He watched us—" She stared at

him with accusing eyes. "You knew he was there."

"I did not. I should have known, but I was lost in the moment. I offer my apologies for allowing my brother to sneak up on us. I am sorry, Rachael-wife."

Lost in the moment. From any other man, his words would have sounded shallow and false. But on Storm Dancer's tongue, the words rang true. They had both been lost in the moment, hadn't they? She lowered the knife. "Stop calling me wife! I hate it when you do that and you know it!"

"But you are my wife and it is time you accept and make the best of what Wishemoto has given you."

"Wishemoto? I know no Wishemoto!"

"He is God in your tongue."

"God? And what do you know of God?" she said.

"I know he delivered you from a burning death by my arms. I know he has given you another chance at life and you must take that chance. No one is coming for you, Rachael. You must know that. You must also know that I would not allow you to go if someone did. You are my wife now and I will fight to the death to keep you at my side."

Tears stung Rachael's eyes at the truth and finality of Storm Dancer's words. "Accept? How can I ever accept being a prisoner?"

"You would not have to be a prisoner if you would be my wife."

"You said I already was your wife."

His black eyes pierced hers, preventing her from looking away. "No, you are pretending to be my wife." He took another step forward, crossing his arms over his chest as he considered her. "How foolish do you think I am that I cannot see through you? You do what I ask of you, but you have offered me nothing of yourself. I know you wait for the man who left you behind—the coward who will not return. Truly become my wife and you will be as free as the red bird that flies, as free as any Mohawk can be."

"Be your wife truly? What do you mean? You mean let you—"

"No!" he barked, losing his patience. "Listen to my words. Do not change them to suit your own ideas. I told you, I would never force you to give of yourself. I want you to come willingly into my arms. I want you to ask me to take you to my bedskins and love you as you deserve to be loved. But for now I would be pleased to see you try to be a good wife. I would like to see a little gratitude."

"Gratitude? For what?" she spit. "What do I get out of this *marriage* other than my life which seems rather worthless at this moment?"

When he spoke again the anger was gone from his voice. "What do you want?"

"I want you to take me home to Philadelphia."

He shook his head. "You know I cannot do that. Something else."

She looked away, staring out at the water. What did she want? She couldn't think of anything to ask for! Then suddenly she thought of Dory. Dory had not been taken by the French along with the other women captives. Too fat and old Rouville had said. Rachael turned back toward Storm Dancer. "I want you to free Dory."

"Dory?" He frowned. "Who is this *Dory?*"

"The woman I take food and water to every day. She's my friend."

He shook his head. "I cannot free her. She belongs to Pretty Woman."

"Then buy her." She looked up at him. "She's going to die sitting there in the sun."

"I cannot take her back to her homeland wherever that might be."

Rachael understood the Mohawk ways enough to realize that. "I know," she said, going on faster than before. "But you could buy her for our slave, couldn't you."

He fingered his beaded belt thoughtfully. "The price would be high."

"Please, Storm?"

He smiled. He liked the sound of her voice when she called him by name. Storm. She spoke the word as if it were an endearment. "And in return?"

She met the challenge of his gaze. "In return I will try to accept my circumstances." *At least for the time being,* she thought.

He considered her offer for a moment and then nodded. "If it is in my power, I will buy this Dory for you, Wife."

She smiled. "Thank you."

He draped an arm around her shoulder. "Come now, it is nearly dawn. Let us lay down and take our sleep. It has been a long night."

Rachael took the blanket from the knapsack and shook it out. He caught the other side and helped her to lay it out on the ground. "What happened to Broken Horn?" she asked, as she stretched out.

Storm Dancer laid his weapons on the edge of the blanket and lay down beside her. "He has gone home."

Rachael pushed up on her elbow, looking down at Storm Dancer's face. She wondered what was so humorous. "Gone?"

He reached out and pulled her down so that her head rested on his shoulder. "I have dealt with my brother. Now, sleep, Wife, and in the morning we will catch fish to take home to our lodge."

Rachael relaxed in his arms and Storm Dancer gave a comfortable sigh. For the moment all seemed right in the balance of the world. He reached down to touch his brother's scalplock that hung from his belt and smiled.

"The Viscount Moreover to see you, sir."

Gifford's gaze wandered from the framed buttery specimen on the wall to the housemaid standing in the parlor doorway. "Who?"

She cast her eyes downward. "Lord Moreover, sir. Lady Rachael's brother."

Gifford considered sending him away with word that he wasn't well enough to receive visitors yet. But he thought better of it. He glanced into a Venetian mirror that hung on the wall and smoothed back his hair. Perhaps it would be better to receive Thomas while he was still looking so pallored.

Gifford glanced back at the young girl still hanging in the doorway. "Well don't just stand there like an addlepated chit, Anna. Send him in!"

She dipped a quick curtsy and hurried down the hallway.

With a sigh, Gifford went to the cherry sideboard beneath the window and reached for a bottle of bourbon. He poured himself a healthy portion and lifted the glass to his lips. He closed his eyes. Once this was taken care of, he could forget about Rachael, about the Indians, about those dreadful weeks, and go on with his life.

He smiled and took another sip of his bourbon, his eyes scanning the wall lined with butterflies from all over the world. Once this was taken care of he could go on with the construction of his house. Though the costs were running higher than he'd anticipated, it was all going to be worth it when he held his first ball in the ballroom of the thirty-seven-room house overlooking the Delaware river. Then he'd be the talk of Philadelphia—the talk of the entire colony. Philadelphians would be pining for invitations to the great Langston estates. Everyone would want to be his intimate friend. His capture by the Mohawks and escape had make him popular, but this home was going to make him renowned!

The Honorable Thomas Moreover cleared his throat.

Gifford spun around. "Thomas." He offered a sad smile and hurried to take his hand. "So good to see you, Thomas."

Thomas crossed his arms over his chest and leaned against the door frame. "Spare me the sensitivities, Giffy. I just came into port last night. They say my sister's dead. They say she had married you."

Gifford hung his head. "True. All true."

"How the hell did you get captured by Indians in Philadelphia?" Thomas barked. "How the hell did you get away and not Rachael?" His voice cracked as he said her name.

Gifford brushed his blond hair off his forehead and took a gulp of the liquor still clenched in his hand. "Please don't ask me to go over the details again." he shook his head. "I just can't bear to think of it right now. My Rachael, my poor little wife."

Thomas glanced out the window unable to stand the sight of the whimpering ass his sister had married. "You're certain she's dead?"

He nodded. "Saw it with my own eyes. Ah, Thomas, it was horrendous. Those savages—" he cut himself off. He had found that in relating his tale his audience enjoyed drawing their own conclusions.

"So when did you marry? She swore to me she'd wait until I returned from Jamaica" He met Gifford's gaze, but Gifford looked away.

"Just that day, in fact." He smiled at the fabricated memory. "My cousin Reverend James performed the ceremony."

Thomas's eyes narrowed. "No witnesses?"

Gifford couldn't resist a smile. "The good reverend of course, but he's dead."

"Documentation?"

Gifford shrugged and tipped his glass again. "Destroyed or lost by the savages, of course. There are only the betrothal papers and the death certificate my uncle down at the courthouse was kind enough to provide."

Thomas swore foully beneath his breath. "I can't believe you let her die, you little bastard!"

Gifford looked up, his eyes cold with hatred. "Had I been able to save Rachael, I would have, but it was beyond my control. My wife is dead, God rest her soul, and I will have to live with that for the rest of my life."

"Where are these sons of bitches, these Mohawks? I'll go there myself."

"And you'll never come out alive." Gifford went to the side table to pour himself another drink. "Take my advice, friend, and accept Rachael's death as I have."

Thomas crossed the hardwood floor in four long strides. He grabbed the mulberry collar of Gifford's coat and spun him around. "Tell me where the Indians are!"

Gifford never flinched. "I don't know. Now, unhand me before I call my man to escort you from my house."

Thomas held him a second longer and then released his collar, giving him a shove. "There's more to this story than meets the eyes, Giffy." He shook a finger. "And let me tell you, if I discover you killed her yourself, I swear to Christ I'll kill you with my bare hands. You say these Mohawks tortured you, well let me tell you, you don't know what torture is!"

Gifford smoothed the collar of his coat. "Please leave my home."

"Gladly." Thomas turned around and headed for the hall.

"But, Thomas . . ."

Thomas turned and glared.

"I'll expect the balance of my deceased wife's dowry in thirty days."

"You pettifogging bastard!"

"I've checked with my barrister. You are under legal obligation to provide the balance in one month's time or your business holdings will be frozen until the court can deal with the matter." He paused. "And heaven knows the English courts can be slow. It might be a year or more before your business accounts would be open to your use again."

Gifford couldn't resist a smile as Thomas walked out of the parlor and slammed the door so hard that a framed African monarch butterfly flew off the wall, the glass shattering as it hit the floor.

Chapter Eleven

Rachael and Dory knelt side by side at the stream's edge washing cooking utensils and discussing where they would go berry picking in the morning. For the hundredth time in a week Rachael glanced at Dory and smiled. It was so good to have a friend.

Storm Dancer had kept his word. Though the price had been steep, he had purchased Dory from Pretty Woman and Dory was now Rachael's personal slave. Once the deal was made, Rachael had gone immediately to Dory and untied her. The older woman had been so grateful that tears had filled her blue eyes. She vowed to give her life to Rachael for saving her own.

Of course Rachael didn't want Dory for a servant. She'd had enough servants to last her a lifetime. All she wanted was a companion and Dory had become just that. Despite their difference in age and life experiences, they found they truly enjoyed each other's company. Dory was anxious to help Rachael adjust to her new position as wife to Storm Dancer in any way she could. Because she had lived in a Seneca village she had many skills necessary to an Indian wife. Not only could she do a task and do it well, but she had a good sense of humor about it. Working side by side, Dory made the tedious daily chores seem almost fun.

And then of course she adored Storm Dancer. When Rachael had confessed that she had not had sexual relations with her husband and that she did not intend on staying, Dory had become angry. She said most women would give anything to have the kind of husband Storm Dancer would be if Rachael would just give him a chance. Dory had also made it quite clear that she would not help Rachael try to escape. She said she would not be responsible for her friend's death. But Dory had not held this difference of opinion against her. She in fact made it a personal objective to unite Rachael and Storm Dancer who now moved cautiously around each other. Storm Dancer was giving her time for adjustment and Rachael was trying to deal with her obvious feelings for her husband, feelings she passionately wanted to deny.

Dory elbowed Rachael in the side and glanced knowingly downstream. Rachael leaned forward, shaking the water from a wooden stirring stick. It was Pretty Woman and Gull. Rachael smiled mischievously. Dory got a great deal of pleasure from annoying Broken Horn's wives and though Rachael didn't encourage her, she could not help herself when the opportunity arose.

"Tell Pretty Woman how much you like 'er new skirt," Dory whispered, scrubbing a copper pan with a great deal of vigor.

Rachael glanced sideways.

"Go ahead," Dory urged. "I always did enjoy a cat fight."

"What are you talking about?" Rachael whispered.

"Just tell 'er."

Rachael leaned over the edge of the bank and nodded politely. In her best broken Mohawk she spoke.

Pretty Woman looked up suspiciously. But her vanity got the best of her and she stroked the blue damask. "My warrior brought it to me. He paid much for such fine English cloth," she said in English.

Gull cast a sideways glance at Rachael. "The skirt was mine," she said partly in Mohawk, partly in English. "Our husband gave it to me."

"He did not," Pretty Woman protested. "I am first wife. All gifts come to me and you get what I cast off."

Gull stood up and threw a pewter plate to the ground in anger. "That is not the truth. Your name should not be Pretty Woman, but She-Who-Tells-Lies! You took the skirt from me when I slept."

"Ha!"

"It is true. Our husband gave the skirt to me because I please him on the sleeping mat." Gull took a step toward Pretty Woman, pushing her face into the other wife's. "He said you bored him."

"And now look who lies! My husband says you sound like a cat hung from a tree the way you scream in his ear!"

In fury Gull reached out and yanked on Pretty Woman's blue skirt.

Rachael couldn't resist a snicker at the sound of tearing material. "We'd better go back to the lodge," she told Dory as she picked up her basket and held it out for Dory to put the clean cooking utensils in.

"I think we should stay put." Dory craned her neck to get a better view of the two Mohawk women. "One's bound to push the other into the stream any minute."

Rachael prodded her friend in the side. "Come on. We'd best get back to the village before they realize who started it."

Side by side the two women hurried down the path, casting glances over their shoulders as they went. By now Pretty Woman and Gull were shoving each other back and forth. Both women held strips of the prized blue brocade which had only moments before been the skirt.

Rachael was still chuckling to herself when Storm Dancer pushed aside the doormat and came into the lodge where she was putting away her cooking utensils. She'd sent Dory off to return a borrowed clay pot to She-Who-Weeps.

Rachael's laughter died at the sight of her husband's face. His usually suntanned face was pale, his mouth pulled into a tight frown. He came in and immediately began to pack his knapsack.

"What is it?"

"I must go, Wife." He held up his palm. "You are to stay here."

The sound of his voice frightened her. Something was terribly wrong. "Tell me. What's happened? Where are you going?"

"It would be better that you did not know." He reached for a quiver of arrows that hung from the birch rafter.

Rachael touched his bare forearm. His skin was cold and clammy to the touch, his muscles as hard as iron.

"Storm?" Her voice trembled. Suddenly his problems had become hers. "Tell me . . . Husband."

He lifted his gaze to meet her eyes. "My brother has gone too far this time. I was not able to stop him once—" he nodded, "but this time I must."

She shook her head refusing to release his arm. "What are you talking about? Please tell me."

His black eyes clouded with hostility. "My brother will attack St. Regents Mission at dawn. I must warn them."

Rachael's hand found his and for a moment she forgot that she was his prisoner, or that he had forced her to marry him. For a moment she was his wife. "You can't go. Speak to the council. There's no one there but old priests and children! They're unarmed but for a squirrel musket or two. Surely the council would not allow the attack of harmless civilians."

"You do not understand. My brother had become the council. He can do what he pleases."

"There's no way for you to stop him?" Her blue eyes searched his face for understanding.

"No. I am one man against too many. I cannot stop Broken Horn, but I can warn Father Drake."

He pulled away and went back to gathering his things.

Rachael thought for a moment and then spoke. "Take me with you."

"Maata. Impossible." He added arrows to his quiver.

"It's not safe for me to stay here without you. Since you shamed him by cutting off his scalp lock you know Broken Horn's been seeking a way to have his revenge."

"It looks as if he has found it."

"You mean—"

"I do not have the time to talk of this matter now. Broken Horn is leaving in a few hours. You will be safe while I am gone. I will go the mission, warn them, and return before Broken Horn and his men return."

"And what if you don't come back?" Her ominous words hung in the still air of the lodge. "You know what will happen to me if you are killed."

"I will not die. I will return for my wife."

"You could cross paths with Broken Horn, or the English. Anything could happen out there!" She grabbed his arm and forced him to turn and look at her. Her voice was stark with the reality of their situation. "If you don't come back, I will become your brother's woman."

Storm Dancer looked away, obviously torn.

Rachael went on quickly. "I won't slow you down, I swear it. I'm much stronger than I was when I first came here. Maybe I can even help once we get to the mission."

"Mohawk women do not travel with their men. This is not a Mohawk woman's right."

She reached up to touch his cheek. "I am not a Mohawk woman. I want to go with you. I want to help you."

"Why?"

"Because what you are trying to do is right. It's honorable." She took a deep breath. "Because Broken Horn must be stopped."

He rested his hand on her shoulder. "Speak with a true tongue. You do not ask to go with me so that you can run from me?"

She shook her head. "I will go with you to the

mission and I will help you get the children out before Broken Horn and his men come."

When Storm Dancer made no reply she brushed her fingers against his cheek. "Please."

He gave a sudden shake of his head. "This is not the way of my people. Women are to stay at the camp and keep the lodge fires burning."

"Is it your people's way to murder innocent men and children?"

He looked off into nothingness, remembering a time of long ago. "Once, no. Now?" He met her gaze. "It seems it has become the way."

Rachael lifted the knapsack from the floor and began to stuff necessary items inside—flint and steel, dried venison and berries, a thread and needle and Storm Dancer's precious medicine bag. "I have to tell Dory we're leaving."

"You cannot tell her where we go." He shrugged on his quilled vest. "Tell her we are going fishing, but instruct her not to tell anyone who does not ask."

Rachael grabbed a waterskin and put the strap over her head. She then put the knapsack on her back so that Storm Dancer would only need to carry his weapons. They would do this together, as equals.

Rachael stepped out of the lodge and glanced up at Broken Horn's scalp lock flying from Storm Dancer's lodgepole. She shivered despite the warmth of the August evening.

Dory was seated on the ground, scraping the hair off a piece of rabbit hide. "Dory." Rachael tried to sound nonchalant. Though she was trembling inside, her voice was steady. "Storm Dancer wants to go fishing again. He insists I go."

Dory grinned. "He's wooin' you, Rachael-honey. Wish I had a man like him. Believe you me, I wouldn't let him out of my lodge." She winked.

"Yes, well, I don't know when we'll be back. Sometime tomorrow, I suppose." She paused, lowering her voice. "Dory, don't tell anyone where we've gone unless you're asked directly."

Dory lifted a bushy eyebrow suspiciously but asked no questions. She returned her attention to the rabbit hide in her lap. "No need to worry 'bout me, Rachael, honey. I don't speak to them 'less they speak to me. Then I pretend I'm too stupid to understand. After a while, they just leave ol' Dory to herself."

Storm Dancer stepped out of the lodge and took Rachael's hand. She waved good-bye to Dory and started through the camp at Storm Dancer's side.

The other villagers paid little attention to them as they meandered through the camp. Two braves called out to Storm Dancer as he and Rachael passed the ceremonial longhouse. He made some comment about the trophy hanging from Storm Dancer's lodgepole and the three men laughed. To those around him, Storm Dancer seemed to be calm and relaxed.

No one seemed to question his taking Rachael with him. Honeymooners often left the village on expeditions. It would be tales of those escapades that would keep the men amused when the long dark winter settled upon them.

Two Crows called out from his lodge. He made some lewd remark about Rachael, but Storm Dancer ignored him, giving a friendly wave.

Storm Dancer and Rachael had nearly made it out of the village when Broken Horn suddenly appeared out of nowhere to block their path.

He had plucked his shorn head bald, making his deformed ear appear even more grotesque. He smiled. "Good evening to you, half-brother." He spoke in English for Rachael's benefit. "You and your wife going somewhere?"

Storm Dancer's eyes met Broken Horn's. There was a sense of amusement that hung in the air. "Fishing."

Broken Horn arced an eyebrow. "Fishing with your wife again." He grinned. "Your appetite is great."

His eyes raked over Rachael and it was all she could do to keep from stepping back a step. But she didn't. She remained beside her husband, her chin held high.

"Would you like me to bring some fish back to your lodge?" Storm Dancer took a casual stance, crossing his muscular arms over his chest. "I hear your wives complaining that you are too busy to bring them decent meat."

Broken Horn's pitch eyes narrowed at the insult. "Yes, do that. I've a taste for fresh catch." He turned to Rachael. "What women do not understand is a man's responsibility to the politics of the world. I have little time for trivial matters."

"Then let me not stand in the way of your importance." Storm Dancer nodded farewell. "Until tomorrow, Brother."

Broken Horn hesitated, but then backed down and stepped aside and off the narrow path that led out of the village.

Storm Dancer took Rachael's hand in his and together they walked off into the forest.

They walked nearly a mile in silence before Rachael spoke. They traveled single file, with Storm Dancer paying close attention to be certain no one approached them from any direction. They traveled quickly, but Rachael was not having a difficult time keeping up. These last weeks in the Mohawk village had strengthened her, both physically and mentally.

"How far is the mission?"

"If we hurry we will be there in two maybe three hours before the dawning light." He spoke curtly, but his voice was not unkind.

"I'm glad you let me come." She stepped over a bulging root and ducked beneath a low-hanging elderberry branch.

"You may yet regret your choice."

"I think not. You might need my help."

He glanced over her shoulder. "I have never before needed a woman's help."

She frowned, her forehead creasing. "You don't seem to like women much."

"I have not had much luck with women." He thought of Ta-wa-ne. "I lost my first wife."

"You were married before." It was a statement that she hoped would lead to further discussion.

"Yes."

She wanted to ask how his wife had died, but she could tell by the tone in his voice that this was not the time to question him on the matter. Instead she asked, "Why then did you marry me?"

"Fate. You were delivered from the flames and into my arms."

"I was in one of your *seeings,* then?" Storm Dancer had made mention several times that he sometimes *saw* the future in a waking dream. She'd heard of men and women with such abilities in London, but she had never believed in it. Seers were for country fairs and young impressionable children.

He held back a branch for her. "I did."

"Well, I don't believe in such silliness." She passed him, unable to resist reaching out and brushing her finger against his chest as she went by.

"It does not matter if you believe."

"It doesn't?"

He shook his head. "What you believe or do not believe does not change the world, Rachael. Life goes on as it always has. You need not believe to be a part of it."

The path northwest widened and she fell into step beside him. By stretching her legs with each stride, she was able to keep up. "What do you see of the future?" She hesitated. "Our future?"

He thought of the sound of laughter he had heard the night he rescued Rachael from the evil flames of Broken Horn. Had that been a prediction of future good times, or only a wish? He didn't know. "I cannot command the sight. It comes and goes with necessity."

"Yet you said you saw a future in us."

He shrugged. "How long is the future? A lifetime? A year? A month? A moment? I cannot say, Wife."

She stopped, shaking her head. "I don't understand you when you talk like that."

He caught a thick lock of dark hair and pushed it back off her shoulders. She was as beautiful in this twilight as any woman he had ever laid eyes on. He pressed his lips to hers and she responded as he had hoped. Storm Dancer was tempted to take her into arms right here in the forest. He could lay her on a bed of moss and make love to her as he did now only in his dreams.

But he had a mission to carry out.

"Come, Wife," he murmured against her honey-lips. "We must hurry. My brother will not be far behind us." He reluctantly released his hold on her and waved for her to hasten.

Rachael smiled in the dim light of sunset. "I'm coming Husband. I'm coming."

Chapter Twelve

A silence fell upon Rachael and Storm Dancer as they traveled northwest toward St. Regents Mission. But it was a comfortable silence that gave them both time to reflect on what they were about to attempt.

Rachael's mind ran wild as she tried to digest all Storm Dancer had said. His first wife, fate bringing him and Rachael together, the Mission, Broken Horn. It was all a jumble in her mind. Nothing made sense, and yet out of that tumult of thoughts and emotions came an overwhelming sense of equanimity. Somehow for the first time in her life, Rachael had found a cause greater than herself. Her entire life she'd had nothing to think of but her own happiness or unhappiness. It wasn't that she had purposely become self-centered and self-serving, she'd just never been exposed to any other type of thinking. She had lived her life in a glass jar like one of Gifford's poor butterflies.

Rachael glanced up at the man who walked several strides ahead of her. Storm Dancer. Here was a man to be reckoned with, a man with a purpose. Here was a man trying to save his people from the destruction of their race. A smile rose on her lips as she watched his muscles ripple in the moonlight as he strode.

Storm Dancer . . . her husband.

Not really, of course. But she wondered for the first time what it would be like to live as his wife. Just for a flickering moment she allowed her mind to wander. Was there any way she could help him bring the Mohawks around to understanding the English? Was there some way through her and Storm Dancer that the Mohawks could learn to live beside the English? Was there a way to end the hate and killing?

She wondered if she could adjust to village life if she truly tried. The work wasn't so bad and she enjoyed the hours spent in front of the community campfire hearing the tales of Mohawk ancestors past.

She didn't care for the way the women of the village were treated, but the reality of the matter was that it was no different from life in Gifford's circle of friends in Philadelphia. Just as the Mohawk men retired to the ceremonial longhouse to talk of politics, Gifford and his friends retired to a nearby alehouse to talk of whatever men talk about when they're alone. Rachael would no more have walked into that tavern than she would ever walk into the ceremonial longhouse.

Yet Storm Dancer seemed to treat her differently from how Gifford had. Though Storm expected her to behave in the proper manner in public, those mores seemed to fall away once they were in the privacy of their own lodge, or on a fishing trip, or just sitting alone on the streamback talking of the weather. Storm Dancer had an underlying regard for who she was.

When they were alone he seemed to respect her for

her opinions. He even asked her for advice on occasion. When had Gifford ever asked her her opinion on any matter? For a year he had been building that great big monstrosity of a house for her on the Delaware River and yet not once had he asked for her counsel. This was supposed to be his wedding gift to her and yet she hadn't even picked out a single sheet of wallpaper or a stick of furniture.

Storm Dancer held back a thorny branch so that she might step by without being scratched.

And Storm is a gentleman, she thought. Certainly Gifford could be a gentleman, but only when it suited him. Only when it looked good and then it was for his own benefit, not hers or anyone else's.

How can I be comparing the Viscount Gifford Langston to a naked savage? she asked herself. *How could I think for even a moment that I could stay with Storm? He's a heathen savage, I'm the daughter of an earl. I belong on a country estate with servants to bring me tea, not in the forest, foraging for berries to save for winter!*

But do I?

Storm Dancer suddenly squatted, bringing his finger to his lips and snatching Rachael out of her reverie.

Rachael immediately imitated him, thankful for the short leather skirt that enabled her to move quickly and quietly. In the first days that she had worn the Mohawk clothing she had been embarrassed by the revealing leather skirt and bodice, but she quickly learned to appreciate the advantages. Not only was her movement unrestricted but for the first time in her life she was cool on a summer day.

"Manake."

Men. Rachael breathed evenly, watching in the direction Storm Dancer pointed. Not a moment later she heard footsteps. Soldiers, she thought. She could hear the squeak of their leather boots as they marched.

"French or English?" Rachael kept her voice as low as possible.

"French I fear. Rouville's men. I think they seek my brother."

"How much further is the mission?" Rachael laid her hand on his bare arm to steady herself.

"Not more than a few miles." He looked at her with his dark eyes. "I know a place you could wait. A place where you would be safe and if I should be—"

She pressed her finger to his lips. "I came to help you and help you I will. I am not afraid."

He brushed the back of his hand against her cheek, his dark eyes searching hers. "You truly are not, are you, Rachael-wife?"

Rachael liked this feeling between them. Not just the physical response but the sense of oneness that came of having the same goal. It excited her. "They've passed," she whispered. "Let's go."

He took her hand and raised her to her feet. "Keep down and walk as a shadow in the trees. We must not be seen until we are inside the mission."

She fell into place beside him. "Why?"

"Because there may be French inside the mission who would betray us. I must get to Father Drake without anyone knowing we have come."

Rachael walked at Storm Dancer's side, trying to concentrate on each step she took. She admired Storm Dancer's ability to walk through the dark forest in complete silence, and now that she understood the need for that ability she wanted to imitate him. As she walked she became more aware of her surroundings. Each step she took, she felt with the souls of her feet, allowing the leather moccasin to protect her but not hinder that ability to feel the earth beneath her.

When the outline of the mission came into view an hour later, Storm Dancer stopped and pointed to the high log wall. The mission looked much like a wilderness fort jutting from a clearing in the middle of the forest, its log walls built high, and guarded by wooden palisades, its gates closed tightly against intruders.

"It looks like a fort."

"At times Father Drake has thought it such. It was built to keep the savages out."

"But I thought you said Father Drake always welcomed the People of the Seven Nations."

He smiled in the darkness, amusement in his voice. "Only invited savages may go beyond the palisaded walls. Those who wish to come and study, to hear the word of the Lord are welcome. Those who wish to thieve and murder are not."

"The walls look so high, how will we get in?"

"*We* do not."

Moonlight fell to the clearing in a wide beam that illuminated Storm Dancer's handsome face. "What do you mean?" she challenged.

"I mean, Wife, that you stay here. When all is safe, I will come for you and bring you through the gate."

She shook her head. "No. I won't do it. I won't stand out here in the dark and wait for Rouville or Broken Horn to find me."

"I would not leave you if I did not think it was safe. It

will be hours before my brother attacks. I know his ways well. He is like the lazy brown bear. He cannot change his habits even in the face of battle. At this moment his men are drinking French whiskey, gathering their war clubs and painting their faces in bloodpaint."

Rachael dropped her hands to her hips. "I've come this far. I'm going with you."

Storm Dancer's onyx eyes narrowed with irritation. "I should have left you home, where a woman belongs."

"But you didn't." She suppressed a smile of conquest. "And I'm going with you."

"Over that wall?"

He was trying to scare her. She looked at the log fortress and its formidable wooden spikes jutting along the top meant to impale the man who tried to scale the wall. *You can't get over that!* "Yes. I can do it, Storm. Just don't leave me here."

With an indignant sigh he removed a length of rope from the knapsack on her back. Attached to the end of the rope was a peace of wood fashioned into a straight-edged hook. "Once I am over, you must come quickly, Rachael."

She nodded. He was already heading for the log wall. She prayed as she neared the wall, asking for the courage to carry through her attempt to scale it.

Storm Dancer threw the wooden hook high in the air. On his first attempt it caught and held tight. He looked over his shoulder. "You could wait for me."

"I'll see you on the other side." She tried to sound confident, though her insides were quaking with fear.

Rachael watched as Storm Dancer climbed up the

rope, his movements agile and swift. He reached the top in a few moments and lifted himself cautiously over the wooden spikes. A moment later he appeared again, waving to her. Apparently he'd not been seen anyone.

Taking a deep breath, Rachael grasped the rope and lifted herself up. Five feet off the ground, she wished she'd remained in the forest as Storm had suggested.

I'll never make it to the top, she thought, sweat beading on her forehead. Her palms burned from the rough rope and she felt like she weighed half a ton.

"Hurry, *ki-ti-hi,*" Storm Dancer whispered from above.

She-Who-Weeps had told Rachael that *ki-ti-hi* meant *my heart* in Lenni Lenape, her people's language. Rachael lifted hand over hand and hauled herself up another body's length.

"You are almost there, warrior-woman," he teased. "Hurry."

Rachael grunted and pulled up again, using her feet wrapped around the rope to propel her. She was panting heavily now. She looked down at the dark ground below. It would be so easy to let go. She probably wouldn't even break a bone falling.

"Rachael."

Her arms felt as if they were being ripped out of their sockets. She could see the stain of her own blood on the rope. But the sound of Storm Dancer's voice drew her. She took a deep breath, squeezed her eyes shut, and with every ounce of strength she could muster, she strained, lifting her body up the rope.

The next time she raised a hand, she felt Storm Dancer's grip. Her fingers wrapped tightly around his and he pulled her up and over the wall, the sharpened spikes covered by his quilled vest.

Rachael struggled to catch her breath as she felt her feet touch the wooden slats of some sort of flooring. When she opened her eyes she saw that she stood above the wall looking down into the inner courtyard of roughly hewn log buildings.

Storm Dancer gathered up the rope and crouched, bringing her down with him. He grabbed his vest and slipped into it, leaving the leather ties unbound. "There is the chapel." He pointed to a log building with a crude wooden cross rising from its peaked roof. "Behind is the rectory where Father Drake sleeps."

She nodded. "Are there guards?"

"Two, but one sleeps. He pointed below.

At first Rachael saw nothing, but then as she concentrated, a dark shadow formed. A man sat on a rain barrel, his head propped against the wall of the church, his musket balanced in his lap. "The other?"

"He walks the perimeter."

"You saw him?"

"He passed as you climbed up."

"And he didn't see you?"

Storm Dancer smiled. "I am like a ghost seen by some, but not by others."

Rachael thought to laugh at such nonsense, but somehow coming from his mouth, the words didn't seem so irrational. "And where is he now?"

"He has stopped to take his man's relief. There."

Rachael squinted to see, then felt herself blush at the sight of the stream arcing from the shadow's body.

Storm Dancer chuckled, patting her knee. "Come let us hurry, Wife. I want you to meet Father Drake. You will like him, I think."

Storm Dancer led Rachael to a ladder and she shimmied down after him. Creeping in the shadows they crossed the compound to the rectory. Outside the door a mangy dog growled and lifted its head to bark, but with a smooth signal of his hand, Storm Dancer silenced the animal. He crouched to pat the dog's head and waved for Rachael to follow. Rachael passed the dog, glancing over her shoulder at him. "How did you do that?" she whispered.

"Shhh." He offered his hand and she accepted it, finding comfort in its warmth.

When they reached a door, he lifted the latch. The door squeaked and scraped on its leather hinges. The dog whined and wagged his tail, but did not move or bark to warn the humans in the mission of the intruders.

In total darkness, Storm Dancer led Rachael down a narrow corridor that smelled of green wood shavings and must. Their footsteps barely sounded on the hard-packed dirt floor.

Storm Dancer slipped into a room to the right, lifting the door as he pushed it open so that it made no noise. He closed the door behind them and leaned Rachael gently against it. There was a slit of a window hewn in the wall through which moonlight filtered in. In the shadows of gray and black Rachael could make out the bare outlines of a few meager sticks of furniture. The room smelled of fresh pine needles and some sort of medicinal tonic. On the far side of the room Rachael spotted a bed with a sleeping form.

Father Drake, she guessed.

Storm Dancer walked to the bed and stood. The form stirred, and from the sound of the man's altered breathing, Rachael could tell the father had awakened.

There was a second or two of silence when Rachael feared the priest might raise a pistol and shoot Storm Dancer, but he made no move. The two men remained perfectly still, regarding each other.

Then Father Drake chuckled. His voice was harsh and rich with age. "Dancer of Storms. I wondered where you had disappeared to. It's been months."

Rachael's French was a little rusty, but she could understand the father.

Father Drake slid his feet over the side of the bed in painful jerky movements. He reached to the bedside and lit an ill-smelling tallow candle. It spit and sputtered until dim yellow light flared, illuminating the old man's crusty face.

Father Drake appeared to be nearly seventy. His cheeks were gaunt, his skin wrinkled and leathery. He had a thatch of milk white hair that stuck up in spikes on his head. He was an odd-looking man, but there was a sparkle in his dark eyes that Rachael immediately recognized. Father Drake was a friend.

"I am sorry it has been so long, Father," Storm Dancer spoke easily in French as he knelt on one knee and allowed the old priest to lay his withered hand on his head.

"Just the same, it is good to see you."

Storm Dancer rose. "This is my wife, Rachael."

"I wondered who it was you hid in the darkness." Father Drake smoothed his wrinkled nightshirt. "Come, come, child. Let an old man see you." He opened his hand to Storm Dancer. "My spectacles. Do you see my spectacles?"

Rachael approached the bed. Storm Dancer handed

Father Drake his spectacles and the old man perched them on the end of his nose. He squinted. "Holy, Virgin Mary!" He looked back at Storm Dancer. "A white woman?"

Storm Dancer couldn't resist a smile. "The Lord works in mysterious ways, does he not, Father?"

Rachael nodded. "It's good to meet you, sir," she treaded awkwardly in French. "Storm Dancer has told me much about you. I'm glad that I could meet you for myself."

He nodded, still regarding her. "You must be an extraordinary woman to catch the eye of this brave."

Her cheeks colored. She saw no need to go into the explanation of how she became his wife by default. It felt good to pretend that they had chosen this union rather than been forced into it.

Father Drake looked back at Storm Dancer. "But you have not come to introduce your new wife, have you, son?"

"No, Father." Storm Dancer's voice turned grave. "I have come to warn you. My brother and perhaps some of Rouville's men will attack your mission at dawn."

The priest swore beneath his breath. "Your brother was the work of the fallen angel, I always said." He stood with Storm Dancer's help and ran a hand over his matted white hair. "Even when he was a child, I saw malady in the boy's eyes."

"You must hurry, Father. Is there anyone inside the walls who might be a part of my brother's scheme?"

Father Drake shook his head. "We are few. Children. A half-wit man, Boswick, who sleeps on guard and his brother, a deaf-mute. Two women who escaped Rouville's whorehouse up river. Then there is one other priest who sleeps in the next room."

"How many in all, Father?"

He shrugged, reaching for his robes. "Twenty-seven of God's creatures, one worthless dog that refuses to bark when you approach."

Rachael went to turn away so that the father could dress, but all he did was pull his black priest robes over his blue-striped tick nightshirt.

"There is a Huron boy who is sick. Rot of the legs. I thought I would have to amputate, but he is better. I don't know that he can be moved."

"He must be." Storm Dancer began to gather a few of Father Drake's possessions. He dropped a few leather-bound books, a shaving kit, and a gold crucifix from the wall into a flour sack. "I would guess my brother will not be happy unless he sets a torch to your walls. You must take anything you wish to keep."

The old priest shook his head as he reached beneath the thin mattress and brought out a loaded pistol. "My possessions are few. What matters are my students." He looked up at Storm Dancer. "Why? Why would Broken Horn want to come here? Why would he want to murder us in our sleep?" He tied a rope around his waist and slipped the musket into the belt.

"In his own sick mind he sees you as a threat. He sees you trying to help our people to live beside the white men."

Father Drake shuffled toward the door. "I will pray for your brother's soul, but if I get the chance," he turned back to Storm Dancer, "I will kill him."

Rachael couldn't suppress a small gasp.

Father Drake turned toward her. "Please do not think ill of me, Rachael." He smiled. "My mother's name was Rachael." He went on. "You must understand that the ways are different here than anywhere else my feet have tread."

"My husband has taught me not to judge. People are not always what they appear."

"None of us are." He waved her on. "Now come and help me with my children. I know a place where we can flee to." He gave a chuckle. "If only I could be here to see Broken Horn's face when he finds no one here." He slapped his knee, his gruff laughter echoing in the tiny log room. "What a sight to miss. One almost worth dying for."

Storm Dancer followed behind them. "You cannot stay, Father. The children will need you."

"I know, I know. Just an old man's wishful thinking." He stopped in the dark hallway and touched Storm Dancer's arm. "You will not wait to face him?"

He shook his head. "The time approaches. I feel it. But tonight is not the night. I have Rachael to think of."

"Wise man." He patted Storm Dancers' arm. "Now come along, Dancer of Storms and help me to save my children."

For the next hour Rachael and Storm Dancer worked side by side to gather the Indian and half-breed children of the mission and lead them safely through the walls of the fortress and out of danger. When the rag-tag group of priests and children had been assembled, they started north toward an old English fort where Father Drake thought they would be safe. Storm Dancer had fashioned a litter for the sick Huron boy which the Boswick brothers carried. With some food on their backs, and a few blankets, the priests led the way, praying for their own safe deliverance.

Storm Dancer and Rachael accompanied the group for two miles, but then Father Drake insisted they turn back. "You have done enough," the old man said. "I thank you. Now go."

Storm Dancer stood for a moment in the shadows of the forest looking down at the priest. Though the sun had not yet appeared, the black of night had turned to gray. "I will not see you again, Father."

Father Drake nodded. "You will, if not in this world, then in the next."

Storm Dancer smiled. "I thank you for all you have given me."

"It was naught a bit more than you deserved." Father Drake reached for Storm Dancer's hand. "Now take your wife called Rachael and leave this colony. Go forth and make your own life far from the evils of this place."

Storm Dancer shook his head. "I cannot abandon my people."

"So instead you will face your sentence?"

Storm Dancer nodded. "As is destined, I think."

Father squeezed his hand. "Then may God protect and keep you on your journey wherever it might lead you." He touched his forehead, breastbone, one shoulder, and then the other in the sign of the cross and Storm Dancer did the same.

As Rachael stood aside watching the farewell an inkling of fear rose in her mind. She tried to shake it off, but it slithered up her spine like a snake waiting to strike.

Father Drake walked away, hurrying to join those who were disappearing into the forest. For a long moment Storm Dancer watched him in silence and then he turned back to Rachael.

"Come Wife. We must be gone from this place before my brother comes."

Rachael lifted her chin to stare directly into his dark eyes. "What did Father Drake mean by facing your sentence? Will you be punished by the village for what you've done here even though everyone knows what Broken Horn does is morally wrong?"

"Ea."

He tried to break from her gaze, but she brushed her fingertips across his cheek, forcing him to look at her. "You didn't tell me, but you must tell me now. What is the sentence if you are found guilty, Storm?"

Even as the word slipped off his tongue, his voice did not quaver. "Death."

Chapter Thirteen

Rachael thought she had heard him wrong. But she knew she hadn't. When she spoke again, her voice was barely audible. "They would kill you for this?"

He took her trembling hand in his and led her in the direction of the mission as if she were a lost child. The plan was to circumnavigate Broken Horn and his men and head for the village. "There are many meanings to our words."

"No." She pulled on his hand, angry that he would accept such retribution so easily. "No, Storm. There's only one meaning. Dead. Cold. Six feet under the ground." She held onto his bare forearm, forcing him to halt. "You can't go back and let them kill you. You have to run while you have the chance. You have to get far from here before Broken Horn discovers what you've done!"

"Shhh," Storm Dancer soothed. "Your voice can carry for miles. Now come. We must hurry. I want to be far from the mission before my brother arrives."

When Storm walked off, Rachael had no choice but

to follow. Or did she?

It suddenly occurred to her that she could have asked Father Drake for asylum. She could have told the priest what had happened to her—how she'd been captured and then forced to marry Storm Dancer to save her own life. But would he have believed her? She appeared willing enough when she'd entered the mission with Storm.

And then of course he was Storm's friend. Would he have helped her if she'd asked, against Storm's will? Storm had made it clear that he would not permit her to leave him.

Rachael stood on the game path twisting her moccasin in the dirt in indecision. If she turned and ran, she might reach the priests before Storm could catch her. She could go with them to the fort and perhaps a soldier could help her get back to Philadelphia.

Or perhaps she could die in some fort in the middle of the wilderness. Even with the priests for protection, what would be the chance of her escaping a fort full of soldiers with her maidenhead intact? At least the Mohawks had not harmed her in that way. Dory had said they thought it was bad medicine.

Storm Dancer turned back to Rachael. "Come, Wife. Why do you stand there?" He signaled with his hand for her to hurry.

Rachael bit down on her lower lip. She wanted to go home to Philadelphia, didn't she? But what were her chances if she ran now? Slim. She looked up at Storm Dancer who seemed to sense her dilemma. He had made no move toward her, yet even in the dim light of the coming dawn she could see his muscles tense. His hand rested lightly on the hilt of his knife in his belt. Would he kill her rather than lose her? Perhaps . . .

"Rachael." His voice was strained. "Rachael, I said come." This time it was an order.

She dared to look over her shoulder. Though the priests and children had disappeared from sight, she could still hear their footsteps.

She looked back at Storm Dancer.

"You gave me you word that you would not run if I brought you with me. I have trusted you, Rachael-wife."

Her lower lip trembled. She still didn't know what to do. Storm Dancer said he was going to die. He said they would kill him for what he had done here tonight. She'd be a fool to walk back into that Mohawk village if her protector was going to be put to death.

"You said they will kill you." Her voice trembled, but only slightly. "Where does that leave me?"

"I said that if I am found guilty, I will be sentenced to death . . . the walking death."

"I don't understand what you're talking about." She brushed away the hair that stuck to her perspiring forehead. "You have to talk so I can make sense of it. I don't understand this Indian gibberish." She was trying not to cry, but she could feel the tears welling up in her throat.

"The walking death. Banishment. If I am found guilty and am sentenced, I would become dead to my Mohawk brothers and sisters forever."

She laughed without humor. "They just pretend you're dead?"

"There is no pretending. Their eyes will no longer see me. Their ears no longer hear my voice. Their hand will no longer feel mine when we touch. I will be banished forever from the village, from my family, from my way of life."

Rachael stared at Storm Dancer as he approached her. His face was etched with pain, and perhaps even fear. The realization of what he had done abruptly hit her. In a moment's time she forgot the priests and her chance to escape. Suddenly there was only her and Storm Dancer.

Knowing he would face banishment, Storm Dancer had come to the misson to save an old man and some half-breed orphans. In saving these few forgotten children he had sacrificed all he loved.

Rachael reached out to her husband. "Storm. Storm, I'm so sorry." Tears slipped down her cheeks as she raised her arms to embrace him. "Why did you do it if you knew they were going to banish you?"

"Because I had to," he whispered resolutely as he smoothed back her hair and kissed her cheek.

She shook her head. "Then why go back to the village? I don't understand. We should run. Go far from here. Far from these evils."

"Run? Run where? This is my home. I am Mohawk. My ancestors have lived on this lake since the beginning of time. I have no other home."

"What about others from your tribe?" She grasped wildly for answers. "You could just go to another village."

"No." He spoke calmly as if it was another man he spoke of rather than himself. "Word of banishment travels quickly. I will be welcome nowhere among my people. To be banished is to be dead and yet not dead. It is a punishment worse than death."

"You could go back to Philadelphia with me."

"And what then, Wife, live with you and your Gifford? Perhaps I could be his manservant?"

"No, of course not. That's not what I meant. We could think of something. Perhaps . . . perhaps you could work for my brother, Thomas, on one of his ships."

He kissed her forehead, seemingly amused. "I do not belong among white men. I could not survive."

The truth of his words stung. He really had nowhere to go. "So you will face the council?"

"Every man is due a fair trial. I will tell the council my reasons. I will try to make them understand one final time what Broken Horn is doing, not just to the English but to us as a village, as a nation of men."

"Will they listen?"

Storm Dancer ran his fingers through Rachael's dark hair. "I don't know," he answered honestly. "They have not listened before, but perhaps this time they will. I cannot believe that my father would approve of the killing of innocent children . . . ever."

Rachael lifted up on her toes and kissed Storm Dancer on the mouth as a wife would kiss her husband.

"What was that for?" He slipped his hands around her waist, surprised by her gesture.

"I don't know." She looked up into his onyx eyes wondering how she possibly could have fallen in love with a savage. When had it happened? Just a moment ago? Sometime in the last weeks? Or was it the night Broken Horn had led her into the village and she had first laid eyes on Storm Dancer of the Mohawks? "I kissed you because you are a good man . . . Husband."

His mouth softened into a bittersweet smile as he

pressed his lips to hers. This time the kiss was deep and filled with urgency.

"Let me love you," Storm Dancer whispered, his voice husky with desire for her. "Let me take you in my arms here beneath the sycamores and make love to you as a husband should a wife."

The words were on the tip of her tongue before she could think. "Yes," she murmured desperately. "Yes, love me, Storm."

Rachael knew it made no sense to give her virginity to this wild savage who called her wife. Without her virginity how could she ever go back to Philadelphia and pick up her life where she left off? Yet her virginity was the one gift she could give to only one man in a lifetime, and it was Storm Dancer she wanted to give that gift to. No matter what happened in the future, whether Storm died, whether she went home to Philadelphia, she would always have these few moments to treasure and the knowledge that she had given to Storm of her own free will . . . out of love for him.

He kissed her gently again and again, his hands stroking her through the thin leather skirt and bodice until she was lost in a flood of sensation. He crooned soft words of encouragement, words Rachael did not understand, yet found stirring.

Everything seemed to happen so quickly. The sound of the wind and the rustle of the trees faded into the distance, replaced by the sound of Storm's voice and her own labored breathing. Rachael saw nothing but Storm, she heard nothing but his husky voice, she tasted nothing but the sweet taste of his mouth on hers.

When he eased her to a soft bed of summer grass, she was barely aware of it. All that mattered were the emotions that had been building inside her since that first night she had laid eyes on him.

When his capable hands unlaced her leather bodice she lay quietly watching him, waiting in tense anticipation until his mouth touched the bud of her breast. She cried out in the sweet morning air, overcome by joy and sorrow in the same breath.

When Storm kissed her again it was hard and demanding, a kiss that left them both breathless, wanting more. Rachael's hands glided over his corded muscles as she explored every ripple and plane of his sun-bronzed skin.

"I never imagined," she whispered. "I never imagined it could be like this."

He kissed her cheek and his mouth brushed her ear, his breath sending hot tingles of desire through her limbs. "I have wanted to love you, my wife, since that first night you appeared in the village. All of this time I have wanted to take you in my arms and show you what a woman as beautiful as you was meant for."

She pushed his quilled vest off his shoulders, her innocent fingers skimming over his back and buttocks in exploration.

"So sweet," Storm Dancer murmured, pushing the hair back off her face so that he could drink in her blue-eyed gaze.

Rachael touched the leather thong of his loincloth. "Take it off," she heard herself say. "I promise I won't turn away, not this time."

Her smokey blue-eyed gaze was filled with hunger. He wanted to take her now hard and fast, and yet at the same moment he wanted to prolong her pleasure indefinitely. "How is it," he asked as he slipped the leather thong from his hips, "that in losing all, I have gained everything?"

Rachael didn't know what he was talking about. She didn't care. Rather than frightening her, the sight of his engorged shaft made her breath go short and her flesh quiver with want of him.

Suddenly he was touching her again, his experienced broad hands seeming to know her body better than *she* ever had. He made her sigh, then moan as he stroked her breasts, her stomach, her thighs.

The first time his fingers brushed her woman's place beneath her skirt, instinctively she tensed. But he stretched over her, kissing her softly, promising to go slowly . . . promising pleasure.

The sound of his voice and the touch of his inviting lips calmed her fears. Gradually she relaxed, letting the newfound pleasure taunt her senses until she was again lost in the pleasure of her husband's caress.

Intuitively, Rachael found herself pressing against Storm, wanting to feel his hard, flat muscles against her soft curves. When he eased over her, she parted her legs, wanting him, needing him.

"I . . . I don't know how," she confessed.

He silenced her with a tender kiss. "It is a husband's duty to show his wife the act of loving. Above all gifts this is greatest."

Rachael moved up and down against his hips, feeling his hardened manhood touching her, stroking her in just the right place. She threaded her fingers through his midnight hair, moaning as he caught her nipple between his teeth and tugged gently.

"Please, Storm, please," she murmured. "It hurts." She laughed, throwing back her head, sighing. "No, it feels so wonderful."

He smiled, reveling in her pleasure as he gently guided his way into her.

At the first thrust, Rachael gasped. But Storm pressed himself against her, cradling her. Barely inside her, he kissed her chin, her cheek, her trembling lips. "There will be only a little pain," he whispered. "But then never again. Only pleasure, *ki-ti-hi.* I promise you."

When he slowly began to move, she moved with him, cautiously at first, then with more confidence.

By the light of the dawn Storm Dancer thrust again and again. He wanted to make Rachael's first time memorable, yet he could feel his body growing impatient. It had been so long since he had loved.

"Rachael," he whispered in her ear. "Rachael, Wife."

She moved faster beneath him, unsure of what she sought and yet knowing the direction. Faster and faster they moved as one until suddenly Rachael cried out in ultimate pleasure.

Storm Dancer followed an instant behind her, driving home and reaching his own fulfillment.

Rachael panted heavily, amazed, in awe of what had just happened. Her Aunt Geraldine had told her of relations between a man and a woman, but she had not spoken of pleasure, only of duty and necessity.

Rachael hugged Storm Dancer tightly. She could still feel him inside her, making her giddy. He lifted himself up on one elbow and kissed her on the lips. It was the kiss of a butterfly's wings, soft and fleeting. "Sealed," he told her, his voice still husky with spent passion. "A marriage truly sealed in the heavens."

She smiled pushing back his hair so that she could

get a better look at his bronze face. "Had I known it would have been like this I'd have demanded my wifely rights sooner."

He laughed, rolling off her and onto his side. "Would you have believed me if I had told you?"

"No." She smiled back. In the time they had spent making love the sun had risen and now soft rays of golden light poured through the trees, bathing their faces in warmth. She reached out to stroke his high-boned cheek. "But I thank you."

He took her hand and kissed the pad of each finger. "I would like to lay here beneath the father elms for days," he told her. "Among my mother's people there are days after marriage when a man and a woman spend time alone learning to give each other pleasure." He looked away for a moment, then back at her. "I wish we could have that time. But we must go. My brother and his men grow near."

Rachael's eyes went wide and she bolted upright. She covered her breasts with her hands. "You hear them? Why didn't you say anything?" She slipped on her bodice and fumbled with the ties. "Why didn't you tell me?"

"We are safe. I can hear them only when I press my ear to the ground." He stood and offered his hand to help her up. When she was standing, he pushed aside her nervous hands and began to deftly lace her leather bodice. "There is still time to pass by my brother and his men without them knowing."

She shook her head. "This was dangerous. We shouldn't have—I shouldn't have—"

Storm Dancer caught her chin and kissed her soundly. "It was the right moment. You knew. I knew.

Had my brother passed by a hand's breath from this spot, I do not think he would have known we were here. There is a powerful magic that protects love."

Rachael reached for her skirt and wrapped it around her waist. *Love?* Was he saying he loved her, or was he speaking of the act? He had admitted he wanted her many times, but there had never been an admission of love. Had he just told her he loved her in his man's way?

Rachael brushed the grass and leaves from her hair. She didn't know what Storm meant. She didn't know anything except that they had to get out of here, and quickly. Right now there wasn't time to worry about feelings. Now was a time for action. Storm Dancer needed to make it back to the village to speak with the elders of the council before Broken Horn returned.

Dressed, she reached for the knapsack that had been thrown carelessly to the ground in their ardor. Storm Dancer was dressed and ready to go.

He slung his quiver over his broad shoulder and picked up his bow. "Come, Wife. Walk beside me and let us go to the village."

Rachael stepped up to him and side by side they pressed for home.

Broken Horn swore in Mohawk and then in English. He stood in the light of early morning staring up at the fortressed walls of the St. Regents Mission. Not only had Father Drake escaped, but to add to the insult, he had left the gate open as if welcoming Broken Horn. The sly old bastard had known they were coming, but how?

Two Crows loped up to Broken Horn, his war club in

his hand. "There is no one here," he said in Iroquois.

"I told you we would not find a living creature." Broken Horn pulled back his mouth in a frown. "Even the mangy dog has fled."

"Perhaps they will be back," Two Crows offered his leader. "Perhaps he has only gone to the river to get supplies. If we wait, the priest will come back and we can kill him then."

Broken Horn continued to stare up at the log walls. He had come here to learn the written and spoken word of the English. He had been eager for knowledge just as Storm Dancer had been. But the priest had taken an immediate liking to one brother and a disliking to the other. Broken Horn didn't know why Father Drake had always hated him.

Broken Horn hocked and spat on the ground in remembrance of his days here at the mission. It was Father Drake's fault Broken Horn was disfigured. If the old man hadn't sent him out to hunt that one summer evening so many years ago, Broken Horn wouldn't have met with that Shawnee warrior and his war ax.

"If we are not going to wait for the priest, what do we do now?" Two Crows asked, breaking Broken Horn from his thoughts.

"We return to the village where I think we will find a rat dug deep in his hole."

"You think someone warned the priest?" Two Crows looked up anxiously. "You think it was your brother?"

"He is my brother no longer."

Two Crows grinned baring a blackened tooth. "He dies and you will have the white whore. A brother is expected to marry his dead brother's wife. It is custom."

The flicker of revenge caught in Broken Horn's heart and fanned into a flame. "You speak the truth, fair friend."

"So we return to the village. What of the mission?"

Broken Horn glanced up once more at the fortress walls he had come to hate. "Set fire to it." He spun around and strutted away. "Then gather the men. We must hurry to meet with the council before my once-brother does."

Chapter Fourteen

The hollow pounding of the drums and the shake of the bone rattles grated on Rachael's nerves. Six hours had passed and still the high council meeting dragged on. Anxiously, she peered outside her lodge. Despite the heat of late August, a column of odorous smoke rose from the roof of the ceremonial longhouse.

Dory snapped the lodge flap shut. "You go stickin' your nose out there and they're likely to bite it off."

"It's been so long." Rachael ran her fingers absently through her hair. "He's been there for hours and still they keep playing those damnable drums!"

"Redskins ain't known for their haste in anything. You just got to be patient."

"I feel like walking right in there and asking them what the bloody hell is going on!"

"You do that and you and that man of yours'll both be in the stew pot." Dory took Rachael's hand and led her away from the door. "Now quit your cursin' and sit down and I'll braid yer hair for you. It's too hot to have it all pullin' on your face."

Not knowing what else to do with herself, Rachael followed Dory's bidding. Seated cross-legged on a hide mat she stared at the door flap. "Why doesn't anyone come out and tell me what's happening?"

"Because nobody cares what you think." Dory pulled a porcupine brush through Rachael's thick, dark hair. "You don't matter a cat's spit to them redskins in there."

"But he's my husband! I have a right to know."

Dory smiled in the dim light of the lodge. "That he is, but worryin' ain't gonna do him a peck a good right now. You got no choice but to sit and wait just like your man told you."

Rachael sighed heavily. "What's Storm going to do if the council won't listen, Dory? What's he going to do if they banish him? His whole life is this village and these people. It will kill him."

Dory methodically braided Rachael's hair. "It won't kill 'im. He's not the first one to hit on bad luck. You and me seen our share too, but it ain't kilt us. If they throw 'im on his ear he'll get up, dust off, and go on the same way I done, the same way you done."

Rachael shook her head. "It's not the same thing to a man as to a woman. We've spent our lives with others in control, others making our decisions for us and then having to adjust. Storm knows nothing but these people and this way of life."

"He'll learn a new way. It's that or shrivel and die and I don't think that buck's ready to give up yet. It ain't in his nature." She tied a piece of thong around the end of Rachael's single braid. "'Sides, he's got *you* now, Rachael-honey."

Rachael frowned. "He's got me, has he?" she

murmured more to herself than to Dory.

Since arriving back at the village Rachael had been too busy with her concerns for Storm Dancer's trial to think about herself. But now that she had made love with him, had she committed herself to a lifetime with him? She couldn't imagine living the rest of her days here in this village where the women hated her and the men scorned her. Then of course there was Broken Horn. Could she live with the constant fear of him? If she and Storm were to have a child, would that child also be in danger of Broken Horn's hatred?

Such thoughts were too difficult to deal with right now. *Better to cross that path when I come to it,* Rachael thought. But whether Storm Dancer was banished or not, Rachael knew that at some point she would be forced to make decisions. Could she leave Storm now, after what they had shared? If she stayed with him, wherever he went, would she resent his love forever because she had been forced to marry him? She couldn't honestly say. A part of her wanted to stay at his side forever, but a part of her still desperately wanted to go home.

Dory patted her friend gently on the shoulder. "Done."

Rachael ran her hand over her neat hair and offered a grim smile. "Thank you, Dory. You—" She halted in midsentence. The rhythm of the drums had changed. They were beating faster. "Something's happened. Listen."

Dory paused, listening intently.

Rachael jumped up and ran to the door. She had been instructed by Pretty Woman that she was to remain in Storm Dancer's lodge, but Rachael didn't care. She had to know what was happening.

"Rachael!" Dory called after her, but it was too late. Rachael had already ducked out and was running across the compound.

Rachael spotted Storm Dancer flanked by two braves as he emerged from the ceremonial lodge. His face was grim, but from his expression she could tell nothing.

The women of the village were spilling out into the compound now. Everyone was gathering to hear the outcome of the trial.

Pretty Woman stepped out to block Rachael's way but Rachael gave her a hard shove, pushing her to the ground. She heard Pretty Woman cursing after her, but Rachael didn't care. "Storm, what's happened?" she called as she ran toward him.

"Stop her," Broken Horn shouted as he strutted out of the longhouse wearing some sort of ceremonial robe decorated with dyed feathers.

Two women grabbed at her arms to stop her, but Rachael twisted free. She wanted Storm Dancer! She wanted to be with him!

"I said stop her!" Broken Horn bellowed as Rachael broke from the women's grasp.

Two Crows reached out and caught Rachael in an iron grip, his blunt, dirty fingernails sinking into the soft flesh of her arm.

"Let go of me!" she screamed.

Two Crows clamped his hand over Rachael's mouth and she bit until she tasted blood.

Two Crows grunted and swung his hand to strike her, but suddenly Storm Dancer was there. He caught Two Crows' wrist in midair and held it, his onyx eyes filled with menace. *"Ye-ta-a e-a-yeye-an-ti tey-a-ken-i-ti-ro*. Strike she who is mine, and I will curse you and your children and their children's children unto eternity, brother."

Two Crows paled. Like his fellow Mohawks, he was a superstitious man. He released Rachael's hand and took a step back.

Storm Dancer turned his gaze to Rachael, cupping her chin with his hand as he spoke so that only she could hear him. "You must stand back with the other women. A woman who cannot control her emotions shames her husband."

"I want to be with you. Tell me what's happened, Storm." Her gaze searched his for some clue as to the outcome of the trial.

"I have been found guilty, now step back with the other women. I am to be sentenced by the chief here among my fellow brothers and sisters."

Tears stung Rachaels eyes. He spoke as if he were telling her when he would return from a hunting trip. There was no emotion in his voice whatsoever.

Rachael wanted to say something more, but the look on Storm's face made her bite back her words. If he needed her to stand submissively among the women while he was sentenced, then she would do it, but not for them, not for those who would cast him out, only for Storm Dancer.

She brushed her hand against his, nodding. He dropped his hand and strode back toward the men, his head held high as if he were about to receive some award.

The old chief, Meadowlark, slowly hobbled from the ceremonial longhouse. He seemed to be growing older and weaker by the day. Behind him trailed Storm Dancer's father.

A silence settled on the village. Even the children grew quiet as the chief and the shaman made their way to the accused.

Rachael stepped back into the line of women, watching Storm Dancer's face as the old men came toward him. Storm followed his father and the chief with his eyes. Instead of anger or resentment, Rachael saw only compassion in her husband's gaze. Storm felt sorry for the old chief and his father who would condemn him to death.

Meadowlark spoke quietly, keeping his eyes averted. Two Fists avoided his son's gaze as well.

Rachael wanted to shout at Two Fists and ask why he would do this to his son, but out of respect for Storm Dancer, she held her tongue. As the chief rambled on in Iroquois, Rachael watched the crowd of villagers. It was too late for Storm Dancer to save these people. Even if he could stay, Rachael could see that it would do no good. They all seemed to be so certain that Broken Horn guided them in the right direction that they were long past listening to Storm's reasoning. These villagers hated the white men, they hated Storm Dancer, and they hated her.

Better to leave this place, Rachael thought. *Better to go elsewhere and make a life of your own, Husband.* Rachael wondered if she meant to stay with Storm wherever he went. She didn't know.

Meadowlark's final words penetrated Rachael's thoughts. Though she understood only a little Iroquois, his last words were obvious.

". . . And for this crime of betrayal against your

brothers, and for the crimes you have committed in the past, you, Storm Dancer of the Bear Clan, of the Mohawk tribe, of the seven nations, are sentenced to the living death." Meadowlark turned to his people, raising his hands above his head. "Let—"

"Wait!" Broken Horn commanded, stepping forward, a hand held high. "Wait, great and mighty chief. I have a demand to make of the prisoner before he is comdemned."

Hushed whispers rippled through the crowd of men and women. What was his request? Would the dying man concede? A strange flow of energy moved among the people of the village.

Broken Horn turned toward his half-brother. Storm Dancer barely glanced at his adversary.

"I ask that you return that which is mine. The woman"—Broken Horn paused—"and that which hangs from your belt."

Storm Dancer's hand fell to his belt and he thoughtfully fingered Broken Horn's scalp lock. "I would sooner slit my wife's throat and let her die in my arms than give her to you—"

Again, the sound of unintelligible voices broke among the villagers.

". . . And as for this." He indicated the stolen scalplock that had left Broken Horn shamefully bald. "It is mine to keep as proof of the final outcome of the struggle between good and evil."

"Give it to me!" Broken Horn shouted, descending on Storm Dancer. "You have no right to jinx me by taking it with you unto the world of the dead."

Broken Horn's face was only inches from Storm Dancer's, and yet Storm Dancer did not flinch. "You do not believe in those foolish ancient superstitions, do you, brother of mine? You are too smart for that. We all know it is but a fool's tale told to children. How could a man be cursed with ill luck simply because another man holds his scalp?" Storm Dancer tugged at the black scalp lock hanging from his belt.

"Make him return what is mine!" Broken Horn demanded of Meadowlark. He suddenly sounded almost hysterical to Rachael. He did believe in the curse!

"Enough pettiness!" Meadowlark shouted. "No one believes ill luck will fall upon you because you are without your scalp lock. Now step back, Broken Horn, son of Two Fists, and let what must be done, be done.

Broken Horn stood for a moment in indecision, but eventually stepped back.

Rachael let out a little sigh of relief as the old chief picked up where he had left off.

"And so," Meadowlark declared, "People of the Flint let your eyes no longer see, your ears no longer hear this man who has violated the laws of the people."

A woman wailed behind Rachael . . . She-Who-Weeps, no doubt.

Two Fists raised a wooden bowl that hung from a string and spun it in the evening air. He chanted gruffly, seeming not to care that his son had just been banished. Great clouds of stinking green and yellow smoke rose from the pot and formed a screen between Storm Dancer and the others of the village.

Broken Horn stood off to the side and crossed his arms over his chest, a smug grin on his face as the smoke engulfed Storm Dancer until he was no longer visible.

The crowd began to break up. Some women whispered quietly as they gathered their children and started for their longhouses. It was time for the evening meal and they had duties to attend to. One of the older woman rested an arm on She-Who-Weeps' shoulders and led the mother of the dead man toward her home.

The men, too, scattered, some in silence, others talking nervously. The green smoke grew thicker and Rachael coughed. "Storm?" she called. Not only had the smoke covered him but now her as well. "Storm, where are you?"

A hand touched her on the small of her back and she spun around, relieved that he had found her. His arms came around her waist and she sighed. "Storm—"

But it was not Storm who held her in his arms. It was Broken Horn. She could tell by the stench of his breath.

"Let go of me," she demanded through clenched teeth.

He brought his leering face to hers. "Now that your husband is dead you have the right to come to my longhouse. Please me and I will marry you. Please me greatly and I will make you first wife." He ground his hips against her, his erect manhood straining against his loincloth.

Rachael stumbled backward, as if she'd been burnt. "Get away from me!" she cried. "Leave me be!"

Broken Horn laughed. "Think about my offer," he told her as he released her.

Rachael fell back hard, hitting the ground. In the confusion of the smoke she lost sight of Broken Horn. She didn't call to Storm for fear Broken Horn would find her again.

When she felt a hand on her shoulder, she flailed her arms, trying to escape.

"Ki-ti-hi," Storm soothed. "It is me."

Rachael fought back tears as Storm helped her to her feet. "I . . . I couldn't find you. The smoke." He opened his arms to her and she gratefully rested her head on his shoulder.

"What's all the smoke?"

"When it recedes, I will be gone."

She gave a little laugh. "Gone? They really think so?"

"It is so."

"Let's just go, Storm. Let's go far from here."

He wrapped his arm around her waist and guided her through the smoke. Slowly it dissipated as they drew closer to their lodge. The village seemed abnormally quiet, save for the sound of Two Fists chanting from inside the ceremonial longhouse.

"They will stay inside their lodges tonight for fear of spirits. Tomorrow I will be gone, nothing but a memory, and in time even that will fade."

"That doesn't make any sense, Storm. How can they do this? Didn't you tell them what happened? Didn't you tell them that Broken Horn was going to kill those children?"

"My people are tainted by my brother's evils. They are no longer able to think with their own mind, only with his." He pushed back the door flap to their lodge and let Rachael pass.

"So what will happen now? When you leave, I mean?"

"I hope they will remain safe, but my dreams tell me they will perish." There was a bitter note in his voice. "Now that I am dead I cannot even lead anyone away with me."

"I got all the stuff together you tole me," Dory told Storm Dancer. "All packed in them sacks just like you said."

"You mean we have to go now?" Rachael stared at him in disbelief. "Tonight."

"I must go." He reached for his bow. "As the wife of a dead man you of course have the right to join another man's lodge and take Dory with you."

"And that's what you want me to do now?" Rachael turned to him, surprised by the fury in her voice. "You want me to go to your brother?"

"No." His dark eyes met hers and though he made no move, she felt his touch. "I would not let you go. I would take you with me if I had to tie you to my back. You are my wife and you belong at my side. I was only telling you what is the custom of my people."

She paused for a moment, sorry for her harsh words. "You said we must leave tonight." Her tone was gentler. "Why can't we wait until morning at least? If you don't know where you're going it seems foolhardy to leave at night."

"We must go because they may burn the lodge." He managed the barest smile. "To send away any demons that might lurk behind."

Rachael couldn't help but smile back at him. She didn't know how he managed to see humor in such a humorless situation, but she admired him for it. She reached out and ran a finger down the muscled line of his forearm. "So tonight it is. Suits me fine. I want to get as far away from Broken Horn as I can."

Storm Dancer looped his medicine bag over his neck and one arm. "Let us go, then, Wife. Let us leave this village and its sourness behind and go."

Rachael picked up a knapsack, but allowed Dory to strap it on her back. "But go where?" Rachael asked quietly, her blue-eyed gaze following Storm across the lodge.

"I do not know except to tell you that the wind will guide us."

Rachael's first thought was that that was a ridiculous statement, impractical, even dangerous. But she held her tongue. Storm Dancer had surprised her so many times, that she almost believed him. "You have the other bags, Dory?" Rachael looked up at her red-headed companion.

Dory was grinning. "Good riddance to this place, I say. I never did like a Mohawk."

Storm Dancer pushed back the flap of his lodge and stepped back so that Dory and Rachael could exit. As the women passed through the doorway, he turned back for one final glance of the place he had called home for many years.

A few strings of dried herbs still hung from the rafters, their shadows dancing on the walls. Several empty baskets lay on the hard-packed dirt floor where Dory had dumped them in her haste to pack. Storm Dancer closed his eyes for a moment and allowed himself to remember only the good he had experienced in this village. He remembered himself as a child and the days that had stretched into adulthood. He thought of those early happy days with his first wife. Then he thought of Rachael. He conjured up the feel of her asleep in his arms, her head resting on his shoulder. He allowed himself to taste her on his lips as he had tasted her on their wedding night.

"Storm . . ." Rachael lay her hand gently on his shoulder. "I think we should go. It doesn't feel right out here. I can hear them all waiting, watching in the darkness."

"They wait for the spirit to leave their presence. If it does not leave, they burn it out." He stepped out into the cool night and let the flap of the lodge swing shut. Then he took Rachael's hand and led her through the silent camp. Dory took up the rear.

There was not a single human to be seen as the three walked quietly through the village. The dogs stirred as they passed.

The eerie green smoke from the shaman's pot still hung in the air, slightly distorting images until nothing seemed real. Rachael felt gooseflesh rise on the back of her neck. *It's as if we are dead,* she thought.

She shook her head sadly. She could understand Broken Horn's hatred but not Storm Dancer's parents' apathy. And what of his friends? His cousins? How could they all turn on him like this?

At the edge of the village Rachael spotted She-Who-Weeps. "Your mother," Rachael whispered to Storm Dancer. "Speak to her."

He shook his head ever so slightly as they approached the beautiful older woman. "She couldn't hear me."

"Don't be silly. She's waiting for you, Storm. Tell her good-bye."

He squeezed Rachael's hand to silence her. "Just as I do not understand some of your ways, Wife, you do not understand mine."

"She's not allowed to speak to you?"

"To speak with spirits is forbidden except to the shaman."

Rachael looked at her mother-in-law standing beneath a tree limb. She-Who-Weeps looked at them, but to Rachael's amazement, her eyes did not see.

Storm Dancer held his head high and proud as he passed his mother and for the first time Rachael saw a resemblance between the two. As Rachael, Storm Dancer, and Dory passed, She-Who-Weeps spoke in a soft lilting voice.

"Though my son is dead to his old and ugly mother, he is not dead to her people. Let him go unto them so that they may welcome him to their bosom. Let him find a new life where there will be happiness again."

She-Who-Weeps spoke so softly that Rachael wasn't quite certain she had heard her. Yet she had. The three passed by her without speaking or looking in her direction.

Only when they had passed out of the village and into the forest did Rachael speak. "Did you hear what She-Who-Weeps said, Storm? What did she mean?"

He shifted his bow onto his shoulder and looked up into the dark sky that hung in a canopy above the treetops. "She said we are to go to her people, to the Lenni Lenape and there we will be welcome."

"To her people? They would take you there?"

"The Seven Nations are enemies of the Lenni Lenape and their Algonquian brothers. To them the walking death is a tale to frighten children around the campfire. They do not believe in it and so its powers do not affect them."

For the first time Rachael heard a glimmer of hope in

his voice. "Do you know where they are?"

"I have never been to the great bay of the Ches-a-peake."

"But can you find it?"

"The sun and wind will guide me. It is south and east."

South and East, Rachael thought. Philadelphia was south and east. Did he mean to take her home? When Gifford or Thomas never came for her, she began to contemplate the thought that she might not ever see Philadelphia. If the chance came now, what would she do? Did she want to go home?

Rachael allowed Storm to take her cold hand in his warm one and lead her through the forest. As they crossed a small stream she looked up at him. Even in the dim light of early evening he was a strikingly handsome man. Just to look at him made her blood stir. She thought of what they had shared yesterday morning and wondered if this was what love felt like. Did love mean being willing to leave behind all you believe in, all you think you ever wanted?

She wished she knew.

Chapter Fifteen

Rachael rested with her head against an elm tree, her eyes half closed as she watched Storm Dancer jiggle his fishing line in the water. They had stopped traveling at sunset and while Dory set up camp, Rachael and Storm Dancer had come down to a slow running stream to catch a couple of fish for the evening meal.

It had been nearly two weeks since the three outcasts had left the Mohawk village. For two weeks they had traveled steadily and though they covered less distance than Rachael had been forced to cover each day with Broken Horn and his men on the march north, Rachael was still relieved when evening came and they could rest for the night.

But for all the hardship, Rachael could see some good in the trek south. In the past two weeks she had learned a great deal about her husband. They had talked for long hours as they walked side by side, giving her a true insight into Storm's complex character.

Storm Dancer was not nearly as disturbed by his banishment as Rachael had anticipated. After the first few days of travel in near silence, he had awoken almost a new man. It seemed that as if after a period of mourning for the death of the brave he had been among the Mohawks, he brightened. His mood turned from black anger to white hope. He began to talk of his mother's people, the Lenni Lenape, relating the tales she had told him as a child of his grandparents and great grandparents when no one in the Mohawk camp had been listening. Storm Dancer told Rachael about the many differences between the Mohawks and the Lenni Lanape, differences she would approve of.

Once Storm Dancer had accepted the fact that he could no longer help his people, that they had refused his help, he accepted their future as their own fate. While he had once believed their destiny could be altered by his deeds, now he seemed to feel absolved. It was oddly wonderful for Rachael to see such logic in Storm Dancer. She had anticipated an entire gamut of emotions from anger to self-pity, even to resentment of her for adding fuel to the fire of discontent in the Mohawk village. But she had misjudged him. Gifford would have experienced all those emotions and taken his anger out on her, but not Storm. She should have known better of the man who called her wife.

Rachael smiled to herself. Despite Dory's presence, Rachael and Storm Dancer had made love several times since they'd left the Mohawk camp. Storm Dancer would lure her away from the camp on the pretext of going fishing or gathering some unusual plant for his medicine bag. Then once they were a safe distance from the camp, he would seduce her, and Rachael would find herself making love with the forest for a bedchamber. It was not until the third time they coupled in the forest that she realized each expedition was planned and orchestrated by her husband. When she had accused him of purposely enticing her into the woods for illicit purposes he had been amused, acting the innocent. The discussion had ended in a waterfight in a small stream and lovemaking on the grassy bank beneath the stars.

Each time that Rachael made love with Storm Dancer, she found she lost a little bit of herself to him. He played her like the bone flute he carried in his bag and she reveled in the new discoveries of womanhood. If he would just once proclaim his love for her and express sorrow over how they came together, Rachael thought she might surrender to him and give up all thoughts of returning to Philadelphia. So far Storm had made no such declaration.

It disturbed Rachael that in the past two weeks not once had Storm Dancer brought up the subject of their future. She knew they had to be nearing Philadelphia and yet he had said nothing about taking her home, not even for a visit. The further south they walked, the more agitated Rachael became. When she pointed out the fact that they would have to pass Philadelphia to reach the Chesapeake Bay to Dory, her friend had told her to hush her mouth and be grateful for the life that was being offered to her. Dory said she had no intention of ever returning to white civilization. Storm Dancer had promised to find her a good husband once they reached the Lenni Lenape. Dory joked that she thought she might take two.

Rachael wiggled her bare toes in the soft, springy green moss and watched Storm Dancer artfully set his hook and pull up a silver-bellied fish. Twice she opened her mouth to speak, then clamped it shut. On the one hand she was enjoying the closeness she and Storm shared so much that she hated to shatter it, on the other hand, she could not accept the fact that she was still a captive. She didn't know if she really wanted to go back to Philadelphia, but she wanted that option.

Storm Dancer tossed the fish high up on the bank and dropped his hook into the water again. He stood naked, waist-deep in the running stream, his blue-black hair rippling off his shoulder in the wind. The sight of his bare bronze chest, his flat stomach, and sinewy buttocks sent a familiar flutter in Rachael's chest, but she ignored it. This was it. It was time to deal with this matter.

"Storm . . ."

He glanced over his shoulder, then back at his line in the water. "I wondered when you would finally speak. You have wanted to say something for days."

She frowned. She didn't know how he did it, but he always seemed to know what she was going to do, even what she was going say before she did so, and it annoyed her. "Storm we've been walking southeast for two weeks now. Fifteen days to be exact."

"Yes."

He wasn't going to help her out with this, she could tell by the edge in his voice. He already knew what she was going to say. Deep in her heart, she already knew his answer. "I want to go home to Philadelphia."

"To the coward who left you behind."

He was jealous; she could hear it in his voice. "No. I told you. That was over before I was kidnapped by your brother. I am not in love with Gifford and I want nothing to do with him—ever."

"Even once you were my wife you waited for him. You wanted him to come back for you."

"I waited to be rescued."

"Have I been unkind or cruel?"

"No."

"Have I struck you?"

"No."

"Have I tried to help you adjust to your new life?"

Her throat constricted. *I won't cry,* she told herself, *I won't do it!* She took a deep breath, taking her time to reply as was the Indian way. "Yes, you have helped me; you've helped me so much."

He turned to look at her, his face stony. "Then what have I done to make you want to leave me, Wife?"

She wanted to look away, but she didn't. Her gaze locked with his. "You have not given me a choice," she managed as she rose to her feet, her hands clenched in fists at her sides.

He turned back to his fishing, his voice cold when he spoke again. "You are my wife and you will remain with me. It was the bargain. I saved you from the fires of death and you agreed that in payment you would be my wife."

She fought the tears that clouded her eyes. "I know what I said, but—"

"But you lied?"

"No! Yes . . ." She exhaled slowly. "I wanted to live."

His voice became void of any emotion. "But not to be my wife?"

"Storm, you don't understand." She stared at his broad back, wishing he would look at her. She loved him and she didn't want to hurt him. "Storm, it's just that my entire life has been controlled by men, first my father and my brother, then Gifford, then Broken Horn, and now you. I want to be allowed to make my own decisions."

"If I took you to the place called Philadelphia, you would leave me."

She thought a long moment, wanting to be certain she meant what she said before she replied. "I don't think so."

He jerked another fish out of the water. "Then there is no need to go to this Philadelphia." He waded to the bank and climbed out of the water, attending to the fish as if that was the end of the argument and both parties were in agreement.

Rachael's first impulse was to walk away. It's what she would have done six months ago, but today she would stand her ground. "Storm, we have to talk about this."

"Women talk too much."

He made her so angry she wanted to strike him. She dropped her hands to her hips. "You say you want me to be your wife. Do you really want a wife that is your wife only because you force her to be so?"

He knelt facing away from her and picked up his knife from the grass and began to clean one of the fish. "I want you to be my wife. But I want you. I will take you willing or not."

She pushed her hair off her face, trying hard to understand him. It was difficult to talk to him when he put his back to her. "You could live with yourself knowing the mother of your children was forced?"

"In time you will know that you and I are meant to be."

She lay a hand on his bare shoulder, suppressing the urge to touch his shining black hair. "If I am forced to be your wife . . . if you do not take me back so that I might be sure that it is you and your life I want, I'm afraid I will come to hate you, just as I hate your brother."

Storm Dancer spun around so quickly that Rachael stepped back in fear.

"Listen to me and listen to me well, Wife," he shouted in a voice Rachael had never heard. He pointed an accusing finger at her. "You are my wife, you are mine—body and soul. I have lost one wife, but I vow before God I will not lose another. Be content in what you have, or be not content, but you will remain at my side if you must be tied to it. Do you understand my words, Rachael-wife?"

Rachael narrowed her eyes, oblivious to her tears. "So you're better than the rest of them, are you? A savage. All of you . . . Gifford, Broken Horn, Storm Dancer," she spit. "I see no difference!" With that she turned and strode away, beating at the branches to make her way through the trees toward the camp.

Dory looked up as Rachael came through the trees into the small clearing where they'd set up camp. The red-haired woman shook her head. "Tole 'im you had to go to Philadelphia, didn't you?"

Rachael wiped her tears with the back of her hand. Dory was supposed to be her friend and here she was siding with him! "Yes. He said no. He said he'd tie me up before he let me go."

Dory frowned and went back to tending the small campfire. "Use your head, Rachael-honey. He loves you and he don't want to lose you."

"Loves me? Hah! He's incapable of loving. He comes from a place where they eat people for God's sake, Dory!" She wiped at the tears that were still flowing down her cheeks. "You don't understand, either. I don't even know that I want to go back, I just want to know that I could. If he really loved me, he'd let me go."

Dory snapped a stick over her plump knee and pushed it into the fire. "Men don't look at things that way. All he knows is he loves you and you love him and he wants you with him the rest of his days."

"Love!" She laughed without any humor in her voice. "I could never love that man. I don't know that I could ever love any man."

"You're just sayin' that 'cause you're mad with him. You do love 'im and you know it." Dory slowly rose to her feet. "But both of you been hurt. You by Gifford, Storm Dancer by his wife I'd suspect."

"Gifford never hurt me!"

"Sure he did, 'cause he made you not believe in yourself. He almost made you think you needed a man to live. He made you think you didn't have a peck of brain in your head."

Rachael shook her head. "I don't know what you're talking about. I don't know anything about his"—she hooked her thumb in Storm Dancer's direction—"other wife and I don't care. I don't care about any it. All I know is I'm not going to be held prisoner anymore." Rachael grabbed the knapsack she carried on her back during the day. "I'm not going to do it!"

"Where you think you're going, missy?"

"Home. Home to Philadelphia. And if he won't take me, I'll take myself!" Rachael started in the opposite direction of the stream.

"So go off in the woods and get your bein' mad over with," Dory shouted after her. "But if your arm or leg gets ate by wolves, don't be cryin' to me!"

Determinedly, Rachael pushed a lock of hair behind her ear, and stepped into the woods line. Now that it was dark, she wasn't even sure which way Philadelphia was. Her tears blinded her and she pushed through the heavy undergrowth. *Was nothing ever going to be right again? Why did she have to love Storm Dancer? Why?* It wouldn't hurt so much if she didn't love him.

Rachael knew she should turn around and go back to the camp. It became dark quickly and it wasn't safe to be in the forest alone after dark. She knew her behavior was childish. But why did he have to shout at her like that? Why couldn't he understand how hard this all was for her? Why couldn't he have taken her into his arms and told her he loved her so much that he couldn't let her go?

Rachael was so lost in her thoughts as she tromped through the woods that she never heard the man until he stepped out of the bushes. She cursed her own stupidity. Hadn't Storm taught her that the most important thing about surviving in the forest was always being aware of the sights and sounds around you? It could cost you your life he had said.

"Oh," Rachael breathed. She stood perfectly still, staring at the man, trying to decide if he meant her harm. Perhaps he was just lost. She glanced at his clothing. Even in the semidarkness of dusk she could tell he was wearing a tattered English uniform.

Her blood went cold. A deserter. A man beyond the law.

Rachael took a step back.

"Hey there, little lady. My name's Reuben." The tall, painfully thin stranger grinned. "Fancy finding you here. An answer to our prayers, wouldn't you say, Beauregard?"

A snicker from behind made Rachael stiffen. "An answer to prayers . . ." a deep bass voice answered.

"I . . . I have to get back to camp," Rachael managed, trying not to let the sound of her fear affect her voice. "My . . . my husband is expecting me."

"Husband is she, that fat-assed redhead tendin' the camp? Funny lookin' husband if you ask me. What do think on the matter, Beau?"

"Funny lookin' husband, fat-assed redhead," the man behind Rachael echoed.

Rachael rested her hand on her waist and slowly let it slide until her fingers touched the hilt of her knife. There was nowhere to go. She looked sideways out of the corners of her eyes, but the underbrush was so thick that she knew she'd not get far.

Suddenly Reuben made a quick move forward. Rachael leaped back, right into the arms of the one called Beauregard. She screamed, flailing her knife. She felt it meet resistance and there was a howl of pain.

Even in the darkness of the moonless evening she could see the black stain of blood on her attacker's cheek.

"Let go!" She screamed, but the sound was muffled as the big man behind her slapped his dirty hand over her mouth and lifted her off the ground. He stank of gunpowder, sour sweat, and grum.

Rachael struggled, kicking her legs and twisting. Anything to get free. Reuben clawed her knife from her, cutting her palm in the process. She sobbed beneath the grimy hand as her only defense was yanked from her fingers.

"Nice knife," Reuben muttered, tilting his cocked hat to get a better look. "Injun knife. Sharp sucker."

"Sharp sucker," Beauregard repeated as he twisted a soiled cloth around Rachael's mouth and tied it so tight that she could only breathe out of her nose.

"Got her tied?"

Beauregard yanked her hands behind her back and whipped a piece of rawhide binding her wrists. Next he tied her ankles together. "Got her tied."

"Well then, don't just stand there, Beauregard." Reuben slapped his partner on the temple. "Let's get our tails out of here. Now that we got ourselves a woman, we won't be so lonely in that stinking cabin of yours come winter. You can do the trapping, friend, and I can tend to more homey pleasures."

"Got ourselves a woman," her captor snickered as he lifted Rachael and threw her over his shoulder like a rag doll.

Hanging upside down over the big brute's shoulder, it was all Rachael could do to keep her head about her. Her stomach turned inside out and her mind spun in confusion as the man ran through the forest, his footsteps pounding the ground, jolting her with every step.

Oh, dear God, how could I have been so stupid? Rachael thought in agony as she gritted her teeth. *How could I have let this happen? If I hadn't been so stupid! If I hadn't stomped out of camp . . .*

But surely Storm would come looking for me. He

said he wouldn't let me go, not matter what. So even if he didn't love me, I'm still his wife. He'd still come for me, wouldn't he, she thought desperately.

Please, Rachael begged in silence. *Please come for me, Storm, and I swear I won't leave you, not ever, Husband. I swear it!*

Chapter Sixteen

Storm Dancer stood by the edge of the river for several minutes after Rachael stalked off. He watched the way the smooth surface of the water rippled with skating water bugs, then broke into circles as fish came up to claim their meals.

Storm twisted his jaw in thought. He knew he had made the right decision in not taking Rachael back to Philadelphia. She was his wife and she was bound by the vows of marriage to remain at his side. Taking her to the place she once called home would be giving her the chance to leave him, to perhaps even run into the arms of the coward, Gifford. Storm had had one wife abandon him; he wouldn't tolerate it from another.

Yet he knew deep in his heart that he didn't have the right to compare his first wife Ta-wa-ne to Rachael. He didn't even have the right to speak their names in the same breath. It was too great a dishonor to Rachael.

He thought about what Rachael had just said. She had spoken of choices. She had said she wanted only to be permitted to make her own decision to stay with him. But what if he took her to the place called Philadelphia and she changed his mind? What if she left him just as Ta-wa-ne had left him? Ta-wa-ne's absence had caused injury only to his pride, but to lose Rachael would be to tear a part of his beating heart from his chest.

Storm turned toward the direction she had run. He could not take her to Philadelphia, but perhaps he could make her understand why.

Leaving his fish on the bank, Storm picked up his bow and quiver and hurried back to the camp. He found Dory sitting alone by a newborn campfire. "Where is she?" he asked, his voice tense. It had grown dark and the thought that she was in the forest alone concerned him.

Dory looked up from the corn mush she was mixing. "'Bout time you come lookin' for her." She pointed. "She done strutted off that way sayin' she was headed for Philadelphia. I didn't tell her she was goin' the wrong way."

Without another word he started in the same direction, following the obvious tracks Rachael had made in her haste to be rid of him. Storm Dancer had not gone but a few hundred strides when he came to the place where she had been captured. An English curse slipped from his tongue as he knelt to study the signs that were but a few minutes old. Stretching once again to his full height, he stared through the darkness in the direction the two man carrying Rachael had gone. He prayed that she was unhurt both for her sake and for that of her captors. After another moment of contemplation he took off in an easy run, certain he would catch up with the kidnappers in a matter of minutes.

Storm Dancer leapt out of the darkness like an apparition in a dreaded nightmare. He let out a piercing whoop of terror that frightened even Rachael who knew who he was.

It was astounding to her that one moment she was alone with her captors in the oppressive, dark forest and the next moment Storm Dancer was there, all power and muscle, his nude bronze body gleaming in the little natural light of nightfall. Even in the darkness she could see the gleam of danger in his pitch black eyes as he notched an arrow in his bow.

Rachael's captor, Beauregard gave an involuntary cry of fear and stumbled backward with her still slung over his shoulder. An arrow flew from Storm Dancer's bow and whistled through the air stripping leaves from the branches of the trees above the kidnappers' heads.

Reuben managed to fall on one knee and discharge his musket, but he was so taken off guard by the appearance of the naked whooping savage that his weapon fired uselessly into the treetops, expending his only bullet.

"Holy Mary, Mother of God, I've pissed my drawers!" Reuben cursed, his voice shaking, as he fumbled with his powder box. "Shoot the bastard, Beauregard, shoot him!"

Another well-aimed arrow whizzed through the air, striking a tree trunk only inches above Beauregard's head. They were striking closer with calculated intention. The giant of a man dumped Rachael into the brush and attempted to raise his musket.

The moment Rachael hit the leafy ground she rolled, pushing herself to her feet. Still tied, she couldn't run, but she had the good sense to dive for cover as another of Storm Dancer's arrows pierced the air. With each arrow he let out a blood curdling cry and it was the sound of his voice that seemed to terrorize the two men even more than the onslaught of feathered arrows.

Beauregard pulled the trigger of his musket, but it misfired, kicking him backward with a cloud of smoke.

Reuben threw a glance over his shoulder at his partner reeling backward under the impact of the misfire. "Jesus H. Christ, Beauregard! We're going to be skinned!"

"Skinned!" Beauregard echoed as he pushed onto his feet.

The next arrow lifted Reuben's battered felt hat off his balding head, drawing a rattling scream from his throat. Rachael inched her way behind a large tree trunk and peered out from behind.

In the dim light she spied Storm notching another arrow with quick fluid motions and for a moment Rachael forgot her fear. It was like watching some ancient, mystic dance to see Storm Dancer slip an arrow from his quiver, notch it, pull, release, and reach for another. There was no break in his movement, no beginning or end to the cycle, just a deadly dance.

Neither Beauregard nor Reuben had managed to reload their muskets. Beauregard had lost his when he fell. Now both men stood in stark terror, without cover or weapon, staring at the naked red man who held another arrow steadily on them.

"One . . . one of us has time to make it, Beau, old friend," Reuben insisted under his breath. "You . . . you cover for me and I . . . I'll give it a try."

"Like hell!" Beauregard shouted the first original words Rachael had heard out of his mouth as he made a dive for the thick camouflage of a clump of mulberry bushes.

The moment Reuben realized he'd been abandoned by his partner, he fled after him, his long legs pumping as hard as they could.

Rachael watched as the two men disappeared into the darkness of the forest, making so much noise as they ran that they sounded like an army.

Another moment passed before Storm lowered his bow and called out softly. "Wife?"

With the gag around her mouth, Rachael could only make a garbled sound, but she moved against the tree, rustling branches so that Storm could find her.

Slinging his bow onto his shoulder he came through the trees and brushed back the hickory limbs that hid her from view.

"*Ki-ti-hi,* are you hurt?"

She shook her head. Tears filled her eyes as she looked up at him, so thankful he had come for her. She wondered how she could love him so deeply, want him so badly, and yet still resent him so much.

He knelt and reached behind her head to cut away the filthy gag with his knife.

"Oh, Storm, I was afraid you wouldn't come looking for me after what I said," she rushed. "I was afraid they were going to carry me away. I—"

He wrapped her in his arms and lifted her, brushing his lips against hers to silence her. "You should not have run. I like it better when you stand and fight, Wife."

"I'm sorry. It was wrong. It was childish."

"Enough talk," he soothed as he carried her into the small clearing where the men had fought and began to cut away her bindings.

Rachael rubbed her raw wrists as he cut the ties that held her ankles together. "I don't know where they came from! I never heard them until they were suddenly there. It was so stupid of me not to hear them coming."

"Shhh," he hushed, rubbing her chafed ankles. "They are gone, Rachael and you are safe."

"Who were they? What were they doing out here?"

"The closer we get to the world of the white man, the more evil we will come upon. They were deserters of the king's army. Bad men . . . confused by war, but not dangerous."

"That's why you didn't kill them?" She looked up into his black eyes.

He nodded. "I do not kill without reason. Those men were too insignificant to waste an arrow upon." He brushed her cheek with his fingertips. "They had not hurt you, had they?"

"No. Just scared me." She looked up at him anxiously. "But they said they were going to take me to their cabin. They said they—"

"You're safe," Storm Dancer assured her. "Think no more of the men."

"Safe," she murmured against his lips, suddenly

intoxicated by the masculine scent of him, the closeness of his naked body, and the feel of his bare chest beneath her palm. She let her eyes drift shut as the familiar tingles of pleasure radiated from the center of her being outward . . . Suddenly her eyes flew open. "My knife! They took my knife, Storm."

His warm lips trailed over her cheek. "I will make you a new knife, a better knife, Rachael of mine."

She smiled as their lips met.

"You taste of honey," he told her, his tongue darting out to flick her upper lip, then the tip of her tongue. "A honey that sets my heart afire."

Rachael's fingers glanced over the powerful muscles of his shoulders and slid down his bare back. He lowered his head and pressed his mouth in the valley between her breasts.

Rachael arched her back, leaning into him, moaning in anticipation as his fingers found the bindings of her bodice and ripped at them. There was a desperation in their touch, an urgency in their kisses as hand flew over flesh seeking that which seemed fleeting.

"Storm," Rachael murmured as he brought the tip of her love-swollen breast between his teeth and tugged, sending pulses of pleasure through her veins. "You make me feel what I don't want to feel."

"It is not wrong between a husband and a wife," he told her, his voice thick with passion. "I have told you it is a gift of God."

She shook her head as his palms cupped the cheeks of her buttocks and massaged them rhythmically. "No, no," she insisted. "You make me love you, but I can't. You're the enemy."

"I am not." He went down on one knee kissing a hot, wet trail between her breasts across her stomach and downward. "I am not the enemy, but your husband—yesterday, today, tomorrow, and for all tomorrows."

She rolled her head, her fingers tangled in his glossy black hair. He was making it hard to think, hard to speak. "But you took me against my will. Still you hold me against my will."

"Only out of love for you do I do these things, Rachael, wife of mine."

"Love?" She caught his face between her palms and lifted his head until their gazes locked. "You have said nothing of love for me, Storm Dancer. You speak to me, of me, as if I were a possession."

He took her hand and pressed it to his bare chest so that she could feel the pounding of his life's blood. His smoldering black gaze held her in rapture as the poetic words slipped off his tongue. "You are a possession of my heart, *ki-ti-hi,* that I cannot give up. I have lost once; I cannot lose again."

"Tell me what happened," she begged. "Tell me about your wife so that I can understand."

He shook his head no, his lips again touching the bare flesh of her flat stomach. "To speak of her would be ill-luck. Let me forget her and love only you, Rachael. Let me love you as you should be loved."

"Yes, yes," she whispered, leaning back against the rough bark of a tree, her hands guiding him as he kissed her where she longed to be kissed.

Storm Dancer taunted her with the rough skin of his fingertips and the sweet hot tip of his tongue, until Rachael gasped for air . . . for release. And only then

The Publishers of Zebra Books Make This Special Offer to Zebra Romance Readers...

AFTER YOU HAVE READ THIS BOOK WE'D LIKE TO SEND YOU

4 MORE FOR *FREE*

AN $18.00 VALUE

NO OBLIGATION!

ONLY ZEBRA HISTORICAL ROMANCES "BURN WITH THE FIRE OF HISTORY"

(SEE INSIDE FOR MONEY SAVING DETAILS.)

did he rise.

She pulled at the ties of his loincloth and was rewarded with a handful of leather. She tossed it aside and slid her hand down his taut belly. The groan that rose in his throat but did not escape his lips excited her. Slowly her fingers glided over the thatch of crispy dark hair and found what they sought. Storm Dancer inhaled sharply as Rachael touched the swollen tip of his engorged shaft. She watched the expression change on his face as his eyes fell shut and he breathed heavily. She kissed him and he responded hungrily, enraptured by her caress.

After only a few moments of stroking, he gently pushed her hand aside. "No more, sweet wife, or there will be nothing left for you."

"That would be all right," she whispered, darting out her tongue to moisten his ear. "You have done no less for me."

He shook his head. "No. I want you too much. I need to feel you, Rachael-wife."

But instead of lowering her to the ground, he lifted her in his arms and with one well-directed tilt of his hips, he sank his tumescent shaft into her. Rachael cried out with pleasure, throwing back her head as she gripped his shoulders, her nails digging into the flesh of his back. For a moment their rhythm was awkward and irregular as Rachael adjusted to this new, exhilarating position, but after only a few strokes, she seemed to find her way. She tightened her legs around Storm Dancer's waist, kissing him, stroking him, moving under the guidance of his palms cradling her buttocks.

The strength of Storm Dancer's arms and shoulders

amazed her as he held her in midair, diving deeper and deeper with each thrust. Rachael felt the rough bark of the tree against her back but felt no pain, only the rhapsody of the rocking motion and the urgency that drove them faster.

Storm Dancer took his time, allowing Rachael to adjust to one rhythm only to change it again. Fast, slow, shallow, deep, he plied her with wave after wave of ecstasy, stopping each time he heard the change of pitch in her voice and felt her muscles contract on the verge of her ultimate pleasure. Finally when he himself could prolong his own need no longer, he drove hard into her, crushing his mouth against her as together as one they reached utter, complete fulfillment.

Rachael found herself laughing and crying at the same time as Storm Dancer sank to the soft leafy ground still cradling his love in his lap. She rested her cheek on his shoulder, waiting for her breath to return to her and her heart to slow its explosive pace.

"Did you really mean it?" she asked when she could finally speak again.

"Did I mean what, *ki-ti-hi?*" He kissed her neck, his fingers brushing back tendrils of hair that stuck to her damp skin.

"What you said about loving me."

"You ask if I love my wife? Every man must love his wife."

"No, do you really love me?" She leaned back a little so that she could see the shadows of his face. "Would you love me if I weren't your wife? Would you love me if I were someone else's wife," she dared.

He seemed amused. "Would I love you if you were

the Gifford's wife? It is too late, you are already mine."

"Hypothetical, Storm. Just tell me if I were another man's wife . . . Broken Horn's even, would you still love me?"

"It is wrong to covet that which belongs to another," he paused for the bat of an eye and then went on, "but to answer you with truth, Rachael-wife, yes I would love you if you were another man's wife. I would come and steal you from my brother's wigwam and carry you into the wilderness to make you mine. I would scale the stone wall of your Gifford's house and take you through the window. I would carry you to his gardens and lay you in a bed of rose petals where I would love you as no man could ever love you, where I could brand you mine."

She smiled. "You would do well at court with a tongue like that. You sound so sincere that I almost beieve you."

"I speak only the truth. Only the truth will I ever speak to you." He kissed her lips as if to seal his vow.

She caught a lock of his crow's wing hair and fingered it thoughtfully. "You speak the truth and yet you won't tell me about your wife."

"You are my wife."

She smiled slyly. "No, your other wife. The first one. The one who came before me."

"I speak the truth when I say it is bad luck to speak her name. I speak the truth when I tell you that only you, wife Rachael, live in my heart."

Rachael shifted her weight. She could still feel him inside her, but now his manhood seemed to be pulsing, growing within her. She decided to let the subject of his dead wife drop, at least for the time-being. She kissed his shoulder, his neck, the lobe of his ear and then whispered, "I suppose we should get back to camp. Dory will be anxious."

"We should return," he answered, his breath warm and caressing in her ear, but first . . ." He moved so quickly that all Rachael could do was hold on as he lowered her onto her back on the moss-covered ground and rose up over her, his burgeoning shaft still buried deep inside her.

Rachael laughed, a slow, sensual laugh. A truce had been met. She knew it. He knew it. Rachael would speak no more of Philadelphia for now. They would go to the Delaware village on the Chesapeake and hope they would find acceptance there among She-Who-Weeps' family. Rachael would be Storm Dancer's wife and try to live up to the meaning of the covenant. Perhaps there would even soon be a child.

But the subject of Philadelphia would arise again. She knew it. He knew it.

Rachael moaned as Storm moved against her, guiding her down the path of loving once more and she released all conscious thoughts, letting them be replaced by the sensations of physical pleasure that were too strong to resist. One day she would go back to Philadelphia. One day she would see her brother Thomas again and say a proper farewell. Only then could she truly give herself to Storm Dancer and the love he offered.

"Tell me again," Rachael whispered to Storm, her

hand in his.

"I have told you, Rachael, the Lenni Lenape are not like the Mohawk. Life will be different here for you, you will see. You have nothing to fear."

They walked with a tall, slender young Delaware brave, Kolheek, and his identical twin brother, Kumhaak. Just after dawn Storm Dancer, Rachael, and Dory had come upon the young men. They had drawn weapons at the sight of the Mohawk warrior and his two women, but Storm Dancer kept his hands at his sides and spoke to them in Algonquian, their native tongue. The young warrior Kolheek had responded hesitantly, his voice strained, but his suspicions had eased as Storm spoke.

In the tongue of the Delaware his mother had taught him as a boy, Storm Dancer explained to Kolheek and Kumhaak that he was looking for his mother's people. The braves not only knew of Shaakhan, the man of the wind and his wife, Hongiis Opaang, who was the chief of the village, but came from that same village. Storm Dancer's eyes had danced at the thought that the grandparents he had never known still lived. Now the two young men escorted Storm Dancer, Rachael, and Dory to the village, with one brave walking in front of them and one behind.

"Tell me that you love me, anyway," Rachael murmured in his ear.

He sighed with exasperation, but his spirit was not dampened. The trip from the great lakes of Iroquois country to the salt bay of the Chesapeake had been long and tiring. It felt good to know that they had finally reached their destination. It felt good to know that soon he might well have a home to take his wife to . . . a home to raise sons and daughters in. "I love you, Rachael. I love you as the moon loves the stars. I love you as the darkness loves the sunshine. I love you as—"

She sank her elbow into his side, laughing. "Enough poetics. You embarrass me with such nonsense."

Dory gave a snort, hustling along the path, clicking her tongue between her teeth. "The two of you sound like a pair of lovesick fools acooin' and abooin'. Makes me want to retch just listenin' to you." Her voice was harsh, but she was smiling as she hurried to keep up. She hadn't asked about the truce Storm Dancer and Rachael had made, but she made no bones about being pleased that the three of them were going to the Lenni Lenape village together. She began to talk of children and what good parents the two of them would make.

The September sun was straight overhead when the taller of the two young men cupped his hands over his mouth and made a trill bird-sound. Rachael couldn't place the exact bird that made the sound, but she knew it was something familiar. The sound was immediately echoed and then the group moved onward.

By the time Storm Dancer, Rachael, and Dory entered the well-guarded Delaware camp, word had already spread by way of the sentries that unusual visitors approached. As the three strangers and their escorts came into the camp, bronze villagers were already hurrying toward them.

Rachael immediately noted a difference between her arrival here in the Lenni Lenape village and her arrival in the Mohawk camp only a few months earlier. The villagers still chattered among themselves, but their voices echoed different emotions. They were curious, even excited, but there was no obvious hostility. As they approached, their faces were unlined by frowns, their body language unhindered by fear or hate.

Kolheek stepped forward and gave introductions, seemingly proud of his find, while Kumhaak hung back, embarrassed by the attention.

A hushed gasp of surprise rose among the villagers as Storm Dancer lowered his eyes in greeting, then lifted his head to speak of who he was. He told the Delawares who his mother had been and that she had sent him. Though Storm Dancer was a Mohawk, and therefore, an enemy to the Delaware, they all seemed to be familiar with the story of She-Who-Weeps' kidnapping so many years ago. Because Storm Dancer was the child of She-Who-Weeps, who his father was, be he Mohawk or the devil himself, seemed of little consequence.

After Storm Dancer introduced Rachael and Dory and then fell silent, there was a moment when all eyes were upon him and Rachael. It was as if everyone chewed his story thoughtfully. Then suddenly the villagers were coming forward in greeting. They hugged and kissed both Storm and Rachael as if they were all long lost brothers and sisters. There was a slapping of shoulders among the men and giggles among the women.

Rachael noticed at once that just as Storm Dancer had promised, a woman's position in this village seemed much different from that of one in the Mohawk village. Men and women mixed without thought, rather than always dividing with men on one side and women on the other. There also seemed to be a great deal more affection between men and women—not sexual contact, but friendly, warm touching. Rachael could immediately spot several couples of varying ages. Rachael also noticed that some men had children with them, while women stood beside them talking with free hands. One father held his tiny daughter across his shoulder, the little girl laughing, her voice filling Rachael's heart with hope. Another father carried a sleeping baby on his back in a cradle board.

And then of course the fact that Storm Dancer's grandmother could be the chief, set apart the Lenni Lenape from the Mohawk. While among the Mohawk the women were not even permitted to sit in on council meetings, here, a woman ran them!

There was so much confusion as the anxious villagers all tried to introduce themselves at once that Rachael gave up trying to keep track of who was who. It seemed that everyone was Storm Dancer's cousin. Some of the Delawares spoke English to her, while others just smiled and nodded. Rachael hung on to Storm Dancer's arm smiling, happy to see him smiling.

After twenty minutes of introductions, a Delaware brave approached Storm Dancer. He gazed at him with a strange mixture of wonderment and familiarity.

"The Dancer of the Storms has come to us," the newcomer said in Algonquian.

Storm Dancer nodded respectfully, but then looked up with a quizzical glance. "You know me, friend?" He spoke English for Rachael's benefit.

"I am called Tuuban." Tuuban's English was without flaw, as he too lapsed into the language of the guest, as was customary. "And yes I know you, yet I do not." He smiled, crossing his arms over his chest as he still stared at Storm Dancer. "For two years my grandfather has told me of how a storm will come out of the north to lift our people to safety."

"I do not know what to say," Storm Dancer spoke carefully. "I fear that I am not who you seek."

"Oh—you are he." Tuuban grinned. "There is no doubt in this man's mind, nor will there be a doubt in Grandfather's once he hears your voice."

"Who is your grandfather?"

"He is the wind, Shaakhan, and your grandfather as well. My father and your mother are brother and sister. I am sorry that my father was not here to great you properly, but he has gone to the white settlement of Annapolis to trade." He nodded in the direction of the wigwams. "I was sent to bring you to our grandparents. They wait, but they are impatient."

Storm Dancer nodded and turned to Rachael. "My grandparents ask that I come to their wigwam—their home."

Rachael released his hand. "Then go. I'll be all right." She looked around her. Though quite a few people had wandered off to return to chores, there were still many villagers standing around in clumps talking and laughing as if they were on an afternoon outing. "I'll come to no harm among these people."

"No." He took her hand securely in his. "You must come. If I am to be accepted into the clan of my mother's people, you too must be accepted as my wife. I will not go where you are not welcome."

Rachael's eyes glistened with unshed tears. Since they had agreed to disagree on the subject of Philadelphia things had been good between them. Each day she found herself more and more thankful that she had Storm, no matter what the circumstances had been leading to it.

Rachael squeezed his hand. "We go together, then."

Storm Dancer gave a nod to Tuuban and they were off. Storm Dancer was to meet the grandparents he had never known . . . the woman who was chief of the village and made the final decision as to whether he was welcome or not, and the man who had declared war on the Mohawks some thirty years ago.

Chapter Seventeen

As Rachael and Storm Dancer passed through the Lenni Lenape camp, Rachael took in her new surroundings. The village barely resembled that of the Mohawks. The homes the Delaware lived in, called wigwams, were made for single families, rather than for communal living as many longhouses were among the Mohawks. The wigwams were round structures with dome roofs. Storm Dancer related from his mother's memory how small saplings were driven into the ground and their tops bent and tied with twisted reeds or strips of inner bark from basswood. Smaller limbs were then threaded crosswise through the framework. The outside and inside walls were covered with bark shingles or mats made of cornhusk or grass. A cornhusk mat covered the doorway for privacy and there was a center hole for the firepit smoke to escape through the roof which could be covered when it rained.

The homes, Rachael could see, were also arranged differently. In the Mohawk camp there was a definite structure to the camp, with your importance in the village playing an important role in where your longhouse was situated. Here in the Lenni Lenape village there seemed to be little rhyme or reason to the haphazard arrangement of the houses, other than that they formed an approximate circle, all doorways opened to the east and that there was a ceremonial house in the center.

Tuuban reached a wigwam that looked like the others and came to a halt. Rachael noticed a sudden tenseness in Storm Dancer's touch as he held her hand. She smoothed his muscular arm. "They will be glad to have you," Rachael whispered.

Storm Dancer stared at the open door of the wigwam. "The Mohawk are the enemy of the Delaware. We have fought their braves, burned their villages, stolen their women. A Mohawk, my father, kidnapped Shaakhan's daughter thirty years ago. He despises the Mohawk and curses our children. There is a strong hate in his heart for the People of the Flint Country." His gaze shifted to Rachael's face. "He may have hate in his heart for me as well."

"Nonsense. You have forgotten all that you have told me, Husband. Here among the Lenni Lenape you are your mother's child. You don't think she would have told you to come if she hadn't known they would accept you."

"She spoke to a spirit. Perhaps I misinterpreted."

Rachael couldn't resist a smile. She appreciated a little hesitancy in her strong, confident husband. It made him seem more human . . . more like herself. "Tuuban says your grandfather knew you were coming. He says he has been expecting you. Now let's go meet your grandparents."

Storm Dancer took a soul-cleansing breath and then turned to Tuuban who waited patiently. Storm Dancer nodded and Tuuban led them inside the wigwam.

Tuuban made no introduction, but simply stepped aside. Rachael stood beside Storm Dancer, her fingers tangled in his.

The Shaakhan of the Delaware sat cross-legged on a padded cornhusk mat chewing contentedly on a drumstick. The man's face was a mass of leathery wrinkles, his hair a pure silvery gray that fell below his waist. His eyes were the white clouded eyes of a blind man.

"Dancer of the Storms!" Shaakhan chuckled as he tossed his turkey bone into the air and an old woman leapt up with a basket and caught the bone in the basket in midair. He wiped his greasy lips on a bit of cloth she pushed into his hand.

Horgiss Opaang, Rachael thought. *Starlight, Storm' grandmother—chief of the village.*

"Good day to you, great Shaakhan, wind of the Turtle Clan, of the Lenni Lenape." Storm Dancer went down on one knee in reverence.

Rachael copied him, lowering her head, listening carefully to the Shaakhan's strong voice as he spoke his native tongue.

The old man waggled a finger. "Come, come and sit with me, Grandson. There are no formalities in my wigwam." He patted the mat beside him. "Come sit and tell me who this white woman is that smells like the heavens. I warn you. No matter what poor habits you may have learned among those man-eaters, you will not be allowed to continue them here. We take no captives. It brings ill-luck to a people."

Storm Dancer rose. "This is my wife, Rachael, Shaakhan. She comes of her own free will." He said it in Algonquian, then in English as if to verify with Rachael the truth of his statement. He took her hand and lifted it so that she stood beside him.

Shaakhan seemed to stare at her, though he was obviously blind. "With babe, is she yet?"

"No, Shaakhan, but we hope God will bless us soon with sons and daughters."

He gave a hrrumph. "Enough of this Shaakhan this, Shaakhan that. I have waited long for you, grandson of mine." He hit his bare chest, which was surprisingly muscular and well-formed for a man of his obvious years. "Call me grandfather!"

"Forgive me for words, sir, but how do you know I am your grandson? We have never laid eyes on each other. My mother was taken from you at least thirty years ago. I could be an imposter."

He made another disgruntled sound. "This is something a man knows. Besides, I have seen you. I have seen you in my dreams. I heard you coming like a great storm that blows over our forest, all power and strength."

"You are rude, Shaakhan!" the old woman said, first in Algonquian and then in English for Rachael's sake. "I stand here being the dutiful wife, waiting for you to introduce my grandson to me. I have waited patiently long enough!" She came across the clean swept dirt floor and threw her thin arms around Storm Dancer in a great hug.

Rachael saw tears cloud her eyes as Storm Dancer returned the embrace. Starlight was a beautiful woman despite the wrinkles of time and the snow in her hair.

Shaakhan groaned. "Hush your mouth old woman, else I'll throw you to the bears and find myself a new young maid to take as wife."

Starlight stepped back and wiped her eyes with the back of her hand, unashamed by her tears. "Oh hush your own mouth, old man. What maid would have you with a worm as shriveled as yours?"

Shaakhan laughed, slapping his knee. "Still does the job though, doesn't it wife of mine?"

Starlight switched back to English again, her voice teasing. "The poor old fool. He's not right in the head. Ignore his babbling, Grandson and Granddaughter."

"She speaks the English tongue because she thinks I know not the words," Shaakhan said carefully in English. "But, I would be a fool not to learn my enemy's language, wouldn't I, Grandson?"

"It is always wise to know the opponent," Storm Dancer replied, amused by his grandmother and grandfather's antics.

Rachael laughed with the elderly couple, enjoying the playful banter between them. It was obvious the two were deeply in love with each other, even after many years of marriage. Rachael couldn't help wondering if her and Storm's marriage would ever be this wonderful this many years down the path of life.

"Sit, sit, Grandchildren," Starlight insisted, ushering both Rachael and Storm Dancer to the place where guests of honor sat. "Sit and I will bring you food and drink. I know it has been a long journey here on both heart and soul."

Storm Dancer sat beside his grandfather and Rachael sat beside Storm Dancer. The old man reached out and took Storm Dancer's hand, seeming to know exactly where it lay without having need to see it. "I should never have doubted my waking dreams, Grandson," he said, the joy obvious in his voice. "I should have known you would come to save us."

"I am glad that I have come to be at your side, Grandfather, but I fear I cannot save you from whatever harm has come your way." He looked away. "I could not save my own people."

"Ha! That is because we are your people, not those savages who paint their faces blue and fornicate with animals!" He patted Storm Dancer's hand. "Now tell me how it is that you finally come to us." The old man's eyes shone brightly despite their lack of sight.

Starlight brought Rachael and Storm Dancer a feast of turkey, stewed corn, and sweet blueberries. As they ate, he related to his grandparents how he came to lose favor with his father's people and how his eventual shunning came about.

Rachael was surprised to find that she understood much of what Storm Dancer said to his grandparents. She was glad that he had spent so much time on their journey south teaching her the language of the Lenni Lenape because suddenly it was very important to Rachael that she be able to communicate with those around her. If she and Storm were to be accepted among the Lenni Lenape, she wanted to truly be one of them, rather than just a guest. It struck her as odd that these complete strangers were so thrilled to see their long lost relative who was half enemy simply because he was also half Lenni Lanape. On the other side of the coin, it mattered not that Rachael was a white woman, again the enemy. Because she was Storm Dancer's wife, on the condition that she was worthy of the honor, she would be adopted into the village and would never be thought of a *manake-equiwa* again.

Storm Dancer's tale of his life as a Mohawk finally drew to an end. For a moment or two there was silence in the wigwam. Rachael could almost hear the minds of Starlight and Shaakhan chewing over the information their grandson had provided, and storing it in the proper categories of their minds.

Shaakhan called for his pipe and Starlight fetched it for him, lighting it between her own teeth with a coal from the firepit just outside the wigwam door.

Shaakhan took several puffs on his pipe before he finally spoke. Once upon a time, Rachael would have grown impatient with the silence, but Storm Dancer had taught her the importance of contemplating one's words. Like her husband, she had grown to relish the peacefulness of silence.

"It is a sad thing that you lived so many years as you did, struggling to be a creature you could never be," Shaakhan said. "I wish that my daughter had never been taken from my arms. I wish that you had never been born into a place so far from here where ways are so different than our own." He sucked on his pipe. "But who am I to say that this was not all a part of the great plan of life? It is said that every word is spoken for a reason, every gesture, a purpose. It is sometimes hard for us to think that maybe we have little control over what happens to us. It is hard to admit that it may be fate that controls every moment we live from birth unto death . . . even beyond."

Starlight let out her breath in a hiss. "I think that is quite enough philosophical talk for one day, man of great wind. Let our grandson take his wife and rest. There will be tomorrow to talk and many tomorrows after that."

"But I have many things to discuss with the Dancer of Storms!" Shaakhan shook the stem of his pipe at his wife. "He does not look tired to me!"

Starlight rolled her eyes as she lay a hand gently on Shaakhan's shoulder. "I was trying very gently, Husband, to tell you that it is time for your nap."

Rachael laughed, rising off the cornhusk mat where she had sat for much of the afternoon. "I don't know about you, Shaakhan—"

"Call me grandfather. Your sweet young voice is music to these ears."

"Grandfather, then." She gave a nod. "I'm tired even if you aren't. I'd love a nap."

"Tuuban will see that you are taken to the guest's wigwam. Take your man and go and I will see you in the evening. My guess from the sounds outside, would be that there will be much celebrating tonight."

Storm Dancer stood. "I want to thank you, Grandfather, for taking me in so easily. I—"

"Enough, Dancer of the Storms. You will make this old man weep with joy and embarrass himself. What kind of man would I be that I would not take my only daughter's son as my own?"

"But after what my father did to you in taking my mother, I could not blame you great Shaakhan, if you did not wish to lay claim upon my tainted blood."

"Tainted! Ha! You are good luck, I should say,

Grandson. And you will be of great help in the months to come. You have been sent for a reason. Prophesy is always fulfilled given time."

"You speak of this prophesy, but you do not say why I have been sent to you, Grandfather. Tell me so that I may know what I am to do."

Shaakhan waved Storm Dancer away. "All in good time. Now take your bride and leave me to lay this old worthless body down for a rest so that I can join in the festivities tonight."

"But, Grandfather—"

Rachael pulled on Storm Dancer's arm. "You heard Grandfather, all in good time," she said gently.

Starlight winked at Rachael and pushed back the corn husk door flap so that Rachael and Storm Dancer could step out into the fading shadows of afternoon. "What would these men do without women?" she teased.

"Where is my pillow, Wife?" Shaakhan complained as he stretched out to sleep. "Stop flapping your tongue and come do my bidding as a good woman should."

Starlight smiled at Rachael and let the deerskin fall behind Rachael and Storm Dancer. "Coming, old man! I'm coming."

Rachael rested her cheek on Storm Dancer's muscular shoulder. "I like them," she whispered. "It's almost like home here, only better."

He brushed back a strand of hair that had fallen from her neat braid. "Life is good, isn't it?"

She lifted up on her toes and kissed him. "Life is good."

Tuuban stood by the door of Shaakhan's wigwam,

looking away discreetly as he allowed the couple to have a private moment together. Then he spoke. "Let me take you to your wigwam. It has been prepared."

"Dory? My friend Dory?"

"She is well. My cousin, Laughing Rain, is a widow. She has asked Dory to join her in her home so that you and Storm Dancer may be alone. It is not right for a man and a woman to have to share time in marriage with others."

"You're certain she's all right?"

"I can take you to her, if you so wish." The brave pointed across the camp. "Last I saw her, she and Laughing Rain were going to gather honey from a beehive."

Rachael looked up at Storm.

"I would think Dory could care for herself, Rachael," he suggested softly. "Come let us see our new home."

The sparkle in Storm Dancer's eyes made Rachael think that perhaps he had ulterior motives for wanting to get her inside their new home. Her heart skipped a beat and she felt her face flush. How unfashionable she would have been in London to be so taken with her husband. How wanton she was to want to touch him the way she wanted to touch him right now.

Storm Dancer's arm fell casually over her shoulder as they followed Tuuban. Several villagers waved a greeting. Two young girls in their teens giggled as they walked by, their eyes on Storm Dancer's handsome physique. Rather than being jealous, the girls' attention made Rachael proud. They could look all they wanted. It was she he took home to his wigwam. It was she he would make love to on the bed mats tonight.

The wigwam Tuuban led them to was almost identical to Shaakhan and Starlight's except that, because it was the guest quarters, there were only a few baskets and strings of herbs and dried vegetables hanging from the rafters. The wigwam was cool inside and smelled faintly of fresh pine boughs. A sweating gourd of water had been left in the doorway as well as several wooden bowls of various berries, sweetened corncakes, and other tasty morsels.

Tuuban hung outside the doorway. "If there is anything I can get for you, please call upon me. I would be honored to help you in any way I can."

Storm Dancer turned to Tuuban, and spoke in Algonquian. "You have been kind, Cousin. I will not forget the hospitality you have offered a man with nowhere to go."

"Nowhere to go? You fool yourself. This home has waited your arrival for many years. Shaakhan the great medicine man said you would come. He saw you in his dream and you came as he promised. I am only glad I did not have to wait another coming of the seasons to finally meet you." Tuuban glanced at Rachael who had sat down to take off her moccasins. "Your wife is very beautiful even with her pale skin. I envy you."

Storm Dancer couldn't resist a glimpse at her. "She is indeed beautiful and with the temper of a crazed bee."

The two laughed easily as if they had been friends for a lifetime and Rachael looked up, wondering what was so amusing.

Tuuban gave a wave over his shoulder. "Rest,

friends, for tonight we celebrate," he said slipping into English. "You will not be disturbed, I will see to it myself."

For a moment after Tuuban had gone and the cornhusk door had dropped, Rachael and Storm Dancer looked at each other in silence.

Rachael smiled, patting the mat beside her, indicating that he should sit down. "It's almost too good to be true, but it is true, isn't it, Storm? We are welcome here."

He came to sit beside her. "It seems my mother was right. My grandparents have taken us in with open arms. I only wish that I knew what they spoke of when they said I was part of a prophecy. I don't know what they expect of me. I do not know why I did not see a future here in a waking dream."

"What is it you tell me sometimes? I think too much and live too little? Stop thinking, Dancer of the Storms, and live as you tell others. Your grandfather and grandmother are wise. They will not expect what you cannot give."

He caught a lock of her hair and brushed it between his fingers. "I think we could have a good life here, Rachael. I think that you will be glad you came with me. There was no life for you in the Philadelphia with the coward."

Rachael looked away. She didn't want to spoil their happiness with an argument over Gifford. Nor did she want to discuss the idea that she still thought it was wrong for him to have not given her the opportunity to say good-bye to her brother.

She turned back to him, raising her arms to rest them

on his broad shoulders. She smiled as her fingers found the edging of his vest and she tugged it off. She pressed her lips to the warm skin of his shoulder, then to his neck, then his ear. She kissed her way to his mouth, enjoying his sighs of pleasure.

"I think we should celebrate, Husband."

"Celebrate?" His voices was husky and warm. "Do you wish to dance? To sing? This is the way our people celebrate," he teased.

"Mmmm, that all sounds wonderful, but I had something else in mind. Something more intimate. Wifely duty you could call it." She kissed her way across the hard muscles of his chest, her lips finding the nub of his nipple. When she took it between her teeth and tugged gently, he groaned.

"Oh, Rachael, Wife, I promise we will be happy together, you and I, in this new land." He pulled her into his lap, kissing her. "And I promise there will be children to love and be loved," he added against her lips.

She unlaced her bodice, letting her breasts free so that she could brush her bare chest against his. "You want my child?"

"It is what every man wants who loves a woman."

"If I had a child, you know I could never leave it. I could never leave you. Is that why you want a babe?"

He pushed her hair back off her cheek. "No," he answered firmly. "I want a child to love as I love you. Do you not wish for a papoose to cradle in your arms?"

She nodded ever so gently. "I do, Storm Dancer. A baby would make our life complete, wouldn't it?"

His thumb brushed against her nipple as his lips

sought hers. "A life is never complete until you breathe your last breath, Wife. But yes, a son or a daughter would make my heart sing."

Locked in an embrace, they rolled onto the sleeping mat, limb entangled in limb. As Storm Dancer pushed away Rachael's clothing so they could be flesh against flesh she felt a rush of happiness she had never experienced before. Too good to be true, her own words echoed in her head.

Chapter Eighteen

The leaves fell from the trees as fall blew into the Chesapeake with its blustering winds and cooler temperatures. With the help of Starlight and the other women in the Lenni Lenape camp, Rachael kept busy with the harvest season ritual of preserving food for the long cold winter ahead. She was so occupied by her new duties and position in the village that the days and weeks slipped by like grains of precious salt slipping from her fingers.

Side by side the women worked to gather *the three sisters*—squash, corn, and beans—from their small but prosperous summer gardens. The wives of the village were so anxious to help the newlyweds set up housekeeping that they showered Rachael with baskets of fresh vegetables and herbs grown lovingly all summer. They took their time to patiently demonstrate to her how each item could be preserved and then stored so that she could provide for her husband throughout the winter. They worked tirelessly at her side, guiding her, laughing with her, teaching her the ways of the Lenni Lenape.

The women not only tended the garden, but fished and clammed beside their husbands as well. Their catch from the shores of the great Chesapeake bay and Metuksit River were smoked on racks and stored in the wigwams on long strings. The women and children gathered honey and stored it in wax-sealed pots. Pits were dug outside the wigwams, lined with dried leaves, filled with fruits and vegetables, then buried to protect the precious foodstores from freezing temperatures. It was a busy but contented time for the Lenni Lenape when the men hunted and cared for the children while the women prepared for winter.

Rachael was overjoyed with the new life she and Storm Dancer had been *exiled* to. It was better than she could ever have dreamed. Her entire life she had always experienced a strange sense of detachment from the world around her, but suddenly she felt as if she were in the center of the universe. For the first time in her life she felt as if she belonged.

Not only did she enjoy the company of the women of the village but she thrived on her husband's attention. They fished together. They dove for oysters off the shore of the bay. He made baskets for her from the reeds of the riverbank to store her foodstuffs. He sat across from her at their firepit and played haunting tunes on his bone flute for her. They swam in the cold bay and made love on the shore by the light of the moon.

As the weeks enfolded into months, Rachael saw Storm change subtly. He became more relaxed, less moody, less brooding. Shaakhan began to train his grandson for the honorable position of shaaman of the village and Storm Dancer excelled under his grandfather's rigorous instruction.

Despite the fact that Shaakhan insisted that Storm Dancer begin his study immediately, the old man remained elusive concerning Storm Dancer's purpose for coming to the village.

Rachael suggested that it was the position of shaman that Storm had been meant to take when his grandfather died, but Storm Dancer insisted his grandfather had ulterior motives. Shaakhan was a crafty old man who had more up his sleeve than he cared to bare.

The entire village treated Storm Dancer as he were a gift from the heavens. They all seemed to know the path he would follow to fulfill the prophesy Shaakhan had related to them, but no one was willing to speak of the matter with Storm Dancer or Rachael.

While Shaakhan had aided Storm Dancer in cultivating his ability to see *waking dreams* to the point that Storm Dancer could often invoke them, Storm Dancer found it very frustrating that he could not foresee events concerning himself or Rachael. Though Shaakhan expressed great pleasure in his grandson's progress, Storm Dancer was impatient with his seemingly trivial accomplishments. When he expressed his concerns to his grandfather, the old man only laughed. "In time, grandson of mine," he offered often. "All comes to the man who waits in good time."

At the sound of Storm Dancer's voice, Rachael glanced up from the stone and mortar she knelt at, forgetting for the moment the corn meal she was grinding. She smiled at the sight of her husband standing beside a wigwam speaking to one of the men,

Yesterday's Thunder. Storm Dancer wore a new sleeved vest and the new leggings she had made for him with the help of Starlight. The wind whipped the long inky black hair that fell across his shoulders, framing his high, bronze cheekbones, making him a striking sight to any woman.

With the coming of winter, Rachael had realized her and Storm Dancer's immediate need for warm clothing. They had left the Mohawk village carrying only what was necessary to survive. Upon their arrival on the Chesapeake, Starlight had put herself immediately in charge of the newlyweds' winter clothing needs. One morning she appeared at their wigwam with a pile of soft tanned leathers and sat down to instruct Rachael on the rudimentary steps of sewing. Rachael was delighted to find that she had far more talent sewing vests and leggings than she had ever had embroidering her father's household bed linens. Within a few days both she and Storm Dancer and Dory had several modest but warm, well-sewn winter outfits. By using some of her own basic sewing knowledge Rachael found that she could even improve on the Lenni Lenape standard garments with darts and attached sleeves. The other women admired the betterments so much that they were soon asking for her help in sewing clothing for their own families. Rachael's current project, a rabbit fur coat, was the talk of the sewing circles that gathered in the late afternoons. All the women were so envious of the fuss Storm Dancer made each time he presented his wife with more rabbit skins that they all went home to their husbands and insisted on having new coats of their own.

Storm Dancer caught a glimpse of Rachael out of the corner of his eye and his expression softened. He continued to listen to what the brave standing next to him said, but his thoughts were obviously on Rachael.

She felt her face flush and she returned her attention to her cornmeal. If anyone had ever told her she would feel like this toward a man, toward a *savage*, she would have called them a liar. It amazed her how the differences in her and Storm Dancer's upbringing seemed to be of little consequence. They weren't just in love; they honestly liked each other and enjoyed each other's company, something unknown in the life-style Rachael had grown up in.

Occasionally Rachael wondered what she would be doing if she were back in Philadelphia. She thought of the afternoon teas and the balls she had missed . . . she would miss. She thought of the excitement a duel or illegitimate child created. She thought of the hours spent shopping or standing for a matuamaker to have gowns made for her. The delightful thing was that it didn't matter. She felt no sense of loss when she thought of the lace and silk she had once worn and the exotic foods she had sampled. She didn't miss the servants or the feather tick mattresses or the glitter of crystal.

Suddenly Rachael realized Storm Dancer was crouching in front of her and she gave a startled gasp. He laughed when she jumped and he reached out to pull a thick dark braid playfully. "Do you dream of lovers past?" he teased.

She looked up, a smile tugging at the corners of her mouth. She wondered how it was that every word that came from his mouth was poetry to her ears. "You know there's no one else but you. I was just thinking of how happy I am at this very moment."

"Making cornmeal makes you happy? You are an easy woman to please, Rachael-wife," he teased as he took the grinding stone from her hands and began to grind the corn for her. Her laughter brought a smile to his face as he watched her dust the cornmeal from her hands. "I am glad you like it here," he murmured.

She added more kernels of corn to his mixture. "And what of you, Husband?" she questioned thoughtfully. "Do you like it here?"

He thought for a moment before responding. His gaze strayed to the scalplock that flew from the lodgepole he had erected outside their wigwam. "I sometimes miss my village. I miss the man I was as a Mohawk." He chuckled. "There is more work to being a Lenni Lenape man." He looked up at her. "But I think, perhaps, I only miss my old life out of habit."

"You're going to be a shaman here. It's what you've always wanted. You said yourself that your brother would never have allowed you to become the shaman of your village among the Mohawks."

His face seemed to darken at the mention of Broken Horn, and Rachael wished she hadn't spoken of him. She saw him again look up at the black scalp lock blowing in the breeze high above their heads. She had no desire to bring back the bad memories he seemed to be dealing with so well.

"I do not wish to go back, but I wonder how my family is. It hurts my heart to know they are doomed and yet not be able to help them."

"We all make choices in our lives, Storm." She took the pestle from his hand and set it aside. She pressed her lips to his palm. "They made the choice to banish you because they didn't want to hear what you had to say. They chose to follow Broken Horn, all of them. Whatever happens to them, they're responsible, not you."

"Shaakhan speaks the same words. He tells me I must accept that my brother is evil. He did me great harm. More harm than any man should do to another, no less his only flesh." Storm Dancer still looked at her, but his eyes were unfocused. "I wonder if he came to me today, if I could forgive him."

"If you could, you'd be a better person than I am."

He patted her hand, pushing aside thoughts of Broken Horn. "It is true that I have lost one life, but I have gained another. I now have new responsibilities, don't I wife?"

"You do." She smiled. "And I hope you'll have more. I hope I can give you a child. Maybe many children."

It was his turn to kiss her hand. "You worry too much over papooses. I told, you long ago I heard a child's laughter mingling with yours. Our God will give us a child in good time."

"But what if he doesn't?" She thought for a moment, then lifted her head to stare directly into his loving, dark eyes. "You said Father Drake read to you from the Bible. Did he ever tell you who Rachael was in the Old Testament?"

"The wife of the man Jacob."

"Yes." Against her will, tears filled Rachael's eyes and she looked away. "And she was barren."

He reached out to touch her cheek with his fingertips, forcing her to look upon him. "Do not cry, Wife, that I love more than the moon and stars. We will have a child to call our own." He caught a tear with his fingertip. "I promise you. Now let me tell you why Yesterday's Thunder stopped me."

She sniffed. "Why?"

"Because as Dory has no father or family, Yesterday's Thunder has asked me permission to court Dory."

"He wants to marry her!" She laughed, wiping away her tears with the back of her hand. "He was serious? What did you say?"

He shrugged. "I granted him permission to woo her."

"You didn't tell him that Shadows Man has already asked permission?"

"I told him, but he said he didn't care. This village has a shortage of women. He says he will win your friend over."

"But she's so much older than Yesterday's Thunder."

"He said it mattered not. She is still well within the years to give him sons and daughters."

Rachael glanced across the compound to where Dory stood, a water basket in her hand, talking to Yesterday's Thunder. Her laughter carried on the wind. It was difficult to believe that any man, let alone two, would be interested in Dory with her spiky cropped orange hair and short round stature, but it did Rachael's heart good to see that someone recognized her for the fine person that she was.

Rachael and Storm Dancer watched the exchange between Yesterday's Thunder and Dory for a moment, before Rachael spoke with amusement in her voice. "It's certainly going to be interesting to see who she chooses."

"That it will be, Wife." Storm Dancer stood and

offered his hand. "It is time to put aside your work and change your clothing. You forget that tonight is the great dance of the corn festival. The other women are already brushing out their hair and donning their ceremonial dress."

"I didn't forget, I just wanted to finish this basket of corn." She rose, wrapping her arms around his neck. "I thought I would wear the white buckskin dress Starlight gave me. She said it's very old, but it's beautiful."

"The beauty is in the woman who wears it, not the cloth that covers her body." He nuzzled her neck, then whispered, "Come inside my wigwam, woman of mine, and I will help you dress for the festival."

The throaty sound of his voice sent a shudder of exhilaration through her veins. "Help me dress, will you? You're not much help with dressing, Husband, but I've grown rather fond of your undressing abilities."

"If you want a baby, Rachael-wife, you must work for it." He lifted her easily into his arms, not caring who saw them. The villagers who passed by the wigwam, politely averted their eyes. "Let me take you inside and show you the way to make a child," Storm Dancer whispered provocatively.

She rested her forehead on his chin, laughing as he ducked into the wigwam. "Storm! They all know what you're doing . . . what we're doing. We're not better than a hutch of rabbits."

"And why, Wife, do you think our forest is so plentiful with the hare?"

She slid out of his arms, letting her moccasins touch the clean mats of the wigwam floor. She snaked her arms around his neck. "We'll be late for the dance." She touched his lower lip with the tip of her tongue.

"So we will."

"But, the shaman must be present to begin the festival."

"I am not shaman. My grandfather can begin the ceremonies." He slipped his hand between the bindings of her bodice and brushed the rough pads of his fingertips against her breast. "A man cannot be reproached for attending to his husbandly duties."

Rachael sighed, letting her eyes close as she savored the exquisite touch of his hand on her breast. "Promise me something, Storm."

He kissed her throat. "If it is my power . . ."

"Promise me I'll always be your wife. Promise me nothing will come between us. Promise me it will always be as it is now."

"There is nothing that could break this union, Rachael-wife." He pushed back the silky hair that fell across her face so that he could stare into her sky blue eyes. "Nothing."

They kissed a kiss of lovers, at first soft and gentle, but then their mouths twisted hungrily as conscious thought slipped from their minds and fierce longing took control. Storm lifted Rachael into his arms and lowered her to a sleeping mat, their tongues meeting in a dance of love as she pulled the ties of his loincloth.

When her fingers found the evidence of his desire, he moaned words of encouragement. Enjoying the power she had over him, she raised up, straddling his body so that she could sit up and he could watch her unclothe.

Shivers of anticipation flowed through Rachael's body as she watched his dark luminous eyes take in the curves of her naked flesh. She took her time undressing, wanting to prolong his erotic expectations as long as possible. When she had thrown aside her leather skirt and bodice and woman's loin cloth, she stretched out over him, her flesh hot when his tumescent shaft brushed against her inner thigh.

Their lips met in a hard and demanding kiss that left them breathless, but wanting more. Rachael leaned over Storm Dancer, running her hands through his thick black hair as she drank in his dark eyes clouded with passion. "Now?" she whispered, moving her hips against his in a slow, sensual dance of love. "Now, husband?"

"Yes, *ki-ti-hi.* Love me now."

Rachael lifted her hips, her gaze still locked with his as she lowered herself onto him.

Storm Dancer groaned, closing his eyes, as he struggled for control. After a moment, Rachael began to move slowly, rhythmically. The corded bands of Storm's arms tightened and relaxed as he guided her with his hands.

Outside the cozy wigwam, hollow drums began to beat calling to the villagers, beckoning them in a dance of Thanksgiving. But the sound of the drums and hollow gourd rattles were lost in cries of passion to Rachael and Storm Dancer as they found ecstasy in each other's arms once more.

Broken Horn sat hunched over the firepit outside his longhouse, a stinking bear hide wrapped around his shoulders for warmth. The fire spit and sputtered, giving off little warmth with its wet uncured wood.

Broken Horn drew the hide tighter around his shoulders and picked a bit of gristle from between his teeth and chewed it again. His fingertips brushed against his smallpox-scarred cheek and he cursed foully beneath his breath.

Winter had set in early this year, just one more strike of bad luck in a long line of ill-fated events. Since Storm Dancer had taken his white woman and Broken Horn's scalp lock and walked off to the south, the Mohawk village had been barraged with bad luck. The drought had left the women with little harvest to gather for winter from the few rows of corn and beans they had bothered to plant. Fishing had been poor and game sparse.

One courageous Mohawk had suggested that perhaps the area surrounding the village had been hunted out. After all, it had been years since they had moved, whereas it was custom to move yearly so as to not overhunt or overfish one place. Broken Horn had smacked him square across the face with the butt of his rifle, breaking his jaw in punishment for suggesting it was Broken Horn's fault they were hungry.

Then the sickness had come. Broken Horn and his men had traveled far east to raid a little village of white settlers. They had stolen fine horses, some pewter, a wagonload of flour, sugar and salt meat, and a pile of warm wool blankets. It was in those blankets that the smallpox had been carried. In the excitement of their kill, the Mohawk braves had not realized that many in the white settlement were ill.

Within a week of returning from the raid, the Mohawk villagers began to fall sick. The old men and women were the first to die. Meadowlark and Two

Fists lasted less than five days. Broken Horn made himself both chief and shaman of the village.

Then the fever and weeping sores began to take the lives of women and children, and lastly the younger men. The few that had survived, like Broken Horn, were ghastly scarred.

By the time the snow blew the plague from the village, it was too late to go far for game. Now the few villagers left lived on the meat of their dogs and what was left of the stolen rations. Women began to cry for what they had lost, and men began to whisper behind Broken Horn's back, wishing they had listened to Storm Dancer.

Broken Horn tossed a stick onto the fire, looking up to see Two Crows coming toward him. Broken Horn grunted and his friend squatted by the fire. It was obvious he had something to say, but he took his time in speaking.

"There is talk of joining the Seneca across the river."

"Seneca!" Broken Horn hocked and spat into the fire. "They are dogs."

"The dogs have food. There are no more than twenty of us, brother. They would take us in. They would keep us from dying."

"You are a traitor. All of you. You think this is my fault!"

"Any fault lies in our own laps," he answered softly in Iroquois. "We should not have allowed the women to become so lazy that they planted no gardens. We should have been hunting all summer and into the fall, storing our meats instead of raiding. Had we been able to feed our sick children they might have lived." He took a long stick and poked at the burning wood in the firepit. "We have no one to blame for our devastation but ourselves."

"No, no, brother Two Crows, you are wrong." Broken Horn turned slowly, the scabbing sores on his joints making it difficult to move. "It is Storm Dancer that is to blame for this. He took my scalp lock and with it my luck. With my scalp lock I could have led our village to great victories. I could still . . . if I had it once more."

Two Crows pulled his ragged muskrat hat down further over his ears. "You forget, Storm Dancer is dead."

Broken Horn glanced across the flickering fire, a sneer on his scarred face. "He is not dead, fool, only gone."

"I saw him disappear in the smoke of the shaman's magic."

Broken Horn grimaced viciously as he peered back into the firelight. "I saw him leave."

Two Crows' bloodshot eyes went wide. "You saw his spirit?"

"I saw him! Him and the white whore. I saw them pass through the village, walking south." A strange light sparkled in his dark eyes. "My mother saw them. She spoke. I think I know where he went, but my mother knows."

He turned his head to the lodge behind him and barked a command. To conserve heat all twenty villagers now lived in the longhouse which had once been the ceremonial lodge.

A moment later Pretty Woman appeared in the doorway of the lodge. She was bent over with pain in her joints, her harelipped face gaunt with hunger. "Husband?"

"Send the old woman out and bring me food. I am hungry."

"So are we all hungry. There is nothing to eat." She turned away. "I will send the old woman."

She-Who-Weeps came hobbling out of the lodge a moment later. She was frail, her skin transparent with age and starvation, but unscarred by the smallpox. She was still a beautiful woman. "You call for me, Son?"

"Tell me where he went."

She came closer to the fire. "Who?"

"My half-brother who is my brother no more."

She lowered her gaze to the snow-covered ground. "Dead. Dead are all my children, but you, *great chief.*" She spoke her last words with all the ridicule she could manage.

"Liar." Broken Horn rose, the bear hide, still wrapped around his shoulders. "I saw him and the whore leave. I saw you standing near the trees. You spoke to him. You told him where to go."

"There were many spirits that night my son died. Many spirits."

Broken Horn reached out and smacked She-Who-Weeps in the face.

Two Crows gasped, but dared not interfere. He still had one wife and a child to care for. If Broken Horn killed him, they would surely die.

She-Who-Weeps rocked back under the force of her son's hand, but did not fall. Slowly she lifted her head, to stare at him, her gray eyes mocking. "This old woman is sorry she displeases you."

Broken Horn grabbed the scruff of her squirrel cape and jerked her frail body up off the ground. "Tell me where the man who has cursed me has gone, or I will kill you, old woman!"

She-Who-Weeps let her eyes fall closed. She was cold and tired with no one left on this earth to love her or be loved. Death would not be such a terrible thing. "My son, Storm Dancer is dead," she said, in the words of the Lenni Lenape. The sound of the words were music to her ears. She wondered numbly how long it had been since she had dared speak her native tongue.

Broken Horn pulled his knife from its sheath. "Tell me, old woman! Last chance!"

She-Who-Weeps heard the pause. She felt the bitter wind on her cheek, and she smiled. Death would take her home to her Lenni Lenape village. Though she had never made it back in life, in her death she would return to the place where she had been happy.

She-Who-Weeps did not feel the agony of the knife as it tore through the wall of her chest and sank into her still heart.

Chapter Nineteen

Snow came early to the Chesapeake in the winter of 1762. It broke with gale-force winds and bitter cold. For two days Rachael and Storm Dancer remained inside their wigwam where it was warm and cozy, waiting for the snowstorm to blow over. To pass the time they played checkers with seashells. Storm Dancer repaired his weapons and began the painstaking task of making a new ax. Rachael busied herself sewing for one of the elderly women in the camp who could no longer see well enough to thread her own needle. They made love in midafternoon snuggled beneath the bear hide blankets. They told stories of their childhoods and tentatively talked about their future.

On the third day Rachael and Storm woke to the deafening sound of silence. The tempest winds had ceased and the deep cover of the snow muffled the natural sounds of the forest. After a quick morning meal of hot corn mush sprinkled with dried apple bits, Rachael and Storm dressed in their fur coats and mittens and went to see how nature had transformed the Lenni Lenape village.

The camp and surrounding forest was covered in a thick blanket of pristine white. The pine, cedar, and oak trees were heavily laden, their branches weeping beneath the weight of the bountiful snowfall.

Hand in hand Storm and Rachael walked out of their wigwam into the biting cold. The morning sunshine radiated from above, warming her face despite the low temperatures, and setting their surroundings ablaze with white light.

"It's beautiful," Rachael sighed, as enchanted by the snow as any child could ever be.

He shook his head as he gazed out over the camp. "You would think that after all of these years of seeing Father Winter come and go, we would not be so amazed by his splendor." He turned to Rachael. "But it is beautiful, isn't it?"

The sound of childish laughter came from one of the wigwams as two round-faced children came bounding out into the snow. It seemed as if everyone had the same idea as Storm and Rachael. The villagers began to spill from the safe havens of their wigwams into the crisp morning air dressed in hooded fur coats and knee length otterskin boots.

Storm Dancer scooped up a handful of snow and balled it in his mittens. Before Rachael could open her mouth to protest, he threw it at her, striking her in the chest. The snowball exploded in her face, showering her with bitter cold snow.

She spit and sputtered, shocked by the cold, but laughing as he ducked behind their wigwam. "All right!" she called, scooping up a big handful of snow.

"This is war, Husband. Expect no mercy!"

A snowball flew from behind the cover of the birchbark-shingled wigwam, but she managed to dodge the missile. Catching a glimpse of his black hair, she threw the snowball as hard as she could and was rewarded by a grunt as she struck Storm Dancer in the back of the head.

Rachael howled with laughter and leaned over to grab another handful of snow. Just as she straigthened up, Storm Dancer leapt from behind the wigwam, and bombarded her with several snowballs.

Rachael squealed with laughter, throwing two more. To her delight, both hit their mark, showering him with powdered snow.

He dove for the cover of the wigwam again and Rachael grabbed for more snow. "Coward!" she shouted. Behind her she could hear other villagers young and old laughing as they threw their own snowballs.

Rachael began to stalk Storm Dancer, several balls of snow cradled in her left arm. "Come out He-Who-Dances-In-The-Snowstorms," she coaxed in her sweetest voice. "Come out wherever you are!"

When he made no reply, she whipped around the corner of the wigwam, a snowball ready to fire clutched in her mittened hand. To her surprise, he wasn't there. She looked down at his footprints in the snow and smiled mischievously. In the snow, even an amateur like Rachael could track a man!

Chuckling to herself, she leaned over slightly, following his tracks. She walked around their wigwam, past another, then another, then under a tree. . . . Rachael stood upright suddenly, glancing behind her.

The tracks ended abruptly.

She looked around. There was no sign of him. He had disappeared! Only last night Storm Dancer had been telling her about a famous shaman who could make himself truly disappear in a puff of green smoke. Rachael had declared such a claim nonsense, but suddenly she wondered if it was true.

"Storm?" She bent to look behind the tree. He wasn't there. She glanced out into the center compound where one of the men was pulling his two children on a flat hide sled. She lowered her hand to her hip, still holding the snowballs. "Very funny, now where are you?" Rachael called.

She heard the slightest noise above her, but in the split second it took to look up, Storm Dancer flew out of the tree, knocking Rachael to the ground. She screamed with surprise as his body hit hers and they both fell headlong into the freezing snow.

"Storm!" She laughed as she struggled to lift her face from the snow. "It's cold! Let me up!"

He rolled onto his back, pulling her over him. He shook a bronze finger in her face. "You must be more cautious. Were I a mountain lion, fair Rachael, I would dine on you this evening."

She leaned over his chest, peering into his liquid black eyes. "Were you a mountain lion," she said saucily, "I wouldn't be chasing you with snowballs!"

He threw back his head, laughing as he lay back in the snow. Rachael stretched out over him, leaning to kiss his cold lips.

"I love you, Rachael of mine," he murmured, looking up at her.

"I love you, too," she answered, then looked away.

"I'm sorry that I've disappointed you by not becoming with child."

He sat up, the smile falling from his face. "You have not disappointed me." He grasped her arms, forcing her to look at him. "I told you, with or without children, I will love you and keep you as my wife, always." He brushed a bit of snow from her eyelashes. "Besides, it's only been a few moons. My grandmother explained to you that there are only certain days when a child can be made. You must learn to have more patience in this, Rachael."

She compressed her lips tightly, knowing he spoke the truth, but somehow not being comforted by his words. She wanted so desperately to carry his child. It was almost as if that event would seal the covenant of their marriage. If she became pregnant she knew she could never go back to Philadelphia. By having his child she would really become one of the Lenni Lenape.

Storm Dancer stood, and pulled her to her feet, brushing the snow off her soft rabbit coat. "Now kiss me, Wife, and let me go about my man's business. We are in need of fresh meat as are the others. I think it would be a good day for a hunt. Many of God's creatures will be out searching for food after such a heavy snowfall."

Rachael kissed him soundly as she patted the snow off his winter coat. "Go on with you then and bring back a buck. I've a taste for fresh venison."

"Rachael!" Dory called from the distance.

Rachael looked over Storm Dancer's shoulder and waved.

Dory came toward the couple, her cheeks rosy with cold, her breath frosty in the morning air. She was wearing an immense patchwork squirrel and rabbit coat with a soft white fox cap . . . a gift from one of her suitors.

"Good mornin' to you!" she exclaimed, patting both Storm Dancer and Rachael on the back. "Good to see you came out of that rabbit hole alive. With the snow blowin' the way it did for the last two days, I was afraid you two would wear each other into your graves pawin' all over each other!"

Rachael felt her cheeks grow warm, but she stuck out her tongue good-naturedly. It had taken her a while to accept how freely the Native Americans spoke of what she had always thought to be personal matters. She still had a difficult time discussing with others so candidly about making babies, but she was no longer offended by such talk. Every woman in the camp had a suggestion for fertility from a particular sexual position, to a kind of food she should be eating.

Storm kissed Rachael again and with a wave of his hand, left the women in search of a hunting partner or two.

For a moment Rachael and Dory stood side by side in silence watching the children and adults alike play in the snow. Yesterday's Thunder walked past them, murmuring a greeting and smiling at Dory as he made his way toward the gathering of men on the far side of the camp.

Rachael waited to speak until he had passed. "So which one's it going to be?" she asked in a teasing manner. "Yesterday's Thunder or Shadows Man?"

Dory rolled her green eyes heavenward. "Such a decision! I don't know. Shadows Man, he's my age. Had a wife that died and needs a mother for his two youngins. He's all loud and full of fun."

"He'd make a good husband for you, Dory," Rachael offered.

"Yea, he would, but then there's Yesterday's Thunder." She whistled between her teeth. "That man's got a hell of a young body on him and never had a woman. He's quiet and gentle. He says he don't care if I'm old and fat and used up from men. He don't care that I sold myself for a coin for supper when times was hard." She pulled off her white fur hat and ran a mitten through her orange-colored hair. "He says he likes me just the way I am. He says he wants to make babies with me."

"He's a good man," Rachael commented.

Dory sunk her elbow into her friend's side. "Already tried to have his way with me, that young buck did."

Rachael couldn't resist a chuckle. "I would imagine both could be rather persuasive. They keep bringing us gifts, hoping Storm Dancer or I will sway you one way or the other." She threw up her arms in exasperation. "I keep telling them they don't have to give me things, but they keep leaving them at the door to our wigwam.

Dory tucked her hat back on her head and crossed her arms over her chest. "Yea, it's gonna be a mighty hard decision to make."

"Well, take your time." Rachael looked directly into Dory's clear blue eyes. "Choose the man that will make you the happiest. After all you've been through, you deserve to be happy, Dory."

There was a moment of silence as Dory contemplated the decision she would soon have to make. Then she changed the subject. "Dove is going to tap some syrup. We thought we'd make the children some candy in the snow. Want to come?"

Rachael looked back at her wigwam. "I have those boots of Storm's to finish sewing up. I wanted to put that waterproof lining in that Starlight showed me how to make."

Dory grasped Rachael's mitten-covered hand and tugged. "Oh, come on with you. The first snowfall only comes oncest a year. Leave your sewing behind and come have some fun."

It took Rachael only a moment to decide. She turned toward Dory, her face bright with laughter as she waggled her finger. "All right, but if Storm's angry with me tonight because his feet get wet hunting, I want you to take up for me."

"I'll do better than that." Dory raised a chubby balled fist. "He gives you a hard time and I'll crack him."

The women's laughter mingled as arm in arm they hurried toward the other women headed on the syrup expedition.

A few evenings later a council meeting was called by Chief Starlight. She was very secretive with Rachael and Storm Dancer about why the meeting was necessary, but it was evident that Storm Dancer would play a vital role in the dialogue that was to take place. Because of the importance of the subject to be discussed, not only would all council members be expected to attend, but every able-bodied adult in the village.

There was a strange sense of excitement in the air as the villagers prepared for the eminent meeting.

Rachael was introduced to the sweat house where she sat naked in hot steamy air to the point where she grew so light-headed she thought she would faint, and then was instructed to run out and jump into the snow.

To Rachael's surprise, the shock of the cold snow on her overheated body was exhilarating. She truly did feel cleansed after the experience and not only in body, but in soul as well. She dressed carefully in the white buckskins Starlight had given her, and braided precious eagle pinfeathers, given to her by Storm Dancer, into her hair.

Storm Dancer, too, took great care in preparing himself for the council meeting. First he fasted through the day, spending his time in deep meditation. Then he had gone to the sweat house where he had drunk some strange concoction with other braves, a drink meant only for significant occasions.

When Storm Dancer returned to the wigwam, Rachael sensed his need for silence. Though she wanted to speak to him of her apprehension concerning the evening's agenda, she respected his wishes.

Storm Dancer took great care in choosing his attire this night. Seated near the firepit, Rachael watched in fascination as he dressed. After donning a loincloth, he slipped into the new leggings she had made for him, wearing the rabbit fur on the inside. Despite the winter season, he added a porcupine-quilled, sleeveless vest given to him by Tuuban as a welcoming gift. On each of his biceps Storm Dancer wore a copper band, the glimmer of the metal seeming to emphasize the hardened muscles they enclosed.

Using Rachael's porcupine brush, he brushed out his damp hair and attached a single eagle wing feather by a piece of leather so that it trailed down the back of his head. Using the hues from a small tin paintpot he carried in his medicine bag, he painted his face in burnt umber and sky blue. The lines, dots, and squiggles meant nothing to Rachael, but she could tell by the way he concentrated as he worked, that each mark symbolized something specific and that it was extremely important that he use the correct icons. He painted not only his face, but his arms and chest left bare by the open vest.

Then to Rachael's astonishment, he came to her with the paintpot held in his hand. "Stand, wife of the Dancer of Storms," he bid in a voice that sounded strangely detached.

Rachael raised up off the mat to stand before him.

"Wear these symbols," he said as he stroked her cheek with his index finger, "as a sign of your position and of the bravery you have demonstrated."

She stood perfectly still as he stroked her cheeks with his finger. The scent of the paint was pleasantly odd. It smelled musty and rich like ground peat and some unknown minerals. She felt slightly dizzy, but she wasn't certain if her light-headedness was from the odor of the paint or from her own nervous excitement.

Storm Dancer carefully closed up his paintpot and returned it to his medicine bag. Then he came back to her, his pitch eyes searching her face until he had her utmost attention. He traced her jawline with the tip of his index finger and Rachael smelled a whiff of the dark red paint that still smudged his hand.

"I do not know what is in store tonight. Both my grandfather and grandmother have been secretive. I believe the cloak of the village shaman will be passed on to me tonight, but there is something more brewing in the night air." He lowered his voice an octave as he reached for her hand and intertwined his fingers in hers. "Do you hear it? Listen beyond the pound of the drums."

They were silent for a moment.

"Do you smell it?" He tapped her temple. "Do you see it in your mind?"

Rachael concentrated. Yes, yes she could feel something different about the air tonight. She glanced up anxiously at him. "I'm certain that whatever the village has in mind, Storm, you will be worthy of the honor."

He released her hand and stepped back to strap his quilled belt around his waist. "I only hope that you are right, Wife." With his belt in place, he offered her his palm. "Come, the drums beat for us. We have been called."

Storm Dancer and Rachael entered the ceremonial longhouse in reverent silence. They were ushered through two lines of villagers all dressed in their ceremonial clothes, some painted, some unpainted. Men and women stood side by side with only the children and the feeble absent.

Rachael's hand trembled in Storm's as they made their way through the people she now claimed as friends into the longhouse and across the great room until they stopped and paid homage to Shaakhan the great medicine man and his wife and chief of the village, Hongiss Opaang, Starlight of the Lenni Lenape.

Storm Dancer went down on one knee in honor of his grandmother's position; Rachael followed only a beat of the drum behind him. Starlight signaled with a wave of her long-stemmed pipe for them to be seated on the mats laid out between her and Shaakhan and they obeyed.

With the guests of honor inside, the villagers entered the longhouse in silence. One by one they filed inside and took their appropriate seats. Not a sound could be heard as they walked, but the spit and crackle of the fire and the steady rhythm of the drumbeat.

When everyone was seated, the flap of the door was closed and laced from the inside. A log was added to the center firepit and a blaze shot up, filling the entire room with golden light.

Starlight gave another wave of her hand and the drums ceased. She took her time in speaking, her gaze moving from one villager to the next. When she finally spoke it was in the clear, strong voice of a leader, not of an old, frail woman.

"Greetings to you, brothers and sisters of the People." She spoke the Lenni Lenape native tongue, but slowly, so that Rachael could follow the conversation. "I thank you all for attending this high council meeting and I ask that you send your prayers heavenward in request that the God almighty, Wishemoto, will watch over us this night and guide us in the decisions which must be made."

Starlight set her pipe aside. "As you know, our shaman, the great Shaakhan of the Turtle Clan, has asked that he be permitted to step down from his position. After more than sixty summers of devotion to his people, he believes it is time for a younger man to take his place."

She indicated with a nod, Storm Dancer who sat

between Rachael and Shaakhan. "You also know that my long lost grandson was returned to us only a few months ago, fulfilling the prophecy that a storm would dance out of the north to bring us salvation." She took a deep breath. "Because Storm Dancer was born into the birthright of the shaman, through his mother our daughter, Shaakhan took it upon himself to begin teaching his grandson the ways of the medicine man. With the knowledge Storm Dancer was born with and the help of his grandfather, it is my belief and the belief of Shaakhan that this man is ready to stand before you as shaman."

Starlight raised her hand, telling Storm Dancer to rise. "I ask now that you speak to me of this man. Tell what is good in his heart, what is bad. Tell me why he should be shaman of our village and why he should not. This is the time to speak because once the decision is made, once you accept this man who lived among our enemies, he will be one of you forever. His sins will become ours, and he will be your shaman as long as he lives."

Rachael watched and listened in fascination as Starlight called on one villager after another. Though her Algonquian was still weak, she understood much of what was said. Most villagers spoke only good of Storm Dancer and those who had an objection, were worried only by the fact that he had once been a Mohawk.

More than an hour lapsed while Storm Dancer stood and the villagers spoke before Starlight raised both palms and a hush settled in the warm ceremonial house.

"If that is all there is to say, then it is time we vote,

brothers and sisters." She picked up a basket and a bundle of pine needles and handed them to a young boy who served as runner. "Because of the importance of this decision, I ask that you choose a needle and place it in the pot. Whole if Storm Dancer is your choice of Shaman, half a straw if he is not." She waved the boy on, and he began to make his way around the great circle of villagers.

When the entire village had cast their vote, the boy returned the woven container to Starlight.

The old woman startled Rachael by handing the basket to her. "We ask Rachael, wife of Storm Dancer, to do the honor of the count," Starlight said.

Rachael peered into the basket and scooped out the brittle needles. *Long, long, long* . . . After a moment she glanced up at Starlight. "Not a short needle in the basket," she murmured.

Starlight gave a sweep of her hand. "Then tell my people of their decision."

Rachael took a deep breath and spoke slowly in Algonquian. A murmur rose among the villagers.

Shaakhan rose from his mat, clasping his hands in obvious pleasure. One by one the others stood, including Rachael, until only Starlight remained seated.

"You may do the honor of passing the cloak," Starlight told Shaakhan, her voice filled with emotion. It was obvious she was proud not only of Storm Dancer, but of Shaakhan, her husband of over fifty years, as well.

With a great deal of ceremony, Shaakhan removed the cloak of the shaman he wore and rested it on Storm

Dancer's shoulders. He chanted huskily as he turned Storm Dancer around three times and then faced him toward the villagers. Tears glimmered in Rachael's eyes as she watched Storm Dancer present himself to his friends and relatives.

The cloak was the most exotic, beautiful garment she'd ever seen in her life. Floor-length, the entire cloak was sewn of a single woolly hide from an animal unbeknownst to her and not native to the area. The color and texture of the fur could only have come from some arctic region and Rachael was fascinated with the wonderment of how the Lenni Lenape came to possess the rare garment.

The villagers clapped and stomped and whistled their praise and when the room was silent again, Starlight rose with the aid of her grandson's hand. She kissed him on both cheeks, then on the mouth.

"I wish the wind always upon your back and the sun forever shining on your face, Storm Dancer, grandson of mine and shaman of my village."

Storm Dancer thanked her quietly, and then thanked his friends and relatives who all supported him. Lastly, he clasped his grandfather's wrinkled hand and pressed a kiss to it.

Starlight took Rachael's hand and laid it in Storm Dancer's, then turned back toward the villagers who still stood. "Now that the Dancer of Storms is our shaman, he can be set to the task of leading his people out of the clutches of the white men, west where we will find safety and contentment once more."

Storm turned in shock to face his grandmother. His bronze face was ashen. "You mean to leave this place where your grandmother's grandmother walked?"

"I mean to save my people from firing guns and measle sickness before it is too late," she said firmly. "I am too old, but you, my grandson, have both the years and the strength to do what an old man and an old woman cannot."

Rachael could tell by the look on Storm Dancer's face that never in his wildest imagination had he speculated that this was what Starlight and Shaakhan had in store for him. As startled by the thought of moving as he was, he was even more startled by the fact that they had chosen him to lead the people.

Storm Dancer looked from his grandmother to his grandfather and then back at his grandmother again. "Surely there is someone else . . ."

She smiled, resting her hand on her grandson's strong shoulder. "We appreciate your modesty, Grandson, but no there is no one else. A task as crucial as this must come through bloodlines. Tuuban is the only other man or woman of direct descendence who lives, and he has not had the calling. You remember, it was long ago that your grandfather saw his vision. This is not up to you, or even to me. It is in the stars. We can only be thankful that we have been blessed with the ability to read them."

With the matter seemingly settled, Starlight gave a few words of closing. Shaakhan sprinkled some soft magical dust over Storm Dancer and the meeting was adjourned.

Outside in the cold night air, Storm Dancer and Rachael were approached by many well-wishers. There was laughter and a hot apple and spice cider to share.

Several campfires were built to chase away the darkness and the cold.

Someone began to beat a drum while another shook a gourd rattle. Several men and women began to sing as food was brought out to serve the entire village.

Rachael stood by Storm Dancer's side, trying to take in all that was said. Her mind was a flurry of confusion as they were ushered to the seats of honor and stuffed with slices of wild turkey and corn bread stuffing.

After they had eaten, Storm Dancer offered his arm to Rachael, bringing her close to him beneath the magical shaman's cloak. He kissed her forehead and she touched his cheek, speaking to him the first personal words all day.

"You had no idea the village wanted to go west?"

He shook his head as he sipped from a pewter cup. "None. It's a daring attempt." He lifted a finger. "But perceptive. My grandparents are right in saying we must flee if we are to save our world as we know it."

"Then you'll do it?"

He gazed into the bright firelight that illuminated the dancers. "I am frightened by the thought," he looked back at her, "and yet at the same moment I am exhilarated." He took her hand and slipped it beneath his vest so that she could feel his rapid heartbeat. "Do you feel the excitement?"

"I feel it."

"Will you help me, Rachael? This is too big a task for one shaman. I will need your help." He swept his arm indicating the villagers. "I will need everyone's help."

She kept her hand beneath his vest, enjoying the feel of his warm skin on this cold night. "Where do you mean to go?"

"West, to Ohio country I would think. That is where our Shawnee cousins have fled. Where other Lenni Lenape villages have gone."

Rachael gazed into the firelight, lost in thought. "If we go, we will never come back, will we?"

His voice was soft. "No, wife of mine. We will never come back." He paused as he took her hand in his. "Will you go with me? Will you turn your back on all you once were and give yourself to me? Will you walk into the sunset at my side?"

Rachael needed no time to think. The sounds formed on her lips before she knew it. "Yes," she whispered. "I'll go with you, Husband. Wither thou goest, I will go; and where thou lodgest, I will lodge; thy people shall be my people . . ."

Storm Dancer brought his mouth to hers and kissed her as she never remembered being kissed before.

The sound of barking dogs and a ripple of commotion among those around them broke the moment.

"What is it?" Storm asked.

"Someone approaches," Kilheek offered. "The sentry has sent her on."

"This is a strange time for a visitor, a winter night," Storm Dancer mused as he rose.

Rachael stood with him, their hands still clasped. "Who could it be?"

The crowd around the fire parted to allow the strangers to approach. When Rachael spotted the Indian woman beside him carrying a baby on her back, she glanced at Storm Dancer. The look on his face made her blood run icy, her stomach sick.

"Wh . . . Who is it?" she beseeched.

A strange silence settled over the camp as the villagers observed Storm Dancer's reaction to the man and woman. For a long moment he said nothing, then slowly he turned toward Rachael and spoke, his voice audible only to her. "It is my wife, Ta-wa-ne."

Chapter Twenty

His wife. Rachael felt strangely numb. There was a buzzing in her ears. The sound of the villagers' hushed talk faded into the background. The cold of the winter air, the heat of the campfire, and the rich smell of roasting venison and burning pine was gone. She could still feel Storm's hand in hers, but there was none of the intimate warmth she had felt only seconds ago. He was watching her, but his handsome bronze face was a blur in her vision. All she could see was *her*. The Indian woman was splendidly beautiful despite the obvious hardships she'd encountered traveling in midwinter. And she was young . . . younger than Rachael.

"Rachael . . ." Storm's voice barely penetrated her thoughts. "Rachael," he repeated firmly, squeezing her hand.

She was aware of the villagers all watching them. She would not dishonor herself by making a scene. It was not the Lenni Lenape way. She would not shame Starlight and Shaakhan; they had been too good to her.

Slowly Rachael lifted her chin, her gaze riveting to Storm Dancer's face. "It cannot be. She's dead."

"She is not."

"You *said* she was dead." There was a desperation in her voice that bordered on hysteria. Rachael's life was crumbling in her palm and she had no recourse, no ground to stand on.

"I said she was gone," he answered decisively. "She left me almost two years ago with a red-bearded trapper who called himself Malvin."

Rachael felt as if all time had slowed to a crawl. She looked up at the Indian woman. Tuuban was speaking to her in Algonquian but supplementing his words with basic hand signals.

The *wife* stood beside Tuuban, speaking with him, but she was staring at Storm Dancer as if she were seeing a ghost. Rachael watched as the stricken look of surprise on her face softened into a delicate smile.

Rachael looked back at Storm, trying to control the tremble in her voice. "She can't be your wife. *I* am your wife."

"You are. Ta-wa-ne was my first wife, but she is no longer."

"What do you mean she is no longer!" Rachael flared. "There she stands!"

"Among my people—"

"I don't want to hear it!" Rachael's eyes narrowed as she jerked her hand from his grasp. She wouldn't let this man destroy her. Once she might have, but not now. She'd learned too much these last months to be defeated by such treachery. She didn't need a man to live. All she needed was herself and that she would always have; she knew that now. "I don't want your sweet words and logical explanations!" she spit venomously. "You married me knowing your wife still lived. You have made me an adulterer! You betrayed me! You betrayed my love for you by not telling me all these months—by making me think I was your wife!"

Rachael attempted to speak quietly, to keep their conversation private, but already she could see the villagers craning their necks with interest. They were all talking at once. All anxious to know who this Iroquois woman was and who she was in relation to their shaman and his wife.

"Rachael! You must listen to me!" Storm Dancer raised his voice in mounting anger, the corded muscles in his neck bunching as he spoke.

"Listen to you—" She cut her words short upon the sudden realization that the wife was standing right there in front of them. Despite her gaunt cheeks, she was even more beautiful up close. She had almond-shaped eyes and coal black hair that fell from her fur-trimmed hood. Rachael glared at the man she had thought to be her husband until only a moment ago. "Aren't you going to introduce me?"

Storm Dancer's attention turned to the woman he had once been in love with but had never loved the way he loved Rachael. Rachael was his heart of hearts. Ta-wa-ne had never been more than an infatuation. He knew that now as he stared at her lovely face, feeling very little of the furied resentment, and bitter pain he had felt for so long after she had gone. Ta-wa-ne had left him for the trapper. "This . . . this is Ta-wa-ne of the Wolf Clan."

Ta-wa-ne smiled sweetly. "Greetings, Storm Dancer," she said in a velvety voice, speaking English quite well. Her gaze never strayed from his face. It was as if Rachael were not standing there. "For a moment I thought you to be a ghost."

"It is good to know you still breathe," Storm Dancer observed quietly. "I did not think to ever see you again. You vowed never to set foot in my shadow again when last we spoke."

"I was a fool." She brushed his shaman's cloak with her mitten. "But I truly did not think to see you again but in death. I passed through your brother's village moons ago. He said you had died a dishonorable death. I don't know why I believed his words. He always spoke a lie as easily as the truth."

"In his eyes I am dead. I was sentenced to the walking death for alleged crimes against him and our village."

Her laughter echoed in the cold night air. "I no longer believe in such nonsense of superstitions. A man cannot be dead when his heart still beats. You cannot kill a man with a puff of smoke and a turn of the back." She looked down for a moment, her dark lashes cloaking her eyes, then looked up at him again. "As for crimes, I know you could be guilty of nothing."

Storm Dancer crossed his arm over his chest uncomfortably. "What bring you so far south into Lenni Lenape territory? How did you get here? How did you find us?"

She looked away. When she spoke again, the clear confidence was gone from her voice. "Malvin travels far to trade. There is much coin to be made. The trapping has been good here along the Chesapeake."

"So where is the redbeard?" Storm Dancer glanced over her shoulder mockingly. "You entered this village alone but for the child."

"He . . . he left me on the water's edge. The boy was cumbersome. He will check his trap lines along the river and then he will be back. A day or two, no more." By the sound of her voice, the wife did not sound certain to Rachael.

There was then an awkward silence that gave Rachael a moment to look at the two of them. Ta-wa-ne watched Storm Dancer with steady black button eyes. He looked away, not daring to look either wife in the face.

Storm Dancer nodded, indicating the sleeping child strapped to her back. "I see you and the trapper have a son."

She paused for one blink of an eye, then smiled, reaching to touch Storm Dancer's forearm. "It is true I have a son, but the boy's father is you, great Dancer of the Storms . . ." She took careful note of his ceremonial cloak. "Yes, his father is you, a great man who is now shaman to the Delaware."

A slap in her face could not have startled Rachael more. She opened her mouth to speak, but not a sound escaped her lips. She struggled to take a breath, tears welling in her eyes. Turning on her heels, Rachael ran toward the safety of her wigwam.

She refused to let Storm Dancer see how much his dishonesty had hurt her. She refused to let him see what a fool she had been to believe his lies . . . his promises of love and devotion forever. Rachael knew that the Indians practiced polygamy. Storm Dancer had explained that in lean years it was a matter of survival, but he also knew how she felt about marriage. Because of her religious beliefs she could never condone polygamy. He knew she would never have agreed to marry him knowing he had another wife, so he had simply not told her.

The snow crunched beneath Rachael's moccasins as she raced for the wigwam, fearful she would collapse before she reached it.

"Rachael-honey?" Dory called after her, following in her footsteps.

By the time Rachael ducked in the wigwam, she was blinded by her tears. Great sobs wracked her body as she fell on her knees, throwing aside her wet mittens and covering her face with her palms.

"Great God a'mighty! What ails you?" Dory demanded, huffing to catch her breath as she came inside. "Who's that trapper and the Injun woman?"

"His wife!" Rachael wept.

"What?" Dory knelt beside Rachael, pulling her hands away so that she could see her face and understand her words. "What are you saying? I can't understand what you're saying, Rachael-love."

"His wife!" she repeated, another wave of tears overtaking her. "That . . . that woman is his wife!"

"Whose?" Dory asked, utterly confused.

"S . . . Storm's. That woman is Storm's wife."

"Oh." Dory sat back on her heels, in utter shock. "You're certain?"

"He said so himself." Rachael fought for control over her emotions. She wouldn't let this devastate her. And . . . and the b . . . baby . . . the b . . . baby is his."

"Son of a rot-guttin' bitch!" Dory exclaimed, looking away.

Rachael glanced up through tear-reddened eyes. "He made me love him, Dory. He made me trust him. All these months I lived in sin thinking he was my husband.

I felt I owed him for he what he did for me, but I didn't owe him. I didn't owe him a bloody thing."

"There, there." Dory reached out and pulled Rachael to her bosom. "Don't cry, Rachael-love. We'll get to the bottom of this pickling barrel, I swear to Christ we will."

She shook her head wildly. "I don't want to talk to him. I don't want to hear his explanations. He took advantage of me, damn him." Her gaze met Dory's, her voice bitter. "And I hate him for it."

Just then the deerhide flap of the door moved and Storm Dancer stepped inside. "Rachael—"

"Get out!" she shouted stumbling to her feet to point at the door. "Get out of here!"

"You must let me explain to you—"

"I don't want your explanations! I don't want your lies, mighty shaman! Why don't you go tend to your wife and child? You never told me *she* had given you a babe!"

Storm Dancer turned to Dory. His shoulders were thrown back, seemingly even wider beneath the ceremonial shaman's cloak. His face was stony with anger. "Leave us."

Rachael grasped Dory's arm before she could move toward the doorway. "She stays!"

"I wish to speak in private, Wife."

His endearment sent off a streak of rage in Rachael that she had never known she possessed. She whipped around, looking for a weapon, anything to silence him. The closest thing was the firepit that glowed red with hot coals. With a scream of fury, she grabbed a half-burned stick as big around as her wrist and two feet long and she brandished it. The red embers of the tips glowed brighter and smoke curled from the stock. "Get out!" she shrieked, taking a step in his direction. "Get out before I set your hair on bloody fire!"

Instinctively, Storm Dancer took a step back. It was obvious there was no reasoning with Rachael at this moment. He understood her pain. He knew he should have explained to her about Ta-wa-ne, but he had just never found the right moment. He didn't now how to make her understand. The ways of his people were different from hers and sometimes that gap of understanding was difficult to bridge.

"Dory, I wish to speak with you outside."

Rachael glowered, still holding the burning stick.

Dory glanced from Storm Dancer to Rachael. "You stay put," she told Rachael. "I'll be right back."

"You don't have to go," Rachael insisted as she went on faster than before. "You don't have to do it if you don't want to, Dory. You're a free woman. He doesn't own you. No one can ever own you again."

Dory walked around Rachael, cautiously, not certain just what Rachael might do in her state. Reaching the doorway Storm Dancer had just exited, Dory put up her hands. "All right now, missy. He's gone. Now you throw that firewood back in the pit and get ahold of yourself afore someone gets hurt. I'll be back in just a bit."

Dory watched Rachael reluctantly toss the firewood back into the firepit, and then Dory stepped out into the night air.

Storm Dancer stood in the shadows of the wigwam, his broad shoulders hunched over, his hand resting beneath his chin in thought. When he saw Dory he looked up. "She will not give me the chance to explain.

She wished to have the right to speak but does not give me the same right."

"Phew-ee! I never seen Rachael hot like that afore, I'll tell you that." Dory looked up at Storm Dancer. "But I ain't saying' she ain't got reason. Why didn't you tell her your first wife was still livin'?"

He looked down at the snowy ground. The camp had grown still, the celebration cut short by the arrival of the Iroquois woman. Everyone was gathering up the food from the feast to store and settling into their wigwams for the night. "I saw no reason."

Dory dropped a hand to her ample hip. "You saw no reason to tell her she was wife number two, 'stead of the one and only wife?"

"Rachael is my only wife."

"But I thought you must said that sweet little she-bitch Ta-wa-ne was your wife?"

"She was. But we are divorced. She ran away with the trapper, Malvin, two winters ago. She never came back. I divorced her so that I would no longer be responsible for her."

Dory exhaled slowly. She understood that the Indians accepted divorce as a natural part of life. Here among the Lenni Lenape a woman could divorce her husband by simply leaving his moccasins and weapons outside the wigwam door. But Dory also knew that Rachael did not recognize divorce. A marriage was a marriage for life. To her, she and Storm Dancer had never been married at all. At the very least, she was his second and therefore lesser wife. Dory chewed her thoughts carefully before she spoke to Storm Dancer. She truly felt for him, but Rachael was who she had to remain loyal to if sides had to be chosen. "Fine kettle a fish you got here, I'd say."

"I never thought to see Ta-wa-ne again," Storm Dancer replied honestly. "I thought her either dead or sold when the trapper had tired of her. The redbeard Malvin was a hard man; dishonest, cruel. He would sell his own soul for a gold coin and a bottle of whiskey."

"So now he's returned her to you?"

"They could not have possibly known I was here. He simply left her at a camp knowing someone would not let her and the child starve."

Dory watched his face carefully as she asked her next question. "And what of the little one? He yours?"

"I did not know Ta-wa-ne was with child when she left me."

"But the little'n could be yours?"

He lifted his head slowly until his dark-eyed gaze met hers. He could not lie. He had to accept, no matter how much he wished not to, the truth of the matter. "From his age, he could be."

Dory looked heavenward. The stars were brilliant tonight. The sky was a dark canopy that stretched into eternity covered with pinpricks of white light. "That kinda tangles the web, then don't it?" She twisted her lips thoughtfully. "What do you intend to do?"

"Ta-wa-ne has asked nothing of me." He sounded hopeful.

"But her man's left her. She's got no place to live, no man to hunt for her, and she says the boy is yours. You got a responsibility, don't you?"

"I do not know." He clenched his fist. "But what I do know is that I will not lose Rachael. I need her. If we are to make the trek west, she must be at my side."

"She thinks you betrayed her. I can tell you right

now she ain't gonna be too willin' to listen to you."

He touched his chest beneath his cloak taking the defense. "If she loves me as she says she does, that love cannot be altered. Ta-wa-ne should be insignificant."

Dory frowned. "Should be, hell. What should ain't got a lick to do with the matter. I'm afraid you got a lot to learn about women."

"I will just go into my wigwam and explain to Rachael that I no longer consider Ta-wa-ne as my wife. As for the child—had my wife died, she would have not resented a child by that previous union."

"It ain't gonna be that easy. I can tell you that right now. You ain't dealin' with no ordinary woman. See if it was me, what would I care? A poor slattern like myself counts herself lucky to have anyone, but Rachael—" she shook a finger in the direction of the wigwam—"that woman's sewn of a different cloth than most of us."

"I will make her understand."

"I got the feelin' you ain't gonna *make* Miss Rachael do anything. She's come too far these months—with your help, granted. She ain't gonna let no man push her around. Not even you."

He rubbed his temples, suddenly tired beyond reason. "Why is it that the sky falls when you least expect it?" he inquired softly as much to himself as to Dory. "She was so happy only a few moments ago. She had agreed that we had to take our people and go west. She had agreed that we would go together." He thought for a moment and then spoke again. "You are a woman. Tell me what it is she wants me to do now. How can I make what has turned so wrong right again?"

Dory rubbed her hands together, the cold seeping through her thick cloak making her shiver. "I can't tell you what to do except to get that Ta-wa-ne slut out of this camp as fast as you can. Marry 'er off, feed 'er to a wolf, somethin'. And if you ask me, I'd say you'd best let Rachael simmer overnight before you try to talk to her again. You go in there now and she's liable to turn that fancy animal coat of yours to cinders."

"That is my home." He pointed toward the wigwam. "I have a right to sleep on my own mat."

Dory shrugged. "Do as you please, but I'm tellin' you, was it me she was mad at, I'd let her cool down first. She's hurtin' inside and when you hurt you don't always think right."

He pulled his cloak closer. The temperature was dropping quickly. A light snow had begun to fall. "I will do as you say and wait until the dawn to speak with my wife." He glanced toward his wigwam. "But I will give her tonight and only tonight. I will not have this unrest. There are too many important problems to be dealt with in this village."

Dory watched him stalk off toward Tuuban's wigwam where she assumed he would spend the night with the bachelor. With a long sigh, she turned and headed toward Rachael's wigwam wondering how she could possibly comfort her friend.

Chapter Twenty-One

Rachael sat cross-legged in front of her wigwam firepit huddled under a doeskin robe. It was nearly dawn. Dory still slept on the far side of the firepit, gently snoring.

Rachael had found little rest all night and what scant hours of sleep she did get, were fitful and filled with dark, angry nightmares. She shivered and tossed a small log onto the glowing coals at her feet. The fire crackled and spit, flames leaping up to lick the dry wood.

Her gaze strayed to the deerhide door covering. She knew Storm would come. She was only astonished that he had not yet been here.

Rachael didn't think she had ever felt so bitter, so angry and so hurt in the same breath. Storm Dancer had betrayed her and her love for him by not telling her that his wife still lived. Her marriage to Storm had been a lie. He couldn't marry her when he was still married to Ta-wa-ne!

The worst thing was that Rachael felt stupid. She

should have known better than to have trusted Storm with her love. He was a man wasn't he? It didn't matter if their skin was red, white, or green, a man was basically an untrustworthy soul and she knew that. Hadn't she learned that from Gifford?

Certainly Storm Dancer had appeared to be different. Look how many months he had fooled her! All this time she had thought he really loved her. They had been so happy. But he didn't love her; he couldn't. No one would do this to a person they loved. . . .

Rachael heard the sound of snow crunching outside her wigwam and instinctively she drew her robe closer. The door flap moved and Storm Dancer stepped inside.

At the same moment, Dory stirred and looked up from her mat, rubbing the sleep from her eyes. Spotting Storm Dancer standing just inside the wigwam, she bolted up, taking her sleeping robe with her.

"You don't have to go," Rachael said, ignoring Storm Dancer.

"'Course I got to go. Got to every morning," Dory answered, circumnavigating the firepit. "You two go on and talk and I'll be back to check on you later, Rachael-honey."

Rachael felt a certain sense of abandonment as she heard Dory slip out the door and then her footsteps dispel in the dry snow.

Even after Dory was gone, Storm Dancer stood near the doorway, having yet to speak a word.

Rachael took her time in looking up at him. She could feel his black eyes boring into her and she took a deep breath. She wanted to be certain she had control of her emotions before she spoke. She didn't want to cry and she didn't want to shame herself. If there was one thing she had learned in her months among the Indians, it was a sense of self-pride and honor. She wished Dory had stayed; having her friend nearby gave her a sense of strength.

Storm Dancer was the first to break the brittle silence. He came forward and squatted beside her, staring into the building fire. "These arms missed holding you last night," he said so softly that Rachael wasn't certain he had spoken at all. He looked at her and she was drawn to turn her face so that she could see his. "I would that I could change what has happened." He paused. "I did not know this would hurt you so greatly, 'else I would have told you."

Rachael curled her upper lip in an incredulous chuckle. "You thought I wouldn't be hurt by the fact that you have *another wife?*"

"I told you, but you do not listen to my words." He tapped his ear. "She was *once* my wife. She is no longer."

"So you say." She looked back at the fire. Even now when her heart ached so badly that her chest hurt, she still felt a stirring for him. He was so damned handsome. She was ashamed to admit that she wanted him, even now. Even after what he had done to her. "Of course, you said she was dead."

He lifted a bronze finger. "I never said she was dead. I said she was gone."

Rachael turned to him in fury, smacking aside his accusing finger. "You let me believe she was dead, knowing she lived!"

He crossed his arms over his chest, giving a nod of agreement. "I did and for that I have regret. I should have told you Ta-wa-ne still lived."

"Why didn't you?"

A moment of silence hung in the air as he thought about his reply. "Because you would not have married me, or perhaps not made your vow in truth." A black sheet of hair fell off his shoulder and brushed his cheek. "Had I told you of my first wife you might never have loved me."

The sound of his soft, regretful voice was difficult for Rachael to deal with. She wanted him to shout at her, hit her even. That she could deal with. But the tone of his voice made a part of her want to reach out and touch his calloused bronze hand. A part of her wanted to kiss away the etched lines of hurt on his face and tell him she still loved him.

Of course she knew she did still love him, no matter how much she didn't want to love him. But that didn't change anything. She'd not be a second wife.

Feeling warmer, Rachael loosened her robe. "Come spring someone will take me as far as Annapolis. From there I'll find a way to Philadelphia on my own. You can have your wife and your child. I'll not get in the middle of it."

Storm stood abruptly. "You are my wife. You'll go nowhere!"

She threw her heavy robe off her shoulders and jumped up, her hands dropping to her hips. "She says she's your wife. You say she's your wife."

"I said she *was* my wife. We are divorced. I told you once long ago that my people divorce. I know it is not common among our people, but it is done. Why is it that you cannot accept a mistake righted?"

"Once you're married, you're married for life. She's

your true wife."

"Why should a man be punished the rest of his days for an error in judging another? Why should a woman be forced to marry a man she says is cruel to her."

"You were cruel to her? You hurt her?"

"I did not want her sleeping with my brother, with my friends, with every trapper and soldier that passed through our camp and offered her a bauble for her flesh." His dark eyes watched her closely. "Had you married Gifford coward and he had beaten you, don't you believe you should have had the right to no longer be his wife?"

How many women had Rachael known in England who had poor marriages? Too many to count. Some wives were beaten, locked up in abandoned country estates, or verbally abused, but most were simply ignored, which almost seemed worse. What if she had married Gifford? What if he had beaten her? Wouldn't she have wanted the right to divorce him. She might have wanted it, but it would not have been a option in Philadelphia.

"Why do you not answer me?" Storm challenged.

Rachael's lower lip quivered. The Indian reasoning sounded logical. Storm made sense. But he was good at that . . . making her see his way. She felt tears well in her eyes and she looked away. "That little boy is yours. You should be with him. You should make amends with your wife and be a father to your son."

"I do not know that he is truly mine. Ta-wa-ne has not asked anything of me. Her man abandoned her. I am certain she wants only a roof over her child and food to feed him."

She looked back at him, scrutinizing him. "So she's

joined the village. You're going to have to take care of her. She has no other protector."

"I will marry her off to a man from another village."

"And what of your son?" Rachael asked. "You are willing to give him to another man to raise when I have been unable to give you a child?"

"A child belongs to his mother among the Lenni Lenape. I have no right to the boy even if he is mine, unless his mother offers that right."

She wiped a tear that threatened to slip down her cheek. When she spoke her voice was strained with emotion. "I feel so betrayed, Storm. You've been dishonest with me. I can't help wondering what other half-truths I've been gullible enough to believe."

He took her hand and pressed a kiss to her palm. "There is nothing, I swear it upon this land."

His warm lips felt so good against her hand . . . She pulled away. "I can't think." She touched her temples. "I'm so tired I can't think. I knew you had once been married, but that was different. She was dead then."

She looked up at him, her hands falling lamely at her sides. "But how can I compete with that? Even if I can accept this married-but-now-divorced nonsense that's so foreign to me, how can I compete with her? She's so beautiful. She gave you a son, something I seem unable to do."

"I love you," he said simply. "I do not love Ta-wa-ne. I have never loved her. As for our child, I have told you before, I see him in our future. And even if there was no babe, I would love you no less, I would want you no less."

"I don't want to talk about this anymore right now." She shook her head. Her mind was reeling. She was so confused by all she felt and thought. "I want you to go," she whispered. "Now."

"This is my home." He suddenly became irritated. "I gave you the night to think, Wife, but it is time to settle this matter and go on with our plans. You and I have much planning to do if we are to move our people when the spring showers come."

"Oh, no." She waved her hands. "It's not going to be this simple. You're not just going to say I'm sorry and have it done with. You lied to me, Storm! You betrayed my trust in you and in your love for me." She reached for her doeskin robe. "I don't know that I can be your wife knowing that."

"You are being hardheaded, Rachael. You can have anger for me. You can burn my venison, you can turn me away at your sleeping mat, but you cannot destroy all we have had these months over Ta-wa-ne."

"I can't?" She threw her robe over her shoulders. *"I* can't throw it all away? You think this is *my* fault?" She grabbed her basket of sewing things from near the door. "Just like a man, isn't it? You futter things up and then act as if it's all my fault!"

"Rachael-wife, that is not what I—"

"If you won't get out, then I will. It's my right isn't it? If I really am your wife and not your captive then I have the right to leave you?"

Rachael saw him clench his hands into fists. He was getting angrier by the moment, but she didn't care. As mad as he could possibly be, she was madder!

"Among the Lenni Lenape you have that right as the wife of this man."

She jerked up the hide flap that covered the door. "Then I'm exercising that right, *Husband!* You can go to hell!" Rachael ducked through the door, her sewing basket clenched in her hand and stomped across the camp. Other villagers were beginning to rise. Several people looked up to see where the domestic commotion came from and then discreetly turned away.

Rachael marched through the center of the camp to Starlight and Shaakhan's wigwam. It was the first place she thought to go . . . the first place she thought she would find comfort. Calling to Starlight, she waited for a reply, then entered the older couple's home, but not before she spotted Ta-wa-ne headed straight for Storm Dancer's wigwam with her bundle of clothes and her baby on her back.

Storm Dancer spun around in utter surprise that Rachael would return so quickly. Though he was not accustomed to the English-*manake* habit of cursing, a foul word escaped his lips at the sight of Ta-wa-ne.

Storm Dancer watched her as she lowered her bundle to the floor and swung her baby down off her back. She released him from his pack and set him on the floor. Then, shrugging off her cloak and hanging it by the doorway, she dug into her pack and pulled out a tiny packet of cornmeal. She kept her eyes averted as she hurried toward the firepit, her head lowered in a submissive pose. When she spoke it was in the Iroquois tongue. "It is morning and you have had no food in your stomach, Husband. Let this ugly woman feed you."

Now that he was accustomed to the Algonquian language, the word of the Seven Nations rung oddly in his ears. "I have no hunger. Tell me why you are here, Ta-wa-ne. Why do you no longer cook for the redbeard, the man you left me for?"

She turned up her small nose. "He was a bad man. He was not this woman's husband. He said he would marry this woman but he did not. You are Ta-wa-ne's husband. This woman had been an ill-behaved wife but she has returned to make all well. She will be a good wife to you. Her lesson has come hard but it is a lesson well learned."

"I divorced you when you left with the trapper." He watched in disbelief a she went on mixing the cornmeal and a little water in a stone bowl she found near the firepit. It was Rachael's favorite bowl with the seagulls painted on it. "You said you wanted a divorce. You said it would be too soon if you saw my face in the afterlife."

She shrugged her delicate shoulders. "I am a stupid woman who has harmed my husband greatly. I will make it up to him." She patted out a corncake and laid it on the cooking rock that had grown hot by the fire. "I will bake his corn bread, I will clean his game." She looked up through the fringe of her lashes. "I will give him pleasure on the sleeping mat. I will give him payment twofold for the manner I have wronged him."

"I have another wife."

"The white whore?"

Storm Dancer's palm itched to cuff Ta-wa-ne. He had once thought she was the most beautiful woman he had ever set eyes upon, but now the evil in her heart shadowed any beauty he had once seen. He saw her only as the conniving woman that she was.

"Do not speak of Rachael in that manner again 'else I will be forced to strike you!" he said through clenched teeth. "She is now my wife. That honor you gave up the day you left with the redbeard."

Ta-wa-ne lowered her lashes, taking another tact. "If there is nothing to be done with the white woman, I would not argue your need for a second wife. I could use her help with the cooking and the child."

For the first time Storm Dancer allowed his thoughts to stray to the little boy who sat quietly by the door in the exact same place his mother had left him. The two-year-old played with the thong of his moccasin. Storm Dancer searched for some indication that he belonged to him, but could see no resemblance. He looked like a masculine version of Ta-wa-ne, giving no clue as to his sire.

"You are no longer my wife, Ta-wa-ne. You betrayed our vows and I released you as wife. You must leave this village. I will give you food and an escort. You are not welcome here."

"You would have this woman leave and take your son?"

"I don't know that he is mine. He could be anyone's. You were quite free with what should have been mine."

"He is yours." She turned the corncakes which were browning nicely. The wigwam smelled faintly of baking corn bread. "I have nowhere to go. The trapper has left me behind."

"You cannot stay here, Ta-wa-ne! You have brought my life to near ruin once. You will not do so again!" He shouted in Iroquois, the words tasting foul on his breath.

She stood. "And what of your son? You want to see him die of starvation in the forest? You want him to die of the cold or be eaten by wolves?"

The little boy looked up at Storm Dancer at that moment and clapped his chubby hands, his lips turning up into a smile and dimpling his round cheeks.

He was a beautiful child. Storm thought of the baby he and Rachael yearned for. "What is his name?" He had not meant to ask Ta-wa-ne about the child. He had not meant to allow himself the opportunity to form any attachment. Ta-wa-ne was a liar. The child was probably not his.

"I call him Ka-we-ras, the great thunder of his father's storm."

"He is a well-mannered boy."

"He is a troublesome child forever in need of punishment." She didn't even bother to look at her son. "He is in need of a father to teach him the ways of a man."

Storm shook his head. "You must go from my lodge, Ta-wa-ne. Go now."

She looked up from where she knelt at the firepit. "I have nowhere to go. Redbeard says he will kill me and my son if I cross his path again. I cannot travel in the winter with such a small child. I have nowhere to protect my son from the cold but your lodge, Storm Dancer. Surely a great shaman like yourself would not throw a child into the snow on a day like this."

"You did not know I was here, Ta-wa-ne. It was but luck that you found me. You do not want me. If I had not been here, it would be another man who would take you in and feed you." He looked away and then back at her again, his pitch eyes boring down on her. "I will give you food and then you must go from here."

She placed two corn cakes on a wooden trecher and set it on his mat. "It is not luck that brought me here, but fate, my dear husband. Now, come eat, before it grows cold."

What is it with the women this day, Storm Dancer thought. *Do they not hear my words with their ears?*

But what could he do if the trapper had truly turned Ta-wa-ne away? He could not let the child starve or freeze to death because he had no protector. Even if there was the barest chance the child was his, he could not see him come to ill-fate. And even if the child wasn't his, he had a moral obligation to any of God's children.

Storm Dancer grabbed his winter cloak and threw it over his shoulder in fury. He did not like being forced into anything. As if his problems were not great enough with Rachael so angry with him, and the new burdens of shaman upon his shoulders, now he was being forced to provide shelter and care for Ta-wa-ne and her child.

Of course he could not stay here now. He almost laughed at the irony of the fact that yesterday morning he and Rachael had made love here in the cozy haven of their wigwam and this morning it was no longer theirs. He snatched his bow from its resting place in angry frustration.

"Where do you go? You have not yet eaten," Ta-wa-ne protested getting to her feet.

The little boy whimpered and put out his hands to her but she slapped him away, concerned only with Storm Dancer's departure.

"Feed the child," he ordered. "There is foodstuff in the baskets and plenty more. Use what you may." He slung the bow over his shoulder and headed for the door. "You may sleep here for now. I will go elsewhere."

She caught his arm. "You need not leave your own home. If the white woman has left you, you will need a woman to attend your needs." She rubbed his arm with her palm in a coy gesture, her voice honey-sweet. "Let me care for your needs. I know what you like." Her sexual innuendo was blatant. "It has not been so long that I cannot remember what it is you like. How you like to be touched." She lowered her hand to the bulge beneath his loinskin and Storm Dancer jerked from her grasp, disgusted by her attempt to bribe him with her body.

He stepped around the little boy, and ducked through the doorway. "Just do not get in my way, Ta-wa-ne," he shouted over his shoulder. "'Else I will be forced to kill you, woman!"

Chapter Twenty-Two

Rachael lifted a small basket of precious clothing and tucked it under her arm. Waving to Starlight who was busy stitching a new ceremonial medicine robe for Storm Dancer by the warmth of the fire, Rachael stepped out of the wigwam.

She had decided to take advantage of the mild winter day to wash the two men's shirts Starlight had given to her. By the cut of the muslin garments, Rachael knew they were old, but they were still in good shape and she had found them to be quite comfortable when belted and worn with a pair of rabbit skin leggings. The wide beaded belt one of the women had made for her was not only fashionable among the Lenni Lenape, but like all of their articles of clothing, useful as well. In her belt she carried her knife and a small leather pouch, much like the drawstring reticule she once carried. When she went outside, she often carried a small hatchet for cutting kindling as well.

Rachael had to chuckle at the thought of wearing men's pants and shirt, even of the Indian style, but it simply made good sense. She was far more comfortable and far warmer in the leggings and muslin shirts than she ever would have been in the cumbersome, drafty woolen skirts that had once been her winter uniform. The clothing the Indians wore was practical and made Rachael's daily tasks easier.

While staying with the old couple Shaakhan and Starlight, she made herself useful by taking over many of their daily chores. The old couple was satisfied to remain in the warmth of their wigwam, sparing their brittle bones the brunt of the winter wind by letting their daughter-in-law care for them.

The business of tending to Shaakhan and Starlight's needs and running their errands took up most of Rachael's time, for which she was thankful. It gave her less time to think about Storm Dancer . . . less time to have to deal with her feelings. She didn't know how she felt. At one moment she wanted to walk out of the camp to Philadelphia on her own, the next, she wanted to run into his arms and forgive him. Even though she was furious with him, she had to admit if not to him, then to herself, that she missed his touch. She missed his company . . . his subtle sense of humor, his sense of purpose among his mother's people . . . his devotion to her.

It had been nearly two weeks since Ta-wa-ne had appeared in the village shattering the new life Rachael had thought was secure, but it seemed like a lifetime. Ta-wa-ne's trapper came and went, making the village his home base along his trap lines, but the young Indian woman had turned all her attention from the redbeard Malvin to Storm Dancer.

After Ta-wa-ne moved into the wigwam Rachael

and Storm had shared, Storm moved out and in with Tuuban. Rachael was of course pleased that he had not remained in the same home with Ta-wa-ne, but that did not absolve him of his wrongdoing.

Storm had made several attempts in the last two weeks to make up to Rachael, but she'd wanted no part of his apologies. He had hurt her deeply and she was scared and confused. She loved her life among the Lenni Lenape. She really didn't want to go back to her way of life in Philadelphia or to the person she had been in Philadelphia. She loved Storm, but she didn't know how to deal with him or the rift between them. Only two days ago he had become enraged when he had invited her to come dine with him and Tuuban and she had refused him. He didn't understand why she was so hurt by his deception; he thought she was being unreasonable. He was angry that there was such vexation in his life at a time when he needed peace and time to contemplate the future of his mother's people that had become his people, and he blamed her.

Rachael suggested that she just needed some time apart from him. She also indicated that there would be no truce until Ta-wa-ne was dealt with. If they were divorced, if Rachael was his true wife, than there was not room for the both of them in the village. Rachael detested the woman, not just for what she had been to Storm, but for the person she was now.

Ta-wa-ne was a taker. She spoke with a soft sweet tongue, luring villagers into her confidence to procure things or trust. She made it quite clear to anyone who would listen that Storm Dancer was hers before the white whore had come and that it was she who would be leaving, not Ta-wa-ne. The woman was also a poor mother. She left her little boy crying in the wigwam while she moved from home to home visiting. When she did take him out she was short-tempered and harsh with him. She shouted at him, pulling him along behind her in the snow, forcing him to keep up with his short little baby legs. Ta-wa-ne seemed to have no love for the child and none of the maternal instincts that Rachael assumed all mothers were born with.

Rachael secured her laundry basket under her arm and headed toward the river where she would wash her clothing. Though the sun shone warm on her face, she was thankful for the rabbit fur coat she wore. The morning air was crisp on her cheeks; her breath formed frosty clouds above her head as she exhaled a greeting to a passing friend.

"Good morning to you," Laughing Spider hailed. She carried a baby on her back in a cradleboard and by the hand led a two-year-old that was so bundled up with winter furs that she could barely walk.

"A good morning to you," Rachael answered in Algonquian. She smiled. Laughing Spider was friendly and had been quite helpful to Rachael when she'd first arrived in the camp. She was one of the Lenni Lenape villagers that she considered a true friend.

"You go to the river?" Laughing Spider stopped. Her daughter kept going, watching the trail she made with the stick she was dragging through the snow.

"Some wash to do. If you have any I'd be happy to take care of it. No sense in both of us getting cold hands." Rachael laughed. Out of the corner of her eye she spotted Ta-wa-ne dragging her little son behind her. Rachael ignored the woman, keeping her attention on what Laughing Spider was saying.

". . . I thank you for the offer, friend-Rachael, but I sent my husband to do our washing early this morning. I think he'll not pester me before the morning meal anymore."

The two women laughed at the joke, and Laughing Spider called out for her daughter to wait for her. Laughing Spider indicated with a nod the wigwam where Dory lived. "So has your friend made her decision between her two suitors?"

Rachael grinned. "Not as far as I know."

Laughing Spider nodded. "I would have a difficult time making such a choice were I in such a position." She looked up to check where her toddler was. The little girl, Kiisku had stopped to pet a dog by her aunt's wigwam. "Both men would be good providers. I like them both for different reasons."

"That's what Dory says is making her decision so difficult. She likes them both. She thinks she could love either one given some time."

"With one hand I am envious of her to have two such fine men ask for her hand. But my other hand feels a sorrow for her. Choosing a husband is a hard task for any woman."

"It makes you see the good sense in arranged marriages."

Laughing Spider frowned. "No. Arranged marriages are easy. A man and a woman make no choice. They never feel responsible for each other because they have not made that choice."

Rachael nodded in understanding.

"Well, this woman must go." She looked up in the direction her daughter had gone. She had abandoned the dog and wandered out of sight. *"Kiisku!* Did your mama not tell you to wait for her?" Laughing Spider gave a wave of farewell to Rachael and hurried to catch up with her toddler.

Rachael had not walked more than a few more feet when Storm Dancer stuck his head out of Tuuban's wigwam. He had to have been watching for her because he was not dressed, yet he called to her. Both his chest and feet were bare.

"A word with you, Rachael."

The sight of Ta-wa-ne a few moments ago had raised her ire. She knew it wasn't fair to take out her anger on Storm Dancer, but she couldn't help herself. "Later. I'm busy."

He stepped out into the snow in his bare feet, rubbing his cold arms. "I'll be but a moment dressing," he called to her in English as she walked by.

"Later," she repeated in Algonquian.

He exhaled angrily and stepped back into the wigwam, dropping the door flap with a loud snap of leather.

Rachael continued on to the river. At the bank, she found a washing hole that had already been used that morning so she didn't have to break ice. The Metuksik River was funny. In some places the ice was a good foot and a half thick, but only a few feet away, it might be paper thin.

Rachael knelt and pulled off her mittens. Taking a shirt, she dipped it into the icy water and swished it vigorously. The water was so cold that in a moment's time, her hands were too numb to feel the bite of the icy water.

Just as Rachael began to ring out the second shirt, she heard a giggle. She looked up to see the little boy that belonged to Ta-wa-ne walking out across the river. He clapped and laughed as he chased a feather blowing in the wind. The child's mother was nowhere to be seen.

"Maata!" Rachael called out instinctively. *"Maata ilauishit!* The ice isn't safe!"

The child stopped and looked in the direction of the adult voice. When he spotted Rachael, he grinned innocently. The feather fluttered again catching his attention and he ran, reaching out with a mitten-covered hand to try and catch it.

Rachael dropped her wet shirt into the snow and stood up, glancing around. No one was to be seen. She looked back at the little boy who was straying farther and farther toward the middle of the river where the ice was at its thinnest.

"Maata," she shouted again, waving her hands.

Again, the little boy stopped, a big smile dimpling the rosy red apples of his chubby cheeks.

Rachael walked well around the hole that had been cut in the ice for washing and stepped cautiously down onto the frozen riverbed.

She held out her arms to the little boy. *"Buumska,"* she urged. "Come to Rachael."

He turned toward her.

"That's right." Rachael smiled and he smiled back. She took a step and he took one.

"Good, good," she called. "Come on, come to Rachael like a good boy and I'll find you a new feather—something even better." She took another step and the ice groaned beneath her. Rachael quickly spread her feet and lowered her body closer to the ice to redistribute her weight as Storm had taught her.

The little boy stopped coming toward her and

squatted, mimicking her.

"*Maata!* No," she called. She held out her arms to him again. The ice groaned and a crack zigzagged its way past her. She wasn't going to be able to get to him. The little boy would have to come to her. "Come to Rachael!"

After a moment's hesitation he giggled, clapping his mittens together and started toward her again.

"That's right, that's right," she coaxed gently. "Come to Rachael and I'll give you a present. A few more steps and she would be able to reach him . . .

The little boy stopped and started again twice more, but finally he made it within arm's length of Rachael. She reached out and swept him into her arms. He wrapped his arms around her neck and hung on, smiling up at her as she slowly made her way back to the safety of the riverbank.

When Rachael felt the solid footing of the snowy ground beneath her knee-high moccasins she gave an audible sigh of relief. She hugged the little boy tightly, forgetting that he was her enemy's child, forgetting that he might well be the son of her husband's first marriage. All he was to her was a precious tot who was safe from imminent danger.

Rachael lifted him over her head and he squealed with laughter. She smiled up at him, thankful he was safe, no matter whose child he was. "What's your name?" she entreated softly. "Tell Rachael what your name is and why you're out here all alone. Where's your mama?"

He was busy playing with the soft rabbit fur of her hat, blowing on the fur and laughing.

Rachael lowered him in her arms, tucking his legs

around her waist so that she could get his attention. She touched her chest lightly. "Rachael. My name is Rachael." She tapped him on the chest. "What's your name?"

"Wa-chael," he said.

She laughed. "Rachael, that's right. What a smart boy!" She touched him again. "But what's your name? What's my smart, brave little boy's name?"

He hit himself with a fist in a great exaggerated manly gesture. "Ka-we-ras!"

"Ka-we-ras, oh, I like that name." She shifted him onto her hip. "Well, let's go find your mama, Ka-we-ras. I know she must be looking for you. You mustn't run off, else your mama will be very sad." Rachael spoke to the boy in Algonquian and though the child didn't know the language, it didn't seem to matter.

Still holding the toddler, she retrieved her clothing, threw it into her basket. Her fingers were so numb that she had a difficult time getting her mittens on while holding the boy, but she managed.

With the boy balanced securely on one hip and the basket of wet clothing on the other, Rachael started down the path back to the village. While walking she pointed a cardinal out to Ka-we-ras and then a rabbit hopping through the drifting snow. She told him the names of the rabbit and bird in Algonquian and he mimicked her words making them both laugh.

When Rachael reached the village, she left her basket by Starlight and Shaakhan's wigwam and headed toward the one she and Storm had shared so happily since their arrival in the Lenni Lenape Village. At the wigwam, she tried to put the boy down so that she could push him inside without having to actually encounter Ta-wa-ne but the toddler refused to let go of Rachael. He tightened his arms around her neck and whimpered when she tried to put him down.

Finally with an exasperated sigh, Rachael called out to her husband's first wife. When Ta-wa-ne made no response on the second call Rachael pushed back the flap to see that no one was in. "Your mama must be looking for you, Ka-we-ras. She's not here."

Rachael heard a woman's shriek and turned to see Ta-wa-ne hustling toward her shouting in Iroquois.

Rachael gritted her teeth. The woman was saying something about Rachael stealing her child.

"I did not steal him, you addlepated twit!" Rachael shouted back in English. "I found him out on the ice on the river. Shame on you for not keeping a better eye on him. He could have drowned!"

Reaching Rachael and the boy, Ta-wa-ne put her arms out for her son. Ka-we-ras flinched, flattening himself against Rachael.

Tears of rage rose behind Rachael's eyelids. What kind of mother could Ta-wa-ne be that her two-year-old wouldn't go to her? When the boy wouldn't come, Ta-wa-ne grasped him by the back of his little cloak and tore him from Rachael's arms, shouting at him in a shrill fishwife's voice.

"You're the one to blame for this, not him. He's two years old!" Rachael pointed a threatening finger. "You hurt him and I swear on the great Wishemoto," —her hand fell to the hilt of the knife she wore on her belt— "I'll slit you end to end!"

Ta-wa-ne swept up her screaming child and brushed past Rachael, going into the wigwam that had been Rachael's two weeks prior.

For a moment Rachael stood with her head hung slightly, taking time to catch her breath and calm herself. When she looked up, Storm Dancer was standing there in front of her grinning the widest grin she'd seen on his face in two weeks.

His smile was infectious. "What's so funny," she asked, almost happy to see him.

"You, hellcat. I've never witnessed such anger. You have not even been that angry with me."

She lowered a hand to rest on her hip. His face was drawn and he looked tired. For some reason she gained no satisfaction in knowing he hadn't been sleeping any better than she had.

"That little boy was out on the middle of the river chasing a feather. He's no more than a baby, Storm! She should be watching over him more carefully. He could well have fallen through the ice and been swept away by the current. She'd never have even known what happened to him."

Storm pulled off his leather mitten and reached out to brush her cheek with his fingertips. "You were a brave woman to walk out upon the ice to get another woman's child . . . your enemy's child."

She shrugged, a little embarrassed.

"Not many would do such a thing," he went on in a low, caressing voice. "I cannot say that I would have saved the child."

"Of course you would have." Her gaze met his. "The boy is not responsible for who his mother is . . . who his parents are," she added quietly.

He stroked the soft skin of her cheek, his finger brushing over her lips. "I have missed your sky-eyes upon me, Rachael-wife."

She swallowed, feeling a little light-headed. His touch felt so good. *God I miss him.*

"Come to Tuuban's wigwam tonight and eat with me. I have some matters to discuss with you."

She covered his hand with hers. "I'm just not ready to talk about us, Storm," she said, not unkindly.

He shook his head, lowering his hand, but threading his fingers through hers so that he held her hand. "I want to speak of us, but I can wait. What I truly need now is your thoughts on our village moving west. There is so much to be done before spring. So many decisions to make. There are questions in my mind that I cannot settle. I thought that you could help me."

She hesitated. She wanted to be with him. She wanted to sit beside the firepit and eat beside him. She wanted to feel his hand in hers, to see his dark eyes look at no one but her, to taste his lips on hers. "I suppose I could come for a little while."

He smiled. "I will cook you a feast."

"I . . . that's all right. I can make the meal." There were butterflies in her stomach. She was warm and flushed from Storm Dancer's attention.

He squeezed her hand. "You will be my guest tonight. Guests do not cook their own meals. It would be an insult."

She smiled. "All right, then. I will come tonight and we will talk of the village. Nothing else."

"Nothing else," he repeated.

She laughed again, feeling silly. He was just standing there holding her hand looking at her. She thought of Ka-we-ras and the promise she had made to the little boy. "Storm . . ."

"Wife?"

"Could you do me a favor?"

"If it is in the power of this man, the shaman of my people."

"A simple yes would suffice." She pulled her hand from his and wrapped her arms around her waist securely. "Will you come to your grandparents' wigwam later and let me give you something for the boy. I promised him a present if he came to me out on the ice."

Storm Dancer hesitated for a moment. He was trying to avoid Ta-wa-ne's child. But he was fast becoming attached to him. "I have need to see my grandfather. I will come now."

"Good." She smiled at him, her gaze lingering over his handsome face before she turned and walked away, excited by the little trip in her heartbeat.

Chapter Twenty-Three

Rachael didn't truly realize how much she missed Storm Dancer until she was with him again. The evening meal in his wigwam was wonderful. In a Dutch oven he made a succulent venison stew chockful of vegetables and cooked in a rich gravy. For dessert there was sugar-sweetened blueberry corn bread and a strange hot drink that tasted like cocoa, yet was not a milk base.

Once Storm Dancer cleared away the supper dishes, the two sat across the firepit from each other and began to discuss the strategy of such an immense undertaking as moving an entire village hundreds of miles west.

For hours they poured over precious maps provided by Shaakhan, bought in Annapolis in anticipation of the move they would one day be forced to make. Not only did Rachael and Storm Dancer discuss the path they would take to the Ohio country, but the practical aspects of the move as well. How would they transport the old, the sick, and the young? What belongings would they take, what would have to be left behind?

Should they purchase horses in anticipation of the more open land west of the Ohio River? The village owned only a dozen pack ponies and a few horses because the forest was too dense in the Chesapeake area for a horse to be of any good. It was only near towns such as Annapolis where there were trails or roads where a horse could be used. Both Storm Dancer and Rachael agreed that with horses the trip west could be made easier, even if it would be slower at first, and the horses would be useful in their new land. But where would they get the money it would take to purchase horses?

The moon rose high in the dark winter sky before Storm finally rolled away his maps and tucked them into the leather pouch that protected them from the weather.

Rachael rose, stretching like a cat. It was so warm and cozy in Tuuban's wigwam here with Storm that she could have easily stretched out by the firepit on a bed of soft pelts and gone to sleep.

Rachael turned to reach for her coat and Storm intercepted her. He wrapped his arms around her waist, staring at her with those black onyx eyes of his. "I thank you for the advice you have given me tonight."

Her hands fell to his shoulders as if it was the most natural thing. "I did little. Just listened."

"Your suggestions were worthy." He tapped her temple teasingly. "You are intelligent for a white-*equiwa.*"

Her mouth turned up in the barest smile. "Oh I am, am I?" she asked in a silky voice. She could feel his warm breath on her face; she could smell that woodsy masculine scent that clung to him stimulating her senses.

He brushed back her hair with his hand. "If I kissed you, would you sink your knife into my chest?"

She chuckled, looking up at him through the veil of her dark lashes. "I don't know. Dare you try?"

In an erotic gesture, he brushed her lower lip with the calloused pad of his thumb. "This man thinks one kiss might be worth the thrust of a blade."

When his lips met hers, his kiss was hot and demanding. Rachael shut her eyes, savoring the taste of him as he thrust his tongue into her mouth. *It's been so long,* she thought. *Too long.*

His hand cupped her breast through the thin muslin of her man's shirt, his fingertips brushing against the hardening nub of her nipple. "I have missed you, Rachael-wife," he murmured in her ear. "I have missed the touch of your hand,"—he brought her hand to his chest—"the taste of your fire honey lips,"—he kissed her softly—"the sound of your voice when you call me," he whispered in her ear.

Rachael could hear the throb of her heart. She could feel her hand shaking as she slipped it beneath his vest to feel the hard sinewy muscles of his bare chest. Dear God, but she'd missed this. She needed Storm so badly.

He pressed his lips to her throat, sprinkling her silken flesh with molten kisses as he made his way to the swell of her breasts.

Rachael looped her hands around his neck in encouragement as he untied the ribbon of her muslin shirt. A sigh escaped her lips as his rough hand caressed the curve of her breast, squeezing gently.

This time it was she who kissed him, her need rising in the flames of his touch.

"Let me love you, *ki-ti-hi,*" he cajoled.

She shook her head, trying hard to concentrate. It was so difficult to think when he was touching her like this . . . kissing her like this. She could feel his great stiff manhood pressing against her from beneath his loin cloth. That familiar ache of desire was spreading through her veins overpowering logic. She wanted to stroke him and be stroked. She was lost in a whirlwind of sensation.

Through the haze of mounting passion, the thought of Ta-wa-ne flashed through Rachael's mind. She thought of the child that was her husband's. "No . . ." She caught Storm's hand and lowered it from her breast. She lay her cheek on his chest and waited for her breath to come more easily before she spoke.

Storm waited, his muscles tense. He encircled her in his arms and held her tightly, kissing the top of her head. "What is it, wife of mine, love of my heart? Why do you stop me? Why do you deny yourself?"

"Storm . . . I can't." She swallowed hard, trying to get control of herself. Her heart still pounded wildly, the blood in her veins rushing in her ears. She wanted him so badly that she hurt physically. "Not yet. This matter has to be settled."

He exhaled in a long sigh. "You are my wife. We love as few can ever hope to love."

Rachael looked up at him. "I know you don't understand." She smoothed his cheek with the back of her hand. "I do love you. These last weeks have taught me that."

"Then come back to my fire. Let me make love to you. Let this man sleep with you in his arms."

"It wouldn't be fair to you."

His arms fell, his dark eyes narrowing, his passion fading in the blink of an eye. "You still want to leave me?"

She lowered her gaze, then lifted her chin so that she could look directly into his eyes. "No," she answered her voice gaining strength with each word. "I don't want to go back. I want to stay here and be your wife."

"You make no sense, Rachael."

She smiled. "I don't make much sense to myself either." She took his hand in hers. "I want to come to you as your wife by my own choice this time, not to save my life, not to do what is right. I want to make that decision on my own."

"You want me as husband, but not yet?"

She nodded.

He looked at her for a long moment. "These words I can understand. I do not like them, but I can understand. What can I do to bring you home to my wigwam sooner. I need you at my side, Rachael. I need your strength to carry me through the difficult months that lie ahead."

"Ta-wa-ne," she answered honestly. "She must leave here, 'else she will forever be a burr between us."

"I have offered to find her a husband in another village. She refuses."

Rachael studied his expression carefully. "She still thinks you will take her back."

"I will not. She will go when the weather breaks and it is safe to travel, whether it is with a new husband or alone. You are my wife, now and into eternity. There will be no other, ever."

Rachael could tell by the sound of his voice that she had less to worry over Ta-wa-ne than she had thought.

There was nothing but contempt in Storm Dancer's tone for the woman who had once been his wife. Rachael believed him when he said he loved her and she was certain this time that it was not wishful thinking that made her trust his words.

The child must be dealt with as well, Rachael thought. *There can be no more walls between us if we are to make this love of ours work.* "I understand that you feel a responsibility to Ka-we-ras because he may be your son.

"The child—"

She lay a finger on his lips. "Let me finish. I understand that you must care for him. Ta-wa-ne is a poor mother; the boy needs you. She doesn't seem to be interested in him. Perhaps she would consider leaving him here with you when she went."

Storm Dancer cupped her chin, lifting it so that he could stare into her heavenly sky eyes. "You would take my child by another woman to raise in your wigwam?"

"He's a good little boy. We may never have any children, Storm. If Ta-wa-ne will give you your son, you should take him."

He smoothed back the wisps of her hair, touched by Rachael's words. "I will think on the matter. I will talk with my grandparents and then with Ta-wa-ne. They know a Shawnee trapper near Annapolis who is looking for a wife."

She smoothed his arm. "It would be wise to speak with Shaakhan and Starlight." She lifted up on her toes and kissed him. "Now I must go."

"You will not stay the night?" He lifted his broad bronze palms in confusion. "I thought all was settled between us, Wife."

She laughed, reaching for her coat and pulling it on. "This is Tuuban's wigwam. I can't sleep here with you, and Mistress first-wife-now-divorced is in our wigwam."

"Tuuban could find another mat to sleep upon. I have only to say the words." Storm followed her to the doorway. "I will set Ta-wa-ne outside with the dogs."

"Perhaps another night," she whispered, stroking his sharp jawline with the tip of her finger. "I need just a little more time." They kissed once more and then Rachael stepped out into the frigid midnight air, feeling more confident about her future than she had in weeks.

"It's time you made your decision, Dory," Rachael insisted. "You can't lead Yesterday's Thunder and Shadow Man around by the nose forever. It's only right."

The two women knelt side by side at the frozen river's edge breaking pieces of ice to take back to the camp for water.

"I ain't doin' it on purpose, Rachael-honey. I can't honestly make up my mind. One day I think to myself, a young man would keep me young, I should marry Yesterday's Thunder. But then I think a man closer to my own age would be a better suit, and then there's those poor motherless children . . ." She clicked her tongue between her teeth. "How could I deny them a mother? 'Course I ain't never been a mother for long. Don't know that I could do it."

Rachael dropped a final chunk of ice into her bucket

and stood. "You'd make a wonderful mother, Dory."

She let out an exasperated sigh as she stood and picked up her own basket. Side by side the women headed for the village. "I like 'em both so much that I don't know how I'm gonna tell the other once I made my choice."

"Maybe you should talk to Starlight. She's always a good one to ask advice."

"I hadn't thought of that. Her bein' the chief and all, she might know what to do even if this poor old girl don't."

"Exactly." Rachael looked up as they passed through the maze of wigwams to see little Ka-we-ras seated on a hide outside his mother's wigwam. As usual Ta-wa-ne was nowhere to be seen.

Rachael thought it would be wise to stay away from Ka-we-ras. She didn't want to become attached to him. She didn't want to have any contact with Storm's ex-wife.

But was it the baby's fault that he had a terrible mother. Was it his fault that he had no one who cared for him but a man who might be his father?

Rachael stooped in front of the little boy. "Good morning to you, little man," she said slowly in Algonquian. "How's my best ice-skater?"

Ka-we-ras' face lit up at the sight of Rachael.

"Wachael!"

She laughed, setting down her ice bucket to take him into her arms. "You out here all alone again? Where's mama? Ta-wa-ne?"

"Mama gone," he answered in Algonquian. "Make visit."

Rachael pulled aside the flap of the wigwam that was

rightfully hers. Sure enough, Ta-wa-ne was nowhere to be seen. She thought for a moment and then dropped the flap. "You want to go with Rachael, Ka-we-ras?"

"Go Wachael," he echoed, getting to his feet.

Dory gave a low whistle. "That woman's gonna be hot with you if'in she comes home and finds the boy gone."

"I'll just take him back to Starlight's wigwam for a little while. I'll give him something to eat and drink and then bring him back. She'll never miss him." Rachael scooped the little boy into her arms and started toward her wigwam. Up ahead she spotted Ta-wa-ne standing in a group of several men. Storm Dancer was among them.

Rachael debated whether to speak or not. But the sight of the woman standing so close to Storm while he talked with the other man ruffled her dander. Storm was hers whether they were presently living together or not and Ta-wa-ne no longer had any right to him.

Rachael walked right up to Storm Dancer, while Dory hung back, chuckling to herself.

"I found the boy sitting alone," Rachael told Storm Dancer. She glanced at Ta-wa-ne standing beside him. "If the woman doesn't mind, I'll take Ka-we-ras to my wigwam. I have a gift for him, a carved dugout that Shaakhan made."

Storm Dancer fought back a smile. The talk last night with Rachael had warmed his heart. He had not lost her. Rachael was still his. He looked down at Ta-wa-ne, lifting an eyebrow.

The petite dark-eyed woman shrugged. "This woman cares not. The boy is trouble. The white woman will bring him back soon enough."

Rachael shifted Ka-we-ras on her hip. "Your grandparents want you to come for the evening meal tonight, Storm. They want to talk about the Ohio country. Shaakhan's been there with the Shawnee, you know, when he was a young man."

Storm Dancer's dark eyes danced with amusement. His *manake*-wife was suddenly a wild she-cat with her hackles raised. "I will come."

"Good." On impulse she leaned over and kissed him on the mouth. She heard Ta-wa-ne gasp. There was a murmur among the men as Rachael's kiss lingered. "I'll see you after nightfall," Rachael said to Storm Dancer when she finally stepped back.

"Until tonight, then," Storm responded with a wave as she walked away.

Dory gave Rachael a playful punch in the arm the moment the two women were out of earshot of Ta-wa-ne. "Good God a Jesus, Rachael-honey! If you could have seen the look on the witch's face when you kissed that man of yours. I thought her eyes was gonna bug right out of her head!"

"It was an evil thing for me to do, Dory, but I just couldn't help myself. She doesn't care who takes the boy as long as he's out from under her skin!"

"I don't know who was more surprised over that kiss, Storm Dancer or Ta-wa-ne."

Rachael laughed. "Come in and speak with Starlight. I'm certain she'll be able to help you decide between Yesterday's Thunder and Shadow Man."

Dory stalled. "Aw, I don't want to bother her; I know she's busy doin' whatever it is chiefs do."

Rachael dropped her ice bucket by the doorway, and took Dory's from her hand and set it beside her own.

"Come on, don't be a coward." She tugged at her friend's hand.

Reluctantly, Dory followed Rachael inside the wigwam.

"Look who I've brought, Grandmother," Rachel said to Starlight.

The old woman turned from where she was digging through a basket on the floor. At the sight of little Ka-we-ras, she threw out her arms.

Rachael set him down on his feet and he darted around the firepit toward Starlight as fast as his little legs could carry him. "Gwand-mudder!"

Starlight scooped him into her arms and squeezed him tightly. "Ah, it's so good to have a little one in this wigwam. It has been too many years."

Rachael stepped inside. "I also brought Dory."

"Greetings to you, Chief Starlight." Dory gave a nod.

"She has something to discuss with you, Grandmother."

"But . . . but if'in you're busy, I can come back."

Starlight gave a wave of her hand. "Nonsense." She had taken Ka-we-ras's winter coat off and seated him by the firepit to play with the new toy dugout Shaakhan had carved for him from a piece of beechwood. "Sit, sit and drink tea with us, Flamehair." Starlight waved a hand. "I even have an English teapot the old man brought me from Annapolis as a present last springtime."

Dory sat on the guest's mat and Rachael began to serve the tea that stayed warm on a rock beside the firepit. "I have asked Storm Dancer to our evening meal, Grandmother, so if you do not mind I will work while you speak with Dory."

The old chief slurped loudly from a handleless porcelain teacup. "The Storm Dancer graces our meal with his presence, does he? I'd say it's about time, wouldn't you?" She winked at Dory.

"Yes, ma'am, 'bout time I'd say."

Starlight set down her teacup and folded her hands as a signal that she was giving her undivided attention to Dory.

Rachael moved about the wigwam gathering herbs and vegetables for supper while she listened to Dory explain in broken Algonquian her dilemma to the village chief. Starlight was a superb listener, occasionally asking a question, but allowing Dory to relate her problem as she saw it. Starlight offered no comments through the entire conversation, always saving her words for last.

When Dory had exhausted her story and grown silent, Starlight stroked her wrinkled chin in contemplation for only a moment before speaking. "The solution is simple you silly *equiwas!*"

"It is?" Rachael was kneeling beside Ka-we-ras feeding him a corncake with honey on it. "What is the solution then, Grandmother, great chief of the Lenni Lenape?"

Starlight reached for her pipe, smugly. "Marry them both."

Dory choked on a swallow of sassafras tea and Rachael reached over to pat her roughly on the back. "Marry 'em both? Pardon my sassiness, Chief Starlight, but are you jerkin' my tether?"

The old woman laughed, striking her knee with her hand. "It's the only choice. Both men need you. It would be only fair."

Rachael came to stand beside Dory and rested her hand on her friend's shoulder. "She could marry two men?" She couldn't believe she was honestly contemplating such a choice for her friend.

"It's a man or a woman's right to marry a second spouse under special circumstances when permission is given by the chief." She poked her sunken chest with the stem of her clay pipe, cackling with pleasure. "That's me and I'd say," she stuck the pipe between her teeth and reached with a straw to light it, "it's been a matter of survival at times."

"Two husbands!" Now Dory was beginning to chuckle. "If that don't hang all!"

"Both men would have to agree to this compromise."

"They wouldn't, would they?" Rachael asked, still a little shocked.

Starlight shrugged her shoulders. "Depends on how badly they want her, I would say."

Dory smiled. "Two husbands," she said more to herself than to Rachel and Starlight.

"You aren't really considering such a thing, are you?" Rachael squatted beside Dory.

Dory looked at Rachael, a grin from ear to ear. "And why not? I'd be a good wife to 'em both."

"I know you would, but—"

"But what, Rachael-honey?" Dory stood. "These people got different ways than our people, but they ain't bad, just different. It all makes sense in a funny kinda way."

Rachael glanced at Starlight. "You're serious?"

"That I am child." The old woman puffed on her pipe. "Think it over, Flamehair, and talk to your men.

If they say they are willing to share you, send them to me so that I may be certain their intentions are true. If there are no objections from the village and all parties agree, you may wed as soon as a feast can be prepared." She indicated Ka-we-ras who had curled up in a ball on a sleeping skin and fallen asleep. "This village is in need of more little ones. We do not delay in marriage these days."

Rachael handed Dory her winter cloak and walked to the doorway with her. "You're serious, are you?," she whispered.

Dory looked up at her friend. "I know you don't think it right, but you know there was many a man in the Bible that done had many a wife. Why can't I have two husbands if my heart's in it and theirs is too?"

Rachael had to smile. "I never thought I'd hear myself say this, but you're right. If Yesterday's Thunder and Shadow Man are willing to share you, I know you'll have enough love to go around." She kissed Dory's pock-scarred cheek. "So, go talk to your men and let me know what they say." Rachael was still smiling when Dory stepped out into the frigid air and let the door flap fall behind her.

Chapter Twenty-Four

"We cannot leave in the darkest of winter," Pretty Woman hissed in Broken Horn's ear. She looked up to be certain no one else heard her. The dozen villagers who had not yet died of starvation or consumption still slept in the lodge, huddled together for warmth near the firepit. "We will freeze to death. There is little game. We will starve."

Broken Horn stuffed a mangy hide vest into his bag. "We must go. There are evil spirits here—spirits who will kill me."

Pretty Woman pulled her cloak tighter over her thin shoulders. "We'll die in the forest with no one to bury our bones! No one to bury us and we'll rot on this earth, never rising into the heavens to meet our children."

He glared at her. "We'll die if we stay here."

"Spring—"

"We will never live until spring with this evil luck that has settled upon us." He nodded in the direction of the sleeping Mohawks. "Look at them. Death hovers over them." He wrinkled his nose. "I can smell its rancid scent. I hear its wings flutter in the darkness. I can see it lurking in the shadows."

"Should we not gather our brothers and sisters and take them from this evil with us? Surely if death presses so close, they will not survive until their great chief can return."

Broken Horn turned his attention to a pile of weapons at the door. He carefully made his selections. "They will only slow this man down. I will not drag corpses behind me."

Pretty Woman glanced at the pitiful sleeping forms. Two Crows wheezed, his chest rattling with each breath he took. Pretty Woman knew Broken Horn was right. Such starvation and illness could not befall a village so quickly except by a curse. She looked back at her husband, thinking that it would only be a matter of time before she too had the death rattle in her chest. "I will go with the chief, my husband."

"You will not."

She picked up Broken Horn's bag from the floor and tossed a few cooking utensils into it. "I will prepare your meals and fetch your water so that you, my great chief, will not have to be concerned with such menial woman's work."

"You could not keep up. It will take months of walking at this time of year."

"If I cannot keep up, you can leave me behind, or kill me if you wish." When she saw that he was considering her proposal, she went on faster than before. "This woman would care well for her husband the great chief. She would be there to fulfill any need he might have, be it one kind of hunger or another." She ran a hand over his lean buttocks.

Broken Horn thought for a moment and then gave a nod of assent. "Very well, Wife, you may accompany this great chief, but he warns you—" he lifted a finger, "if you are trouble I will leave you behind to feed wolves. Now hurry. We leave before the sun lifts on the horizon."

"You will not wait to tell the others?" She grabbed items at random off the floor and walls, fearful he would leave without her.

Broken Horn's black eyes narrowed dangerously. He grabbed Pretty Woman by a hank of her hair and jerked her backward making her drop her leather journey bag. "You think this chief needs permission from his people to make a journey to save himself . . . to save them?"

Her hand flew to her head to ease the pain. "How . . . how can you save them if they are already dying?"

He jerked her head by her hair again. "Silence!" he shouted as loudly as he dared. "If these people die then I will find a new people, but first my luck must be restored! The evil spirits that haunt this camp must be driven out. I must take back what is rightfully mine!"

"Yes, yes, this stupid woman understands the great chief's words."

"Now hurry about your task of packing, and do not show me any airs you picked up from the white whore Rachael. You speak to this man in that tone again and I will break your jaw." He let her go with a smack to the back of her head.

Pretty Woman knelt to gather her belongings that had spilled from her fallen bag. "The white whore is it? Is she the reason you try to leave this woman behind?

So that you can take her as wife?"

"I have said nothing of taking the white woman Rachael! I will kill her the same as I will kill my brother. Now hurry or I will leave you to die with the others." He swung a quiver of arrows over his back and reached for the best bow on the wall. A musket already waited for him beside the doorway. "Get what you must and dress warmly. Bring snowshoes."

"Mine rotted."

"Take someone else's. They'll not be needing them. Put everything together in one pack you can carry. A chief does not carry anything but his weapons." He stood tall, thrusting out his chest in a manly stance. "We will travel south to the Chesapeake and I will find my mother's people. I will take back my scalp lock from my half-brother and with it my luck." He smiled at the thought, his voice growing softer and more thoughtful as he spoke. "I will kill the Dancer of Storms." He slammed his chest with his fist. *And then I will take his white whore for myself.*

Because of the frigid January temperatures, Dory's marriage to Yesterday's Thunder and Shadow Man was held in the great ceremonial longhouse. After a touching wedding ceremony presided over by Chief Starlight and the new shaman, Storm Dancer, the villagers lavished the bride and grooms with gifts and the feasting began. Storm Dancer excused himself to discuss some village issues with the elders of the council, but promised to search Rachael out later in the evening.

Lanterns hung from the ceiling joists of the ceremonial longhouse casting the large room in golden sparkling light. The longhouse was filled with villagers dressed in their finest clothing, all there to celebrate the covenant of marriage. A great fire in the firepit in the center of the room kept the wedding guests warm and filled every nook of the bark ceremonial house with bright light in the dead of the dark winter.

Rachael soon found herself heady from the loud drums and rattles, and the spicy food and the friendship. Dressed in her white doeskin dress, she laughed and danced with the men and women of the village until she was hot and sweaty and her head was reeling.

As she whirled with Tuuban she watched Dory who was seated between her two bridegrooms, the children crowded around them. Surprisingly, when Dory had made her offer, there had been little protest from the two men. When each considered that he might not be the choice, should Dory have been forced to choose, they both readily agreed to the arrangement. If each man could not have her to himself, he would share her. It was decided by all parties involved that each man would continue to live in his own wigwam. Dory would live in both wigwams and the children would always be welcome to come and go in both homes. It seemed that this odd arrangement had provided Shadow Man's children not only with a mother, but an extra father as well. Yesterday's Thunder enjoyed the activity of Shadow Man's large family and doted on the children like a favorite uncle. When he presented Dory with a wedding gift of a short feathered cape, he gave the children gifts as well.

Tuuban whirled Rachael around and she threw back her head in laughter as she stumbled. She was caught by a pair of strong arms banded with copper armbands and when she looked up, Storm Dancer was there and Tuuban gone. Holding her in his arms, he bent to press a kiss to the throbbing point of her throat.

"Business finished?" she asked, intoxicated by his nearness. The wedding ceremony had touched a place deep in her heart, bringing embarrassing tears to her eyes. She wanted so badly to love and be loved. She wanted to make her marriage to the Dancer of Storms work.

"No, business is not complete, but the elders insisted I join you before another man carries you off to his wigwam." He dropped an arm around her shoulders, nuzzling her neck. "You are by far the most beautiful woman here tonight, the most beautiful woman on the Chesapeake." He scanned the crowd, his voice husky in her ear. "The men look at you with appreciation for your beauty, at me for my foolishness at not yet bringing you home to the wigwam where you belong."

She looped her arms around his neck. "I saw you speaking with Ta-wa-ne. Have you been able to reason with her?"

"She refuses the offer of marriage to the Shawnee trapper I spoke of."

"And Ka-we-ras?"

He brushed his lips against hers. "She says I may have him for a price."

Rachael's mouth dropped open in horror. "She will sell you your son?"

"My supposed son."

She gave an incredulous laugh. "It makes no difference. He's only a baby." She rested her hands on his broad shoulders. "What are you going to do?"

"Her price is too high. She wants white man's coin." He paused. "That or to wed me."

She chewed on her lower lip. He was testing her; she could hear it in his voice. Rachael dug deep within herself to grasp the trust she knew she must have for her husband. "If you turn her away, she may leave and take Ka-we-ras with her. If she's willing to sell him to you, she'd just as easily sell him to another."

Rachael glanced at a knot of young braves that surrounded Ta-wa-ne. She was deep in conversation with them, their tones bawdy. One brave rested his hand possessively on her buttocks. Another tried to steal a kiss. Rachael could hear her bell-like laughter, even in noise of the celebration. Ka-we-ras was nowhere to be seen.

Storm Dancer ran a hand through his midnight hair in thought. "Yes, something must be done to protect the boy. I only wish I knew what."

"We must make her give him to you, Storm. Threaten her. Kill her if you must."

A smile crept across his sensuous lips. "I cannot kill her. She has not yet done anything wrong."

Rachael crossed her arms over her chest. "You have to do something to get the child in your care." She paused. "In our care."

He studied her intently. "You would take another woman's child?"

"He's yours; as your wife I have a responsibility to you to care for your child."

Storm brushed his knuckles against the apples of her cheek. "You would do this for this man?"

"I would do this for my husband." She closed her eyes and pressed a kiss to his lips. It felt so good to be so near him, to taste his lips on hers again.

"I will speak to Starlight and Shaakhan on this matter of the boy tomorrow. For tonight I can only offer my prayers into the heavens."

"For tonight we give our prayer for the child," Rachael whispered, guiding his hand until it rested possessively on her hip. "And what do we do in the matter of Storm Dancer and Rachael?"

He kissed her again, harder this time, and she melted into his arms, wanting nothing but to be his again.

Their lips parted all too soon and for one intense moment their gazes locked and then Storm Dancer swept her into his muscular arms. Rachael rested her head on his shoulder not caring who saw them in such an intimate embrace. When Storm started for the doorway, she protested. "Our cloaks. Tis cold outside," she murmured in his ear.

"I will keep you warm," he answered as he carried her out of the ceremonial house and into the frigid night air. "Come back to me Rachael-wife and I will hold you so tightly in my arms that you will never know the cold again."

She threw back her head and laughed in the bitter night air. "You ask and yet you already carry me away. Is this not kidnapping?"

He nipped at her ear. "If I do not get you onto a sleeping mat, I think I will take you here in the snow."

"Brrr, too cold." She left a string of tantalizing kisses along his jawline. "Better to go inside where it is warm and slightly more private."

"As you wish."

Despite the bitter cold of the winter night, Rachael felt a warmth in the pit of her stomach that was radiating outward to her limbs. Storm whispered words of love in Algonquian in her ear and though she did not know all of the words, it made no difference. Rachael did not know how this problem of Ta-wa-ne and Ka-we-ras would be settled but she had the faith to know that all would be right if left to time and God. There was a peacefulness she felt in her heart as Storm carried her through the doorway of the wigwam he shared with Tuuban.

Once inside, he slowly lowered her, flesh brushing against flesh until her moccasins touched the floor. "What of Tuuban?" Rachael asked. "This is his wigwam."

Storm stepped back to lace the inside door, guaranteeing their privacy. "He will sleep elsewhere tonight."

She went to where Storm's bedskins lay and brought them near to the firepit where she shook them out. "You planned this all," she teased. "And what if I had turned you away?"

He turned back to her, the door securely closed. "You did not." He pulled at the ties of his buckskin shirt.

She smiled, her hands falling gracefully to her hips as she watched him unclothe.

Realizing that she watched him, Storm Dancer took his time in undressing. He began to sway to the sound of the ceremonial wedding drums echoing in the night, the rhythm undeniable.

Rachael suddenly found her breath quickening. The sight of Storm Dancer's golden bronze flesh in the glow of the fire's embers made her weak in the legs. He was dancing slowly to the music, his sinewy arms and thighs flexing, each movement erotic in itself as he disrobed for her.

Rachael licked her lower lip which suddenly seemed dry. She wanted to go to him, to touch him and yet she wanted to stand here forever and watch him dance to the ancient sounding of the hollow drums.

Storm had cast off his buckskin shirt and his chest rippled with his strength as he unlaced his knee-high moccasins standing first on one foot and then the other. He began to chant to the music in a deep, husky voice that sent shivers down Rachael's spine.

When Storm cast aside his moccasins, he began to untie the laces that held his breeches-like leggings. He moved slowly around and around, his hips lifting and falling to the rhythm of the music in the distance. Aroused by his actions and bare flesh, Rachael made a move to come to him, but he shook his head ever so slightly, a playful smile on his lips.

He moved his hands in a graceful yet masculine manner, forming patterns in the air as his body turned and twisted to the sounds that seemed now to surround Rachael, drawing her in. When he spoke, his voice was fluid and sensual like his movements. "First I will disrobe for you, my wife, then you for me."

That thought made Rachael's heart trip in her chest. Watching Storm dance nearly nude in the firelight excited her beyond her wildest thoughts. She could feel her hardening nipples brushing against the soft hide of her white doeskin dress. She could feel a wetness growing between her thighs.

Storm Dancer hooked his thumbs around the band that held his loincloth and Rachael felt her breath catch in her throat.

"Kahiila?" he beckoned, his dark eyes intent upon her.

"Yes," she whispered. *"Kahiila."* The music had caught her and swept her up. She too was moving slowly to the beat, watching Storm as he pulled away the last remnant of his clothing.

Tossing aside the loincloth he danced in a circle around her, stomping his feet in the intricate purposeful pattern of some ancient dance. He teased her with the sway of his muscled buttocks and the flexing of his corded thighs and forearms.

Rachael laughed, allowing him to take her hands and spin her as she joined in his dance of love.

With the encouragement of Storm Dancer's touch, she found her own hands on her doeskin bodice. She traced the laces of the soft hide, bedeviling him as he had bedeviled, enjoying the way his black eyes began to glisten with arousal. Rachael had never been much of a dancer in Philadelphia or London, but this was different. The pounding of the drums and rattle of the gourds made her feel alive. The rhythm carried her from her inhibitions, lifting her up and guiding her movement.

Rachael swayed seductively, shedding her bodice so that her breasts hung free and bare in the firelight. She felt a surge of excitement at the realization that he was watching her as intently as she had watched him.

Storm moved his hands in a dance that told the story of the creation of the world and Rachael mirrored him, their gazes locking, then straying, then locking again as they spun and dipped.

Rachael's hips undulated in a graceful circle as she

unwrapped her doeskin and threw it aside, dancing nude save for her woman's loinskin.

Storm came to her, catching her hands and bringing his hips against hers, his tumescent shaft brushing against her most private place. Waves of heat and pleasure washed over Rachael as she swayed to the rhythm that had lured them and now controlled them. For the Lenni Lenape the song was a celebration of life, for Rachael and Storm Dancer, it was a celebration of reunited love.

Storm cupped Rachael's bare buttocks, guiding her against him again and again. He was kissing her now, confusing her with his hot hands and hotter mouth. "Love me, *ki-ti-hi,*" he whispered, "love me the rest of the days this man must walk on this earth."

"Yes," she whispered, struggling to catch her breath, caught in the rhythm of him brushing against her in tantalizing intervals. "Yes, I will love you, husband. I will love you always." She fumbled with the tie of her loincloth but could not manage the knot.

He laughed, brushing aside her trembling hands and kissing her deeply as he shed her pieces of clothing for her.

When they were finally both naked in the firelight, he lifted her into his arms and lay her gently on the sleeping fur she had laid out for them. Resting on his side with her on her back he began to touch her, savoring the softness of her flesh, every soft curve of her body.

When he lowered his head, she held her breath in anticipation until his lips touched her peaked breast. Threading her fingers through his midnight hair, she moaned, lifting her hips, needing him, and yet wanting to prolong this exquisite agony forever.

"Come to me," she whispered in his ear as he tugged on her nipple with his teeth, the pleasure exquisite. "Come to me, Dancer of the Storms. Love this woman as she must be loved."

"You are impatient," he teased as he lifted up and stretched over her. "I have but barely found my rhythm."

But Rachael parted her thighs as his hips brushed hers and gently, insistently, he entered her. She cried out in sheer relief, her blunt fingernails sinking into the flesh of his broad back. He let her catch her breath and then he began to move to the sound of the wedding drums.

Consumed by the fire of his shaft deep within her, Rachael lifted again and again to meet his thrusts. A heavy-limbed aching filled her, propelling her upward, lifting her beyond all conscious thought. Without warning she felt herself shatter with pleasure, not once but twice, three times and yet he still moved inside her, deeper, harder.

"Storm," Rachael called, her entire body shuddering. "Storm!"

He raised himself up on his arms so that he could drink in her sky-eyes and for a moment their gazes locked, then suddenly, he, too, was caught in a wave of pleasure that couldn't be denied. Rachael heard him groan as he spilled into her with a final thrust and she smiled, her hands falling to rest on his buttocks as his movement stilled.

For a long time they lay entwined, neither wanting to break from the other. The feel of Storm's hard, male body pressed to her soft curves gave Rachael a sense of security. It was not until she had almost drifted off to sleep that he rolled off her onto his side and drew her into his arms covering them both with a light blanket.

"Sleep, my love, my Rachael-wife," he whispered. "Sleep and tomorrow we will begin our life anew."

Chapter Twenty-Five

The following day Storm Dancer rose early to join some of the younger men in hunting. He kissed Rachael soundly on the lips and covered her with an extra sleeping fur, promising to return by midday. Drowsy, she had waved a good-bye and turned over to go back to sleep, content to dream.

Rachael slept late into the morning and when she finally rose and went to the river to fetch fresh water she found that the entire village was up and about and chattering about the fact the shaman and his wife were obviously together again. Rachael had just returned to Tuuban's wigwam when Dory came hustling toward her calling her name.

"Rachael-honey!"

Rachael turned and smiled. "The wedding was beautiful." She shielded her eyes agaist the glare of the morning sunshine reflecting off the snow. "I'm sorry I didn't get a chance to wish you congratulations properly."

"Well word has it you was busy with a little merry-makin' of your own." Dory winked.

Rachael laughed. "Just the same, I hope you'll be very happy. I know you will."

"Yeah. Yeah," she waved her hand, "enough of that talk. I got serious business here."

Rachael's brow creased. "What is it? What's wrong?"

Dory gave a nod in the direction of the wigwam that rightfully belonged to Storm Dancer and Rachael but was now occupied by Ta-wa-ne. "It's that bitch. You best keep an eye on her. Sometime after you and that man of yours disappeared, the trapper Malvin came back into the village. Ta-wa-ne took him to her bed, leavin' the boy to wander in the ceremonial house."

"Is Ka-we-ras all right?"

"Course he is. I tucked him right in with Shadow Man's little ones and he slept through the night without a peep, but come mornin'," she raised a finger, "his mother was hollerin' for the child."

"Why didn't you wake me? What did you do?"

Dory shrugged. "What could I do? She's still the boy's mama, and Storm Dancer had already left. Shadow Man said to hand him over so I did."

Rachael gripped Dory's arms. "So where is he now?"

"He's in there with his mama, but I just thought you might want to keep your eye on 'em both. Shadow Man told me last night that she had offered to sell 'im to Storm Dancer with a handful o' witnesses standin' right there listenin'!" She gave a low whistle. "That trollop's crazy as a bedbug in bedlam. No tellin' what she might do."

Rachael nodded, glancing across the compound at

Ta-wa-ne's wigwam. There was no one to be seen, but she could tell that the door flap was laced from the inside. "As soon as Storm gets back something will have to be done. We'll call a council meeting if we have to. If she's living with us, she's under Starlight's jurisdiction."

Dory patted Rachael's arm, trying to comfort her friend. "Now don't be gettin' your dander in a ruffle. I just wanted you to know what the woman was about, so's you could keep your eye on her and the little tot. This is the boy's father's affair, not yours. Let him deal with it."

"I suppose you're right. I just wouldn't want anything terrible to happen to him."

"I know you wouldn't. Go on with your chores and I'll keep my eyes peeled too. The men folk'll be back before long. Now I got to get back to my little ones."

Dory took her leave and Rachael picked up her ice bucket and ducked into her wigwam.

Not half an hour later Rachael heard a woman screeching at the top of her lungs. She knew immediately who it was—Ta-wa-ne.

Rachael stepped out into the snow, not taking the time to grab her cloak. She shivered, hugging herself for warmth as she craned her neck to see what Ta-wa-ne was about.

The trapper had come out of Ta-wa-ne's wigwam dressed for travel in a long bearskin coat with packs on his back. Ta-wa-ne was shouting at him in Iroquois as she followed him, dragging Ka-we-ras behind her.

Twice the trapper turned around and barked a reply.

Rachael couldn't understand everything Ta-wa-ne

was saying, but it was obvious she wanted to go with him and he was telling her to stay put. Ka-we-ras was screaming and crying, dragging his feet as his mother jerked him along behind her.

Without hesitation Rachael sprinted across the compound after Ta-wa-ne and the trapper, who was obviously taking his leave. Ka-we-ras was only half dressed with one moccasin on and one off and no mittens. He wore the little otterskin cloak Rachael had made for him, tied over one shoulder and dragging in the snow.

Rachael knew that Ta-wa-ne had a right to go where she pleased, and she'd be thankful to have Storm's ex-wife gone, but Ta-wa-ne didn't have a right to endanger Ka-we-ras. If she was going to run after her trapper in a February cold snap, she was going to have to leave the child behind where he'd be safe.

The moment Ka-we-ras spotted Rachael, he began to cry for her, calling her name and reaching for her with his little cold chubby hands. Rachael stepped in front of Ta-wa-ne crossing her arms over her chest, her teeth gritted. "Go with your trapper but let the boy go."

"Out of my way, white whore who stole my husband. The child is mine; I can take him where I do wish!"

"He is also his father's, a great and powerful shaman. He has as much right to him as you, more because you are unfit to be a mother!" She pointed an accusing finger into Ta-wa-ne's beautiful face. "You don't want Ka-we-ras, you just want him so that you can manipulate others. Leave him here where he'll be safe."

Ta-wa-ne's black almond-shaped eyes narrowed

venomously. "This woman would rather drown him like a pup than leave him to you!" She gave Rachael a vicious shove, shoving her backward into the snow. Before Rachael could get to her feet, Ta-wa-ne swept Ka-we-ras into her arms and began to run after the trapper.

By this time many of the women and children had come out of their wigwams to see what all of the commotion was about. One of the women had run to get Starlight. Ta-wa-ne was shouting at the trapper again, screaming for him to wait for her. She was telling him in a mixture of Iroquois and English how much she loved him and how well she would please him if he would only let her go with him.

Rachael got up and began to run after them. They had passed the outer boundaries of the village and were now headed down the snow-shoveled path that led to the river.

"Ta-wa-ne!" Rachael shouted. "Let him go!"

"Wachael!" Ka-we-ras was crying. He had lost his cloak and was now being carried over his mother's shoulder like a sack of cornmeal.

Tears of frustration rose in Rachael's eyes as she raced to catch up with them. It was not until Ta-wa-ne reached the riverbank that Rachael finally caught up with her. The trapper had walked out on the frozen river and was headed east. Ta-wa-ne had already stepped out on the ice.

"Ta-wa-ne, please," Rachael stopped on the edge of the bank. "Please let me have him. His father will care for him well, I swear it."

"Malvin! Malvin!" Ta-wa-ne called, ignoring Rachael's pleas. "Wait for me, Husband! Wait for this woman! I will give you the boy! We can sell him. We can get coin!"

Rachael looked down at the snow-covered ice of the river, panic rising in her chest. Storm had told her not to go out on the ice, not ever, but Ta-wa-ne was getting away! She was taking Storm's son, the only son he might ever have."

"No Rachael-honey!" Rachael heard Dory cry.

Tentatively, Rachael stepped down off the bank onto the ice. "I'll be careful," she called over her shoulder. "I'm just going to get Ka-we-ras!"

"Get off that ice, girl! It ain't safe!"

Rachael hurried after Ta-wa-ne who was walking a few feet from the bank. "Give him to me!"

Ta-wa-ne spun around in fury. "You want the useless boy?" she shouted. "Take him! He is nothing but a burden to this woman!" With that, Ta-wa-ne threw the boy off her shoulder and hurled him through the air.

Rachael leaped to catch the child before he hit the hard ice and the ice beneath her feet cracked and groaned. Ka-we-ras was sobbing and shivering so hard that his teeth chattered. He clung to Rachael, sobbing her name over and over again.

"Take the boy, but this as well!" Ta-wa-ne shouted as she swung around and struck Rachael in the jaw, stunning her. The next time the Indian woman swung, Rachael had the sense to duck. She ducked, spun around, and shoved Ka-we-ras across the ice in the direction of the bank. "Go to Dory," she told the little boy as he slid across the snow on his bottom. "Go!"

"Wachael!"

"I said go!" Rachael shouted harshly, fearful the boy would come back toward her.

Still crying her name, Ka-we-ras jumped to his feet and ran for the bank toward Dory who waited with open arms.

Just as Dory caught the boy, Rachael felt her feet being knocked out from under her. The ice groaned as she hit it with a loud thump.

The village women who stood on the bank were shouting for Rachael and Ta-wa-ne to get off the ice.

Ta-wa-ne gave a screech of rage, hurling herself at Rachael, but Rachael rolled over and bounced up before Ta-wa-ne's body made contact with hers. Just as Rachael turned to face her attacker she spotted the glimmer of a knife's blade held tightly in the Indian woman's mitten.

Rachael held up her hands in peace. "Enough. Go with you. Your man is getting away."

Ta-wa-ne brandished the knife, lowering to a crouch. "You took my man."

"You left him!"

"You took my son!"

Rachael laughed at the ridiculousness of her statement. "You threw him at me! You said you didn't want him!" She lowered her voice an octave. "Ta-wa-ne, I have no malice toward you. My husband has his son, and he will be well cared for. Now go. Go with the trapper. It's what you want isn't it? To be rid of the child and the responsibility?"

Ta-wa-ne glanced past Rachael to see that the trapper was indeed still walking east.

"Go," Rachael urged gently. "I'll tell Storm you left

the boy for him."

Ta-wa-ne lowered her knife, straightening. Rachael took a step back and aside to let the woman pass. She could hear the ice groaning beneath her, cracks forming around them. She was already hedging toward the safety of solid ground. "Go with him, but go along the bank," she warned Ta-wa-ne, still watching her movements closely. "It's not safe to walk on the ice, the current is too fast. The ice isn't solid."

"Wait!" Ta-wa-ne called to the trapper. "Wait for this woman!" She started toward him.

Rachael had just turned away when out of the corner of her eye she saw Ta-wa-ne's hand snake out. Rachael felt a white-hot streak of pain across her arm as she put it up to protect herself. Immediately her thin muslin shirt turned scarlet with blood. Before Rachael could think, she swung her leg, kicking Ta-wa-ne in the arm to ward off the next blow.

Ta-wa-ne groaned in pain as the knife was knocked from her hand and went skittering across the ice. Rachael looked down at her arm, which was now bleeding profusely. She looked up at Ta-wa-ne and gave a shout of anger as she balled her hand, and sank her fist into Ta-wa-ne's stomach.

The Indian woman went down with a groan of pain.

"Now get up and go," Rachael shouted with authority ignoring the blood that dripped from her arm onto the white snow. "Go from this place and do not ever come back again 'else this woman will slit open your belly and hang you from a tree so that the crows may eat your entrails!"

Ta-wa-ne shrunk back in superstitious horror and

made a hand signal to ward off any evil curses her enemy might be silently flinging. Still watching Rachael, the Indian woman scrambled to her feet and began to run toward the center of the river. She screamed the trapper's name and he hollered over his shoulder for her to go back.

Rachael watched as Ta-wa-ne caught up with Malvin and he spun around, striking her in the mouth with his fist. Ta-wa-ne fell onto the ice and a horrible cracking sound rent the air.

Dory screamed for Rachael to run for the bank as that entire section of the river began to crack. Rachael was just reaching the bank when she heard the first splash and as she turned she saw the river sucking up both the trapper and Ta-wa-ne.

"Ta-wa-ne!" Rachael screamed. Though she hated the woman, drowning beneath the black ice was no way for anyone to die. Without thinking, Rachael turned back toward the river, thinking perhaps she could help the woman out. She could see her dark head bobbing up and down in the hole as the woman struggled to pull herself up out of the water. Each time she caught a piece of solid ice and tried to heave herself up and out, the piece broke dropping her back into the water. The trapper was nowhere to be seen.

"Oh no you don't," Dory shouted, stepping out on the ice to catch Rachael's arm and drag her toward the bank. "Ain't no use in you dyin' too."

"Dory, we can't just let them drown," Rachael protested, struggling to break free from her friend.

"It's too late," Dory shouted, trying to make Rachael understand. "The whole river's breakin' up!"

Just then a huge crack zigzagged toward them and both Rachael and Dory dove for the safety of the bank.

Rachael felt the frigid water on the toe of her moccasin as one of the village women pulled her up off the ice as it broke. Rachael fell onto the snowy bank exhausted and in shock from blood loss. Somehow Ka-we-ras found her and crawled into her arms. Rachael hugged the toddler tightly, crying in relief that Storm's son was safe and in sorrow for the death of Ta-wa-ne and the trapper. Dory came to kneel beside her to look at her wound.

"She's deep," Rachael heard Dory say to one of the other women. "But a few stitches'll fix 'er right up."

Rachael's mind was hazy for the next few hours. She was ushered back to Tuuban's wigwam by the women and given a ghastly tasting concoction to drink. The women then cleansed her wound and sewed it. With the help of the medicinal tea, Rachael barely felt the stitches. She was then stripped naked and tucked into Storm Dancer's sleeping furs with hot stones at her feet. Rachael remembered wanting to get up and care for Ka-we-ras but she was so cold that she couldn't think straight and her words seemed fuzzy . . . and the bed furs felt so warm. Dory kept assuring her that the child was fine and soon Rachael relaxed and drifted off to sleep.

The next thing Rachael knew it was late in the afternoon and Storm Dancer was kneeling beside her carefully rewrapping the bandages of her arm. "Storm?"

He smiled. "I see my she-cat has struck again."

She tried to sit up but he gently pressed her back onto the sleeping mats. "Storm, she drowned, they both drowned, we couldn't save them."

"Of course you couldn't. The whole river has broken today." He kissed her. "But you saved Ka-we-ras."

She closed her eyes, licking her dry lips and then opened them again. "I told her not to walk on the ice, I told her—"

"Shhh," he hushed her. "We all choose our own fate, Rachael-wife. Ta-wa-ne chose hers."

"But—"

He pressed a finger to his lips. "My son is alive and that is what is important." He took her hands. "Now listen, Rachael, I must ask you a question and then I will leave you to sleep." He squeezed her hands in his, waiting until she gazed up at him with her sky-eyes.

"Tell me, Wife, are you certain that you can accept my son in our wigwam, because if you cannot there are others who can take him."

She shook her head, struggling to remain conscious and make sense as she spoke. "I have a responsibility to my husband's child. Now no more of that talk; he'll live with us."

He tucked her hands under the bed fur. "Well enough then, my brave Rachael. Sleep now."

She closed her eyes, snuggling down into the warm blankets. "Storm?"

"Yes, my love. This man is still here."

"I have been thinking about those horses and the supplies we will need to get across the Ohio River."

"You must rest now." He smoothed her dark hair. "We will speak of the matter when you have rested."

"But I have a good idea." She opened her eyes to look up at him and brought her hand out from under the covers to touch his. "Promise you won't get mad or misunderstand."

His midnight hair brushed across his shoulders as he shook his head. "I could have no anger in my heart for you today after you risked your life to save my son."

Feeling dizzy, she closed her eyes. "We could go to Philadelphia, I know it's not far." She opened her eyes to see his expression. She saw caution, but no fear, no anger. "I have money, Storm, money meant to be my dowry when I married Gifford. It's not a lot to some, but it would be a great deal to the Lenni Lenape."

"We do not need your money, my dearest wife."

"I have a right to it, Storm, and I have a right to do with it what I wish. I wish to buy horses and supplies to aid us in our journey west." With that said, she closed her eyes again. Her arm was beginning to throb.

"We will talk more tomorrow."

"Tomorrow," she whispered already drifting off to sleep.

The following morning the bodies of Ta-wa-ne and the trapper were found at the edge of the river a few miles downstream of the village. Warriors carried the bodies back so that they could be prepared for proper burial. Rachael offered to assist the other women in the cleansing of the bodies but Storm Dancer refused to let her leave the wigwam. Instead he gave her Ka-we-ras to entertain and he went to make plans for a proper funeral.

Rachael had just settled down to play a game of clay marbles with Storm's little boy when Storm Dancer came back into the wigwam. His face was pale, his mouth drawn back in a frown. "Ka-we-ras," he called from the doorway.

The boy looked up and seeing his father, he bounced to his feet and ran as fast as his two-year-old legs could carry him. *"Nukkuaa!* Papa!"

Storm lifted him into the air and the boy gave a squeal of delight. He didn't seem to care that his mother was gone forever, all that mattered was that he was to live with his father.

Storm tickled his round belly and then set him gently on the floor and turned him around and lifted up his shirt.

"What are you doing?" Rachael asked. "What's wrong, Storm."

He lowered the boy's buckskin shirt slowly.

"Storm?"

He leaned over Ka-we-ras. "Put on your cloak and mittens and go find Dory in her wigwam. Can you do that, Ka-we-ras?" He had already picked up the toddler's cloak and was helping him into it.

Ka-we-ras nodded. "This boy can find Dory," he answered in perfect Algonquian.

Storm tied his cloak tightly, slipped his mittens over his hands and let him out the door. He stood and watched until the child reached Dory's wigwam and the woman gave a wave.

Storm let the flap fall and turned to face Rachael.

"What is it?" She rose, frightened by the look on his face. "Please tell me, Storm. Is Ka-we-ras sick."

He shook his head, taking her into his arms. "He is not mine," he said, regret obvious in his voice.

Rachael pulled back. "What?"

The boy is not mine. Ta-wa-ne lied to me. Ka-we-ras belonged to the trapper."

"How do you know?" She brushed her fingertips over his cheek. "How can you be certain?"

"The mark of birth on Ka-we-ras's back . . ."

"Yes?" Rachael frowned. "What about it?"

"It is identical to the one on the back of the man called Malvin. Dory found it."

Rachael looked away. "Oh." Her lower lip quivered. What Storm Dancer was saying was that he had no child of his loins. Ta-we-ne had not given him one and Rachael might not be able to either. Tears formed in her eyes. "I'm sorry, Storm. I'm so sorry."

He frowned, and seeing her tears, pulled her against him. "Why do you cry, Wife?" He wiped the tears that rolled down her cheeks with his hand.

"Because I cannot give you a child. Because you wanted a child so badly."

Her thought on her words for a moment, slightly confused. "You do not understand. I come to tell you this, not as an accusation. I came to tell you that you are no longer responsible to this boy. He can go to another. He is not mine, so you do not have to care for him."

"Don't have to!" She laughed. "But I love Ka-we-ras! It's just that I thought you wanted a child of your own blood. I would gladly take him if you're willing."

Storm Dancer pulled her tightly against him. "Of course I would take the child, no matter who he belongs to. I, too, love him, and that love is not greater than the love that could spring from my own bloodline." He leaned back so that he could stare into her sky-eyes. "It is settled, then? The boy is ours?"

"Ka-we-ras is the son of Storm Dancer and Rachael. We will adopt him as is the custom of the Lenni Lenape." She paused. "And when the spring comes you and I will set out for Philadelphia. We will get my money and we will buy the horses and supplies we need to travel west."

He studied her for a long moment and then leaned down to kiss her. "Very well, my wife," he murmured against her lips. "Very well, wise woman."

Chapter Twenty-Six

Philadelphia, Pennsylvania Colony
April, 1762

Rachael stood just inside the woods line, invisible to the passing carriages of Philadelphians. She took several deep breaths to gather her courage as she observed them. Just behind her she knew Storm Dancer stood, waiting, watching.

"You do not have to do this," he murmured in a constricted voice.

"I do," she whispered, unable to resist one last glimpse of his handsome face. It was for Storm Dancer that she would do this . . . for love of him and those who had taken her in. "I have a right to that money and I want your people—our people—to have it." She glanced back at the road just as another carriage rolled by. The passengers were laughing and chattering, but their voices seemed unfamiliar to her. Their King's English sounded awkward and guttural to her ears. It was the sweet melodious language of the Lenni Lenape she now spoke and thought in as well.

"I would go with you, Wife. You have only to speak the words."

She could hear the uncertainty in his voice. They had talked of trust on their trip north to Philadelphia and Rachael had sworn her love for him, promising she would not leave him, but she wondered if he was now afraid. Did he think there was the remote chance she might not come back to him once she was reminded of the life she had left behind?

She lifted her dark lashes to meet his gaze. "We agreed, Storm, that it was better if I went alone. I'll go to Gifford's barrister, get the necessary paperwork, and collect my funds from the goldsmith." They assumed Gifford had never made it back alive. How could he have? "I'll be back by nightfall. Then we can go home to Ka-we-ras. You and some of the other men can go to Annapolis to buy our horses and supplies. It's a good plan and you know it."

Storm knew that, logically, Rachael was right. This was the easiest way to accomplish what they had come for, but just the same, he hated to let her go alone. He felt as if he were throwing her to a den of winter wolves. "Go then," he forced himself to say. "And may the wind of luck be at your back."

"Luck? I need no luck. There'll be nothing to it."

He reached out to touch her hand, to look one last time into her sky-eyes. She was dressed in her best white buckskins, her hair careful braided and adorned with shells from the Chesapeake Bay. Across one cheek she wore the mark of their tribe in blue and red paint. "Come back to me soon, my love."

She laughed, shrugging off the strange sense of foreboding that teased the recesses of her mind. "I'll be back by tonight, now just stay out of sight. Someone spots you skulking in the woods and you'll have the entire city of Philadelphia frightened of an impending Indian attack." She withdrew her hand from his and pursed her lips in the air in a kiss. Then she turned away from her husband and stepped out onto the roadway she had traveled nearly a year ago the day she was kidnapped by Broken Horn.

Rachael had not walked half a mile toward Philadelphia when she heard a carriage approaching from behind. She tried to slow her pounding heart as she waited for the vehicle to draw close enough for her to call to one of the occupants. She didn't want to be here. She wanted to be with Storm and Ka-we-ras back at the village. But somehow this return to Philadelphia was the way for her to break off her last ties with the woman she had once been. She would try to find Thomas or leave a letter so that her family would know she had survived and then she would truly be able to leave the life of Lady Rachael Moreover behind.

She turned around to face the carriage and waved her arms over her head. "Help me! Help me," she cried, trying to sound sincere as she stepped out into the middle of the rutted roadway. "Please help me!" She and Storm had agreed that it was best if she played the role of a captive of the Iroquois who had escaped. If her goal was to get into the city as quickly as possible, this was the surest way.

Startled, the driver of the open carriage jerked on his leather reins, yanking the horses to a halt. The occupants, a potbellied, middle-aged man with a whiskered face, and three young girls, stood to get a better look at the woman dressed in buckskins and to hear her first words.

"Ma'am?" The driver's eyes were wide with uncertainty. He looked over his shoulder at his master.

Rachael's skin was so suntanned and her hair so dark that she knew they were trying to figure if she was English or a savage. "Please help me," she repeated in English, the words tasting funny on the tip of her tongue. "I've been walking for days."

"I'm John Calmary." He tipped back his cocked hat. "Have you need of assistance, young woman?" the gentleman in the carriage called.

Rachael walked around the vehicle to speak with John Calmary. "Sir, would you help me? My name is Lady Rachael Moreover—"

"Precious Mary, Mother of God!" He looked her up and down taking in the braided hair, the white buckskin skirt and tunic, and the face paint. "You're the woman who was captured by the savages last year! You're Langston's bride!"

She was taken off guard. *His bride?* She almost protested, but on second thought she decided it was best to play along until she could figure out what this man was talking about. What would make this man think she and Gifford had been married? "That's . . . that's correct. I . . . I've escaped from the Indians. I need to get to Viscount Langston's barrister's home. I know the viscount is dead but—"

"Dead? Indeed not. Your husband's alive and well. A miracle you both survived." His teenager girls tittered, covering their mouths with lacy handkerchiefs. "I saw the viscount but a week ago at his new country estate on the Schulkil."

For a moment Rachael was too startled to speak. Gifford alive? She'd really not considered the fact that he might have made it back to civilization alive, though now she wondered why she hadn't. Perhaps because she secretly wished him dead. That and because he'd seemed so incapable of caring for himself. She thought of how Gifford, the man who had supposedly loved her, had abandoned her in the forest, leaving her to Broken Horn. She thought of the promise he had made to come back for her if he made it out of Iroquois country alive.

Rachael set her jaw. Alive is he? *So he had told everyone they were married and then passed her off as being dead? The heel.* "Thank God Gifford's alive," she proclaimed. *This way I can kill the coward myself.* She tried to sound meek as she rested her hand on the carriage door. "Would you . . . could you take me to him . . . my husband I mean?" She had a difficult time getting the words out of her mouth, but she'd come this far. She'd not back down now.

"God's bowels!" John Calmary threw up his arms in distress as he hurried to throw open the door and help Rachael into the carriage. "You just had me in such shock, Lady Langston. I . . . I truly am not responsible for my own actions."

Rachael allowed him to assist her into the carriage although she certainly could have leapt in herself. She sat between two of the man's daughters, both as plump and plumed as partridges. She greeted them, but they only giggled.

The fifteen-minute carriage ride to Gifford's house was awkward. John Calmary was anxious for the sordid details of her capture and questioned her extensively, while the three young women giggled incessantly.

Rachael asked John if he knew her brother, but he did not. She was hoping she would get a chance to see Thomas one last time, though she knew there was little chance of it. It seemed he had spent most of his life at sea.

Finally the carriage rolled up Fourth Street to the city residence owned by Gifford. It was a three story L-shaped brick house with extensive gardens in the back. It was here that Rachael had resided with Gifford and his old senile Aunt Emma who was meant to chaperone them. *Chaperone.* That was a joke. It was right here in this stately house, with dear Aunt Emma sleeping upright in a chair in the parlor, that Gifford had tried to seduce Rachael, even offering money for her maiden head!

It all seemed so ludicrous when she thought back now. Why hadn't it then?

The carriage wheels rolled to a halt and John Calmary leaped down, straightened his coat, and reached up to help Rachael out of the vehicle.

"I thank you for your kindness, John." She turned, dismissing him but he followed her around the back of the carriage toward the front steps.

"Let . . . let me escort you inside, Lady Langston."

"No, no thank you," she said firmly. "I'd rather go alone. You understand?" She didn't want to sound ungrateful, on the other hand, she wanted no audience when she came face-to-face with Gifford. What she had to say to that man was for his ears and his alone.

Just then the front door swung open. After assuming Gifford was dead all these months, Rachael thought she should feel some sense of relief to see him alive. After all, he was the man she'd once thought she'd loved. But as she looked at him standing tall and handsome in the morning sunlight, she felt no relief, no joy, only burning rage.

Gifford swept off his scarlet cocked hat. "I say there, John Calmary, what are you— Holy God!"

The woman coming out of the door behind him clamped her hand over mouth with a gasp as she reached for Gifford for support. She was an attractive woman with yellow-blond hair and billowing lemon yellow skirts with a matching bonnet. She was obviously several years older than Gifford, trying to look several years younger.

Rachael stood on the cobblestone sidewalk in her Indian garb looking up at Gifford with a wide-eyed, aggressive stare.

"R . . . Rachael?"

"Gifford . . . She smiled the smile one uses when facing her opponent. Her voice was as smooth as silk and laced with razor-edged steel.

"Sweet Jesus!" He looked from John Calmary to the woman clutching his lace sleeve and back at Rachael again.

For a moment Rachael thought he might faint. Obviously he had assumed she died the night he left her alone in the woods to defend herself against Broken Horn. Obviously he had assumed he would never see her again. Obviously by walking into his life like this, she had set a few matters askew.

Suddenly Gifford snapped into action and came running down the steps. He threw his arms around Rachael like a long lost lover would and pulled her tightly against him. "Praise God, you're alive, dear wife!"

"Wife!" she murmured so that only he could hear her. "Wife, Gifford? I don't recall becoming your *wife."*

He pulled back, holding her shoulders, pretending not to have heard her. "I can't believe you're alive. My prayers have been answered!"

"I found her wandering along the roadway," John Calmary offered with an air of importance. "The poor woman was nearly out of her head. Lucky I came along, 'else I don't know what would have come of her, Viscount."

"Bless you, John Calmary! I will forever be indebted to you. Should you ever need my assistance—"

"Enough of the socializing," Rachael interrupted. "I'll have a word with you inside, *Husband,"* she intoned. *"Now."*

"God in heaven!" Gifford proclaimed. "I've got to get her inside before she collapses!" he apologized to John. He tried to put his arms around Rachael but she shrugged him off.

"Inside, Gifford," she repeated.

"My apologies." Gifford looked up at John Calmary. "Please excuse us. My wife has been through a terrible ordeal. She's not herself."

"I understand fully, Viscount," John answered, still standing in the same spot on the cobblestone walk watching them.

Gifford tried to take Rachael's hand to lead her inside, but she pulled away. "I've gotten this far on my own, I think I can make into the house, don't you?" she asked, unable to control the sarcasm in her voice.

Gifford stepped inside the front door with Rachael

following. The blond woman he had been leaving the house with stood in the hallway, her eyes riveted on Gifford. "Your wife? Your wife has returned? I thought you said she was dead," she said through clenched teeth, speaking about Rachael as if she weren't present.

"I thought she was dead," Gifford responded carefully. "But she isn't. Thank the Good Lord she's alive and well." He clapped his hands. "Margaret!"

His bedraggled housekeeper came wandering down the hall, obviously in no hurry to respond to her master's call. "Yeah, Viscount. I'm comin'." When she looked up she gave a gasp and threw up three fingers to ward off evil. "Holy hell, she's come back to haunt ye, Viscount. She's been reincarnated as an Injun!"

"No, no Rachael hasn't come back to haunt me, Margaret. Now, stop being ridiculous. You'll have the entire household in an uproar. Lady Langston's been rescued. My dear wife has been rescued from the savages. Now have someone start a bath for her and prepare her room. We'll put her straight to bed of course."

"Bed?" Rachael lifted an eyebrow. "I think not." She grasped Gifford's arm tightly and pointed down the hall toward his study. "I think we have some matters to discuss, don't you?" She looked over her shoulder at the woman still standing in the hallway staring. Rachael smiled sweetly, wondering just how long Gifford had waited before bringing the tart into his house. "You'll excuse us, of course?"

"Gifford!" the woman cried. "Gifford, I wish to speak to you immediately."

"Not now, Jesslyn."

"Gifford . . ."

"Not now!" he barked sharply as he walked down the hallway and pushed open the door to his study. Rachael passed him and stepped into the room. "We're not to be disturbed, Margaret, not by anyone for any reason. Make tea and leave it outside the door."

Margaret followed them down the hallway, muttering to herself about how perhaps Rachael was a haunt and she was the only one that suspected it.

The minute Gifford closed the study door, Rachael turned on him. *"Your wife?"* She tried hard to control her rage. "You told everyone we were married and that I was dead?"

He plucked off his befeathered cocked hat and set it down on the cherry sideboard. He reached for a glass. "Rachael love, let me—"

"How could you have done such a thing?" She was shocked, though she didn't know why. This was certainly not beyond Gifford. But what would possess him to make up such lies. Why would he do it? For the sympathy? Perhaps. She supposed he had gotten a great deal of attention after escaping an Iroquois Indian capture. . . . Perhaps the fact that he had lost his wife just added to the story. But perhaps he had ulterior motives. Not that it mattered, because it didn't. Whatever Gifford had said or done in the past made no difference in her life now. She would get her money and she would leave him with his lies.

Gifford poured himself a more than healthy portion of brandy, his hand shaking so badly that the glass clinked as he tried to pour from the bottle. "You must let me explain."

She crossed her arms over her chest. She despised having to even stand in the same room with him, and this one of all rooms. She had always hated this room with its dark paneled walls and cases of dead butterflies pinned to boards and enclosed in glass. All she wanted was to get away from here. To go home to the village. To be with Storm Dancer and their little son.

She looked him squarely in the eye. "I want no explanations. I want my dowry money. I want to see my brother and then I'll go."

She watched him as he took a long swallow of his brandy. He was still as handsome in a boyish sort of way as she had remembered him, though his hairline had receded a good deal. He was dressed in an obviously expensive scarlet brocaded coat and breeches with a laced stock shirt and clocked stockings. On his feet he wore a pair of scarlet heeled shoes. She wondered absently if he knew how utterly ridiculous he truly looked.

"You . . . you want your dowry?" He took another gulp of the fiery liquid. "But, love, now that you've returned we can go on with our life as planned. Our home is done." He looked up anxiously. "You'll love it, truly you will."

"Gifford." Her eyes narrowed dangerously. "You listen and you listen well. I am not the woman you left to die in the forest at the hands of a brutal savage. I will not play your games any longer, and I will not be manipulated by your sweet hollow words. I want my money. You give it to me and I'll walk out of here. I don't care what you tell people—that we were married, or we weren't, or that I was eaten by savages. It matters not. I just want what was rightfully mine and I want it now."

He set down his glass and pulled a lacy orange-water

scented handkerchief from his sleeve and wiped his perspiring forehead. His eyes were darting back and forth like those of a caged rodent. "And where are you going to go with this money?" he asked, taking the defensive. "No man will have you after what you've endured among the savages." He flung out his hand. "Look at you. You look so much like them, I thought you were one when I first laid eyes on you!"

"Not that it's your affair, but I have married now and have a child." She smiled proudly. "I have married Storm Dancer, brother to Broken Horn."

"They forced you?"

She shook her head. "I married Storm of my own free will . . . because I loved him."

"A red nigger." He laughed. "You married one of those futtering heathens when you would not marry me?" He looked up at her for a moment as if he thought she had lost her mind, but when he saw the steady gaze in her eyes, he knew she had not. She was entirely serious. He paused for a split second, then spoke. "All right, Rachael, all right." He lifted his hand, the handkerchief fluttering. "Let me go see about sending for the funds and then we'll see what we can do. It may take some time."

"I'm not jesting with you, Gifford. You give me my money or I'll tell everyone what you did. I'll tell them how you left me to be tortured and killed. Then how popular will you be? Who will want to come to your parties then?"

He backed up toward the door. "I'll be right back. Just wait for me."

She gave a nod, and turned toward the window to look out on the garden. She tried to ignore the cases of butterflies that adorned the walls of his study. She tried to ignore their motionles bodies and sightless eyes. She wrinkled her nose. The room smelled musty and dank. There was a hint of the scent of preservative in the still air.

Gifford closed the paneled study door behind him and leaned against it, squeezing his eyes shut.

"What the bloody hell is going on here?" Jesslyn came down the hall.

Gifford looked up. His fiancée had removed her traveling cloak and hat. He could see she was damned furious. He touched his lips with his finger. "Shh, or she'll hear you!"

"You lyin' son of a bitch!" She slapped him across the cheek, leaving a red palm print. "You said she was dead. I gave you all of that damned money of my father's to finish that bloody house and now you've already got a wife?"

He massaged his cheek as he went down the hallway toward the winter kitchen. "I'll take care of it, Jesslyn."

"Take care of it? Take care of a wife? You swore you would marry me!"

"And I will." He felt calmer now. He had a plan. A plan that could work. This could be handled. He need not lose face among his friends. he need not lose Jesslyn and all her father's money. He just had to remain calm and do what had to be done. "Jesslyn, I want you to go home."

"Go home! If you think—"

He whipped around and caught her by a lock of stiff bleached blond hair. "Are you listening to me?"

She grabbed his hand. "Ouch, you bastard. You're hurting me!"

He brought his face inches from hers, his upper lip curling in dissatisfaction. "Now you go home to your father and you stay there until I call for you, do you understand me?" He released her.

She rubbed her forehead to ease the pain of her pulled hair. "What are you going to do? Tell me. Just how are you going to fix this mess?"

"Go home now!"

"Very well, but I'll not wait long." She tried to smooth her hair. "I'm warning you, you futter this up and you'll regret it, Viscount Gifford Langston. I swear to God you will. I'll see you a pauper on the street!"

A few minutes later Gifford entered his study with a tray of tea and cakes from the kitchen. He was smiling now, once again in control of himself. "I've sent for the funds."

"The goldsmith is coming?"

"It's being taken care of, Rachael." He set down the tea tray. "It will only be a little while."

She turned away from the window. "Have you heard from Thomas? Do you know where he is? I'd like to see him before I go."

Gifford poured a cup of tea and offered it to her. She took it though she didn't know why, politeness she supposed.

He drew in a breath. "I'm sorry to have to tell you this, Rachael love but . . ."

"But what?" He offered her a plate of cakes, but she shook her head. "What Gifford? What's happened to Thomas?"

He lowered his head. "Drowned at sea. Just after we

were captured I'm afraid."

Rachael looked away, tears pooling in her eyes. Her brother never knew she was safe, then. He would never know of the happiness she had found with Storm Dancer and her life among the Lenni Lenape. She took a deep sip of the tea. It had been overly sweetened and tasted bitter, but she drank it anyway.

"Where was he when it happened?"

"Good God, somewhere in the Indies, I think." Gifford poured himself another brandy. "The entire ship went down. All hands lost." He made a clicking sound between his teeth. "A terrible tragedy."

She nodded and changed the subject. She didn't want to think about Thomas now. It hurt too much. She had to be able to concentrate on the reason she was here. "The woman—who is she?"

"A friend."

"You're a poor liar." She finished the tea and set the handless china cup back on the tray. "Who is she really?"

He poured her more tea and handed her the cup. "Why God's bowels, you couldn't expect me to become celibate!"

"She's your whore?" Rachael sipped the tea in her hand, feeling a little dizzy. She didn't like the closeness of the walls and the wood floor felt strange beneath her moccasined feet. The room suddenly seemed stifling. "I think not. Your wife?" She smiled. "Have you married *again,* Gifford, love? And of course the next question would be, does she know you're married?"

He laughed . . . "Witty. You were always so witty, Rachael, in an unflattering sort of way." He was watching her closely now as he sipped his brandy. His voice sounded more confident than it had a few minutes ago . . . almost cocky. "Jesslyn is my fiancée. When I lost you to the Iroquois, I of course had to find another woman to serve as my hostess."

Rachael's tongue suddenly felt as if it were swollen and glued to the roof of her mouth. She was having a difficult time forming words with her mouth. "I . . . it makes no difference to me. Honestly it d . . . doesn't."

"Rachael love, are you all right?" He offered his hand when she swayed.

She blinked and reached to set down the teacup. When she released it, it hit the floor and shattered. She had missed the tray by a good arm's length. She looked up at Gifford in confusion. She didn't know what was wrong with her. She was suddenly sick to her stomach and the room was spinning. She touched her forehead. It felt cool and damp. "I . . . I'm feeling a little faint. I'm not used to being inside like this anymore." She inhaled deeply. "If you could just open a window."

He grasped her arm.

The room was spinning faster now, the dead butterflies in their cases whirling around her. "I . . . I have to go . . . I . . . I'll come back . . . I . . . want my husband." Her lower lip trembled. She was suddenly terribly frightened. "I want Storm . . ."

"There, there, it's just all the excitement, love, Margaret!" Gifford bellowed. "We'll just tuck you into bed so you can get some rest."

"No." She tried to shake her head, but it hurt. "I want to go home now."

"Margaret!" Gifford patted Rachael, holding her up by her shoulders. "But you are home, love, and you'll be fine with a few days' rest."

Margaret stuck her head in the door, but upon seeing Rachael, half draped in Gifford's arms, she came running. "What happened to her?"

"Lady Langston's taken ill, Margaret. I want you to make a bed up for her and . . ."

Rachael could hear Gifford and Margaret talking, but they seemed far away. She felt a sense of panic and blind fear. She wanted to run, but her legs wouldn't move. She wanted to cry out, to call for Storm Dancer, but her vocal cords wouldn't respond. *Please help me,* she thought as she felt herself lose her balance and fall as she descended into blackness. *Someone help me!*

Chapter Twenty-Seven

Storm Dancer crouched beside the firepit he had prepared in anticipation of Rachael's return but had not yet lit. He looked up at the rising moon, guessing the time. Midnight . . .

Midnight, and still Rachael had not returned. When dusk came and she had not appeared, he told himself it was simply taking her longer to get the money than she'd anticipated—or perhaps she had stayed to sup with the brother Thomas who she would never see again. But then darkness had fallen and still she had not returned.

Storm clenched his fists and shook it at the waning moon that hung high above his head. "Where are you?" he demanded. His voice echoed in the treetops before it melded with the sounds of the night forest and grew into silence. "Where are you, my love, my wife? Are you hurt? Did you die along a roadway?" He took a deep breath. "Or have you betrayed me?"

The thought had not even occurred to him until he had said the words aloud. Rachael would not do that to him, not to him and their son Ka-we-ras, who waited for them back at the Lenni Lenape village. She would not have pretended these months since Ta-wa-ne's death to be content. She would not have deceived him in her promise to never leave his side. Or would she?

He sprang up to flex his tight calves, wondering how long he had crouched waiting. Hours.

Was he a fool? Had he been betrayed?

What if Gif-ford Langston the coward had somehow miraculously survived his escape and made it back to Philadelphia? Rachael had been so adamant about the fact that he was dead that Storm had not really broached the subject, but what if? What if he had lured her into his home with the promise of fancy trappings and a life of luxury and ease? What if he had convinced Rachael that an Iroquois turned Lenni Lenape brave was unworthy of her? What if all along she had planned to have Storm Dancer take her to Philadelphia, only to remain in the city and return to the meaningless life she had once had. What if she had only pretended to care enough about his people to offer them her dowry to use to finance their journey west?

For a long time Storm Dancer paced around in the small clearing, watching the moon move across the clear night sky. He waited hour after hour, hoping against hope that his wife would appear with a logical explanation. But she didn't. All night Storm Dancer wrestled with the feeling of betrayal he felt creeping under his skin. He felt like a fool. He had loved Rachael more than he had loved Ta-wa-ne. Why had he not learned with the first wife? Why had he allowed himself to be deceived by a woman of even greater beauty, of greater intelligence? A white woman no less! Had his brother Broken Horn been more correct in his opinion of women than Storm Dancer cared to admit?

Giving Rachael the benefit of the doubt, Storm Dancer remained in the camp until the first streaks of dawn began to paint the morning sky. He waited until he heard the chirping of squirrels and smelled the dew begin to burn off the thick green leaves of pine oaks. Then he packed his sack. He covered the firepit he had made for Rachael and slinging his weapons over his shoulders, he turned away from the evil city called Philadelphia and started home.

Rachael turned and twisted beneath the heavy blankets that had been piled on top of her. The scratchy white nightgown that went from her neck to her toes was tangled around her legs restricting her movement. She was dreaming she was drowning, thick reeds tangled around her drawing her under the surface. She couldn't breath. She couldn't think. She was nauseous and her head pounded so hard that the slightest sound made her cringe in paranoid fear.

Occasionally she heard voices, but few were familiar. *Storm?* She tried to call to him—to tell him she was sick. No sound came out of her mouth. She wanted to see her little boy with the chubby round cheeks. Why were these people pouring this foul tea down her throat and making her choke. She didn't like it. She didn't want anymore. Where was Ka-we-ras? Where was Storm? Why wasn't he here taking care of her? Didn't he know she was sick?

Glimpses of the past drifted through her head. Some were so hazy that they barely registered in her mind while others were as clear as the crystal water that ran from the Metuksik River. She thought of Storm's smile, the sound of his laughter, the feel of his rough calloused hand as it cupped her breast. She remembered the picnic she and Storm Dancer had taken Ka-we-ras on just before they had left—

They had left . . . Yes, she remembered that now, but where had they gone? She struggled to recollect, but her mind was a jumble of sounds and sights that made no sense. She wasn't home; she knew that. She wasn't in her wigwam. The smells were all wrong. This place stank of sickness and closed quarters. There was no breeze, no light, only stifling darkness.

"Rachael?"

A voice penetrated her stupor and slowly she turned her head toward the sound though the sound of the voice was nearly unbearable.

"Rachael, love, can you hear me?"

"Gifford?" Her voice was barely a raspy whisper. She couldn't open her eyes, it hurt too much.

"Yes, Rachael, love."

"W . . ." she tried to think of the words. "W . . . where's Storm. I want Storm."

"I don't know what you're talking about, love." She felt someone pick up her hand and squeeze it. Her muscles made no response. "You're very sick, you know."

"I . . . I want Storm." she insisted. "I want my husband. Please, Gifford, please find him."

"Oh, sweet, love, I am your husband. And I'm right here. I've barely left your side in the two days since you fell ill."

"No. Not my husband. Storm . . . the Dancer of the

Storms. He is my husband. He—"

Gifford chuckled. "You've been hallucinating. You have no other husband, silly girl, just me. It's been a year. We've been married a full year."

She turned away, a sob rising in her throat. "No. I'm Rachael, wife to Storm Dancer."

"You are Rachael. You were Lady Rachael Moreover. You came from London with your brother to marry me."

"T . . . Thomas?"

"Yes, that's right. But he's dead now. Your brother is dead, drowned in the sea. You've no one but me, sweet wife.

"The I . . . Indians?"

He pulled the heavy covers to her chin. She wanted to protest, they were too hot, but she didn't have the energy. "There were no Indians, love."

"Broken Horn, Pretty Woman—"

He laughed again. She heard a chair scrape the wooden floor as it drew closer. "It's just your mind playing tricks on you. You always did have quite the imagination.

Hallucinating? She was dreaming? She dreamed about the Indian called Storm Dancer? It couldn't be. "But, but we . . . we were captured. Iroquois, I remember, I'm certain," she managed, her strength waning. Her lips were so dry that they cracked when she spoke.

"Just a dream, just a bad dream, my love." He leaned over her and though she didn't see him, she felt his presence. "Now drink this and it will make you feel better."

She felt the warm rim of the teacup touch her lip and

she turned away. "No!" It smelled ill and tasted worse and each time they made her drink it she tumbled back into the well of hallucinations. It was then that she dreamed of the Indian village . . . then that she fantasized of the savage lover with the glorious black hair.

"Rachael, you must drink this if you are to ever become well." Gifford spoke firmly.

She shook her head again. "No!" *No, don't make me drink it. Don't make me hurt inside. Help me . . .* someone *help me. . . .*

"Very well, if you don't drink it on your own, I shall have to help you."

Rachael clamped her mouth shut to keep out the evil brew, but he pried it open and poured it down her throat. She held her breath as long as she could, but then she began to choke and when she tried to breath the tea slipped down her throat.

"There, there, that's better."

Gifford was wiping her chin now. She could feel the tears rolling down her cheeks. "Go away," she whispered, feeling herself begin to slip back into unconsciousness. "Go away and leave me to die."

The chair scraped the floor again and when Gifford spoke it was from the far side of the room. "All in good time, my love," he answered in a strange voice. "All in good time."

Storm Dancer stood behind the wall of a dairy watching a young girl in a mobcap hang out laundry. He leaned against the cool brick and waited for her to take her leave.

Storm Dancer had walked an entire day before he had allowed himself the time to go over the past events in his mind. Rachael had not returned so she had betrayed him. Wasn't that right? Or was it? Rachael was not Ta-wa-ne. She had never been Ta-wa-ne and was nothing like her. Rachael loved him. She didn't just say so. He saw it in her eyes, in her touch, in the sound of her voice.

And Rachael was an honorable woman. If she had decided to leave him, she would have stood up to him. She would have said so. He twisted his moccasin into the soft grass. It was unfair to jump to the conclusion that she had betrayed him. Why had he been so quick to condemn her? Because of Ta-wa-ne he supposed. Because of the pain she had caused him and the natural distrust of women she had instilled in him.

No, once the initial anger and hurt had passed, Storm had realized that he had not been thinking clearly back on that road to Philadelphia two days ago. He had jumped to conclusions too quickly. A good shaman did not do that. A good shaman weighed all odds and gave each man and woman a fair chance. He feared he had not given Rachael a fair chance . . . his sweet Rachael.

Of course Storm Dancer knew that there was the remote possibility that she had betrayed their love. In everything there was possibility. But if she had betrayed him he wanted to see her face once more. He wanted to hear her words from her own lips.

The laundry maid in the blue tick skirt and droopy mobcap picked up her basket and wandered back toward the kitchen. Storm watched and waited until she disappeared inside and then he stepped out of the shadows and into the sunlight.

From the clothesline he snatched a pair of burgundy breeches, a white linen shirt, and a pair of white hose. Behind a trellis of strongly scented roses he stripped off his buckskin tunic, loinskin, and ankle-high moccasins. He dressed in the silly white man's clothing and then, having no shoes, put his moccasins back on. He tore a strip from the hem of the shirt and tied back his mane of black hair in a queue. He then hid his bag in the brush, leaving all his weapons behind save for his hunting knife which he tucked into the waistband of his breeches and covered the hilt with his shirt. Now he knew he need only find a hat and then he could walk down the street of this Philadelphia drawing little attention to himself. Rachael had explained to him that there were Indians who frequented the city of Philadelphia, Indians who had become trappers or traders and depended on the white men for business, so he assumed that correctly dressed, he wouldn't be stopped.

As he walked along the backyard and out onto the cobblestone street he mentally thanked the good Lord that he had had the sense to question Rachael on the layout of the city. Though her sketches in the sand had been crowded and disproportional, at least he knew where the law offices were and where the coward resided. Instinct told him to head for the coward's home. He would go there and he would find his Rachael and then he would know for certain if it was by choice that she had left him. Not matter what her words were, Storm knew that the truth would be in her sky-eyes.

Storm Dancer walked down the cobblestone sidewalk with his eyes on the ground. When a pedestrian approached him, he stepped off the walk in an appropriately submissive way, much as an Iroquois woman would have moved for a man. He had not gone a block when he spotted a three-cornered felt hat left on a wagon bench by the driver who was delivering vegetables to a house. The moment the vegetable man disappeared down the walkway that wound around a house, Storm snatched the hat off the bench and stuffed it on his head. Feeling better camouflaged in this strange, noisy world, he hurried northeast in the direction he thought the Gifford house to be.

The houses were so much alike that Storm Dancer feared he would never figure out which belonged to the coward. It was only luck or divine intervention that he passed the house at the precise moment that the coward appeared in the front doorway to speak with an agitated visitor. Taking care to be certain no one saw him, Storm Dancer stepped behind a screen of tall boxwoods just past the house and listened intently to the conversation transpiring.

"You let me see her, you little prick, or I'll have your head!"

"Now, Thomas, I have explained to you that the surgeon has forbidden visitors. She's far too ill. She'll never know you've been here."

Thomas? Was not Thomas the brother of Rachael? Was Rachael ill? Was it she they spoke of?

"I don't care. I just want to see her."

"And you will. She's doing better. She's been conscious several times. I see definite improvement. I imagine that within the week she'll be up and about," the coward went on. He was dressed in some sort of woman's robe made of blue silk.

"What the hell is wrong with her? You haven't said why she's sick."

Storm studied the brother's stance carefully. He had one booted foot planted on the top step and he was shaking his fist. The material of his clothing was good, but he had a certain masculine untidiness that set him apart from the peacock Gifford.

"The surgeon isn't certain. Shock he conjectures. Pure shock at having survived her capture. Pure shock at having been rescued."

"I spoke to John Calmary. He said she wasn't ill when he picked her up on the road into Philadelphia."

"No, she wasn't physically ill yet, but she was obviously mentally off-balance. She was confused and babbling. Why at one point she even denied being my wife." He laughed. "And of course you know I have the papers to prove it."

"Bastard."

"Now, now, that will be enough. Hurtling insults at me will only leave me less likely to let you in."

"When can I see her?"

Gifford stroked his shaven chin. "Tonight . . . perhaps."

"If I return tonight you'll let me see her?"

"As long as she continues to improve, I don't see why that wouldn't be a possibility."

"All right." Thomas lifted a finger beneath Gifford's nose. "I'll wait until evening, but I warn you. If you're jerking me around, Gifford, there'll be no limit to my fury. I won't be held responsible for my own actions."

Gifford stepped back into the doorway. "Come back tonight, Tommy, and we'll see."

The door slammed shut and Storm Dancer lowered himself into the boxwood hedge. He watched the brother Thomas look up at the curtains drawn tightly in the windows overhead. Then, swearing beneath his breath, he turned and headed down the street.

His Rachael sick? Storm Dancer felt ill in the pit of his stomach. Of course the coward could be lying. She might just not wish to see her brother, but she might be truly ailing.

His first thought was to walk into the coward's house and find Rachael. He would see for himself. But a wise shaman did not enter the enemy's camp without preparation, did he? Storm watched the brother turn the corner and disappear. He thought for a moment and then stepped out onto the sidewalk, pulling the cocked hat down low on his brow, and headed in the same direction the brother had gone.

Chapter Twenty-Eight

Storm Dancer followed the Honorable Thomas Moreover down the cobblestone street. As he walked, he tried to mentally gather all the information he knew about this potential ally.

Rachael liked her brother; he was certain of that. She had said he was a simple man, levelheaded and fair. He was a man who sailed on the big dugouts that crossed the endless ocean. He was the man who had told her not to marry the Gifford coward.

Storm Dancer thought that perhaps he would like this Thomas.

In addition to what Rachael had said of her brother, Storm Dancer had the evidence of the conversation that had just taken place between Thomas and the dog, Gifford. Rachael's brother's stance had silently spoken of hatred and distrust for Gifford. But Storm Dancer had also caught a sense of caution in the air. Thomas was wary of what the coward was capable of, which in Storm Dancer's eyes meant Gifford was dangerous . . . or had the potential to be so, something Storm Dancer had not considered.

Was Rachael in jeopardy? Had she caught a fever after she had made the decision to remain with the white coward, or had he taken advantage of her illness to hold her against her will? Was she truly sick at all, or was the man holding her prisoner, keeping her from returning to Storm Dancer?

Thomas turned into a doorway and Storm Dancer slowed his pace. The wooden sign that swung over the entrance read The Swine & Boar. Storm Dancer halted in the shadows of the frame building and considered the tavern for a moment. He could smell the water from here and surmised they were near the docks. Most of the street traffic was sailors. An oxcart rumbled by burdened with hogsheads of some precious cargo bound for England. This world was so foreign to Storm Dancer he felt completely out of his element. It even frightened him a bit.

Then he thought of Rachael, sick, perhaps calling him. Was she frightened? Had this world become foreign to her? He regarded the tavern sign again and stepped inside.

Storm Dancer had not taken but a few strides through the dark, dank public room when a short English sailor appeared out of nowhere and threw up his hand. "No red niggers," he sneered. "Not in The Boar."

Out of the corner of his eye, Storm Dancer spotted Thomas. He had taken a seat at a trestle table near the cold stone fireplace on the far side of the room. He was leaning over the table, resting his forehead wearily on his hand. A young woman in soiled skirts was serving him a leather jack of ale and chattering. Thomas made no response.

Storm Dancer glared up from beneath his cocked hat at the sailor who had made the mistake of barring his way.

"What's matter, boyo, you don't speak the King's English?" The sailor slapped Storm Dancer on the chest. "In case, not, I'll repeat myself for your own stupidity. *I said no red niggers allowed.*"

Storm Dancer's hand snaked out so quickly that the sailor never even had time to flinch. Storm Dancer caught him by his tarred pigtail and lifted him off the floor until his feet dangled in the air. He raised his blade to the sailor's exposed neck. "I have business with a gentleman," he enunciated in perfect English. "Have you a problem with that, sailor mon-key?"

The sailor stared up in wide-eyed fright, his useless legs peddling in the air above the sawdust-covered floor. "No . . . no . . . no mate, I ain't go no troubles with that."

Storm passed the knife a hair closer, drawing a perfect line of blood for emphasis. "This is a good answer." He nodded as he slowly loosened his grip. "A good answer. Now take yourself from this place before I skin you and hang your flesh to dry upon my lodge-pole."

The moment the sailor's booted feet hit the ground, he ran straight for the door.

Storm Dancer slipped his knife back into the waist-band of his English breeches and scanned the dim low-ceilinged room that smelled of rancid tallow and splashed ale. No one seemed to have taken notice of what had just taken place, either that or no one cared. Deeming the public room relatively safe grounds,

Storm Dancer approached Rachael's brother.

Thomas looked up and then back at the jack of ale he held in his hands. "If it's work you seek, see my quartermaster upon the *Lady Rachael.*" He dismissed the red man with a sweep of his hand.

Storm Dancer stood stock still, his obsidian eyes fixed on Thomas.

Thomas repeated himself, not bothering to look up again. "I said if you seek—"

"I do not ask to sail upon your great ship," Storm Dancer responded. "I seek your help."

The tone of the Indian's voice made Thomas look up. "My help? Then what is it?"

"You have a sister called Rachael."

"Yes, yes I do." He took a moment to study Storm Dancer closely, his eyes narrowing in speculation. "Why do you ask? What do you know of my sister?"

Storm Dancer looked behind him. There were only a few patrons in the public room, all still content to mind their own business. "May this man take a seat so that he does not draw the attention of others?"

Curious as to what this soft-spoken Indian wanted, Thomas indicated the bench directly across the table from him. "Please."

Storm Dancer sat carefully on the white man's furniture that always seemed to him to be a little precarious. "I am the Dancer of the Storms of the Lenni Lenape," he said carefully. "A shaman of my people." He watched Thomas for his reaction to his next words. "I am the husband of your sister."

"Her husband?" he flared, half rising in his seat. "That cannot be! You must be the bastard who kidnapped her?"

Storm shook his head. "No, I was not. I love Rachael and I believe in my heart of hearts she loves me."

"My sister wouldn't marry a heathen of her own free will!"

"No." Storm Dancer held Thomas in his black-eyed gaze. "Your sister is good Christian. But I am not a heathen. I spent many years in the walls of a Jesuit mission learning your ways." He laid his palms on the rough wood of the table. "But I have not come here to speak of myself or to justify the marriage of Rachael and Storm Dancer. Ask her yourself when you speak with her."

"So what is it you want, supposed husband to my sister?" Thomas was still not entirely convinced Rachael was married to this redskin but for some odd reason, when he looked into the man's honest eyes, he thought it entirely possible.

"There is something not right here in this place of Philadelphia. My Rachael returned to collect the dowry money she said was hers. She was to return to me three days ago, yet I have not seen her face."

"Perhaps she doesn't wish to be your wife," Thomas suggested carefully. He had once again taken his seat.

"Perhaps, but if you speak the truth, I must hear the words from her own mouth."

"Why do you come to me? How did you even know who I was?"

"I saw you at the Gifford's house. I heard him speak of her illness. I saw him turn you away." Storm Dancer leaned on the table. "You have not seen my Rachael with your own eyes?"

"No." Thomas took a sip of his ale. The red man's story sounded ludicrous of course, but there was something in the tone of his voice that made him think he did know his sister . . . and that he did, indeed, love her. Could it be that his mild sister Rachael had fallen in love and married this virile savage? It was entirely possible. Thomas looked up. "What do you want from me?"

Storm Dancer noticed that he had the same sky-eyes as Rachael. "I wanted first to ask if you have seen her. You have not. I now ask if you wish to join with me. I will see her tonight. Do you come with me?"

"Gifford said he would let me in to see her tonight. Of course he's a lying little bastard too."

"If he will let you in to see her, I would ask that you tell her I wait for her in the gardens below. I would ask that you tell her that I swear on our son's life that I will not force her against her will if she does not wish to go back to our village with me. I want only to hear the words from her lips, so that I can know that she makes this choice of her own free will, that free will which has become so important to her."

Thomas took a long swig of ale. "She has a child?"

"My wife and I adopted a son this winter." He couldn't resist a smile when he thought of the toddler. "He is Ka-we-ras."

Thomas stroked his chin. "So you'll wait in the garden for her. If she's sick, how can she come to you?"

"This man is not certain she is truly sick. Perhaps she does not wish to speak with you or me. But perhaps—" Storm Dancer lifted a finger, "she has not been given that choice."

Thomas thought a few seconds longer and then nodded. He didn't know why he trusted this red man with eyes the color of pitch, but he did. "This is crazy as hell, but all right. I get in to see her tonight and I'll give her your message. What if the prick doesn't let me see her?"

"You will speak your farewell without rousing suspicion, and then you will come to the garden. We will go into the house anyway."

Thomas laughed at the absurdity of the Indian's statement. "The room she's always slept in is on the third floor. It's a flush brick wall. You can't get in a window."

Storm Dancer rose. "I will see my wife before I return to my people. I must."

Thomas stood and watched the red man take his leave. "Tonight then?" he called after him. "When?"

"When darkness falls."

Then Storm Dancer left Thomas and crossed the sawdust floor to step out of the tavern and onto the busy cobblestone street.

Darkness fell on Philadelphia as Storm Dancer crouched behind a fragrant lilac bush. As he waited for Thomas to appear at the front stoop at the designated time, he studied the brick house, which now seemed a fortress. He observed the movement in the windows and quickly surmised which ones led to the room where Rachael rested . . . or where she was being held.

Thomas was correct in saying that it would be difficult to get to the window, but it would not be impossible. While he waited, Storm stripped off his white man's clothing and took off his moccasins, so that he would have better traction with his bare feet. He had strapped his bow and quiver to his back and carried his knife tucked into the band of his leather loincloth. He had spent the afternoon prowling barns looking for any materials he thought he might need. Coiled in the grass within his grasp was a sturdy hemp rope attached to a metal hook taken from a small granary.

Storm Dancer shifted his weight on the balls of his feet, finding a comfortable position. A brave could crouch motionless for hours—a well-trained one for a day.

As Storm Dancer waited for Thomas, he allowed his thoughts to wander. What if Rachael had indeed betrayed him, what would he do then? He thought of her sweet face and the sound of her laughter on a dewy morning and his arms ached for her. The concept of being without her the rest of his days made him physically ill. He had loved her more than he had ever allowed himself to love anyone—no, he still loved her more than he loved anyone. Could he go on without her?

He would have to. He would have to return to the village, to his son, and to his people. They were waiting for him, depending upon him. Without the money Rachael was to have provided, the trek west would be difficult, but not impossible. Storm Dancer, shaman of his tribe, would take his son Ka-we-ras west and raise him to be a fine man, and Storm Dancer would not ever, ever give his heart to another woman. He would give in to Broken Horn's way of thinking and use them as he saw fit, for sex, for work, but he would never love another female as long as he lived.

Broken Horn. This was the first time he had thought of his brother in ages. Storm Dancer had become so wrapped up in his happiness with Rachael among the

Lenni Lenape that he had all but forgotten the Mohawk he had once been and the brother he had once loved.

Storm Dancer could not help wondering if he was forever doomed to be betrayed by those he loved. As children he and Broken Horn had been inseparable. What had happened to draw them so far apart? What had made Broken Horn hate him so much? He wondered how his brother fared. Was he happy now that Storm Dancer was gone? Had he found that fleeting sense of peace within he had sought his entire adult life?

Footsteps on an arm's length away the cobblestone walk startled Storm Dancer. He silently chastised himself for being so lost in his thoughts as he peered through the lilac bushes. Thomas stood on the top step, his cocked hat tucked beneath his hand waiting for someone to answer Gifford's door. After repeated knocking, the housekeeper, Margaret, swung open the door; the lantern she held up illuminated a purple bruise across her cheek.

"The Honorable Thomas Moreover here to see my sister Rachael," Thomas said in a clear voice.

Margaret lowered her head. "Sorry, sir, but Lady Langston is not receivin' visitors." She spoke as if she recited what someone else had told her.

"I'm not a visitor, I'm her brother." He leaned on the door frame, trying to look inside. "If she's ill, I've a right to see her."

"I'm sorry, sir," Margaret repeated steadily. "But I'm not to let you in. Not anyone, 'else I'll catch hell."

Storm Dancer saw Thomas look the woman over, no doubt taking in consideration the fresh bruise that marked the housekeeper's plump face.

"Very well," Thomas said. "I'll not have you in trouble. I'll see Langston, then."

She shook her head. "He's not to be disturbed. I been given strict orders."

Thomas looked away, cursing a sailor's curse beneath his breath. "Can you tell me," his gaze met hers, "is she veritably ill or is he holding her prisoner."

Tears welled up in the rotund housekeeper's eyes. "She's true sick, sir. Bad sick and gettin' worse. I tried everything. One minute she seems like she's comin' out of it and then she's worse again." She took a step back. "I got to go in. I ain't to speak to you or anyone concerning the mistress."

Thomas caught her sleeve. "What's wrong with her?" he pleaded gently. "Can you tell me what sort of illness she's contracted?"

Margaret glanced over her shoulder, obviously fearful of the retribution she would receive if caught speaking with Rachael's brother. "I don't know, sir. Strangest thing I ever seen. She don't know where she is most of the time. She talks gibberish. The master says she's possessed by the devil. It's a punishment for 'er sins against her true husband." She ground her teeth. "The master says she whored for the Injuns to save 'erself."

Thomas wiped his forehead with the back of his hand. "Thank you for your help. You can go in now. If that bastard lays a hand on you over this, you let me know. I can be contacted at the *Lady Rachael* in the harbor. I was to have set sail yesterday on the morning tide but until my sister is better, the goods and Mother England will wait."

Margaret turned away and hurried inside, closing

the door behind her. Before Thomas turned away he heard a bolt slide on the door.

The moment the door slammed shut, Storm Dancer rose to his full height. "He leaves me no choice, Thomas," he said gently. "I must be certain she is not in danger."

Thomas came off the step and followed the Indian into the shadows of the garden. "You would go through with this." He looked up at the brick wall of the building. "You would risk your life on the chance that she may well be sitting above drinking tea with Langston?"

"You heard the woman servant speak. It is the sound of the words more than the words themselves that you must hear. Rachael is very ill," Storm Dancer said gravely. "And whether it is by choice, or nay, that she stays with this man, if she is ill, I must see her."

Thomas exhaled slowly as he looked up at the dimly lit windows curtained on the third story. "That's the window all right." He pulled his cocked hat over his head and pointed. "I can climb the *mainm'st* to her top in a hurricane, but I can't climb a brick wall three stories into the sky, friend."

Storm Dancer glanced up at the wall, unconcerned. "I do not ask that you go above. I will go to her." He picked up the hemp rope and coiled it carefully on his arm. "I have another task for you." He eyed Thomas. "If you are up to it."

"Name it. The chance that that bastard might be holding Rachael against her will makes me so bloody mad I can't think straight."

"Go to the barn and take two horses. Two fast horses. Saddle yours if you like, but on mine I want only a bridle. I never learned to ride the saddle well.'

"Steal his horses?"

"If she is being held against her will, I will take her. We will have to ride fast for the safety of the forest. I cannot defend my wife on stone streets."

"I'll do it." Thomas looked up at the brick wall of the house. "But are you certain that's the way to go? Can't you sneak in from the ground floor and go up the stairs like the rest of us?"

"You heard the bolt slide home on the door. It is obvious the coward expects trouble. I will not kill him unless I must because my position among my people as shaman does not permit me to kill without good reason. In this manner there will less likely be bloodshed and Rachael will be safer."

"All right. It sounds as crazy as hell to me, but I'll get the horses."

Storm Dancer swung the hook attached to the rope well over his head and it caught on the header brick ledge of the second-story window below the window they assumed Rachael to be behind.

Thomas gave a low whistle and started toward the barn that loomed in the darkness beyond a line of other dependencies. "I'll hurry. God speed, friend. You're going to need it."

Storm Dancer tested his weight against the metal hook and rope, and satisfied with its sturdiness, he lifted himself off the ground and began to scale the wall.

With his bare feet againt the cool, rough brick, Storm Dancer made his way slowly up the wall. He leaned back against the rope, using his own weight to steady himself. One foot at a time, he rose above the ground, past the first story window, up to the second. When he made it to the windowsill on the second story, he was forced to perch on the ledge barely half a brick wide.

Storm Dancer breathed carefully as he steadied himself in a crouched position, one bare foot in front of the other. Unhooking his rope from the ledge, he slowly stood inside the window casing. He now had to swing the iron hook up into the next windowsill without losing his balance and tumbling to the grass below.

He heard the soft neigh and snort of a horse and knew that Thomas was about his job. He smiled in the darkness, pleased with his choice for an ally. This Thomas, brother to Rachael, was a good man. He could use his sturdy head among his braves back at the village.

Hesitating for only a moment, Storm swung his hook above his head. On the first try it hit too high and hit the brick above the window. On the second though it hit a glass pane with a silent shattering *clink*. With luck beyond reason, the thin glass did not shatter.

Storm Dancer glanced up into the clear-skied night heavens and whispered a prayer. He then threw the hook again, and this time it caught on the ledge. With one hard pull, it lodged and Storm Dancer was once again scaling the wall upward toward Rachael.

When he reached the third story windowsill and came to rest on the narrow ledge, he realized that he stood further above solid ground than he ever had before in his life. It seemed as if he was so high that if he stretched, he could pluck a twinkling star from the sky, and when he looked down, the grass loomed so far below that it made him dizzy.

Leaving the hook and rope where it hung, Storm Dancer turned in the window, keeping careful balance and shielded his eyes with his hands to look into the dimly lit room.

Across the small sleeping chamber was a bed so heaped with piles of quilts that the form of the person in the bed was obscured. But there was someone sleeping in the bed, and it was Rachael, Storm Dancer could feel it in his bones.

Carefully, he pressed his hands to the glass-paned windowframe and slid it up just as he had watched a maid do so when washing the ones on the bottom floor this morning. When it did not slide smoothly, he slipped his knife from his loinskin and eased it around the tight points. On his next try the window slowly squeaked up.

The first rush of hot air that billowed from the sick room made Storm Dancer wince. As a medicine man he would never understand this white man's way of locking someone already ill in a room of bad air.

With the window up, and no one to be seen, he stepped inside through a haze of filmy curtains. The moment his bare feet hit the hot polished floorboards, he surveyed the room. Rachael lay on the bed on her side facing away from him with nothing but the back of her dark head showing. There was a fire burning in the fireplace making the vine-wallpapered room ridiculously warm. The bedchamber was sparsely furnished with the bed, a chest along one wall, and a table and upholstered chair near the bed. Eyeing the paneled door that led to the hallway, Storm touched the chair with his palm. It was warm, and still indented from the person who had sat there only moments before, caring for Rachael, or guarding her.

Storm picked up the heavy chair and carried it to the door. Tipping it, he wedged it beneath the knob so that the door could not be easily opened. Then he crossed the room, toward Rachael, his bare feet padding on the hardwood floor.

He stood for a moment over her, looking down on her deathly pale face. Her breath was so shallow that a lump rose in his throat. From the sound of her breathing, she was dying, God in Heaven, his Rachael was dying!

He laid his hand on her cheek. She burned with fire, but there was no fever. Storm grabbed a handful of the quilts and ripped them off the bed, throwing them angrily to the floor. He sat on the edge of the bed and grasped her shoulders, rolling her over.

Rachael was so ill, that she didn't look like herself. Her face was a dull gray, the color of a dead man's skin. When Storm Dancer lifted her eyelid, her pupils barely reacted. With a moan, he lifted her into his arms and held her tightly, unabashed tears running down his broad bronze cheeks.

"Ki-ti-hi," he pleaded. *"Ki-ti-hi,* I have come for you. Do you hear this man who is your husband?"

To his amazement, her lips moved, though he was unable to understand what she said. He leaned closer, pressing his ear to her mouth. "Speak to me, my love. I listen."

"S . . . Storm Dancer," she moaned. "Husband . . ."

"Rachael?"

"Storm." Her lips moved, though this time there was no sound.

"Rachael listen to me. You must tell me. Have you

left me for your white man? Do you live beneath this roof of your own free will?"

"Storm?"

He smoothed her hollow damp cheek. Her face was dotted with perspiration, her white gown buttoned to her neck soaking wet. "Yes, I am here."

". . . Take me a . . . away?"

"You want me to take you away?"

"He said . . ." She took a long shuddering breath and then began again. "He said you were only a dream. He said you were never mine."

"Who?" Storm Dancer insisted. "Who Rachael?"

". . . Gifford," she managed on the exhale.

"He took you against your will?"

"W . . . wouldn't get you. Thomas dead. No one help me."

Storm Dancer pulled her tightly againt his chest, his throat constricted with anger and pain. How dare he hold her from him! How dare that coward lie to her when she was sick! For this he would kill him. He would torture him and then he would kill him!

"No. Thomas is not dead. He is below waiting for you. I will take you home," Storm Dancer whispered. "Do you hear me? I'll take you home to the village, home to Dory and to Ka-we-ras."

"Ka-we-ras," she repeatd. "H . . . he said my little boy was just a dream." She rolled her head to and fro, her eyes still closed. "Is he . . . is he just a dream?"

Storm Dancer caught her chin. "Open your eyes, Rachael."

"Can't."

"You can. For me. For our son."

Her eyelids flickered, and opened a slit. They

widened as she caught a glimpse of Storm Dancer's face. "You're not a dream," she whispered. "But even if you are, it's all right. Just take me away." She closed her eyes again, weakened by the talk. "Take me away, lover, take me far from this evil place before I die."

"You're not going to die," he said firmly, giving her a shake. "You're—"

A rattle at the door made Storm Dancer look up, his voice cutting into silence. A key was being jiggled in the keyhole, then the knob was turned. "God a' mercy," a young woman swore from the hallway. "Have I locked myself out?" She jiggled the doorknob hard and hit the door hard with something. The chair slipped slightly.

Storm Dancer lay Rachael on the bed and ran for the door. Just as he hit the chair with his foot, the maid in the hall peered through the crack in the door and the air was rent with a high-pitched piercing scream of terror.

Storm Dancer slammed the door shut and adjusted the chair. This was just what he had wanted to avoid. He could hear the girl shrieking as she ran down the hallway proclaiming the house was under Indian attack.

Storm Dancer knew it would only be a matter of seconds before others came. He ran back across the room and pulled Rachael into his arms. "I'm taking you home now, *Ki-ti-hi,*" he told her. "You must hold onto me." He raised her hands to clasp them around his neck, but they fell useless to her sides.

"Can't," she breathed.

"You must, he insisted glancing at the door. He could hear commotion below now. The household was springing into action.

He looked back at Rachael who was nearly unconscious again. There was no way she could hold onto him while he climbed down the brick wall and he couldn't get to the ground without the use of his hands. The house was already alerted to his presence so he couldn't go out from inside. He thought about jumping, but it would probably mean death to both of them.

There was a man with a deep voice at the door now ramming it with a large object. The girl was still shrieking and there were others in the hallway. Several dogs barked and growled behind the door.

Storm glanced at the sheet that lay damp on the bed. He would tie Rachael to him, that's what he would do. He yanked his bow and quiver from his back. Another bang came at the door and this time wood splintered. Storm Dancer jerked the sheet off the bed and tossed Rachael's unconscious form over his shoulder, looping her hands around his neck. He wrapped the muslin sheet around them both, securing her body to his and then tied her wrists securely around his neck.

The door splintered again. Storm Dancer could hear Gifford's voice now as he came barreling down the hallway to take control of the situation. "Don't let them get away," he shouted. "Those filthy savages are kidnapping my wife!"

Storm Dancer sprang off the bed and ran, his weapons in his hands. His movement was awkward with Rachael tied to his back, but he could manage. Just as he stepped up to the window, the door gave way and instinctively Storm Dancer spun round to face his enemy and protect his wife tied to his back.

He sensed the pistol even before he saw it and his fingers found the arrow and notched it in a breath's time. He released the arrow from his waist and it flew straight and true slicing through the middle of the burly man who had broken down the door. The man screamed and fell back, clutching the arrow that protruded from his stomach. His pistol fell to the floor and misfired filling the room with black powdered smoke and its acrid smell.

Storm Dancer slipped barefoot through the open window and out of the corner of his eye he spotted the coward, Gifford. "You red son of a bitching bastard!" Gifford shouted lifting a musket to his shoulder, so crazed with rage that he didn't seem to care that in taking aim on Storm Dancer, he also took aim at Rachael.

Storm Dancer grasped the rope at his feet and flung his body into the night just as the musket exploded in the window.

Chapter Twenty-Nine

The blast of the musket surrounded Storm Dancer until there was nothing but the shattering of brick, the echo of the shot and the smell of a full charge of black powder. He swung out through the air, praying the rope held, because if it didn't, he and Rachael would both fall to their death.

There was a moment just after Gifford fired that Storm Dancer felt himself suspended in midair without the security of the tug of the rope or the solidity of the brick wall. For that instant it seemed as if he were flying. He thought of the tales his grandfather Shaakan had told him of the shaman who could fly and he wondered if this was what it felt like.

In a blink of his eyes Storm Dancer felt the rope catch and jerk him upward and in toward the wall. Shards of windowpane and crumbled brick still flew through the air as the soles of his bare feet hit the brick so hard that it jarred his teeth. Without wasting an instant he began to climb down the wall with Rachael still tied securely on his back.

"Come back here, you son of a red bitch!" Gifford screamed at the top of his lungs. "Reload! Reload!" he shouted to someone.

Storm Dancer did not take the time to look up. He was nearly to the second story windowsill now.

"I'd sooner see my wife dead than carried off by heathens!" Gifford shouted from overhead.

Storm Dancer felt the glass panes with his bare feet and dropped onto the windowsill.

"Christ, get out of there!" Thomas shouted from below.

Storm Dancer looked down as he jerked his rope from its hold on the third story and began to coil it in. Thomas waited below astride a stolen horse, holding another by its reins.

"He's going to fire again!" he screamed.

"Thomas Moreover, you son of a bitch," Gifford screamed hanging out the third story window. "I'll have you hanged for kidnapping my wife!"

"Catch me first, you sorry son of a bitch!" Thomas shouted shaking a fist.

Storm Dancer had just turned to lodge the rope hook into a crack between the header bricks when he looked up to see Gifford turn out of the window. When he swung back, it was with a loaded musket rifle on his shoulder.

Without thinking, Storm Dancer let the rope fall from his hands. With the lithe spring of a mountain cat he leapt into the air and out of the range of fire. Gifford's musket hit its mark where Storm had stood only a second before, blasting away the glass, wood frame, and surrounding brick of the window. Rachael's arms tightened around Storm Dancer's neck and she screamed a scream of nightmarish terror as they hurled toward the earth below.

Storm Dancer fell with Rachael tied on his back for what seemed an eternity until finally his bare feet hit the dewy grass. He landed on the ground hard in a crouch, using his bent legs to absorb the weight of his fall. "Shhh, *ki-ti-hi,*" he soothed rubbing her bare arm as he ran for the unsaddled horse Thomas held for him.

Storm Dancer leapt onto the horse and jerked the reins from Thomas's hands. He sank his heels into the mount's flanks and whirled it around through the garden toward a manmade wall of boxwood.

"Stop them! Stop them!" Gifford shouted from what remained of the third story window. "They've stolen my wife and my Arabian horses, the bastards!"

Storm Dancer lifted the horse's reins murmuring to him in Algonquian. The horse sailed over a six-foot-high length of boxwood hedge and into the obscurity of night with Thomas and mount a length behind.

In a bed of moss and leaves, Storm Dancer spread a wool blanket from the supplies Thomas had brought along for them. Then gently he lay Rachael down. Her breathing was still shallow and she had not regained consciousness since they had leaped from the window.

Though Storm Dancer and Thomas had little fear Gifford and the authorities would catch up with them, they had ridden at full speed out of Philadelphia and deep enough into the forest that no one would find them.

Upon their arrival, Thomas busied himself setting up camp and caring for the horses while Storm Dancer dealt with Rachael. After settling her on the blanket, he took a clean rag dipped in spring water and bathed her flushed face.

"Storm?" Her voice was barely audible, but he was certain she had called him.

"Ki-ti-hi, I am here." He brushed her cheek with his fingertips and with great effort she lifted her hand until it covered his.

"You came for me . . . Was afraid . . . Said you were just dream . . . Said—"

"Hush, my wife. You are safe now. That man shall never lay hands on you again."

"Dying, Storm." She squeezed his hand, but her strength was no more than that of Ka-we-ras's.

"You're not dying."

"Am. Don't know what's wrong." She rolled her head in confusion and picked at her nightgown. "Take off. Take off filthy thing."

"You want me to take off the sleeping gown?"

She pulled at the buttoned and tied collar. "Hot. Can't breathe. My . . . my tunic in bag."

She wanted to wear her own clothing. He understood. "I can take it off," he assured her as he began to loosen the ties. "Just lay still and rest."

"Don't . . . don't let them take my . . . my body. Want . . ." she exhaled but didn't inhale.

Storm Dancer grabbed her by the shoulders, suddenly more frightened than he had ever been in his life. "Rachael . . . Rachael!"

At long last she took a shuddering breath and he sighed in relief. He dipped the cloth in the cold water again and began to bathe her exposed chest as he unbuttoned its buttons.

"Storm?"

He smiled. "Rachael, Wife."

"You have to promise."

She was still talking about dying. "You will not die. I won't let you," he whispered.

Her eyelids fluttered and slowly lifted until she was looking at him by the dim light of the campfire. Her pupils were dilated and glassy. "If I die you'll bury me here in the woods under the trees. You won't let them put me in a churchyard."

He thought for a moment. He didn't want to admit that she might be dying, but if he were in her place, he would want to know that he would be laid to rest in the right spot—a place where he belonged. He owed it to her. "I promise," he whispered.

She smiled a faint smile as her eyes closed. "I love you, Dancer of the Storms. Care for our son and tell him . . ." She took a deep breath. ". . . Tell him I loved him as if he had been born of my own body."

Storm Dancer leaned over to kiss her lips. They were cool. Too cool. "Sleep and speak no more of dying," he whispered.

She lifted her hand to brush back his hair that fell across her cheek, and then her hand fell as she drifted into unconsciousness.

Storm Dancer fought the moisture that gathered in the corners of his eyes as he made himself busy removing Rachael's sleeping gown. He bathed her flushed body and redressed her in the extra doeskin tunic he had carried in his bag for her.

The fact that there seemed to be nothing he could for her infuriated him. But he didn't know what was wrong with her. He had never seen such a strange illness. It was as if she had taken a medicine man's sleeping potion she could not awaken from—

Storm Dancer suddenly rocked back on his heels and glanced into the flames of the fire. A sleeping potion stronger than one he had ever heard of? A poison? Had the coward poisoned her? He looked back at her gray, drawn face. It was very likely.

When Thomas returned from a walk around the perimeter of the camp he found Storm Dancer crouched by the fire, one hand resting on the pulse of Rachael's wrist. "How is she?"

Storm Dancer glanced at her and then back at the fire. "Not good. Her heart has slowed until it seems it will not beat again, yet it does." He paused. "I think she was poisoned."

"Poisoned!" Thomas knelt to get a better look at his sister now dressed in a doeskin tunic with her hair neatly braided and a necklace of polished stones and sea shells around her neck. "Who would—" he cut himself off before he completed his statement. "Langston." He looked up at Storm Dancer. "But why?"

"He claimed her as wife and yet they were not wed. Rachael broke their engagement in the carriage just before they were attacked by my brother and his men." Storm Dancer had told Thomas briefly the story of Rachael's capture earlier.

"I knew they weren't married! I just knew it!" Thomas came to sit beside Storm Dancer as he contemplated the new information. After a moment he shrugged. "The money. It can only be the money." He raised his hand, splaying his fingers. "As soon as that bastard Langston got back to Philadelphia he had a marriage certificate and death certificate drawn up for

Rachael by a friend in the courts and then demanded the remainder of her dowry."

"He thought her dead by my brother's hands the night he abandoned her in the forest. When she appeared alive at his door he had to dispose of her."

"Quickly," Thomas added. "Before she proclaimed him the liar and cheat that he is."

Storm Dancer looked at Rachael who lay perfectly still, her chest rising and falling in a slow, uneven pattern. "Liar, cheat, and murderer, perhaps."

Thomas rose slamming his fist into the palm of his hand. "If she dies, I will kill Langston."

Storm Dancer gazed into the flickering flames of the fire. "You and I together, my brother. You and I both."

The entire night Thomas and Storm Dancer sat vigil over Rachael. Twice more she stopped breathing and twice Storm Dancer shook her until she gasped for air. Just when it seemed she was near death, color began to return to her face. By some miracle, by dawn she was asking for water and weakly proclaiming hunger. Thomas and Storm Dancer saw no explanation to her strange recovery except that she had been poisoned by continual doses of a drug, an opiate no doubt, and now that she was no longer in Gifford Langston's care, she would recover.

By the following day Rachael could sit up well enough, leaning against a tree trunk, that she joined the men she loved most in the world in the evening meal.

"I still can't believe you're alive, Thomas," she breathed. Her voice was weak, her movements unsteady, but she was still the Rachael Thomas knew and Storm Dancer had come to know.

"I have no trouble believing it," he teased. "I was

never dead to begin with."

"But he told me you had drowned at sea." After what she'd been through she couldn't stand to speak Gifford's name. "He told me they'd not even recovered your body."

"The bastard. It was a cruel thing to do." Thomas offered her a cup of steaming herbal tea Storm Dancer had brewed especially for Rachael to help her get her strength back. Now that the poison had worn off, she had only to fight the withdrawal symptoms that made her shaky and nauseous.

"The question is, what do I do now?" Rachael said thoughtfully.

"Do?" Storm Dancer turned to look directly into her sky-eyes, eyes he had feared would never look upon him again. "You do nothing. As soon as you are well enough to travel, we leave for the village and our son."

"Oh, no." She gave a defiant laugh. "The stinking dog took my money, he told me vindictive lies, and he tried to kill me with some sort of opiate. I want revenge."

Storm Dancer took the cup she held out to him. "You will not risk your life again for coin."

"Our village needs the horses and supplies to get across the Ohio."

"I need you more, *ki-ti-hi,*" Storm Dancer answered evenly.

Rachael looked up at Thomas. "I've never known my husband, a shaman, to back down under siege before." She said it teasingly, but there was a challenge in her voice.

"I do not back down!" Storm Dancer answered. "But I know what is important and what is not. Your life is more important to me than all the wealth in this world and I will not risk it."

"We don't have to risk any lives. All we have to do is go into the city," she glanced mischievously at Thomas, "and frighten him a tad. We use the right persuasion and I know he would return my money gladly."

Thomas couldn't resist a handsome smile. "It just might work."

Storm Dancer looked from Rachael to Thomas. "You conspire with my ill wife against me?"

Thomas poked Storm Dancer playfully with a stick. "Not against you. Against that bastard, Langston."

"It would be easy," Rachael soothed, pushing away from the tree so that she could loop her arm through Storm's. The thought of revenge made her feel stronger. "I've already got a plan." She kissed his bulging biceps above his copper arm band.

"I'll not be a part of it!" Storm Dancer tried to ignore her tender touch. "I'll take you back to the village if I must tie you to my back, Wife."

"But isn't that what we agreed to, Storm," she said gently. "That there would be no more force. That I would be allowed to make my own decisions?"

He exhaled slowly. He didn't like the idea of returning to Philadelphia, not one bit. He had to get Rachael back to the village, home where he understood his surroundings, home where he could protect her. "Yes, this is what we agreed but—"

"But nothing. It's my money and I want it back. I want to go west with our people and I want to help them get there safely. Will you take me to Gifford, Storm? Will you help me put an end to this life once and forever?"

He turned his moccasin in the dark, pungent humus stalling. "I do not like this, but I will take you, Wife." He looked up at her, his obsidian eyes filled with concern. "This man will take you because of his love for you, not for want of your coin."

Rachael raised up on her knees and rested her hands on his broad, bare shoulders so that she looked directly into his raven eyes. "Fair enough." She kissed him, her lips lingering against his, not caring that her brother watched. When she drew back, she turned to Thomas, a smile turning up the corners of her mouth. "Do you want to tell him our plan or shall I?"

Thomas tapped his clay pipe on his boot heel with a chuckle. "Oh, no, it's your idea, I simply gave input." He lifted a hand. "Be my guest, Sister. Your husband awaits."

A week later, Thomas, Storm Dancer, and Rachael rode into Philadelphia under the cover of dusk. Rachael, having gained back her strength, rode horseback behind Storm with Thomas taking the lead. They rode through alleys directly to Gifford Langston's majestic brick home and dismounted in a line of sycamore and poplar trees on the rear of his property.

Storm Dancer dismounted, but before he could help Rachael down, she sprang from the horse's back and landed gently in the cut grass. She wore her doeskin tunic and her dark hair flowing down her back. Across her cheeks and forehead she painted the lines and symbols of her adopted family with paint from Storm's paintpot. She insisted on painting Storm Dancer as well with blue and red markings across his face, bare arms, and chest—for effect, she'd insisted. Eve Thomas sported two diagonal blue lines across on cheek as an icon of his bravery.

Storm Dancer looked to Rachael. He wore nothin but a loincloth and his moccasins. Around his waist h wore a quilled belt with knives tucked into it. From th side hung Broken Horn's scalp lock. "You're certai you wish to do this, Wife?"

"We've been through this a hundred times, Storm. She touched his bare arm and a warm thrill of excitement went through her. "It's what I want."

"If there is trouble, you run for the horses." H caught her chin, forcing her to look up at him, forcin her to take him seriously. "We will meet back at th camp."

She took his hand and lowered it, grinning. "I understand. Now let's go."

Storm Dancer turned to Thomas who waited by th hedges giving Rachael and Storm their moment c privacy. "I warn you, white man whom I call brother, I am injured or killed, my wife is your responsibility. will not see her harmed. If there is trouble, I will dea with it and you are to get her out of the house."

Thomas popped the cork on a flask of whiskey an took a sip. "I promise you she'll come to no harm. almost lost my sister once, it'll not happen again."

Rachael lifted up on her toes and kissed Storm Dancer soundly on the lips. "Let's go, Storm. Grabbing her canvas bag from the horse's withers, sh ran through the dark yard after her brother, who ha already started for the kitchen door.

Rachael and Thomas and Storm Dancer walked directly up to the back stoop where a mother cat and he litter of kittens sat drinking from a plate of milk. Rachael turned the brass knob and let herself in. The men brought up the rear.

The kitchen was dim. The servants had cleaned up and retired to their loft chambers for the evening. The warm, low-ceilinged room smelled of smoke and cinnamon bread.

Rachael crept through the kitchen with the men behind her. Down the dark back hall toward Gifford's study they went. Gifford spent every evening there that he did not go out, so Rachael was betting that he would be there tonight. She couldn't suppress a smile of triumph as she peeked around the corner and spotted light in the crack under the study door.

Just as she turned the corner with Storm Dancer and Thomas on her heels, she gave an involuntary squeak. There was Margaret standing in a flood of candlelight staring at her in her Indian garb and paint as if she were a savage ghost. At the sight of Storm Dancer, Rachael thought Margaret was going to faint.

But Margaret recognized Rachael and for a long moment she considered her carefully. Rachael raised a finger to her lips and pointed toward the door and then to herself. She was afraid to speak for fear Gifford would hear her, but she wanted Margaret to understand that she wanted to see him without interference from the household.

Margaret thought for a moment and then nodded. Rachael knew the old woman had always liked her for her kindness. She also knew that she despised Gifford for his unfairness and cruelty. It was only because of her age that she had not sought out other employment long ago.

With a glance at the study door, Margaret turned away and went back down the hall the way she came, with her candle, pretending she had never seen Rachael.

Rachael turned to flash a grin at Thomas and Storm and then went for the door. Just as she lay her hand on the polished knob, she heard a distinctly female giggle . . . a bawdy giggle. She looked at Thomas. He was grinning broadly, indicating with a wave of his hand that it was now or never.

When Rachael tried to turn the doorknob it was locked. Storm Dancer appeared alarmed, but she only stood on her tiptoes and found the key Gifford always left above the door frame. As quietly as possible, she turned the lock, though from the sounds inside she doubted if Gifford and his friend heard anything.

With the knob unlocked she turned it carefully and stepped back out of Storm Dancer's way. The moment the door swung open, Gifford's head popped up. He was seated on a chair with his breeches around his ankles, his lady Jesslyn only partially clothed, on her knees in front of him.

"What the—"

Storm Dancer leaped through the air like some apparition from hell, and before Gifford could utter another word, he had a knife at Gifford's throat.

"Go ahead, Langston, holler." Thomas said, coming through the door and closing it behind him. "There's nothing that would please me more than to see my friend here slit your throat."

Gifford's woman fell backward in fear and Rachael lifted a foot to place on her bare-breasted chest. Rachael touched a finger to her unsheathed knife. "I can skin a deer in five minutes, do you think skinning a woman would take longer?"

"Oh dear God! Oh dear God!" Jesslyn cried, hyperventilating. "She's gone mad, Gifford. She's gone mad!"

"Wh . . . what do you want?" Gifford managed. His fingers were on the waistband of his breeches and he was trying to figure out a way to cover his exposed parts without moving beneath the knife the wild Indian held on his throat.

"I want my money," Rachael demanded, her moccasined foot still planted squarely between Jesslyn's ample breasts.

"Your . . . your money? I . . . I don't know what you're talking about."

"My dowry money is what I'm talking about and you damned well know it! It belongs to my rightful husband." She pointed at Storm Dancer. "And he's damned mad you didn't give it to me the day I came for it."

"Gifford—" Jesslyn piped up.

Rachael pressed weight on her foot propped on the woman. "I'd suggest you keep quiet."

"I . . . I don't have any of your money. N . . . No way to get it here."

Thomas shook his head. "Pity, because my brother-in-law here, he doesn't understand English very well and he understands the English coin system even less." He shrugged as he poured himself a portion of Gifford's best brandy and swirled it in the snifter. "Let's get more comfortable and then we can speak more freely. Rachael?"

From her bag Rachael pulled out several lengths of

rope and with Thomas's help she tied both Gifford and Jesslyn into chairs. They were not given the opportunity to clothe themselves. Rachael wanted to play upon any vulnerability she could. It had been agreed that there would be no violence unless absolutely necessary. Rachael saw no reason to hurt Gifford, she only wanted to scare the hell out of him.

With Gifford and Lady Jesslyn tied securely, Thomas waved to Storm Dancer, who had yet to speak a word, and Storm took a step back.

Rachael had a hard time suppressing her laughter. Storm Dancer was playing this savage routine to the hilt. He had taken a wide stance and now stood with his knife in his hand, relaxed yet ready to spring, his black eyes intent on Gifford.

"Cozy now?" Thomas went back to his drink.

"I demand that you release me, Thomas Moreover!" Jesslyn shrieked. "My father will have you hanged for this, you bastard!"

Thomas rolled his eyes and Rachael pulled a piece of material from her bag and wrapped it around Jesslyn's mouth so no sound escaped but a garbled protest.

"Better?" Rachael asked her brother sweetly.

"Much better." Thomas lifted his glass. "And Gifford, let's get back to the matter at hand. Fact. You and my sister are not married and were never married. Fact. You abandoned her in a Mohawk village and left her to die. Fact. You came back here and lied about being married to get her money. Fact. When she came back she ruined your proclaimed widowerhood leaving you in a sticky situation. Fact! You tried to kill my sister to get yourself out of this mess!"

"I . . . I . . . I didn't," Gifford moaned. "She . . . she was sick."

Thomas shook his head. "Oh, I forgot the most pertinent fact." He indicated Storm Dancer with a nod. "My sister's husband is damned mad about this entire business."

Storm Dancer bared his teeth and growled.

Rachael looked to Gifford to see that he was visibly shaken.

"Now just what are we to do about this problem, Gifford? Hmmm?" Thomas took a sip of his brandy. "My sister's husband wants the dowry that he believes to be rightfully his." He shrugged. "But you have it."

Gifford's eyes widened in fear. Storm Dancer, who still stood in front of Gifford was now sharpening the twelve-inch blade of his hunting knife on a sharpening stone with an even-sounding scrape . . . scrape . . . scrape.

"My brother-in-law is not happy. You've been among the Mohawks. You know the sort of things they do to get what they want out of people." He took another sip, shaking his head. "I understand it's not a pretty sight."

"Please, please," Gifford begged.

Storm Dancer lay his first knife on a small cherry table beside Gifford and he produced another to sharpen. Scrape . . . scrape . . . scrape . . .

"Oh, God, Oh, God, I'm going to be sick," Gifford moaned, unable to tear his eyes from Storm Dancer.

"The dowry money, Giffy?" Thomas lifted an eyebrow.

Rachael sighed. "I'm very sorry about all of this, but

now that Storm Dancer is my husband, I have to turn my dowry over to him. You understand?" she said innocently.

Gifford retched. "I . . . I have money."

"Money!" Jesslyn argued against the gag in her mouth. "You've got no money but mine!"

Gifford flashed Jesslyn a warning glance. "I can get money for you if that's all you want. Now call him off." He looked up at Storm Dancer. "Call the wild beast off!"

"When can you get the money?" Thomas asked.

Storm Dancer set down his second knife on the table beneath Gifford's nose and removed a third from his belt, this one a thin-bladed filleting knife. He sharpened it carefully on his sharpening stone, his eyes still riveted to Gifford. Scrape . . . scrape . . . scrape.

Gifford looked at the table of knives. "Tomorrow! Tomorrow!" Gifford proclaimed.

Thomas shook his head. "Too late. I fear I'll not be able to hold my brother-in-law back that long."

Rachael watched Storm Dancer pick each knife up from the polished table, check the point, and set it down again.

Thomas put down his glass. "I hear the Mohawks have a fondness for tobacco pouches made out of white men's balls." He shuddered. "I think I'd rather be dead." He shrugged. "But these savages, they don't think that way. They like to prolong your agony. They like to keep you alive as long as humanly possible . . ."

"Tonight! I can get you money tonight!" Gifford sobbed, tears of terror running down his cheeks. "I've but to sign the note and seal it, and you can go to my goldsmith right now!"

Thomas looked at Rachael. "Is that suitable to your husband, Rachael?"

Rachael looked across the room at Storm Dancer. He was still portraying the heathen savage, but there was a sparkle in his obsidian eyes meant only for her. "I think tonight would be quite suitable. And wise. Very wise."

Chapter Thirty

"Rachael!"

"Wachael-mama!"

Rachael looked up from the travois she was helping Dory pack. She smiled and waved at Storm Dancer and Ka-we-ras, a lump rising in her throat. Storm Dancer was leading their son through the camp on a pony bought in Annapolis the previous week. The toddler rode bareback with his fists balled in the pony's mane, a wide grin on his chubby bronze face.

That night in Philadelphia, Rachael had gotten most of her dowry in notes from Gifford's frightened goldsmith. After a tearful farewell to Thomas, who no matter how much Rachael begged him to come with her, said his life was on the sea, she and Storm Dancer returned to the Lenni Lenape village. From there, several braves went with Storm Dancer to Annapolis where they bought horses, drygoods, and medical supplies for their journey to Ohio country to join their Shawnee cousins.

Now it was the first of May and the entire village was

scurrying to pack. The weather was good and the leader of the expedition, Storm Dancer, thought it prudent to leave as soon as possible. With the arrival of spring, the English soldiers were gathering forces again, and to a frightened regiment any Indian face was unfriendly. Storm Dancer hoped to have the entire village headed west within the week and to hopefully avoid any confrontations with the English army.

Rachael watched Storm Dancer and their little boy disappear behind Shaakan and Starlight's wigwam and then she went back to packing bags of flour onto Dory's travois. Dory had gone to Shadow Man's wigwam to check on a napping child.

A few moments later Storm Dancer came up behind Rachael and wrapped his arms around her waist. She laughed, as she leaned back allowing him to plant a kiss in that tender hollow nestled between her neck and shoulder.

"Do you need something?" she asked. "I'm helping Dory right now, but I can come."

"Does a man need something to be with his wife?"

She laughed as she turned to face him. "Everything is going to be all right now, isn't it?"

He traced the line of her jaw with his fingertip. "You have rid yourself of Gifford Langston and the life you led before you came to me. Our people will go west where they will be safe and there we will grow old together. We will watch our grandchildren and great grandchildren grow and become men and women we can be proud of."

She brushed her lips against his, intoxicated by his nearness. "It's almost too perfect, isn't it?"

"Shhh." He touched his fingertip to her lips. "Do not

say such thing, for it is bad luck among the Lenni Lenape."

"Superstitious nonsense." She kissed him again before sliding her arms down from his broad, bare shoulders. "Now go on with you and leave me to my work."

Their lips met again and just as Rachael pulled back she heard Tuuban calling for Storm Dancer.

Storm Dancer's brow furrowed. There was a strained tone to his friend's voice. He turned to see Tuuban running toward him.

"Storm Dancer! You have guests."

Storm Dancer looked aside at Rachael. "Guests?"

Tuuban came to a halt as he pointed toward the wigwam Rachael and Storm Dancer shared. "They wait for you at your firepit."

"Who?" Rachael asked, certain that after the fright Storm Dancer had given Gifford, they would never see him again. No, whoever the visitors were, they came without escort. She'd heard no horses. No commotion. Whoever it was had walked into the camp in relative silence.

Tuuban looked from Rachael to Storm Dancer. "He says he is Broken Horn, Mohawk brother to you."

Rachael's blood ran to ice. She grasped Storm Dancer's bare arm. "Broken Horn, here?" she whispered. "It cannot be."

"A man without an ear." Tuuban brushed his own ear. "And a woman with a harelip. He said she was his wife."

Rachael's lower lip trembled. "He's up to no good. It can be nothing else."

Storm Dancer glanced toward his wigwam, his sight

blocked by other sleeping lodges. "He is still my brother. He has come a long way. I must see what he wants. It is only right."

Rachael slipped her hand into her husband's. "I'll come too."

"You don't have to. I know my brother frightens you. Take our son and go to our grandparents' wigwam. You'll be safe there."

She squeezed Storm Dancer's hand, gathering her courage. "No. We go together."

Storm Dancer nodded, as he turned his attention to Tuuban. "He brought no others with him? You are certain. My brother can be a clever, devious man."

"No. The sentries saw no one."

"They cannot harm us if they are two against a village, but to be safe I would ask that you tell our braves that my brother is in the camp. Warn them to watch their women and children and to keep their eyes open for trouble. Send extra sentries out to guard all perimeters of the camp. I will deal with Broken Horn of the Mohawks."

Tuuban gave a curt nodd and dashed off.

With their hands still entwined, Rachael and Storm Dancer crossed the camp toward their wigwam. She spotted Broken Horn immediately, though his face was blackened with ashes and he appeared thinner than he had last summer. Beside him stood Pretty Woman, her face blackened as well, her clothing in ragged shreds.

"Why the ashes?" Rachael whispered.

"It seems my brother and his wife are in mourning for a family member."

When Broken Horn saw Storm Dancer, he came forward offering both hands in peace. Storm Dancer accepted them with caution.

"Greetings, Brother," Broken Horn said in English.

"Greetings to you, Brother. I thought myself dead to you," Storm Dancer said, getting straight to the point. "How did you find me and why have you come?"

Broken Horn lowered his head in a submissive gesture. "I cannot right what has been wronged in the past. I cannot change the direction of the wind which has already blown. I have come to bring sorrowful news to you and to the Lenni Lenape. Our mother told us where you had gone in the hopes that we could mend our differences."

"You say you have come from the Great Lakes to the Chesapeake to bring news to your dead brother?"

"Do not be so suspicious." Broken Horn opened his hands. "I am unarmed but for one musket that lies at your doorstep, one bow, and one hunting knife. I came because it was the right thing to do." His gaze wandered to Rachael's face, but he looked away before his brother took notice.

Rachael tightened her grip on her husband's hand.

"What news is this you bring?" Storm Dancer lifted his hand. "You come in the ashes of mourning. Who has died?"

"Do you not offer your hospitality to this man and his wife who have come so far?"

"First the news, *Brother.*"

Broken Horn crossed his arms over his chest. "Our mother's spirit has passed into heaven. The entire village died of smallpox, she among them."

Storm Dancer's eyes narrowed. "You do not bring the air of disease with you?" he challenged.

"Look at us," Broken Horn scoffed. "Look closely

and you see we bear the scars of the disease. It was months ago. Winter. We are but two lonely souls without refuge."

Storm Dancer exhaled slowly. It was a kind act for Broken Horn to come so far to give She-Who-Weeps' family the news of her death. It was true, he seemed genuine in his intentions and he apparently had come without escort. Perhaps his brother saw the wrong in his past actions and regretted them. Perhaps the deaths of their entire Mohawk village had brought to him the realization of his evils.

Storm Dancer stepped aside, taking Rachael with him. He spoke so that only she could hear. "My brother comes with good intentions. It is only right I offer him the hospitality of our home."

Rachael's gaze was riveted to Storm Dancer's. "I don't like this. I don't like it at all."

"Perhaps he has repented of his sins. It can happen, Wife."

She glanced at Broken Horn who stood speaking quietly to Pretty Woman. "I have no doubt of that. The question is can Broken Horn change? Can he be trusted?"

"We have but to feed them and give them a place to lay their heads. I will tell Broken Horn that he may rest a day or two and that then he must go. I will offer him the hospitality of my wigwam as is only right, but I will tell him that too much bad medicine has passed between us. He cannot stay and he cannot go west with us."

"You can forget all he did to you so quickly?" She studied Storm Dancer's handsome bronze face, trying to understand. She had a fierce sense of protectiveness that encompassed not only Ka-we-ras, but her husband as well. She wanted to protect Storm Dancer from the pain of the past, but from future pain as well."

"I have not forgotten. I cannot even say that I have forgiven, but as the shaman of our tribe I must be a good example to others. I must show compassion though I may not feel compassionate."

She set her jaw. "You have to trust when you don't feel trustful?"

Storm Dancer looked at Broken Horn who was staring up at his own scalp lock that flew from the lodgepole. "He cannot harm us here in the midst of our people. Once I was in his camp, but now he is in mine."

Rachael wanted to argue the point further, but she could see that it would be of no use. It was that sense of right and wrong that was so strong in Storm Dancer, in all of the people of the Lenni Lenape, that would govern here. She reached up to touch his cheek. "Very well, Husband. I will offer our guests the hospitality of our firepit. Many of the wigwams have been taken down with families sharing so they will have to sleep with us tonight."

Storm Dancer glanced at his brother and sister-in-law. "Better that I can watch him." He looked back at her. "Rachael." He waited until her gaze met his. "I would not jeopardize your safety if I thought for a moment he might harm you or our son."

"I know that." She lifted his hand to kiss his knuckles. "I'll make something for them to eat right away while you take them to Starlight and Shaakan. They will want to know their daughter is dead."

* * *

That evening a light rain began to fall. Rather than eating in front of the wigwam out where Rachael felt safer, she was forced to serve her evening meal inside. Broken Horn and Storm Dancer carried on a light conversation throughout the courses of roasted venison, corn bread, and boiled peas while Pretty Woman sat an arm's length behind her husband in silence. She was not rude to Rachael, but she was by no means pleasant.

After dinner while Rachael cleaned up the pewter dishes Storm Dancer had brought her as a gift from Annapolis, Storm Dancer and Broken Horn smoked their pipes. Ka-we-ras wandered about the wigwam sailing a wooden boat through the air. When Ka-we-ras, being the curious toddler that he was, climbed into Broken Horn's lap Rachael had to suppress the urge to snatch her child from him and run. Broken Horn had done nothing wrong in deed or word since he had come to the camp, but Rachael still couldn't shake the uneasy feeling that had plagued her all day.

She thought to try and talk to Storm Dancer about her concern, but she knew he wanted so badly to believe his brother regretted his past actions that she just couldn't bring herself to speak out against Broken Horn. After all, she had no proof, only a few lurid glances that could have been imagined and a bad feeling in the pit of her stomach. Storm Dancer was the shaman, she told herself. He could foretell the future in waking dreams. Surely he would know if Broken Horn meant harm.

Rachael was thankful when it finally came time to turn in for the night. With most of their belongings packed and ready to go west, there was plenty of room in the wigwam for comfortable sleeping arrangement.

Storm Dancer put Broken Horn and Pretty Woman on the far side of the wigwam while Rachael, Storm Dancer, and Ka-we-ras slept near the doorway. Once the lamp was blown out and Ka-we-ras had settled beside Rachael, she crawled over to rest her head on her husband's broad shoulder.

"I told you he means us no harm," Storm Dancer said in a voice meant only for her ears.

"He's done nothing wrong. That's true enough."

Storm hugged her, kissing her forehead. "You are safe here with me. Now, sleep, Wife. Tomorrow my brother leaves. He thinks to look into the trapping here along the Chesapeake. He understands the thinking of the English-*manake*. He would do well."

Rachael lifted up on one elbow. "I think I'll sleep next to Ka-we-ras if you don't mind."

He smiled in the darkness. "I will miss the feel of your body against mine."

"I'll just feel better if I know he's safe," she whispered.

He kissed her again, but this time his lips lingered over hers. Finally he said, "If that is what pleases you, Wife, I can do without your warmth this one night."

Rachael gave Storm Dancer another quick kiss and then crawled the four feet back to Ka-we-ras's pallet. When she lay her head beside her son's, he was already asleep, his tiny fingers locked around the wooden boat given to him by the uncle he would never know. For a long time Rachael lay awake staring through darkness at Storm Dancer, thinking about him and the love she had for him. Finally she drifted off to sleep.

Sometime in the middle of the night Rachael heard

Ka-we-ras stir and cry out. Thinking he was having a nightmare she reached out to pat him, her eyes still closed.

When he screamed, her eyes flew open in fear, her entire body stiffening. Something was wrong.

Rachael automatically turned toward Storm Dancer as she reached for her frightened toddler.

Her own scream of terror rent the night air. Broken Horn stood over Storm Dancer, a jagged-edged knife stained dark with blood clutched in his hand. Storm Dancer's neck and chest were pooled in dark liquid.

Rachael was petrified for the safety of her son, but the rage inside her was stronger. Whirling around on her knees she shoved Ka-we-ras through a narrow tear in the hide between the wigwam floor and wall that had gone unsewn in the midst of the busy week. "Run for Tuuban," she screamed. The little boy scooted through the hole and out of Rachael's arms and she turned to face her husband's murderer.

She leaped up, the knife she had left near her pillow in her hand. "You killed him!" she screamed in fury, flailing the weapon. "You killed my husband and now you'll die!"

Broken Horn threw back his head in laughter. "I have come to take what is mine. I take back my scalp lock from the lodgepole and with it my luck and now I take you as mine!"

Rachael was slowly coming toward him in a crouched position, with her center of gravity low to the floor. It was the way to stalk a predator and it suddenly seemed instinctive. "I would sooner turn the knife on myself than let you touch me!" she shouted, ignoring the hot tears that ran down her face.

"Brave words for a woman who is once again a slave!"

Rachael leaped forward slashing at Broken Horn's chest and leapt back again before he could reach her. He cursed in the darkness, touching the gash she had sliced at his breastbone. "Caution, bitch," he warned. "You will pay dearly for each injury you cause me. Put down the knife and we go."

"You lied, Husband!"

Rachael turned to see Pretty Woman coming toward them, a musket clenched in her trembling smallpox-scarred hands. "You said you would not take her. You said you came to kill them both, to rid yourself of the bad luck they gave you."

"I lied," Broken Horn sneered. "She was mine the day I took her from her carriage and she will be mine until the day she dies or I kill her! Now put aside the musket before it misfires and you shoot me in the leg!"

Pretty Woman shook her head, waving the loaded musket. "No. You cannot have her. I am your wife. I have stayed at your side when you were ill. I fought wolves to get you meat. I gave birth for you again and again. I am your wife! I am your woman! There can be no other woman!

Rachael took a step back and felt the saplings of the wigwam frame press into her back. She had nowhere to go, and now she faced two deadly adversaries. She could hear dogs barking in the village and the sound of men's voices. Bare feet raced across the compound toward her. Ka-we-ras had reached Tuuban and sounded the alarm.

Rachael's gaze flicked from Broken Horn to Pretty

Woman, who was now pointing the musket at her. She wasn't certain who the greatest threat was, but she surmised that it was Pretty Woman. The woman was clearly mentally off-balance. "Don't shoot," Rachael said, holding up her hands. "I don't want him. I don't want your man. Take him and go."

"He is obsessed with you! He walks half a world to find you! I cannot let you live!"

"Put down the musket or I will strangle you with my bare hands!" Broken Horn threatened, furious at his wife's disobedience. "I will have any woman I please and this white bitch pleases me!"

Pretty Woman shook her head, seemingly dazed. "No. It can't be. I am wife to Broken Horn of the Mohawks." She pulled back the trigger with her thumb. "He will have no other wife, not ever again."

Rachael braced herself for the point-blank shot of the musket. She knew it would kill her, but she was numb. She couldn't call out, all she could think of was Storm Dancer lying unconscious on his sleeping mat, his life's blood flowing onto the floor. He had wanted to believe in his brother so badly that he had mislaid his trust and for that he would die.

Rachael saw Pretty Woman's finger flick over the trigger.

"No!" Broken Horn bellowed as he threw himself between Rachael and Pretty Woman. "Don't kill her! She's mine!"

The musket ball hit Broken Horn's chest and shattered beneath his rib cage covering Pretty Woman and Rachael in bloody gore. He fell backward under the blast of the black powder knocking Rachael down and pinning her to the floor.

Screaming in shock, Rachael dragged herself from beneath Broken Horn's shattered body, just as Tuuban and several other braves ripped open the wigwam door.

Tuuban lifted his bow to his shoulder to kill Pretty Woman, but she had already thrown the musket to the ground and was cradling her dead husband's body, wailing in an eerie voice.

Dazed, Rachael crawled toward Storm Dancer. She leaned over him, sobbing. There was so much blood. She knew he couldn't possibly still be alive. Without thinking, she took the corner of a blanket and pressed it to the gash in his neck that still flowed freely with blood. "Get help," she cried. "Get Shaakan and Starlight. Storm Dancer is hurt! He's hurt badly!" She pushed back her hair from her face. "Dead maybe."

Tuuban knelt beside Rachael and pressed his ear to Storm Dancer's chest. He paused for a moment and then lifted his head. "He yet lives. His heart yet beats for you, Rachael."

She wiped the tears that blinded her. "That's not possible. There's so much blood! He slit his throat!"

By this time someone had lit the lamp that hung in the rafters and by the light of the candles Rachael could see the deathly pallor to Storm Dancer's skin. His breathing was shallow, his face a mask of gray.

"Keep holding that tightly," Tuuban said lifting the corner of the blanket from the gash in Storm Dancer's neck and then replacing it. "The bleeding has slowed."

Rachael looked up at Tuuban in confusion. "He might live? You mean he might be all right?"

"Stay with him. Shaakan will bring his medicine bag. My friend the Dancer of Storms will not leave you without a fight."

* * *

Only a week later Rachael stood at the head of the line of travoises watching Storm Dancer give final orders before the village began the first leg of their journey. He was pale and he moved slowly, his neck covered in bandages, but he had insisted he was well enough to travel.

There seemed to be no explanation as to why he had not bled to death except that it had only been a matter of a minute or so from the time Broken Horn had cut Storm Dancer, to the time Rachael applied pressure to stop the bleeding. If it had not been for the fact that Ka-we-ras had seen what happened and cried out, Storm Dancer would never have lived.

Storm Dancer came slowly toward Rachael, his son's hand in his. "We are ready, Wife."

"We're ready," she repeated. Looking out over the few wigwams they would leave behind, she shaded her eyes to see Pretty Woman seated before a cold firepit. "Are you certain we should just leave her?"

Storm Dancer looked back at Broken Horn's widow. She had cut off all her hair until it was nothing but jagged spikes. She had covered her face in ashes and cut off two of her own fingers before Storm Dancer removed all weapons from her reach. Pretty Woman now sat cross-legged before the empty firepit, rocking back and forth and calling in Iroquois to her dead and buried husband.

Storm Dancer lifted Ka-we-ras onto his shoulder and turned away from Pretty Woman, leading Rachael by the hand. "There is nothing that can be done for her. She has been her own worst enemy. If she is to come out of her madness, it will be on her own. We cannot help her, or feel responsible for her crimes."

Rachael sighed knowing he was right. "Very well." She smiled, pushing away all thoughts of Broken Horn, of Gifford, of Ta-wa-ne . . . of all the bad things that had ever happened to her. Today was the day to begin anew.

Rachael turned to Storm Dancer and reached up to stroke his broad bronze cheek. In many ways he still looked the savage to her, but she loved him, more than life itself. "Lead us on, Husband," she said, smiling up at him and their son.

Storm Dancer leaned down to brush his lips against hers. "You lead."

"I don't know where we're going."

"West, Rachael-wife" he teased. "And wherever thou will goest, I will go." He took her hand and lay it on his chest so that she could feel his heartbeat. "Wherever you lodge, I will lodge. Your people shall be my people . . . your heart my heart."

Ka-we-ras clapped his chubby little hands in laughter as his parents sealed their love with a kiss.

Epilogue

Spring, 1763
Somewhere in Ohio Country

Rachael raced around the wigwam and bolted into the open grassy field with Ka-we-ras and Storm Dancer hot on her heels. The little boy was laughing so hard that he could barely run. Finally his father scooped him up and draped him across his shoulders.

"Two against one! It's not fair," Rachael protested over her shoulder. She ran barefooted, her hair flowing down her back, through the high grass of the open field as hard as she could, knowing they were gaining on her.

The land called Ohio country was distinctly different from that of the land near the Chesapeake Bay. Here, the forest was less dense and there were open fields of grassland that seemed to stretch for miles. Here, across the Ohio River, they had settled only a mile from a Shawnee camp. With the help of the pack animals and the supplies bought in Annapolis they had reached their destination healthy and ready to begin a new life far from the dangers of the white men.

Storm Dancer caught up to Rachael in a few easy strides, and the little boy squealed with laughter when his father caught his mother by the shoulders and twirled her around, forcing her to the ground. Storm Dancer then plucked his son from his shoulders and lifted him down onto his mother's chest.

"Enough! Enough! You win," she declared, laughing so hard that her sides ached.

Storm Dancer dropped down onto Rachael, sandwiching Ka-we-ras between them. Laughter bubbled up out of the little boy. Then he spotted an orange butterfly and scrambled out from between his parents to chase it.

"Don't go far," Storm Dancer warned, lifting up to look out over the waist-high grass of late spring. You'll be lost and I'll have no one to go fishing with me."

Rachael grasped Storm Dancer by a handful of the leather of his sleeveless vest and pulled him down until his nose touched hers.

"And what is it you want, Wife?" he growled playfully.

"A kiss. I demand a kiss."

His lips met hers and their tongues touched in a sensuous dance of love. "If I am the winner, should I not be making the demands?"

She laughed, her fingers going to the binding of her leather bodice. "I thought to shed this for the summer," she told him, arching a feathered eyebrow. "What do you think?"

He watched her as she pushed back the soft leather to

are her breasts, his dark eyes pooling with desire. He
eaned over to touch the tip of his tongue to one dark
ipple. "This man could grow used to this."

She traced the scar that banded his neck. Thoughts
f Broken Horn and all that had taken place in the last
wo years had faded from her mind until they were
othing but a distant, dim memory. "And you won't
nind me baring myself to the others?"

His hand glided over her breast and she sighed,
etting her eyes drift shut. "They may look as long as
hey do not touch."

"No, no, it's all right, Husband." She grabbed the
dges of the unlaced bodice and covered herself, feign-
ng modesty. "You're right. It's best I not take on all the
ustoms of your people at one time."

Storm Dancer sat up, straddling her and grasped the
wo edges of the bodice. He yanked them so hard that
he seams tore and he ended up with two handfuls of
eather.

Rachael broke into laughter as he leaned over to
ury his face between her breasts. The sun felt wickedly
varm on her bare flesh and his nearness made her
remble with pleasure. She threaded her fingers
hrough his inky black hair and lifted his head until he
vas staring directly into her eyes. "Say it," she
vhispered.

"I say it a thousand times a day. I am a warrior,
shaman to my people," he said gruffly. "I can-
ot—"

"Say it," she whispered, a husky catch in her voice.

"I love you," he murmured fiercely, lowering his
nouth to hers. "I will love you until the heavens come

down to lift us, until we become two stars twinkling in the night sky."

Rachael smiled as her eyes drifted shut beneath the glare of the hot sun and the feel of his mouth. She wasn't certain what heaven felt like but she hoped it would be just like this.